THE
HOOLIGANS

THE
HOOLIGANS

P. T. DEUTERMANN

ST. MARTIN'S PRESS

NEW YORK

First published in the United States by St. Martin's Press, an imprint of St. Martin's Publishing Group

THE HOOLIGANS. Copyright © 2020 by P. T. Deutermann. All rights reserved. Printed in the United States of America. For information, address St. Martin's Publishing Group, 120 Broadway, New York, NY 10271.

www.stmartins.com

The Library of Congress Cataloging-in-Publication Data

Names: Deutermann, Peter T., 1941– author.
Title: The hooligans / P. T. Deutermann.
Description: First edition. | New York : St. Martin's Press, 2020.
Identifiers: LCCN 2020009560 | ISBN 9781250263094 (hardcover) |
    ISBN 9781250263100 (ebook)
Subjects: LCSH: World War, 1939–1945—Naval operations, American—
    Fiction. | GSAFD: Historical fiction. | War stories.
Classification: LCC PS3554.E887 H66 2020 | DDC 813/.54—dc23
LC record available at https://lccn.loc.gov/2020009560

Our books may be purchased in bulk for promotional, educational, or business use. Please contact your local bookseller or the Macmillan Corporate and Premium Sales Department at 1-800-221-7945, extension 5442, or by email at MacmillanSpecialMarkets@macmillan.com.

First Edition: 2020

10 9 8 7 6 5 4 3 2 1

This book is dedicated to the memory of the skippers and crews who manned what the Japanese Navy called "devil boats" during the Solomons campaign of 1942–1943.

PART I

ONE

Rain. Pounding, tropical rain. Not comforting; more like scary. Sounding like a waterfall on my steel shipping-box home. My brain telling me: It's just rain. Go back to sleep. But it wasn't just rain: someone or -thing was also pounding on the side of the box.

Go away! I don't know if I said it, but *God!* I was so tired.

"Doc," a voice shouted over the roar of the rain. "We need you. *Now.* Unlock the hatch."

Can't make me, my evil, sleep-deprived brain whispered. I looked at the radium dial of my watch: 0330. I'd gone down for a quick nap at 2300. Almost four hours. An extravagantly long time, and a whole lot more than the perimeter snuffies were getting.

"Okay, okay, keep your shirt on," I shouted back. The banging on the door stopped.

The Marines had taken steel shipping containers, formerly filled with 75 and 105 mm artillery rounds for shipment across the Pacific, and made one-man sleeping quarters for each of the docs. The box was ten by six by six feet, with a hatch at one end. There were screened holes on the top sides for air, a makeshift bamboo rack for clothes, clean surgical gowns, and a Springfield rifle. There was a crude interior lock bar to keep any sleepers safe from infiltrating Japs intent on murder. The boxes lay just outside the maze of ropes

3

and cables supporting the main hospital tent, like a row of olive-drab beehives.

Typical of tropical rain, it stopped when I finally unlocked the hatch and stumbled out into the sauna-like atmosphere of Henderson Field. I was wearing a relatively clean set of "Johnnies," or surgical-gown tops and bottoms, and GI-issue combat boots. I also carried a government-issue 1911 M1 .45 semiautomatic on my right hip in a very non-sterile holster. As a Navy doctor, I was a commissioned officer with the rank of lieutenant (junior grade), US Naval Reserve, in the Navy Medical Corps. The Marine general commanding at Guadalcanal had issued standing orders: *all* officers will carry a sidearm, even doctors. We'd dispose of our hand-cannons when we got inside the main hospital tent, nicknamed the Big Top, but they were never very far away. Just like the Japs.

A Navy hospitalman was standing outside, holding a red-lens flashlight and looking like a drowned rat. I couldn't remember his name, but I knew he was a new guy. Together we slogged through the red mud toward the cluster of medical tents, accompanied by the sounds of muted thunder, intermittent rifle fire, and the occasional thump of an illumination mortar. The tents containing the surgical unit were about fifty feet away from the sleeping containers, partially concealed in a stand of bedraggled coconut trees. I could see them each time an illumination round lit up the sky in a blaze of magnesium, which unfortunately lasted only fifteen seconds or so. Once it burned out the resulting darkness seemed even more intense. I'd caught a glimpse of several litter-jeeps parked around the Big Top, which meant more casualties. Nothing new there.

Another flare went off, behind us this time, and in a single horrifying instant a Jap soldier stepped out of the darkness and bayoneted my hospitalman in the stomach. The youngster went down with a mortal scream, which continued each time the Jap pulled the bayonet out and then stabbed him again. I'd seen lots of dead Japanese in various stages of deconstruction. I'd never actually seen a live one, and this little man was shorter than his rifle but making up for his lack of stature with his zeal for homicide. I stumbled backwards to get away from him just as another flare popped over our heads. I completely forgot to draw my .45, but by then the Marines standing around the casualty jeeps were running toward us, firing as they came. My brain finally engaged and I hit the dirt to avoid the rounds coming in "our" direction. By the time I gathered my wits the Jap was dead and three Marines were pulling me up from the mud.

"Sorry, Doc," one of them said. "Don't know how that bastard got by us."

Nobody spoke the obvious—you with the .45: why didn't you do something? Then I realized they knew that my .45 was mostly for show, and as a doctor, I couldn't be expected to be much of a soldier and most certainly not a Marine. Still, I was embarrassed. I bent briefly to examine the hospitalman, but it was pretty obvious he'd bled out. There was a flare of yellow light as someone in the surgical tent opened a flap and yelled something at the cluster of Marines helping me toward my tent. I assumed that meant: hurry the hell up.

The Big Top was a PSH, a portable service hospital. It was square, forty feet on a side, and made of dark green canvas. Several small portable generators were rattling away along the sides. There was a web of guy wires and ropes holding the thing upright and, inside, three large metal poles supported the ridgeline canvas. The "floor" inside was made up of large tarpaulin sections that undulated when you walked across the interior of the tent. The sanitary condition of the floor did not bear examination, even though two hospitalmen were assigned to constantly sweep, mop, bag, and remove all the bloody medical litter that emergency surgery in an active combat zone produces.

There were four operating tables, each with its own surgical light and the usual clutter of IV stands, instrument trays, a stool for the hospitalman anesthetist and his helper, and the operating table itself. All of this had come ashore from the supply ships once the initial invasion fleet returned to Guadalcanal after the sea fight they were calling Savo Island, and the big bosses regained their nerve. There was a fan in each corner of the tent running on low to keep down cross contamination of the four tables. The fans offered the surgical teams a smidgen of relief from the ninety-degree heat, and that was at night. During the day they'd spray water on the tent in an attempt at evaporation cooling. All of the surgical team members wore masks with Vicks VapoRub smeared on them to deal with the charnel-house smell inside the tent.

Attached to the Big Top were smaller versions, which housed pre-op, triage, and post-op teams. The triage tent had yet another tent attached, where casualties deemed unfit for further medical treatment were laid out on cots and given as much morphine as it took to stop the screaming. When they finally died, the orderlies zipped each one into a rubber body bag. Then the remains were taken out to a truck and ferried over to the temporary burial site, where a bulldozer worked constantly to create and then cover long trenches. The assumption was that the graves-registration detail would map whose bag went where in the trench. If we won the battle for Guadalcanal, they'd eventually be exhumed and sent home in a proper casket. If we lost, well . . .

I had to find a new set of operating clothes. I changed right there in the surgery area, and then scrubbed in at the single scrubbing station in the tent while the surgeon I was relieving watched anxiously. I felt his anxiety. We surgeons worked until we began dropping instruments or went into a prolonged pause while our brains tried to deal with the fatigue. The chief surgeon had finally figured out that we needed one doctor who would float through the surgical area and just watch the other cutters. When a hospitalman raised his hand it usually meant that the doc he was helping was all done for the moment. The floater would step in as the tottering surgeon would be taken over to a dark side of the tent and ordered to lie down on one of the cots there. They'd give him two hours of sleep and then rouse him to go back to a table, where the anesthetist would slap an oxygen mask on him for fifteen seconds. That cycle was repeated twice before we finally got to stagger out to our beloved shipping box and get some real sleep. Day and night had merged into a tapestry of horribly torn bodies, flashing steel, frantic chest massages, overloaded suction tubes, and that awful feeling when your patient's nether orifices opened unexpectedly, telling you he'd just died despite your best efforts. The constant crack and rumble of gunfire and tank engines outside kept us company.

I worked until dawn, although the only indication that daylight had returned was the smell of fresh coffee. It was our one luxury, appropriated by some Marines who'd snuck aboard one of the Navy cargo transports and traded "genu-wine" Jap souvenirs for five-pound cans of Navy coffee. A Jap sword could actually produce canned hams. The fighting entered something of a lull that morning, probably because of the weather, so the emergency casualties diminished. Breakfast was available in the "new" mess tent, the old one, thankfully empty at the time, having absorbed a mortar round. Scrambled eggs made from a yellow powder, precooked bacon strips from cans, and rice. Always rice, all of which had been salvaged from the ration pouches of dead Japs when the fleet withdrew temporarily after Savo. No bread or biscuits because loose flour grew brilliant strains of mold in this wet heat and there was simply no way to store it. Maybe someday. If you wanted starch, you ate rice, and smothered the whole lot in hot sauce. It was food and it was welcome. In the first days after the initial invasion, there hadn't been *any* food when our distant theater commander, Admiral Ghormley, a thousand miles away in Nouméa, had decided to withdraw the partially unloaded invasion support ships the day after almost all our big-gun cruisers were sunk near Savo Island.

I was sitting on an ammo box outside the mess tent in my

bloodstained Johnnies, eyes closed, stomach full if a bit nervous, oblivious to the light rain falling all around while listening to the distant *pop-pop* of pistol fire as the Marines dispatched enemy wounded. That might sound barbarous, but none of them wanted medical help or any help at all other than an honorable death on the battlefield. According to the Marines, they'd make a "gun" out of their thumb and fingers, point it at their head, and beseech any passing Marine to please do the honors. No problem, you Jap bastard, you. *Pow.* I think some of the guys felt bad about doing that sort of thing, but then we learned the Japs beheaded any American wounded they came across, so in a way, it was just business. I was so exhausted by then that anyone wanting to take issue with me about what was going on up in the hills and ridges around the airfield would be told to go down to Graves Registration and tell that small mountain of dead Marines all about his moral concerns.

"Doc Andersen?" a young but weary voice asked. I opened my eyes. A Marine who looked like he'd just crawled out of a mud puddle was standing there. His hands were bandaged in what looked like burn dressings, probably from grabbing the barrel of a heavy machine gun to steady it. His eyes were a reddish color. I recognized him as one of the sentries assigned to the Big Top. I asked him what he needed.

"Doc Garr sent me, sir. Said you're needed over on Tulagi after the big bombing raid last night. Said to tell you to grab your stuff and get down to the landing beach by ten-hundred. Tulagi's sending over a PT boat to pick up you and two hospitalmen, Greer and Miller, down on the landing beach."

"Okay, got it," I said. "Now: can you do me a favor? I need you to go back to the big surgical tent, find HM1 Greer, and ask him to pack up as much medical supplies as he can beg, borrow, or steal."

"Yes, sir, will do."

He seemed to be weaving a little bit as he stood there, so I offered him my canteen cup, half filled with coffee. He gulped it down, burped, said, "Thanks, Doc," and then took off. I launched my weary bones in the direction of my box. My "stuff" didn't amount to much more than a partially filled seabag, but then I wanted to go over to the Big Top to see what I could scrounge in the way of surgical equipment. Garr wouldn't be much help in that regard. He didn't like me, nor, truth be told, was there that much equipment to spare. If I was really lucky Greer might think big and snare an entire surgical equipment trunk. Then we'd have to figure out how we were going to get it down to the beach.

The airfield had come alive now that it was daylight. The gravelly rumble of deuce-and-a-half trucks going and coming, dozers moving dirt, a six-pack of tanks trying to move through all that sticky mud, and the roar of some Marine F4F Wildcats running up their engines filled the air. The operational code name for the island was Cactus, so the Wildcats were part of the Cactus Air Force. Occasionally there'd be gunfire, but it didn't sound serious. Whenever the Japs made one of their nighttime attacks, they'd leave snipers behind, perched like monkeys up in coconut trees. Three Marine rifle teams made it their business to begin each day scouring the trees for two-legged coconuts and then shooting them off their perches. Once discovered, the snipers weren't shy about firing back, so it was a risky assignment. The Marines, of course, thought it was fun.

My team and I made it down to the landing beach just after ten, courtesy of a Marine major who rated a jeep. My helpers were Hospitalman First Class Surgical Assistant Greer and a much younger hospitalman apprentice named Miller, who looked like he should still have been in seventh grade. Doctor Garr had caught us trying to awkwardly "liberate" a 250-pound surgical equipment trunk, one of only three spares. This had led to a noisy argument, which I'd finally won by pointing out that if I was really going over to Tulagi Island as a surgeon and not just as a general medical officer, what was the point if I had no equipment? Supposedly they had at least one doc over there, but no surgeons. Garr relented only when there was a sudden emergency back in the Big Top and he simply *had* to break it off, but not without repeating his standard complaint that I wasn't a real surgeon and thus shouldn't even *be* here on Guadalcanal, much less over on Tulagi, without adult supervision.

While we waited on the landing beach under a palm tree, HM1 Greer asked me what was behind the big beef between me and Doc Garr. The beach was down on Lunga Point, where the First Marine Division had come ashore on the initial invasion day. It was still littered with abandoned gear and the hulks of overturned landing craft, while at the same time abuzz with the diesel noises of small, flat-faced landing craft bringing in desperately needed food, ammunition, medical supplies, and all the other impedimenta that a full Marine division consumed in great quantities every day and night. There was a Navy amphibious ship anchored just offshore, surrounded by hungry boats. The ship was an LST, which stood for Landing Ship, Tank. A second cargo ship lay on its side nearby, the hulk burned out after a Jap bombing attack. If there was a PT boat out there somewhere, we hadn't spotted it, so we'd gone to the beachmaster up in his wooden tower so he'd alert us when it showed up. Then we just moved into the trees to stay out of the way.

"Here's the problem," I told Greer. "When the Japs hit Pearl, I was just finishing up my third year of surgical residency. That's year three out of six, sometimes seven. I left school and signed up like everyone else after Pearl Harbor, and ended up out here with the First Marine Division. Garr was the senior medical officer of the medical team who came ashore right after D-day. He asked me what my credentials were and I told him. Finished medical school and had just finished my third year of a surgical residency at Duke University. He said that meant I wasn't yet qualified to do independent surgery and that I would be restricted to assisting "real" surgeons, as he put it. He also said he'd ship me back to Nouméa as soon as possible, where'd I be assigned to the field hospital there. For further training."

"Ouch," Greer said.

"Well, actually, I couldn't really argue. In your third year of a surgical residency, you're just beginning to realize that learning the procedures is one thing. It's learning how to handle all the things that can go wrong during a particular procedure that takes all those later years. But for me, everything changed when the Japs first counterattacked."

"Remember that night well," Greer said. He was about my age, prematurely gray, solidly built, a man of few words, and utterly competent at the table. He was known around the main tent as a reliable third hand: one of those indispensable and unflappable surgical assistants who could anticipate which instrument was needed next, or who'd go after a bleeder without prompting from the surgeon. Back at Duke the assistants had all been women, registered nurses with additional surgical training. I didn't know there even were male surgical assistants until I'd joined the Navy.

"Yeah, well, when the avalanche hit, they'd just completed the second big top. All the "real" surgeons were overwhelmed so I was sent over to the new tent to see what I could do. By the end of the first two weeks of heavy fighting, I'd probably done more surgical procedures than I would have during all my years back at Duke. Never looked back. Garr was furious when he heard, but then the other docs told him to back off, that I might not have been qualified when the shit hit the fan, but that I was, by God, qualified now, or something along those lines. I wasn't there."

"I *was* there when Garr found out," Greer said. "He did his usual outrage number, got red in the face and loud, until Doc Hennessy said that your work was better than his, due probably to the fact that you were coming fresh from a topflight medical school and that he, Holland Fraser Whitman Garr, probably hadn't cracked a book in twenty years. Admittedly, everybody was pretty tired."

"Wow," I said. "How'd that go over?"

"Never really found out," Greer said. "Garr's face went from red to purple, but then six trucks showed up with wounded from one of our cruisers, and we were off to the races again." He peered into the hazy distance over the strait. "That our coach and six?"

He was pointing out into the Sealark Channel, the strait that separated Guadalcanal and Tulagi, where I could now see a white V approaching. We gathered our stuff, asked a couple of the beach-master's crew to help with the trunk, and went down the short hill to the pontoon landing. All of us were sweating profusely; the morning sun was out and baking the place already. The PT boat rumbled into the makeshift "harbor," backed down, and then came alongside the pontoon and put over two mooring lines. It looked as if the entire crew was at general quarters, wearing helmets and sti-fling in gray kapok life jackets. There appeared to be only one officer, a lieutenant (junior grade) who wore a fore-and-aft cap, khakis, a set of oversize binoculars on a neck strap, and a .45 in a holster. He gave us a brief glance and then resumed a sky search. He definitely looked like a man expecting trouble.

We were escorted to the boat's stern, where we could clamber aboard from the pontoon. Our seabags and the all-important trunk followed, plus some other boxes of medical supplies that Greer had managed to commandeer from Big Top Number One. The boat didn't linger. We were hustled down into the interior by one of the crewmen, along with our gear, and then off we went, slowly at first as we cleared the pontoon landing and went past the ship, whose sides were aswarm with small boats off-loading stuff. Then the engines revved up into a mechanical howl, throwing all three of us back into our chairs. The noise coming from the engine room behind us was overwhelming, so there was no possibility of talking. We could feel that sleek eighty-foot mahogany hull begin to plane through the tops of a light chop out in the strait, bumping rhythmi-cally over the small wave tops and occasionally hitting something bigger, causing the engines to scream momentarily as the props came out of the water. As water taxis went, this one was a humdinger. The surgical trunk was sliding around, so Greer grabbed some kapok life jackets and strapped them to the trunk to absorb the bumps.

Tulagi Island was supposedly twelve miles from Lunga Point. The engines began to slow after just ten minutes, so this boat had to be capable of at least fifty miles per hour. Gasoline exhaust fumes began to blow back into the interior as she slowed down and came off the plane, along with a wave of noxious hot air. The engine noise then subsided as they idled two of her three 2,500-hp Packards. I decided to climb the ladder to the weather deck to escape the engine fumes. A squall of 50-caliber machine-gun fire greeted me as my head popped up out of the hatch, along with the sound of the boat's 20 mm cannon firing back aft. We had apparently arrived at the same time that a six-pack of Jap "Betty" bombers came out of the midday sun and began blowing up everything in and around the harbor.

The boat made a violent maneuver to starboard, and I ended up sliding back down the ladder without touching a single rung. I landed on the deck, where my two hospitalmen were trying to pick themselves up from that sudden turn. For one galvanizing instant, all three of us stared at one another with open mouths, and then came an explosion that lifted the front end of the boat right out of the water and back down again, causing all three of us to smack our foreheads on the deck.

Two seconds later the centerline engine went to full power and the boat accelerated, but not at all like she'd done over on the Guadalcanal side of the strait. A wave of seawater entered our compartment from the direction of the bow, turning us into human flotsam and jetsam whirling around in the rapidly flooding compartment. The engine strained to build rpms but the boat was losing the battle as her forward spaces flooded. There was a sudden powerful jolt just as we started to grab the lower rungs of the ladder, once again throwing the three of us back into the roiling seawater, which was now halfway up the bulkhead. The remaining engine choked and then died, but the guns topside did not. A small avalanche of 50-caliber shell casings rained down through the hatch and, with the engine silenced, we could now hear the roar of aircraft engines flashing overhead, followed by the truly scary sound of large-caliber bullets tearing into the hull behind us. All three of us were submerged into the four feet of water in the compartment. We were then treated to the sting and tugs of rounds coming through the compartment and expending their energy, thanks be to God, in the water.

And then it was over. The three of us crouched on the submerged deck with only our heads exposed. The boat was motionless but the water in our compartment continued to rise. We could hear feet banging around on the deck above and then a face appeared in the hatch.

"Out!" the face yelled. "Right now!"

No problem, I thought. Greer was the closest to the ladder so he went up first. Miller, whose eyes were out on stalks, appeared to be frozen in terror. He didn't move, so I pushed his head underwater. He came back up, spluttering and babbling, and then I pushed him toward the ladder. He froze up again. I shouted at him to go *up* and, miraculously, he did, but then he hesitated again, with his head halfway out of the hatch. I put both hands on his backside and elevated him through the hatch with strength I didn't know I had, generated by the fact that the boat was obviously sinking. I didn't need to climb the ladder: the rising water pushed me up and out of the hatch in a wave of gasoline-tainted foam. Greer was nowhere to be seen. Miller was down on the sloping deck, lying on his back like an overturned turtle, sobbing. I looked around.

Fires, everywhere. We were close to the shore. Ahead of us was a scene of total disaster. I caught a quick glimpse of two dungaree-clad bodies bobbing nearby, their heads and lower extremities submerged. Then the boat began to slide backwards. As it gathered speed, Miller and I rolled off the deck, just in time for the smashed bow to swerve sideways and push me down. I panicked and started kicking to get out from under the boat but it was gone in just a few seconds and I popped up to the surface. The boat was out of sight, but the disaster on the shore was in full swing: buildings burning, palm trees blasted into kindling, another LST aflame from stem to stern alongside the large pontoon pier about a quarter mile away, and a small clutch of natives wandering aimlessly in the dirt streets, the women wailing and the dark-skinned men stupefied.

Directly in front of me was the beach, if you could call that narrow band of black sand a beach. There were five sailors stretched out on the sand in various states of disrepair. The air was filled with the wail of sirens, crackling fires, and the sounds of aircraft buzzing around nearby. Ours, I prayed, and they were. Four Wildcats from Henderson Field were overhead, looking for revenge, but the Jap bombers were long gone on their 500-plus-mile flight back to Rabaul.

Greer. Where was Greer? A shout from behind me answered my question. Greer was fifty feet off the shoreline, trying to tow the surgical trunk as he did a sidestroke. It was barely afloat but those kapoks had done their job. I swam out to meet him and help him with the trunk. The harbor on Tulagi was on the backside of the island with respect to Guadalcanal across the strait, so the waters here were flat calm.

"Miller make it?" he asked as we huffed and puffed our way onto the black beach.

"I don't know," I said. "He clutched up and I had to push him out of that compartment. If he could swim, he should be okay."

Two jeeps slammed to a stop at the shore. One of them produced a Navy captain in wet, sun-bleached khakis who was wearing a pith helmet. He was a big guy, round-faced, redheaded, and with an impressive beard. As Greer and I struggled to pull the trunk up onto the steeply sloping sand, he asked if one of us was the doctor. I raised my hand.

"Thank God," he said. "I'm Dutch VanPiet, CO Tulagi. We need you *now*. You hurt?"

"No, sir," I replied. "I'm wet, scared, shocked, and pissed off, but no, I'm not hurt."

He grinned. "Join the crowd," he said, but then his face sobered. "We had a medical tent, red crosses and all, but the pig-fucking Goddamned Japs machine-gunned it. I—"

He was interrupted by a thunderous blast as that burning LST over in the harbor blew up. The ship virtually disappeared in a 300-foot-wide churning column of fire, smoke, and *things*. To my astonishment, the captain and the people who'd come with him all sprinted past me and into the water. VanPiet grabbed my shoulder as he went by and pulled me in with him, as one of the white hats grabbed Greer and pushed him underwater.

"Down, *down!*" VanPiet shouted before submerging. "Deep as you can go!"

After grabbing a deep breath, I did what he said, clawing for the bottom and wondering why. Then large, heavy objects began landing in the water, some of them smacking the surface with a sound like a lash, others slicing down into the clear water like glittering butcher knives and burying themselves in the bottom muck. This seemed to go on for an hour but it was probably more like thirty seconds. I finally popped to the surface, gasping along with the others. The shore was littered with various debris: gray pieces of the ship's hull, unexploded artillery shells, the carcasses of vehicles still in their shipment wraps, and lots of body parts. Captain VanPiet dog-paddled over to me.

"Welcome to beautiful downtown Tulagi," he said. "It's usually not this noisy on a Sunday."

I just stared at him. He grinned back at me, but it was the savage, hollow-eyed grin of a man who was on the edge of losing it. I knew just how he felt.

TWO

Captain Willem VanPiet was a Dutchman, all right, through and through. My uncle, also a doctor, had served in World War 1. He'd told me that the British Navy had an expression about the Dutch: there's the Rotterdam Dutch, the Amsterdam Dutch, and the *God-damned* Dutch. VanPiet was one of the latter. Loud, intense, profane, red-faced, with a generally bigger-than-life persona. He'd come ashore on Tulagi with the Marines after the Japanese seaplane base and a clutch of flying boats had been worked over by a carrier air group. Guadalcanal had been taken pretty easily at first because the Japs had been completely surprised and most of their people there were civilian construction workers. Tulagi and the surrounding islands, Gavutu, Malaita, and Mokambo, had been a different story. The Japs had put their version of the Marine Corps ashore there to protect the *Kawanishi* base. They had put up a terrific fight and it had taken days for the Marines to be able to declare that Tulagi was finally secure.

Captain VanPiet's official title was Commander Naval Activities Tulagi, and that pretty much described it. Anything and everything that went on here was under his command. Unlike Guadalcanal, which was important because it had an airfield, Tulagi Island was important because it had a harbor. When one of our cruisers got mauled by the deadly efficient Japanese battle fleet in a night action out there around Savo Island, Tulagi provided a place for her to limp in and lick her wounds. The Navy hadn't planned to have a field hospital here, but it soon became evident that one was sorely needed, mostly to deal with shipboard casualties. The Marines accounted for some of the wounded, but a cruiser with her bow blown off might land eighty people ashore for treatment. Captain VanPiet's job was to keep these ships afloat long enough to make them sufficiently seaworthy to get the hell out of Dodge and back to a more secure area.

VanPiet was fully up to the job from what I could see. With fires still burning everywhere from that bombing raid, he got on his jeep radio, issuing rapid-fire orders and yelling at everyone within earshot to hurry up. If his subordinates seemed to be moving too slow, he reminded them that the Japs would be back, and that if the Japs weren't coming back, he, VanPiet, was already here. I couldn't be sure which option his people thought was worse, but his efforts seemed to galvanize everyone around him. Greer, Miller, and I just stood there, dripping wet, waiting to see what happened next. Then Greer remembered there were more medical supplies aboard the PT boat, which had now reappeared on its side in the shallows just off the beach. He and Miller swam out to the wreck and started groping around to see what they could salvage. I didn't know where the boat's crew had gone.

Another jeep appeared an hour later and picked the three of us up along with the precious surgical equipment trunk and some of the medical bags from the wrecked PT boat. Some sailors from the Tulagi command had swum out to the boat and retrieved the bodies of three crewmen and the skipper. They laid them out on the sand, covering their faces with bloody life jackets. Captain VanPiet was now trying to organize a working party to salvage whatever else they could from the wreck of the LST. He waved us toward the jeep while he and his people prepared to comb the bones of the LST for usable equipment.

We were driven past the road leading down to what had been the actual harbor. The 400-foot-long floating pontoon string that had served as the pier was now fifty yards from the water, upside down on the side of a small hill. The stern, propeller, and rudder assembly of the LST lay athwart the road we were taking to the medical encampment, forcing our jeep to go off the road to get around the mess. All the palm trees in the area had been reduced to bare stumps. The ground was littered with every kind of debris imaginable. There were no people visible around the harbor, although I thought I could see body fragments here and there. There was a ghastly feeding frenzy going on in the near harbor as the sharks converged. A complex of small wooden warehouses along the waterfront had been flattened. The only thing standing was a flagpole, whose American flag hung in tatters, as if in mourning. By then I think we were all in shock. I had never seen such destruction.

The medical area was on another low hill at the north end of the island. It, too, was a mix of small wooden buildings with palm-covered roofs but no sides, a string of the ubiquitous artillery shipping containers, and one large medical tent, although not as large as the ones over on Guadalcanal. Three bomb craters were visible crossing the road, creating a line that pointed at the hospital tent. For the first time I could see people, but only when we arrived could we see that most of the buildings and the main tent were riddled with large-caliber bullet holes, despite the large red crosses painted on their sides. Hospitalmen and Marines were extracting wounded men from the slit-trench bomb shelters beside the compound. Some were ambulatory, but many were being brought out of the trench on green canvas stretchers. Our driver, a frightened-looking Navy sailor, turned to me in the front right seat.

"The captain said to bring you here, sir," he announced in a high voice. "Said you'd know what to do next."

Anything's possible, I thought. We got ourselves, the trunk, and the other medical stuff out of the jeep, which promptly sped off back toward the harbor area. I looked around. I could see a small island across the northern harbor approach channel. There appeared to be several PT boats there, huddled in a cove surrounded by dense tropical jungle and palm trees. I sent Greer to find the senior medical officer and told Miller to guard our precious equipment. Miller seemed to be still a bit shell-shocked so I didn't want to tax him with anything important. I remember thinking we'd all be pretty busy soon enough. Then I saw one of the PT boats from across the harbor getting under way and pointing his bow in our direction as we headed toward the tent complex.

The situation at the medical compound was disheartening, to say the least. The senior medical officer on Tulagi had been one Lieutenant Commander Roger Stone, MD. He'd remained behind in the main tent to stay with the patients who couldn't be moved and had caught a 20 mm round. His number two was Lieutenant (Junior Grade) Randy Smythe, MD, a very young-looking GP whose gray face revealed the strain of both the attack and the bloody press of even more casualties. He'd gone into the main tent right after the strafing run and had watched the SMO die with a fist-size hole in his chest. Smythe was sitting against a tree when we found him, covered in blood and looking like he was about to go catatonic. I told him who we were but he just sat there for a moment with one of those thousand-yard-stares I'd heard about. Then he declared he couldn't do this anymore and could I please take over as SMO. Just at that moment the island's air raid siren started up, causing a panic among the survivors of the first Betty raid.

Smythe pitched down on the ground and covered his head with his arms, while the stretcher-bearers tried to decide what to do. The big tent would be the target if the Jap planes came this way, but there was hardly time to get the wounded back down into the trenches. Greer ran to where the stretcher-bearers stood dithering

and began issuing orders. The sound of approaching aircraft engines encouraged the disorganized mob into action. I tried to get
Smythe up off the ground but he went rigid and wouldn't move.
I gave up and ran to where Greer was directing the stream of casualties back down into the bomb shelters. To my horror I saw a
Jap bomber coming over the nearby island just above the treetops.
The nose of the plane was blinking with muzzle flashes and then a
stream of shell splashes began to unzip their way across the harbor,
headed in our direction.

The Mitsubishi G4M twin-engine bomber, nicknamed "Betty"
for the Navy recognition charts, carried 20 mm cannons in addition
to their other armament. Everybody hit the deck as quickly as they
could. I rolled under the trunk of a palm tree that had been cut
down by the last attack. When I heard the sound of 20 mm rounds
whacking their way up the hill I just closed my eyes and prayed.
Then I felt the tree trunk jerk as a round went right through it and
blasted sand into my face. There was a roar of engines as the plane
flashed overhead and I caught a brief glance at the red meatballs
painted on its fuselage and then registered the fact that his right
engine was on fire as he swooped out into the strait. A moment later
a Marine fighter howled overhead and chased the burning Betty
down to a fiery death in the sea. I started to get up but then I heard
more engines and the booming of bombs going off. It sounded like
they were hitting that PT boat base across the harbor.

Things finally quieted down about five minutes later. I got out
from under "my" tree trunk and patted it gratefully. I saw Greer
pop his head out of a trench and scan the skies. There was a fierce
gasoline fire out in the harbor and I thought it might be a bomber
until I remembered the PT boat that had been coming our way.
I finally made it over to the main medical tent and saw that their
first strafing run on the field hospital had done a lot more than just
stitch holes in the tents and the tin roofs of the outbuildings. They'd
torn everything inside into junk, and there were still some small

fires burning from incendiary rounds. The dead had been removed by the time we got there, but evidence of their demise was frightfully clear. Sixteen patients and the SMO had been killed. A series of popping sounds erupted as we stood there taking in the destruction. Everyone flinched, and then we realized what those noises were: the ropes supporting the tent were breaking and in just a few seconds we were all enveloped by the heavy canvas fabric as the tent fell in, pressing us down onto the ground.

I ended up face-to-face with Greer under all that heavy canvas. He could only shake his head. We had to wait for some Marines to cut it off us. Once out, I told Greer we'd have to start over from scratch. "With what?" he asked plaintively, looking around at the crowd of hospitalmen and Marines trying to find someplace to put the wounded being brought out of the bomb shelters. Then I remembered those four longhouses I'd seen when we'd first crawled ashore after our PT boat sank. Wooden pole construction with palm frond roofs. Maybe forty feet long. I asked a Marine sergeant if he had comms with Captain VanPiet. If so, can he send a jeep?

Fifteen minutes later a jeep appeared, grinding its way up the hill to our destroyed medical compound. But this wasn't a jeep for me: this was Captain VanPiet's personal jeep. He stood up in the passenger's seat when he saw the collapsed medical tent, and then he saw Smythe. He began yelling orders at poor Smythe, who stared blankly back at him and tried awkwardly to salute from a sitting position. I hurried over and interrupted VanPiet's gathering verbal fusillade. He asked where the SMO was, so I gave him the bad news. He started to calm down. I told him that I was the acting SMO, for better or worse. Then I pointed to the wrecked medical compound.

"This can't be fixed," I declared. "They shot everything to pieces. We need a new location—and buildings, not tents."

"Oh, ya?" he responded. "And I would like a suite in downtown Amsterdam, soft beds, hot and cold running women, and a gallon of schnapps. Can you get me that, *hanh*?"

"I want those buildings I saw up on the hill where we came ashore," I said. "Longhouses. Four of them. I want them right now."

"The island people use those," he explained patiently. "They were the local provincial headquarters buildings, before the Japs invaded, back when the Aussies were in charge. And they're not buildings like you think. They're more like meeting places where you might host a barbeque."

"Right now," I said, "we have three slit trenches, thirty-six broken cots, a pile of broken medical equipment, and a fully air-conditioned tent."

"Air-conditioned?"

"Yes, sir, as in there are more holes than canvas. We must get our more seriously wounded people under a roof. Then we'll need generators. And screens. And a cemetery, I suppose."

That took the sarcasm right out of him. "Okay, Doctor, Okay. I'll see what I can do. But my bosses in Nouméa have told me not to antagonize the natives if we can help it. We don't need them taking sides with the Japs."

I looked around. The PT boat out in the harbor had gone down. There were two more out there now, probably looking for survivors. The one thing I didn't see were any of the islanders. I asked VanPiet where they were.

"Over there, I assume," he said, pointing to a much larger island across the harbor. "That's Florida Island. Behind that is Malaita. Most of the Tulagi people fled when the Marines came ashore. Supposedly Florida is secure, but the jungle bunnies tell me they're still mopping up pockets of Japs in the area. The natives have mostly gone to ground, probably to see who wins. They're not stupid."

That the Marines were still encountering Japs was not good news, but I was getting tired of arguing. "Well, they're not *here*, Captain," I said. "And we are, and we need basic shelter for our field hospital, such as it is. What if I just take over those four buildings? Nouméa's a thousand miles from here. If someone at Navy headquarters objects, they can come out and evict us. And then we have to talk about standing up a surgery."

VanPiet just stared at me. "Anything else, *mijn heer*?" he asked finally.

"Yes, sir," I said. "I'll need four *more* of those longhouses. With walls, this time. By tomorrow would be nice."

VanPiet grinned, and then shook his head. "Okay," he said. "But tomorrow might be difficult. Things don't go fast here in the Solomon Islands."

"Bettys do," I said.

His face sobered. "Ya, that they do," he said quietly. "Look: I have an idea for your surgery building. I took over a rubber plantation owner's house as my headquarters after the landing. It's about a mile from here. We have a generator. And walls. And screens on the windows, even. Get your surgery set up there and we'll get some longhouses built next to that."

"You have Seabees here?"

"No, but we have Marines. I'll ask them for help. All you have to do is tell them it's impossible and they work wonders. In the meantime, those longhouses up there are yours. I'll get you some transport to move the wounded. What's the matter with Lieutenant Smythe over there?"

I told him, and he made a disgusted sound. "I'll fix that," he said. "We have no time for that bullshit. Japs'll be back soon enough."

THREE

Captain VanPiet delivered. We got trucks to move our wounded from the wreck of the field hospital to the longhouses. He galvanized LTJG Smythe into taking charge of the move. Greer, Miller, and I moved the surgical equipment trunk to the planter's house with the help of VanPiet's four-man staff and a squad of Marines. The sprawling, single-story plantation building had porches on all four sides, a large kitchen, four bedrooms, and an expansive living room. We decided to set up the surgical theater in the living room. The bedrooms had been turned into offices of sorts, with one of them being the island's communications center. Captain VanPiet had kept one bedroom; the staff slept outside in one of those boxy, eight-man Marine tents.

Most important, we had electricity. We took the dining room table, which was an eight-foot-long Philippine mahogany beauty imported many years ago, and made it into the operating table. The Marines kludged up a surgical light fixture by taking four headlights from a damaged truck and wiring them into one of the overhead fans. The surgical equipment trunk had all the essential stuff we needed to operate, but no way to sterilize the instruments. The Marines brought up two fifty-five-gallon oil hydraulic drums from the wreckage of the harbor. They'd cut the tops off and then filled them halfway up with black sand. Then they'd put them on a roller assembly for twenty-four hours, after which the insides fairly glistened. Then they'd cut them in half lengthwise, made a firepit, and set them up as boiling water sinks. That took two days, but then we were in business, but only for the most drastically urgent surgeries, such as amputations to prevent gangrene.

Triage was a painful rite of passage into treatment. As casualties came in, the hospitalmen would scissor off the bandages to inspect the wounds. If they were already showing signs of infection, the patient would get a dusting of sulfa powder, something for the pain, and then be placed aside. The wound would be left unbandaged, on the theory that fresh air was better for it than a blood-soaked and probably contaminated dressing. With only one surgeon available, preference had to be given to casualties with no signs of sepsis. The sulfa powder worked, sometimes, and then the larger injury could be treated. Far too many of them died from general septicemia. Captain VanPiet was unaware of this procedure, but when I explained it to him he sent a message to General Vandegrift on Guadalcanal, in which he summarized what we'd done and what we needed, which of course was everything: anesthetic and a second anesthetist, more bandages, oxygen tanks, sulfa pills and powder, blood plasma, an autoclave, and on and on.

By then the Marines and some locals had erected four longhouses around the planter's house so we could have, however primitive, pre-op and post-op facilities. They made beds using bamboo from the neighboring islands of Tanambogo and Gavutu, scenes of heavy fighting on Tulagi's D-day. They wove netting made of strips of steamed palm leaves hung vertically, which would allow some air in and keep the larger insects out.

Lieutenant Commander Garr responded quickly, again using the PT boat squadron. They sent four hospitalmen and a full bag of surgical supplies, but no docs. About the time we thought we had what we needed to expand our care, a cruiser was towed into the harbor, dangerously down by the bow and showing signs of being worked over by heavy-caliber gunfire. The first eighty feet of the ship's front end had been blown right off by a Japanese torpedo. The cruiser would have normally carried a medical complement of one or maybe even two ship's doctors, a chief hospitalman anesthetist, and four hospitalmen. Unfortunately, they, along with twenty-four patients, had been killed in the battle by a direct eight-inch hit on the main sick bay.

Two destroyers, who had been her escorts, came in with her. We had to send most of their seriously wounded patients over to Henderson Field on a large landing craft escorted by three PT boats. Between what was left of the cruiser's crew and the crew aboard the two tin cans, they made the big ship seaworthy enough to get to Nouméa in New Caledonia. There they would attach a temporary bow structure, sufficient for her to make the long voyage back to one of the West Coast shipyards.

We did what we could for her wounded, which was mostly a triage process, but after our first report to the bosses across the strait, the Navy finally recognized that one surgeon working in a Tulagi planter's dining room wasn't going to cut it. Guadalcanal had no harbor. Damaged ships were ordered to pull in close to shore off Lunga Point and put their casualties ashore with the help of Marine landing craft. Too many of the ships were coming in with double crews: their own and the bloodied survivors from ships that had been sunk out in what they were now calling Ironbottom Sound. Garr and his teams could stabilize the most serious cases, and then seaplanes from Nouméa could transport them to the real hospital that had gone operational there. Once they'd off-loaded their casualties, damaged warships could come into Tulagi harbor and catch their breath. VanPiet's mission now became one of being in charge of a temporary shipyard.

That left my little medical team with a more manageable workload. The Marines had just about cleared out all the remaining Japs, so most of my work came from that PT boat squadron across the harbor. We weren't told anything about what they did operationally, but almost every morning there were stretcher jeeps coming from the harbor to the planter's house. The biggest problems were burn cases. The PT boats had three gasoline engines that used super-high-octane aviation gas. In the hot tropics of the Solomons, burn cases usually did not make it.

A four-man Marine recon unit came to the headquarters and reported something interesting a week after that cruiser limped out of the harbor. They'd been on Tanambogo, combing the island for the remnants of the Japanese naval infantry who'd put up such a fight when the Americans landed. They'd discovered a cleverly disguised observation post inside a hillside cave. The Japs manning it would have had a clear view of just about everything going on over on Tulagi, which was connected to Tanambogo by a tidal causeway. After killing the four Japs inside with a grenade, they'd found detailed drawings of the installations on Tulagi, including our efforts to rebuild the harbor facilities and our makeshift hospital, and an HF radio. They couldn't read the Japanese script, but it was obvious that Rabaul was being kept well informed.

"Why haven't they sent Bettys?" VanPiet wondered.

"Probably waiting for you to make it worth their while," the young Marine first lieutenant replied laconically.

That night Captain VanPiet held a council of war. He pointed out that the sudden silence from Tanambogo would probably provoke the Japs into attacking the Tulagi base again. He went around the table, asking his Marine counterpart, Lieutenant Colonel Mark Bates, USMC, how we could beef up our defenses. That led to a discussion about bomb shelters and dispersal of docked supplies. It was Randy Smythe, of all people, who came up with an idea. Captain VanPiet had forcefully shared his thinking with him after his "fainting spell," and he'd come back on the line, helping me in the surgery when not managing the clutch of patients out in the longhouses.

"What about the PT boats?" he asked.

"What about them?" VanPiet said.

"Well, the ones I've been on have two twin 50-caliber machine gun mounts, a 20 mm anti-aircraft cannon, and two single 50-caliber mounts. The last time the Bettys came in, they came from the east, over Florida Island. There are twelve PT boats over there across the harbor. Why not station them in the waters between Florida and Tulagi so they can welcome the Bettys when they show up? That's a lot more firepower than we have here on the island. The boats go out at night, but the Bettys come during daylight hours, so at least some of them should be available."

Lieutenant Colonel Bates thought that was a great idea. He pointed out that we'd need warning that the Bettys were inbound. It would also be nice to have a couple of fighters from Henderson Field in the area. That meant we had to tie into Henderson Field's warning network. Captain VanPiet told Bates to take charge and make that happen. I later learned that that was about all you had to say to a Marine officer. I wondered how much time we would have now that the Japs' observation post had been eliminated. I also wondered about the PT boats' availability. If they'd been out all night, they'd need rest and repairs during the day. I'd seen enough casualties from that squadron to know that they didn't just go out for a moonlight cruise. Captain VanPiet told me my part in this endeavor was to organize a way to quickly move patients from the longhouses to bomb shelters. He then thanked Smythe for his idea, causing that young man to positively beam. Redemption had been achieved.

We got one day and night to make our preparations. We'd chosen not to mark the hospital area or buildings with red crosses as this seemed to only attract the murderous bastards. The problem was that the Japs had been watching all the activity around the planter's house from that hill on Tanambogo. They had to know that it had become a worthy target for the bombers, along with the new pontoon piers and some ship repair Quonset huts that were going up. Bates came to see me the morning after our meeting. He told me it wasn't possible to dig out real shelters without Seabees and their equipment. He suggested another approach: make the Tulagi medical compound, the planter's house and the longhouses, into an anti-aircraft position. In his planning sessions with the PT boat people he'd learned that when one of their boats came in torn up beyond reasonable repair, they'd strip her for parts and then discard the hull. If two engines were damaged but the third one wasn't, they'd extract that engine. Same with guns, radar sets, radios. Everything would go into storage for another day.

"Thing is, Doc," Bates said, "they have three sets of rescued twin-barreled 50-cals over there. Assuming the bombers are coming soon, I suggest you and your people dig out three AA positions facing east, toward Florida Island. We'll get you some gunners and a bunch of sandbags. Three of those twin mounts can put out a total of forty-five hundred rounds a minute, which damn well oughta make a pilot go somewheres else."

I liked the idea. In fact, we could probably get some of our wounded-getting-better guys to help. I'd have preferred having some deep underground bomb-shelter bunkers under the house, but Bates was right: that would take the Seabees.

"The PT boat guys gonna play?" I asked.

He grinned. "*Hell*, yes, they are. I found out when I was over there that the Japs have equipped a bunch'a *Kawanishis* for night flying. Apparently, they cruise around the Sound until they see a PT boat's wake in the dark. Water here is really phosphorescent at night. They get behind them, quiet down their engines, fly up the wake, and then bomb the boats. Those boys over there got them a serious hate-on for those big seaplanes. They said they'd need about an hour's advanced warning to get set up, but they'll come out on ten minutes' notice if that's all they can get."

The next morning a Marine major came over from Henderson Field to brief us on the latest intelligence regarding Jap aviation units and warships up at Rabaul on New Britain Island. Captain VanPiet called a quick unit-commanders meeting to hear him out.

"The Japs are masters of the night-fight when it comes to ship engagements," the major began, "as we've so painfully learned. Their cruisers and destroyers are faster than ours, more heavily armed, and they both carry what the Japs call the Long Lance torpedo. Our torpedoes, well, lemme just say, are seriously inferior to the Long Lance. Worse, we think their battleships are gonna get into the game here. You've seen the pictures: great big black monsters with guns everywhere and those big pagoda superstructures up front. But: like all big ships, they're vulnerable to air power, so they like to come down through the Solomon Island chain late in the afternoon so as to get here at night, when our planes can't see 'em and they have all the advantages.

"It's the opposite for their bomber force. They have to fly five, six hundred or so miles just to get here, and they need daylight to do their work. So: they launch at oh-three-hundred from Rabaul to arrive down here at sunup, do their work, and then get the hell out of here before our guys can come up and tear them up. In practical terms, this means the Navy ships can expect to fight at around midnight. Anybody who qualifies as Betty-meat can expect an attack in the morning, within an hour after sunrise."

"So why aren't we posting combat air patrols from sunup to mid-morning to intercept the bastards?" VanPiet asked.

"We do," the major said, "but we need advance warning to do it right. Two days ago, we set up a dawn patrol. About the time the fighters had to come back in for fuel is when the bastards showed up."

"From whom do you get warning?" I asked.

"From people we call the coast-watchers. Aussies, mostly, who were here in one capacity or another before the war came and who now hump a radio through the jungle with help from the locals. They watch the Jap ships and aircraft and report to Henderson when they see a Jap cruiser formation or a gaggle of bombers headed our way. The Japs hunt them."

"So, if one of these coast-watcher fellas sees a bomber formation headed south from Rabaul," VanPiet asked, "we get an hour or so warning that a strike is coming?"

"Like I said, Captain, they take off at oh-three-hundred. Coast-watchers might hear them flying down the Slot but that's about all they can tell us—multiple large aircraft headed your way."

"Better than nothing," Van Piet observed.

"Yes, sir," the major said. "*If* his radio works. *If* the atmospheric conditions don't swallow his signal. *If* he actually hears them flying by. You get the idea, right, sir?"

"I certainly do," VanPiet said. "So, we do the best we can. Did Lieutenant Colonel Bates tell you what we've been up to?"

"He did, Captain," the briefer said. "Let me make one suggestion: Station a PT boat east of Florida Island at first light. Tell him to just loiter out there—making no high-speed wakes. If our early-warning system fails, he can give you fifteen minutes' warning."

VanPiet nodded. "We will absolutely do that," he said. "Now, we feel that they're coming sooner rather than later since our recon guys took out their spy nest on Tanambogo. Do your people agree with that?"

The major frowned. "Hard to say, sir. The Bettys have been working hard to stop our supply ships from getting stuff unloaded onto Guadalcanal. I think that's their main mission now: big, fat, slow cargo ships at anchor to put stuff ashore. Tulagi, well, it's becoming a base but not one that's directly hurting the Japs trying to retake Guadalcanal."

"You're saying they may not give a shit about Tulagi if they're getting their asses kicked over there on Guadalcanal."

"Um—" the major began.

"No, no," VanPiet interrupted. "I understand that. We're not looking to invite trouble. We just want to be ready in case they change their evil minds."

"There is one target over here that they may attack," the major said. "That MTB base. The PT boats have been out there every night raising absolute hell with the Jap supply ships. They can't come to the island in daylight because of our fighters and bombers at Henderson. They come at night, and that's when the PT boats are out there."

"Those boats doing good work for Jesus?" Bates asked.

"The Japs are ferrying supplies to their troops on Guadalcanal on large amphibious boats, escorted by their destroyers. The PT guys are claiming a lot of those cargo boats sunk, but..."

"The Jap destroyers are tearing them up, right?" VanPiet asked.

"All I can say, sir, is if they send bombers to Tulagi it won't be for the hospital or the repair facilities—it'll be for those guys across the harbor."

"An even better reason, then," Lieutenant Colonel Bates said, brightly, "that we get as many of those boats as we can out of their cove. That's why early warning is so important."

The major smiled. "Yes, sir, we know that. We'll give you as much warning as *we* get. I just can't promise it will be that hour they want."

"Nor do we expect you to," VanPiet said. "We're gonna do our best. I'm confident you guys will, too. I'll get the PT boat squadron to post a picket east of Florida starting at dawn tomorrow. Then we'll go have a sit-down with the MTB squadron commander, work up the harbor defense plan."

FOUR

As the acting senior medical officer on Tulagi, I went along with Captain VanPiet the next day to that tree-lined cove across the harbor. I used the fact that I hadn't seen their medical facilities as an excuse to come along, and VanPiet seemed to be amenable. Lieutenant Colonel Bates also joined us. We were going to meet with Lieutenant Commander Peter Cushing, USN, commander of Motor Torpedoboat Squadron 3, and some of his boat skippers. VanPiet had met him, of course, but the boats operated under a totally separate command structure which had nothing to do with VanPiet's Tulagi support command.

We rode over on a Navy harbor tugboat, one of two recently delivered with a load of dockside cargo-handling equipment. There was no pier as such, only some pontoon barges tied to trees on the shore. It looked as if one PT boat would be tied up to a tree on the shore, and then three more would be tied up to that boat. Some of the boats were half-overturned, with their noses buried in the sand. Crewmen were underneath, scraping the marine fouling off the hull like the sailing ships of old when they were careened for this very purpose.

Peter Cushing was a long, tall drink of water with buzz-cut blond hair and a hawklike visage supervised by a dramatically hooked nose. His nickname in the squadron apparently was Boss. He was wearing faded working khakis, sea boots, a pith helmet, and he carried a holstered government-issue .45 on his right hip. He introduced his executive officer, Lieutenant James "Deacon" Haller, USN. Haller was at least six foot four and skinny as a rail. He had a mop of wiry black hair reminiscent of Abraham Lincoln and the same awkwardly assembled face. Two other boat skippers were in attendance, similarly attired. One was a lieutenant, Roy Bond; the other was a lieutenant (junior grade), Morgan Stuart; both reservists. The enlisted men within view were all bare chested and wearing nothing more than dungaree trousers and sneakers. Some were just wearing khaki bathing suits and floppy hats.

Cushing gave Captain VanPiet a casual salute, and then VanPiet introduced Bates and me. We were led along a pontoon pier and into a grove of palm trees where there was a single Quonset hut. The air was filled with the sounds of boatyard maintenance: powerful engines being tuned up, hammering and banging as men worked to repair damage to the mahogany hulls, the spat of welding sticks, fuel trucks grinding their way down to the shore to pump high-octane aviation gasoline into the boats' fuel tanks, and the friendly banter of working men, trading insults and sweaty mechanical advice in equal measure.

Inside the Quonset hut there was a single long plank table surrounded by ammunition boxes serving as chairs. There was a fan in each corner and a lone desk at one end of the hut. The floor was pounded sand. There were charts hung along the rounded walls filled with route lines and what I assumed were markings representing known enemy positions. A hole had been cut into the other end of the wall that led to a shipping container that had been made into a radio room, where a single sailor was pressing earphones onto his head and writing down a message. I could hear a generator rattling away outside. The fans were doing their best but it still was at least ninety degrees in that hut. Cushing sat down at the head of the table and the rest of us took seats on either side.

"Sorry I can't offer you water," he began. "The Marines lent us a seawater distiller but once we loaded up the boats going out tonight there wasn't any more left. Captain VanPiet, how can we help you, sir?"

VanPiet prepared to respond but was interrupted by a loud shout from the radio room. "*Air raid, Air raid!* Bettys, *many*, low, inbound from Savo Island!"

A second later a siren began to wail outside. Cushing jumped up and told us to follow him. His exec ran for the boat landing. We bolted out of the Quonset hut and ran to a sandbag bunker fifty feet away. Cushing stood at the entrance and forcefully urged us down into the underground hole. Then he disappeared. The bunker was dark and damp, lined with palm tree trunks on four sides and across the ceiling. The floor was wet; we weren't that far above sea level. The whole thing smelled of rotting roots. There were more of the ammo crates to sit on, so we sat. The boat skippers had disappeared with Cushing. We looked at each other in dismay. The Japs were coming in from the west, not the east. Our picket boat had been outmaneuvered.

"When making war plans," VanPiet observed, calmly, "you must remember that the enemy always gets a vote."

There was a commotion in the narrow passageway leading from ground level above us as several enlisted men tumbled down into our dark little refuge. Then the roar of guns started, followed immediately by the sounds of bombs crumping into the wet sand. One came uncomfortably close. The bunker shook and every one of those palm logs moved around, creating a cloud of sand and dirt raining down on all of us. A second bomb hit even closer, causing the logs on one side to bulge out and then sag into the dirt floor, followed by one side of the bunker's roof. We barely had time to leap over to the other side, where we pressed up against the log wall. Fortunately, the bunker entrance was on the stable side of the bunker. I, for one, was ready to take my chances topside when we heard the sound of massed 20 mm cannons tearing things up above us.

Then it was over. I looked at Captain VanPiet. He just shook his head. Someone in the bunker expressed our collective sentiments: *fucking* Japs. We crawled up the mud-and-log stairway into bright sunshine and even brighter gasoline fires. Give it to the Bettys: they'd bombed the hell out of the PT boat base. While I stood there taking in the God-awful scene of cratered earth, blasted trees, shattered PT boats, and small knots of half-clad men down on the ground tending to the wounded, a sailor who looked like he may have been fourteen rushed up and asked if I was the doctor. After that, it was all a blur for the next twenty-four hours.

Miraculously, the Quonset hut had survived, so that's where I set up the aid station. The boat squadron didn't have a doctor, but they did have a hospitalman chief, Walter Higgins, USN; two petty officers; and two hospitalman apprentices. Chief Higgins had been trained as an anesthetist, qualified to use nitrous-plus, ether drip, and even thiopentone. The chief had wisely dispersed his medical supplies after a previous attack, so his assistants were soon hurrying into the Quonset hut with dirt-covered medical supply boxes unearthed from other hidey-holes back in bunkers out in the trees. Higgins and I did triage and then I went to work as best I could on the most seriously injured, assisted by the chief and one of his petty officers. Two men were clearly beyond hope, one with both legs severed at the hip and the other with his entrails puddled next to him on the stretcher. They were both in agonizing pain. I ordered the chief to give them each a spinal injection of thiopentone. Their trembling bodies relaxed immediately and then they died. Two others were badly wounded, but I thought I could stabilize them long enough for them to be sent across the strait. Eleven others had injuries we could handle, albeit only temporarily.

Although the Quonset hut had survived, the generator had taken a single 20 mm round and had given up the ghost. No fans, no lights, and a growing crowd of stretchers outside. By early evening we knew we were losing the battle, but then help arrived from Tulagi. That harbor tug had evaded a strafing run, so Captain VanPiet had taken it back over to the island and returned with help from our makeshift field hospital at the planter's house, including a surprise: two surgeons from Guadalcanal and, fortuitously, a replacement portable generator. The two docs, both regular Navy Medical Service Corps lieutenant commanders, took over with the fresh team. The chief and I gratefully backed out and went to find somewhere to just sit down and catch our breath. There was a longhouse near the shore where people appeared to be eating, so we trudged in that direction. As we did, we heard the sounds of boat engines lighting off, and then six boats began easing their way out of the cove, headed out for a night's work in the waters around Savo Island.

We realized then that a bombing raid on the MTB base was just another day in the life of being a PT boat sailor. Incredible, I thought, looking at the damage around us. There was a moment of surprised silence in the longhouse when Chief Higgins and I appeared out of the darkness. I think we'd both forgotten what we looked like after an entire afternoon of bloody surgery. Then the squadron XO, Deacon Haller, recognized us and stood up.

"Hey, it's the docs," he said, staring at our blood-spattered clothes. "You guys all right?"

We'd stumbled into what served as a makeshift wardroom for the squadron officers. It was a typical island longhouse, maybe twenty by forty feet, with a thatched palm roof, open pole sides, six mosquito-netting-covered cots at one end, and three oil lanterns hanging from the crossbeams. There were rolls of canvas curled up along the sides that could be let down to keep blowing rain out. There was a single long table in the middle, with the ubiquitous ammo crates serving as chairs. The XO made room at the table for the two of us, and then handed us each a metal canteen cup.

"Have a screamer," he said. "You look like you need one."

I didn't know what a screamer was, but Chief Higgins grabbed his eagerly. It turned out to be canned grapefruit juice, augmented with medicinal alcohol. After a couple of long drafts, I let out a grateful sigh. "Just exactly what I needed," I pronounced, which generated some laughs around the table.

"Wrong, Doc," Higgins said. "You need another, just like me."

Someone brought us each a bowl of what they called Solomon's stew, made with fried SPAM chunks, C-ration beans and franks, ketchup, and hot sauce. It was wonderful. After eating I asked if Lieutenant Commander Cushing was available.

"He went out tonight," Haller said. "Took offense at this bombing raid; said he needed to go out and kill him some Japs."

"I wanted to give him a casualty sitrep," I said. "We lost some this afternoon."

"Word is, you saved a whole bunch of others," one of the boat skippers said. "We've never had a real doc here. Wally Higgins there does the best he can, but someone said you're a real surgeon?"

I had to smile. Not according to Doctor Garr, I thought. But, hell, compared to *no* surgeon, even a resident would be an improvement. "Chief Higgins is no slouch at the operating table," I said. "If we saved some guys this afternoon, he gets at least half the credit."

Higgins, who was working on his third screamer, lifted his canteen mug at me in a Solomons salute, burped, and then put his head down on his folded arms and fell asleep at the table. One of the skippers informed me that Higgins had been up for thirty-six hours *before* the bombing raid, performing some surgical procedures by lantern light while one of the apprentices read the line-by-line instructions from the Navy Medical Corps *Field Surgical Manual.*

The dinner and drinking session broke up. I was offered one of the cots down at the end of the longhouse. Each cot had a single olive-drab sheet, a kapok life jacket for a pillow, and a mosquito net strung over two X-frames. Chief Higgins roused himself and left with one of the boat skippers. The smell of red, raw earth and diesel exhaust filled the air. The roaring bulldozers which were plugging bomb craters nearby acted as a lullaby. It took me at least thirty seconds to drop off to sleep.

I woke to the sounds of the torpedo boats coming back in from their night operations. It was just breaking dawn and already insufferably hot and humid. I availed myself of the nearby latrine and then a rainwater barrel to wash up. By the time I got back to the longhouse, there was coffee going. As I stepped in, I was astonished to see two baskets of hot rolls on the table, along with a can of honey. I just stood there and looked at them until one the skippers laughed and told me, yes, they were real, and to help myself. Apparently one of the cooks had been a baker before the war and provided fresh baked bread and rolls to the squadron messes every morning. Butter would have been nice but no one was bitching. The rolls were wonderful. I wondered how he kept the flour from getting moldy. One of the skippers said he kept the flour in a steel GI trash can, and covered it in a one-inch layer of alcohol.

The longhouse filled up quickly with returning skippers, and I was introduced by Lieutenant Commander Cushing as "our new squadron doctor." It took me hearing that three times before I suddenly realized what he had been saying. He grinned when he saw the surprise on my face.

"That Doctor Garr fella, from the field hospital over on Cactus?" he said. "He told me he was reassigning you to us last night when he sent those other two docs in. They're gonna run that little surgical clinic you set up over on Tulagi for a coupl'a days, but then it'll be shut down. He said they'd send us what you needed to stand up a casualty station here for the boats. Welcome to the Hooligan Navy, Doc."

I raised my coffee mug and tried to make it look like I was pleased. I don't think I succeeded, but, on the other hand, I would now be *the* MTB squadron doctor and not the unwanted orphan from the Guadalcanal medical operation. Garr probably thought he'd gotten his revenge, especially after what that other doc had said to him about not opening a book recently. I went to get another roll but they were long gone, so I refilled my coffee cup and sat down on one of the cots to listen to all the stories about what had happened out there the previous night. I learned that the night's planned operation had turned into a total SNAFU, with boats getting lost, shooting at one another, attracting a couple of Jap night bombers, and firing torpedoes that hit absolutely nothing. Or at least that's what it sounded like; I wasn't really familiar with what these guys did out there. It did sound interesting, though. Cushing finally steered the insults and banter into a more formal mission debrief. That's when Chief Higgins showed up and asked if I could come to the Quonset hut.

As we walked through the grove of palm trees, some of which had been uprooted by bomb blasts, he filled me in on the new arrangements that were being put in motion.

"Those two docs told me you're gonna be our new squadron doc, which I gotta say from my point of view, is medium wonderful. They're gonna go back over to Tulagi this morning. Cactus sent an LCU over to take as many patients as possible back there. One of the docs told me that your new assignment was somebody called Garr's doing. Said to tell you you're gonna be better off with us than with the Cactus operation, on account of there's gonna be a four-stripe Medical Corps captain coming in from Nouméa to run that field hospital."

"A four-striper will bring an admin staff," I said. "If nothing else, I'll avoid the paperwork avalanche that's coming. By the way, I don't think I got a chance to tell you yesterday: I never finished my full seven years of surgical training before I left school and signed up. Did three years of surgical residency at Duke until Pearl Harbor. Garr thinks I'm an impostor."

He stopped on the muddy path. "You listen to me, Doc. I've seen a lot of surgeons in my eighteen years, okay? You're a better surgeon than most of them. Those two docs from Cactus kinda said the same thing. You're gonna do fine here, and that's an f-a-k fact."

"In your humble opinion," I replied, but I was secretly flattered.

"Damn straight," he said as we resumed our walk to the hut. "And, even better, now *you're* the poor bastard gonna be on the hook for all those drug custody signatures and stuff. Instead of yours truly. I like the *hell* out of that."

I had to laugh.

FIVE

The bombing attack had been noisy but the damage wasn't as bad as the attack two weeks ago. The boats were called torpedo boats, not gunboats, but each of our mahogany beauties sported one 20 mm automatic cannon, one twin-barreled, turret-mounted 50-caliber machine gun, and two single 50-caliber pedestal-mounted machine guns in addition to the four torpedo tubes. One of the boat gunners explained the math: A single 50-caliber machine gun can shoot 750 rounds per minute to a range of 2,000 yards or 6,000 feet of altitude. The Bettys typically came in at 3,000 feet to deliver their bombs. With six boats in the cove, they'd run into an anti-aircraft position that was shooting 18,000 rounds per minute at them, *not* counting the 20 mm guns. This storm of fire had apparently distracted the pilots and bombardiers to the point where most of the bombs had fallen into the harbor or the jungle. Three planes had been seen crashing into the sea off Tulagi. Two boats were destroyed, one of the pontoon piers sunk, and a lot of damage to the base camp from the Bettys' own 20 mm guns, and, of course, the bomb shelter would have to be rebuilt. The Quonset hut had survived, which meant the radio station had survived.

My immediate problem was to cobble up yet another medical facility. HM1 Greer was returning to Guadalcanal with the two docs and Miller, his apprentice. Lieutenant (JG) Sykes had been charged to close up our newly minted Tulagi facility and then report across the strait to Garr's operation. Tulagi was now technically "secured," thus there was no need for a medical aid station there. The arrival of a captain over on Cactus meant that he would immediately begin consolidating all medical services in the Solomons theater of operations under his direct command. That made sense, but it didn't solve my immediate problem. I needed somewhere to provide immediate casualty care for the crews of our squadron. Chief Higgins came up with a solution.

"There's a bunch of Seabees over there on Tulagi," he said. "They're fixing up the harbor facilities after that LST blew up. Scuttlebutt says they're building a real pier for the big transports, since Guadalcanal doesn't have a harbor anywhere. How's about I go over there and see what they can do for us."

"Absolutely," I said. "Besides, I think Boss Cushing wants his base operations hut back."

The next day, two LCMs showed up in our cove. LCM stood for Landing Craft, Medium, popularly called Mike boats. One discharged a full-size bulldozer, the other a few hundred wooden pallets piled with bags of cement mix. That was the beauty of amphibious landing craft: they could drive right up to the beach, run aground, drop a ramp, and drive their cargo off. With all that weight gone ashore, the boat could then simply back off the beach and go get more stuff. The chief in charge was called "Tiny Tim" Hauser. He was, of course, a giant, with reddish blond hair, a graying beard, and hands the size of dinner plates. Higgins and I went down to meet him. He introduced himself and then told me in a booming voice what he had in mind.

"We're gonna scrape a big damn trench," he began. "Eight foot deep, twenty wide, a hundred long. Line the damn floor with a cement shell. Then we're gonna line the damn walls with pallets, stood up on end, two high. Then we're gonna fill them pallets with damn cement. Meanwhile, my boys'll cut down a whole damn shit-load of trees, and then we'll put a damn log roof on the trench. Two layers of tree trunks with a layer of damn steel Marston matting in between. There'll be a line of support columns running the whole damn way down the middle inside. That way we can finish it up by putting all that damn sand and dirt on top in a wide mound. I've got two electricians on my team. You give me a diagram of where you want what, and they'll damn well wire it up. Your boss says he has a generator he can lend you. How's that sound, Doc?"

"Like damn Christmas, Chief," I said, somewhat in awe. "Can you really do all that?"

"Can do, Doc. That's our motto. We'll even disguise the damn mound by covering it in the tops of all them damn trees we cut down. They'll all die but then it'll look like damn jungle that took sick. Damn Japs'll never see it."

"Hate to sound like a whiner, Chief," I said, "but we'll need water down there. And overhead lights. I'll get you that diagram, but since we'll be underground, we'll also need some kind of forced ventilation. Our job will be to stabilize casualties so they can be sent over to Cactus, so mostly it'll be cots, a small surgical area, and a safe place, away from rain, insects, Japs, and other undesirables."

He thought about that for a moment. Then he nodded. "Can do, Doc," he said. "We'll figure all that damn shit out. Don't worry about a damn thing."

And, by God, they did. Four days later the entire damn thing was in place. The chief himself was the dozer operator and he had the trench opened up and excavated in one morning of howling diesel engine and lots of smoke. The dozer was enormous and equipped with a 50-cal machine gun at the operator's station, which was surrounded by vertical plates of steel for protection. His tree-cutters began hauling in tree trunks while the trench was being dug out and then they built a crude yard-and-stay crane rig to place the trunks. Others hammered reinforcement bars through the pallet walls, then tacked up plywood over the open boards of the pallets. The cement was next. Bags of the mix were opened into the dozer's huge bucket and then water added. Hauser then mixed it by rotating the bucket up and down and then poured it directly into the vertical pallets. They gave it a day to harden while they placed the tree trunks, which had been cut to twenty-four feet, long enough to rest on the top of the dirt-cement walls. Hauser told me the dirt would subside so that the tree trunks would ultimately rest on the pallet walls.

The Marston matting was the same stuff they used over on Cactus to "pave" the airfield after bombing or shelling damage. Long strips of steel, punctured with a pattern of holes to reduce weight, came off the ships in large rolls. A bulldozer would unroll the steel matting after another dozer had pushed in the crater dirt. They could have a runway back in action within one hour, and the matting gave us a comforting layer of steel in our tree-trunk "roof." Ventilation was achieved using twenty-inch red-devil blower fans from one of the cargo ships. There was no way to provide ducting, so they installed two red devils to draw air down from topside through a section of steel pipe, and then one blower to suck it out of the space and send it back topside. The first thing I noticed when I went down into the space was that it was much cooler than topside. That alone would provide great relief for suffering wounded men.

Boss Cushing and Deacon Haller came to see the finished space. Cushing immediately asked how much of it I would need to provide a casualty aid station for squadron casualties, seeing as that new four-striper over on Cactus was supposedly centralizing all *hospital* functions over there. I'd thought the whole thing would be a medical setup. Silly me. As soon as Boss experienced the cooler and far less humid space, he explained to me that this would be a perfect place for crews that had been out all night to get some real sleep, instead of having to curl up under a salt-encrusted tarp on their boats, fighting off noise, insects, and daily downpours while trying to get some rest. I had to admit, for a casualty triage and first-response medical station, I probably only needed thirty feet of the 100-foot-long bunker. Boss brought the skippers down into the bunker and explained what he had in mind. God, yes, was the unanimous reply. Deacon started making arrangements.

It was a good thing he did, because three days later a smirking and now full Commander Garr and the new four-striper, Captain Horace Benson, Medical Corps, USN, showed up at the PT boat base. Word had gotten back to Cactus that the Seabees had constructed a large bunker to be used as a medical aid station. At 2,000 square feet, it was larger than anything over on Cactus and far more secure than the tent city I'd started out in. The captain, a short, somewhat rotund orthopedic surgeon by trade, was one of those guys who looked like he went through life with a permanent expression of disapproval of everything and everybody he encountered. I could see in a heartbeat that our Cadillac bunker would seem like a direct challenge to the new regime standing up over on Cactus, as I'm sure Garr had been quick to point out. We were saved from a tongue-lashing by Boss, who'd hurried to the bunker when he got word a four-striper was intruding on his patch. He explained in vivid detail to the suspicious captain that most of the bunker would serve as a refuge for his desperately sleep-deprived boat crews, with only one end being reserved for casualty aid prior to transport to Cactus.

Apparently mollified, Benson and Garr left. I heard Garr saying to the captain as they walked off: "*That's* the guy I was telling you about, sir. Third-year resident posing as a qualified surgeon, if you can believe that."

Benson just shook his head and they both went out of sight up the ramp leading to the surface. Boss, unaware of my purple past, asked what the hell that was all about. I told him I'd fill him in at evening prayers, as the after-hours decompression sessions were called. Evening prayers was also where the screamers lived. Then

Wally Higgins and I went to work finishing up the now much-diminished casualty station. I never did get to tell my tale of woe to Cushing because he went out that night, substituting for a skipper who'd come down with some kind of jungle fever. The boats went north up what everybody was calling the Slot, that 500-mile-long stretch of water that runs like a channel from Guadalcanal all the way to Rabaul, down which what was becoming known as the Tokyo Express made its way nightly to raise hell with the US Navy and the Marines around Guadalcanal. The boats were on the hunt for a reinforcement convoy bringing Jap infantry down to Cactus. In a way it was a good thing that the boats went where they did, because that night the Japs sent two *battleships* to Guadalcanal with orders to destroy the airfield and all its works.

These two behemoths arrived off Lunga Point in the middle of the night and began lobbing fourteen-inch shells onto Henderson Field. Each shell weighed about one ton and the target wasn't exactly capable of getting out of the way. The noise of their salvoes was thunderous. Everybody left at the MTB base got up to watch the horizontal bolts of lightning illuminating the western horizon, followed by ear-punishing thumps from the big guns and then a long crescendo of explosions ashore. It seemed to go on forever but probably even longer than that over on Cactus, itself. We never actually saw the battleships, only the enormous balls of fire coming out of each barrel every time they fired. It looked like there were two slowly moving volcanoes out there in the strait. Two to three miles of the western horizon were in flames when they finally stopped firing. Higgins wondered aloud if I thought the hospital had been destroyed. I was afraid to venture a guess, but I couldn't imagine anything around Henderson Field had survived that. "Where the hell are *our* battleships?" he complained.

"Back at Pearl," I said, without thinking.

"Oh," he said, with a sick look. "Right."

The hospital over on Cactus did survive, sort of. One of those fourteen-inch shells had landed in the Big Top itself, which had been evacuated by that time. It failed to explode, which was fortunate. The bad news was that it was still there, with just the base of the one-ton projectile showing from a large sand crater that had pushed over one side of the tent. A bomb-disposal crew had been sent by Catalina from Nouméa. They recommended dismantling the medical tents and putting them somewhere else, and then they'd blow the shell up. Finding a new location wasn't the problem. Henderson Field, its runways, fuel storage areas, aircraft parking revetments, and 80 percent of its planes had been destroyed. The one outfit that had been spared was the Seabees, and those bulldozer warriors got to work even before the smoke cleared. By daylight they had the main runway operational, and by noon twenty-five Navy and Marine Corps replacement fighters began landing.

It was a good thing they did, because right afterwards a division of Betty bombers showed up over the Sound to attack the clutch of transports that was anchored off Tulagi, waiting for their turn to off-load. This time the transports were under the protection of an entire destroyer division, five ships, who were most definitely *not* anchored. Once again, we got a ringside seat while those tin cans flamed one bomber after another with an entire skyful of AA fire. Two Bettys decided enough was enough, dumped their bombs into the sea, and tried to leave the scene. But not soon enough. Four Marine fighters jumped them on their way north and showed us why our fighter pilots called the Betty a flying gas station. I had to wonder what the Jap high command up there at Rabaul would think about the fact that, even after a battleship bombardment, Henderson Field was clearly back in action the very next day and that *none* of their bombers had returned.

Our squadron had been somewhat sidelined right after these momentous events. As the squadron doc, I attended the morning debriefings and then the afternoon pre-briefings, mostly to learn about what these guys did and to get to know the boat skippers.

The boats went out only at night; in daylight they were vulnerable to enemy *and* friendly air attacks. I learned that the squadron, *my* squadron now, was running the eighty-foot-long Elco brand of motor torpedo boats, or MTBs. Their main anti-ship armament was four 2,600-pound MK VIII torpedoes, launched from twenty-one-inch torpedo tubes bolted to the deck. Each torpedo packed a 466-pound TNT warhead and had a range of eight miles, running at forty knots. The boats' propulsion was provided by three Packard 2,500-horsepower marine engines.

I approached Deacon one morning and asked if I could go out on a patrol. He said he'd talk to Boss, but since I was the only doc they had, Boss would probably say no.

Cushing surprised him. He said, hell, yes, I'll take him out. He needs to understand what our people are going through out there. That afternoon I attended the pre-brief, which wasn't very elaborate. In theory they would go out at night in search of enemy ships, which they would then attack with torpedoes. About half of them carried something called radar, which allowed them to see enemy ships electronically in the dark. Their principal tactics involved patrolling at slow speed while conducting a radar search for Jap ships. When they detected one, they'd accelerate to forty-five miles an hour, roar in, release their torpedoes, and then run like hell. The reality was somewhat different. First of all, they were equipped with old WWI vintage aerial torpedoes, which half the time just went over the side and drowned. Secondly, when a PT boat went up to full speed, it made a very large wake, which, in the phosphorescent seas around the Solomons, was a dead giveaway to all those first-class Japanese optics. As soon as they started in for the attack the escorting destroyers would open fire with five-inch guns. Boss pointed out that it made for a pretty simple fire-control problem for the Jap gunners: the boats had to come straight at the enemy ships; the five-inch guns only had to lay their barrels down on the bearing and shoot continuously to wipe out their wooden-hulled tormentors.

Added to this was the problem of night-flying *Kawanishi* seaplanes. They would come down the Slot and arrive in the area of Guadalcanal at about the same time as the Jap transports and their escorting destroyers. They didn't have this radar gadget that we had, but they didn't really need it. From above, the Jap pilots could see those phosphorescent wakes even when the boats were loitering at slow speeds. They'd circle behind the boats, fly up the wake, and release a stick of bombs. Our boat skippers could be forgiven for sometimes thinking that all their efforts were somewhat superfluous, until one night they caught a Jap submarine unloading troops and supplies onto one of Guadalcanal's northern coves. This time the torpedoes did work, followed by several high-speed passes with the machine guns that tore the sub and the troops waiting to off-load her to pieces.

We left at sundown that night and headed out toward the waters around Savo Island, where four Allied heavy cruisers and about a thousand Americans and Australians were asleep in the deep. I was riding Cushing's boat, which had been designated the command boat. We went out at a moderate fifteen knots to suppress the wakes. A crewman took me around to each of the deck weapons—the twin 50s, the single 50, and the 20 mm cannon back aft. I took a quick look into the radar display that was down in the crew room; all I saw was a fuzzy green ring in the center of a small, circular screen which the operator told me was "sea return"—the beam bouncing off the light chop in the strait and reflecting the signal back to the boat's radar receiver. The more active the seaway, the larger that ring would grow, sometimes large enough to conceal a lurking enemy. A single dim ray of light swept around the display. The radar antenna was on a stub mast up above. It squeaked quietly every time it passed the 330-degree mark for some strange reason.

Cushing took his formation of three boats to a spot midway between Savo Island and Cape Esperance on the northern end of Guadalcanal. We shut down two of the three engines and then ran at idle on the third. Supposedly the fleet forces around Guadalcanal had been told that we'd be out there, when and where. The night was steamy hot, with low flying scud clouds, occasional passing squall lines, and not quite enough wind to keep the engine exhaust at bay. Boss made sure I had a steel helmet and a life jacket on, which made the heat even more hostile. The water temperature was eighty-five degrees, barely cool enough to maintain the engine coolant systems. The other two boats were out there in the gloom nearby, also idling. I stayed up in the cockpit area with Boss; the rest of the crew appeared to be dozing on their gun and torpedo stations. The radar operator kept watch down below, where it was even hotter. He, too, wore a kapok life jacket and a helmet. Battle dress, as it was called, was mandatory at all times when at sea on patrol. Trouble came quickly around Guadalcanal.

"Do we know if there are Japs coming?" I asked Boss.

"Sort of," he said, cupping a cigarette lighter in his hands and lighting up. "The coast-watchers keep a lookout from the islands up and down the Slot. If they see a Jap formation—ships or bombers—they send an alert to Cactus."

"These coast-watchers—are they all Aussies?"

"Mostly," he said. "These are men who were here before the war—planters, colonial administrators, missionaries, and some soldiers of fortune. When the Japs came, some of them disbanded whatever they were doing and took to the hills. The Aussie government got them radios and some basic logistical support. They depend on the natives on their islands for protection. If they'd been good to the natives, the system worked. If not, well..."

"So, these guys are our eyes and ears up and down the Solomons chain?"

"Precisely, and they're invaluable. It's a dangerous life because the Japs know about them. They hunt them and try to direction-find their radios. If they catch one, they execute him and any natives who've been helping him."

"Why wouldn't that deter the locals from helping?"

"Funny thing, that. These Micronesians have long memories of conquering invaders: Spanish, Arabs, and even Chinese going back centuries. These islands are their home, and they're not happy when 'occupiers' show up, especially when they turn out to be barbarians—like the Japs. They appear to be docile, submissive. When the strong wind blows, survivor trees bend. But then sometimes whole Jap patrols vanish out in the jungle. Like I said, if a planter goes bush to become a coast-watcher, everything will depend on how he treated the locals who worked for him before the Japs showed up."

The radio speaker in front of us on the control console sputtered to life with a strange squeal, followed by a series of clicks. "Boss, this is five-four-four. Radar contact, three-four-zero, range eleven miles, closing."

"Five-four-four, roger contact," Boss responded. "Track and report." He then called down to our radar operator and asked if he had the contact. Negative. Boss then gave the order for all boats to light off all their engines.

"Why can't our radar see them?" I asked.

Cushing shrugged. "Hell if I know," he said. "We'll wait until one more boat sees the contacts, then we'll set up for an attack."

Our other two engines rumbled to life in a cloud of exhaust smoke, shaking the entire boat. I suddenly realized that this was why a large, four-engine seaplane could sneak up on a PT boat going at full speed: even at idle, those three 2,500-hp Packards made conversation just about impossible.

"If we tangle with destroyers tonight," Boss said, "I want you to get below with the radar operator; it won't help you if we take a five-inch, but the mahogany stops a lot of frag."

"Got it," I said.

The 544 boat came back up on the radio. "Two large, several small contacts. Estimate speed twelve knots, course south."

Cushing ordered the boats into a line-abreast formation for a head-on attack on what he estimated was a formation of two tin cans and some smaller craft, called self-propelled amphibious barges, loaded with troops and supplies. He explained that if he did it right, only the forward two five-inch mounts on each destroyer would be able to fire on us while steaming into twelve torpedoes rushing right at them.

"I've got them," our radar operator called out. "Range nine thousand yards, bearing 350, steady course. Loose column formation."

Cushing acknowledged and ordered the formation up to twelve knots. The hulls wouldn't plane at that speed, so our wakes wouldn't be that big.

"Four minutes to intercept," Cushing told the crew. There followed the sounds of machine guns jacking rounds into their chambers. The torpedo director was turned on to establish communications with the four torpedoes. One crewman took the tube covers off each tube and hand-cranked the tubes out to a ten-degree firing angle to make sure we didn't run over one if it failed to accelerate.

"Two minutes!" Cushing shouted. "Commit the gyros!" Then he began to accelerate the boat. Our other two boats were required to keep station on Cushing's boat, so there was no need for radio orders. I was still standing in the cockpit, my discomfort from the helmet and the bulky life jacket long forgotten. I stared out into the gloom ahead of us and saw absolutely nothing, but when I looked to our sides, I could very clearly see the bow waves of the other two boats as we came up to forty knots.

So could the Jap destroyers. A star shell popped up above us, followed by the boom of the gun that had fired it. By now we were roaring along at full power. Boss raised his hand and dropped it. Four fish fired in succession and drove ahead of us at forty knots toward the by-now alerted enemy. Red flashes appeared directly ahead of us, although how far away I couldn't tell. Boss, still at the controls, began making a wide weave just as ear-cracking explosions began to raise surprisingly large fountains of yellow-tinged water around us. I started to duck down and then realized the futility of doing that: this was a *wooden*-hulled boat. This was a good idea, I kept telling myself, suddenly longing for my bunker.

And then we were among them. I caught a brief glimpse of what looked like an enormous bow coming straight at us, its bow wave rising almost to its main deck. He was obviously trying to ram us, but Boss turned across the onrushing bow and then every one of our guns opened up, sending streams of tracer fire into the upper works of the destroyer. I could actually see rounds ricocheting inside the destroyer's pilothouse. Our gunners shot up his stacks, topside AA gun positions, the boats, antennas, life rafts. Our guns were using APIT rounds on the 50s; armor-piercing incendiary tracers. Every fifth round was painted with phosphorous, and I saw several small fires getting under way along his decks. We were so close alongside that the destroyer's guns could no longer bear on us but that didn't stop them from shooting, their five-inch guns belching fire and smoke right in our faces.

We flashed by the destroyer in seconds, our 20 mm cannon gunner trying desperately to hit the rack of depth charges back on the destroyer's stern. The destroyer's aftgun mount then took up the fight, sending red-hot rounds right over our heads as Boss bobbed and weaved at nearly fifty miles an hour in the destroyer's wake. I couldn't see either of the other two boats until there was a large explosion off to one side of the Jap formation. Then we ran into the troop barges. Once again, our gunners were shooting at everything in sight, and then I realized the everythings were shooting back. We made two very hard turns, which forced me to sit down or fall overboard. Something grazed the top of my helmet, knocking it to the back of my head despite the chin strap.

At that moment I saw one of our other boats thundering past us, her entire stern area a mass of orange high-octane gasoline flames. All the barges were firing at her, and her front-end gunners were shooting back until the boat just exploded. Boss made a few more violent turns to shake off the streams of Jap tracer fire coming our way. In the distance something was burning on the water and it looked too big to be a PT boat or a barge. Maybe one of our torpedoes had struck home. I looked aft and saw some smaller fires on the water astern of us, and then it was all over.

We blasted along at top speed for five more minutes before slowing down to a mere twenty knots. Amazingly, the other surviving PT boat appeared out of the dark and closed in on us from one side. Together we headed for the western side of Savo Island, hoping against hope there wasn't a second Jap destroyer formation behind the island. As soon as we were in the shadow of Savo Island itself and could no longer see the fires behind us, we slowed down to twelve knots, mindful that the Jap destroyers may have called in a *Kawanishi* or two. I tried to catch my breath; everything had happened so fast that I still couldn't take it all in. I could hear the clink of spent machine gun cartridges rolling around on the deck and inside the gun tubs. Then one of the 50s went off, firing a single round that had cooked off in the red-hot chamber, which made everyone jump. The gunner quickly removed the belt and jacked out the next round. All the barrels were so hot that I could see the dull red glow of the steel. They were literally smoking in the dense, humid air.

The 544 boat came up on the radio and reported seeing the 621 boat go down.

"We need to go back?" Cushing asked.

"No, I don't think so," the other skipper said. "When she blew

up, I could see the three engines come out of the water, still attached to their props. There can't be anything left."

"Unless," I offered, unasked, "someone got blown clear off the
deck."

Boss gave me a long look and then nodded. He instructed the
other boat to maintain formation and said that we were going back
to take a look. We turned around and headed southwest, maintain-
ing slow speed. Boss asked the radar operator if he had anything; he
did not. We really didn't know where to begin searching, but every
kapok life jacket had a tiny flashlight pinned to its lapel and a police
whistle sewn into a pocket. If there was a guy out there in the water
with his light on, we might, just might, spot him. *We* couldn't turn
on lights for obvious reasons.

We went back to the area where we'd lain in wait for the Japs to
come to us. Then we moved slowly north, along the line of where
we'd initiated the torpedo attack. It was all an approximation. No
one had been navigating or keeping track. Boss spread the two
boats out to 500 yards distance to increase coverage. Suddenly
we smelled fuel oil. One moment the usual humid warm air of the
tropics, the next the eye-stinging reek of bunker oil.

"Maybe we did get one of those bastards," Cushing muttered.

We slowed even more and then one of our crew said: "Look—
over there."

We all squinted in the dim light available. Then we saw a head.
And then another. Then several. They were bobbing in the sea,
except their faces looked shiny black.

The oil. They were *in* the oil slick.

They were Japs.

"What the hell do we do now?" one the crewmen whispered, as
if he didn't want the Japs to hear him. We realized we were surrounded by at least a hundred men in the water, just bobbing around
in an oil slick. None of them raised a hand or shouted. It was eerie.

"I know what to do with them," the forward gunner said, reaching for his 50-cal ammo belts. Boss raised his hand.

"No," he said. "Their own ships left them here. We'll let nature take its course. Besides, Japs don't surrender. Let 'em die in peace. It's what they want. Our guy was west of here, headed north. That's where we're going."

With that he told our companion to head northwest, same speed, same distance. We searched for three more hours, using the expanding-square technique to cover the most ground. Run north for half a mile, then turn east, run for three-quarters of a mile, then turn south, run for a full mile, and so on. We found nothing, not even a gasoline slick. Two hours before sunrise we gave it up and headed for home, still crawling along by MTB standards. The boat was silent except for the engines and the squeak of our radar antenna. No one had anything to say. I finally approached Cushing.

"You knew it was hopeless, didn't you?" I asked quietly.

He shrugged. "I thought it was, but I can't say I *knew* that it was. You can't know unless you go look. You were right to suggest it."

I had no answer for that.

"And besides, I did it for the rest of the squadron. Guys gotta know that we'll try to find them, if at all possible. Sometimes it isn't. I learned that from the Marines. They don't leave anybody behind, not even their dead, if at all possible. All Marines know that, so they fight harder."

We kicked it up as nautical twilight began to bloom on the eastern horizon and headed for the barn. The *Kawanishis* knew better than to hang around once dawn broke and Cactus fighter planes came out hunting, but the Bettys weren't bashful about making strafing runs on PT boats during the daylight.

The next day at noon we held a memorial service for the lost crew. A chaplain came over from Tulagi to conduct the service. It wasn't the first time and probably wouldn't be the last. The padre said the appropriate words and Cushing made a nice speech about the individuals on the boat. I was impressed—he knew all their names and even some detail about each one of them.

Our nighttime search hadn't been the only one. A Catalina launched out of Henderson Field with fighter protection at sunrise and searched the entire Savo Island area for an hour. They found the big oil slick we'd encountered, but spotted no floating Japs or debris. Either they'd been picked up on the reinforcement convoy's return trip, or they'd succumbed to all that oil and the ever-present sharks.

Somehow word got back to Cactus that I'd gone out on a patrol. A sharp rebuke ensued. Cushing was blasted for allowing it, and I was equally censured for requesting it. Boss shrugged it off. "Screw 'em if they can't take a joke," he quipped. "And besides, I think it's important that you have some firsthand knowledge of what goes on out there."

After the Jap battleship bombardment, the theater commander, Vice Admiral Ghormley, was relieved by Vice Admiral William Halsey, USN. "Bull" Halsey was cut from a different cloth from Ghormley. He immediately detached two of the American battle-wagons escorting the carriers and sent them into the waters around Guadalcanal. The Japs had handily cleaned the clocks of most of our Navy's heavy cruisers in a series of night actions, so when they came back for another heavy bombardment run on Henderson Field with cruisers and the battleship, IJN *Kirishima*, they got a nasty surprise.

USS *Washington* and USS *South Dakota*, both equipped with sixteen-inch guns and radar-directed fire control, laid into the Jap formation with devastating results. *Washington* was the star. *South Dakota* suffered an electrical failure early in the action that disabled her big guns. She then became the main target of the Japanese battleship and suffered a pounding. But, concentrating on *South Dakota*, the Japs failed to even detect *Washington.* She soon smothered the Jap battleship in sixteen-inch armor-piercing shells weighing in at 3,200 pounds each. *Kirishima* went down in the early hours of the next day.

From our vantage point over near the Tulagi harbor, the gun-fight out in Ironbottom Sound had looked like two thunderstorms duking it out in the darkness. We got more of the story when Boss came in with three boats. This time they'd gone beyond Cape Es-perance and set up shop on the northwestern side of Guadalca-nal, hoping to be able to mount an ambush on any reinforcements coming in. They had detected the two American battlewagons as they came up from the southwest. They'd been informed by the coast-watcher network that a Jap battleship had been sighted in the Slot, headed south. The American battleships had come up the west coast of Guadalcanal using radar, hoping to surprise the on-coming Jap formation. Our guys naturally assumed that the large contacts that popped up on their radars had to be Jap ships, because large American warships had been in short supply lately. Ever game, they headed in, lunging out of a cove at forty knots.

The battleships and their four escorting destroyers all sounded the alarm. Then the admiral on *Washington,* Rear Admiral Willis A. "Ching" Lee realized what they were looking at. He came up on the local fleet radio net in plain English, identified himself by name *and* Academy nickname, and ordered the boats to stand clear. After a moment of stunned silence, Boss ordered his three boats to turn away and head back for the cove. Then he answered the ad-miral: "Standing clear," he said. "We've got you covered." What the admiral thought of *that* was never revealed but I thought it was pretty gutsy of Cushing. It was fortunate that the radios worked that night because between them, our two battleships sported *forty* five-inch guns along with their eighteen sixteen-inchers. Cushing and company would have become mahogany kindling in about ninety seconds.

The remaining Jap warships withdrew after this shocking loss, along with the convoy of cargo ships and troop transports they'd been escorting. This meant that the Marines on Cactus got a bit of a breather, but not for long. The Jap base at Rabaul received reinforcement Betty squadrons, and each sunrise in our neck of the woods was announced by air raid sirens. There were more fighters over on Cactus now, so the Bettys got a hot reception, but on two occasions cargo ships in Tulagi harbor were the targets. One ship was set afire and had to be abandoned, another, after being torpedoed, ran herself aground in order to save the supplies. Cushing told us that the Japs knew they were losing to America's growing logistics superiority. Food, ammo, tanks and trucks, artillery pieces, medical supplies, and those all-important reinforcements were streaming in from safe bases like Nouméa and seaports in Australia. There were rumors that the Jap soldiers were starting to call Guadalcanal "Starvation Island." The few, very few, prisoners being taken by the Marines were being described as skeletal.

The underground bunker provided by those amazing Seabees turned out to be a Godsend. The Japs were frantically stepping up their efforts to get basic supplies, especially food, to their troops trying to retake Henderson Field from the Americans. Boss had changed the squadron's tactics once the Jap push began in earnest. Instead of going north and trying to intercept the Jap reinforcement shipping before it got to Guadalcanal, he stationed his night patrols within ten miles of the known Jap landing positions. This saved fuel, which was still pretty tight, and increased the chances of making an intercept. They never knew which route the Japs were going to use to Guadalcanal, but they did know where their various routes all terminated. The Japs responded by beefing up their destroyer escorts that shepherded the barges down the Slot.

Jap destroyers were more lethal than ours. They were fast, capable of almost 45 mph, and armed with six five-inch guns and those monster Type 93 Long Lance torpedoes. A succession of American heavy cruisers limping into Tulagi harbor with their entire front ends blown completely off was a sobering testament to the power of the Long Lance. While their heavy forces came to Guadalcanal periodically, their destroyers were almost always out there at night and they began taking a real toll on the MTBs. My small casualty station at one end of the bunker quickly morphed into a full-scale emergency surgery room. I was no longer running a casualty collection station, and we had to ask for help from our Marine battalion medics.

I duly sent a message to Guadalcanal, but Lieutenant Commander Garr replied that no help was available and reminded me that surgery was no longer my mission. To my surprise, Captain Benson overruled Garr and sent in two senior hospitalman chiefs who'd received special training for burn casualties. He also sent over a much wider range of supplies. The burn cases were our biggest problem, since the MTBs ran on super high-octane avgas. Being able to stabilize these patients belowground in relatively cool surroundings upped their survival rate significantly. The squadron's dreams of using the facility to get a good night's sleep evaporated as more and more Jap destroyers came down from Rabaul to mix it up with the American PT boats.

Cushing decided he needed to change his tactics again. He got some help from a naval aviator one of our boats had rescued over near Florida Island. He was a naval reserve lieutenant, but his prewar job had been as the resident mathematician on the war-gaming staff of the Pacific Fleet commander. He told Cushing that the Jap bombers had crafted an attack geometry wherein their torpedo planes would fly past their target and get out in front of it, instead of heading in from the sides. They would then split up and take stations thirty degrees on either side of their target's course, turn inbound, and release their Type 93s in a converging wedge in *front* of the oncoming target. No matter how their target maneuvered, turning left or right to avoid the torpedoes, at least some of them would hit. The British had lost two battleships, HMS *Prince of Wales* and HMS *Repulse*, to this technique off the coast of Malaya.

He told Cushing that roaring in from the beam of your target gave every advantage to the destroyer: all of her guns could be brought to bear on the approaching boats. Attacking from the front meant that only two of his five guns could be brought to bear on you. "If you know where they're going, get out *ahead* of the enemy formation and reduce speed to idle so your wake becomes invisible. Spread out so that you can fire a spread of torpedoes instead of a single line. Track them on radar, and when they get into five thousand yards, accelerate to whatever speed it takes to stabilize your torpedoes' gyros, and launch." And here was the interesting bit: then, he said, "Keep going, *full* speed now, and run directly *at* the approaching Jap formation. They will see you and they will turn to present all their guns—left or right, it doesn't matter— which will expose their entire length to an approaching swarm of American torpedoes."

I was present for this briefing and saw that Cushing and his boat skippers were entranced. It made so much sense and, if they could take out the escorting destroyers, the amphibious boats jammed with soldiers and supplies would then become easier pickings.

"Practice it," our grateful visiting flyboy said. "We own the daylight; the Japs own the night. Practice the maneuver until you can do it with a minimum of radio comms. You only need one working radar and good comms to set it up. A three-boat formation can project twelve torpedoes. You guys should clean up out there."

Cushing picked three of his best skippers and then took them out into Ironbottom Sound during daylight to practice the maneuver. It was trickier than they had anticipated, especially because they had to wait for the torpedo guidance system gyros to spin up and stabilize on the same heading the boat was running on. Unlike a submarine torpedo, which could be commanded to launch and then turn to the desired heading, the MTBs had been issued older, air-drop torpedoes, which required the plane to remain on a steady course for up to a minute to align the gyros, making them easy pickings for shipboard AA guns. A second problem was that their torpedoes required a boat speed of at least twenty knots to achieve a stable launch if you were in a hurry. At that speed the boats kicked up a wake, which would give the Japs early warning that they were under MTB attack.

Cushing's solution was to separate the two problems. Don't be in a hurry. Steady the boat at low speed and then spool up the torpedo's gyro. Once the gyro was running and stable, close into 3,000 yards instead of 5,000, and do so by letting the Japs close the boats instead of the other way around. Then, at the last minute, accelerate to full power and launch the fish as soon as you were at twenty knots or better. And then keep on accelerating. A Jap destroyer formation approaching at twenty knots, added to the MTB's speed of forty knots, meant that the combined closing speed was sixty knots. That was a mile a minute. The Japs would then have thirty-four seconds to react to the sudden appearance of MTB wakes dead ahead.

They practiced a daylight attack for two more days and then tried it at night. They found that they had to iron out some radar-directed approach problems, but finally it came together. That night they went out at sunset to intercept an approaching convoy of destroyers and small transports reported by coast-watchers. The anticipated time of intercept was just after midnight. What happened next turned into a lethal fiasco. For some reason, the operations of the MTB squadron this night had not been coordinated with the local naval commander. An American destroyer squadron commander had planned an ambush of the approaching Japanese. He, too, was trying something new. Instead of heading up the Slot until they ran into radar contacts, they took a station west of Savo Island and then waited under radio silence. When our four torpedo boats were detected on radar on the *other* side of Savo, the destroyers pounced. Thinking the Japs had done some kind of end-around, Boss let fly with three boats' worth of torpedoes, or twelve fish, keeping his boat's fish in reserve. Then he ran straight at the approaching destroyers. American destroyers.

The destroyermen opened fire first and began landing shells all around the MTBs racing in at them. Then their sonars detected the torpedo boat engines, which is when the squadron commodore realized he might be attacking friendlies and ordered a cease-fire. That order did not reach the twelve torpedoes, of course, and when the tin cans' sonars detected *those* screw-beats the entire confrontation degenerated into a melee of wildly evading destroyers, totally confused PT boats, and a hash of radio communications as each "side" talked right over the other's transmissions. The squadron commodore ordered up illumination rounds. Radar was wonderful but he needed to actually *see* what the hell was going on.

Enter the Japanese convoy, which had watched a sudden explosion of gunfire ahead of them and had slowed down. When the American star shells lit up the sea surface, everybody could finally see everybody. The Japanese squadron commodore ordered his three destroyers to charge. The result was what the fighter pilots called a fur-ball. Everybody shooting at everybody and all of them running at full speed. With the exception of Cushing's boat, the MTBs were, of course, out of torpedoes, so they ran in against the Jap destroyers with their machine guns. The Japs in turn brightened the night with five-inch gunfire. The American destroyers replied in kind and also fired torpedoes at the Japs, who returned the favor. After only a few minutes of this appalling circus, everybody disengaged and withdrew.

Our three boats emerged unharmed. Unfortunately, one American destroyer ate a Long Lance and disappeared in a flash of bright white steam. One wildly maneuvering Jap destroyer somehow managed to cut a second Jap destroyer in half, and then one of our boats nearly collided with the bisected Jap ship. Everyone opened fire with all their guns, which finally caused a magazine explosion on the bisected Jap tin can, finishing her off. Our close-in PT boat went down as well, but almost everyone got off before she sank. The remaining Japs decamped, and the remaining American destroyers picked our guys up an hour later.

The following morning, the American destroyer squadron commodore's flagship, USS *Keene,* pulled into the harbor at Tulagi. The commodore let it be known that he was there for an urgent conference with Lieutenant Commander Cushing and Captain VanPiet, whom he mistakenly assumed were in charge of the MTB squadron since they were based in Tulagi harbor. The meeting was held aboard the *Keene,* anchored in the harbor, because the commodore was senior to everyone else there. There were two Navy cargo ships also in the harbor, so all available harbor boats were being used to get cargo over to Guadalcanal, in addition to the usual clutch of Mike boats from Cactus. That meant that VanPiet and Cushing couldn't actually get out to the *Keene* for two hours, which didn't make the commodore any happier. Boss finally had to call for one of the PT boats to come over to Tulagi and take them to the *Keene.*

Cushing told us the story at evening prayers. They finally got aboard the *Keene* and were escorted to the commodore's cabin, where they found a seething ComDesRon 12 pacing the cabin. Cushing and VanPiet were not invited to sit down, but as the commodore began to wind himself up, the Tulagi air raid sirens announced the arrival of six Betty bombers. The skipper of the *Keene* immediately slipped his anchor and pointed his destroyer out into Ironbottom Sound to avoid being caught stationary by the incoming Jap bombers. The commodore glared at Cushing and Captain VanPiet and then hurried to the bridge as the *Keene* went to GQ.

The PT boat that had been standing off the *Keene,* waiting to retrieve Cushing and VanPiet, followed the destroyer out and joined in the anti-aircraft barrage that was exploding over Tulagi. She tucked close in to the destroyer's stern and added her machine gun and 20 mm fire to the destroyer's five-inch and 40 mm. The *Keene* shot down one of the bombers, which crashed close aboard and pelted the *Keene*'s bridge with wreckage. The PT boat shot down another, and then the Bettys blundered into the rest of Destroyer Squadron 12, which had been loitering outside the Tulagi harbor. When the shooting finally stopped, only one Betty had managed to escape, crapping bombs into the Sound as she fled north.

The appearance of a Jap bombing raid had taken much of the wind out of the commodore's sails, assisted by the sudden storm of bomber fragments blowing out all the *Keene*'s bridge windows and encouraging everyone on the bridge to establish close personal relations with the deck. Captain VanPiet salvaged the situation by suggesting that the commodore come ashore for a calm discussion among reasonable men with perhaps some gin thrown in. To Van-Piet's surprise, the somewhat shaken commodore agreed. The PT boat took everyone to the Tulagi pier. From there they went to the planter's house, where they were joined by a senior intelligence officer on General Vandegrift's staff.

The upshot was that the MTB squadron was folded into the cruiser-destroyer task group commander's daily planning. The days of the MTBs going out at night to more or less raise hell with anything Japanese were over. There was an admiral involved now, and what our squadron lost in terms of independence was more than made up for by being part of a bigger, more centralized picture. As Cushing pointed out at evening prayers, the expansion of the naval command and control structure had to mean we were starting to turn the tide against the Japs here in the Solomons. Now all we needed was for someone to convince the damned Japs.

I was a little surprised to have become part of the command inner circle, although, as the squadron doctor, I reported daily to Cushing on what was going on in my underground clinic, which had been surprisingly busy. Every time we thought we'd be able to clear out and clean up, another ship would limp into Tulagi with casualties serious enough to require my efforts as a surgeon. The two chief petty officer surgical assistants were a true blessing, having lots of experience and used to working under less-than-ideal conditions. I told them both that I was always open to suggestions during a procedure, which I think helped tighten the team. They knew a lot, being chief petty officers, and it would have been stupid of me to maintain the all too common "surgeon knows best, and if he wants a suggestion, he'll ask for it" attitude.

One night a battered light cruiser came in to discharge wounded. Captain Benson arrived from Cactus to observe, without Garr this time. He walked into an imperfectly controlled bedlam of triage: immediate actions for burns, amputations, and a bunker full of men writhing on bloodstained cots. He scrubbed in at once and went to work, which is when I remembered he was an orthopedic surgeon. After three hours of often heartbreaking work, we'd been able to classify the wounded into those who could be transported over to Cactus, those who couldn't for the moment, and those who would not survive the night. The cruiser herself didn't survive the night. She rolled over at about three in the morning and slid down the slopes of the undersea mountain whose top we occupied, leaving behind a lone anchor chain and a small fountain of oily water rising from her grave some 3,000 feet down. Fortunately, they'd seen it coming and managed to get everyone off before she capsized.

We took a break while the chiefs and the hospitalmen who'd come with them tidied up. The entire MTB squadron was in for the night because the higher-ups were still deciding on how to employ us so as to avoid a repeat of the other night. The maintenance people worked all night to catch up. I took Captain Benson to evening prayers and told everybody who he was and also that he was an orthopod of distinction. He was in his early fifties, but he now was a lot thinner, with dark pouches under his eyes that he hadn't had the first time I met him. He was also a lot friendlier. He praised our little bunker hospital and admitted he'd had no idea how seriously overwhelmed our station became if a ship limped in here instead of anchoring off Guadalcanal and transferring wounded. Boss pointed out that most of the cruisers we'd seen here since the landing had their front ends blown off and no longer *had* anchors. The Japs had been overestimating our ships' speed, so their torpedoes often got there early, meaning they hit on the bow instead of amidships.

We went back to the medical station, fortified by one screamer each since we knew we weren't done. Captain Benson made rounds, a procedure I hadn't had the luxury of doing since coming to the Solomons. I found him a cot when he started to totter and he went down like a tree. It wasn't as if he'd been goofing off over there on Cactus, but our pace, when the shit hit the fan, was a big surprise to him. The following morning a small fleet of amphibious craft showed up to take casualties over to the Big Tops. Chief Higgins sidled up to me as the captain and two other doctors from Cactus were supervising the onload.

"What now?" I asked, rather abruptly, and then apologized. I was more tired than I realized. He took it in stride.

"Well," he said, lifting his chin in the direction of the captain. "He's gonna come kiss you good-bye in a few minutes. Tell you what a good boy you've been, after all. When he asks you if there's anything you need, be sure to tell him that our medicinal alcohol is about to run out over here."

I gave him a look. "Are you telling me that the only reason I've been included in the afternoon debrief was that I just might be the only way that evening prayers can keep going?"

"Heavens to Betsy, no," he protested piously. "You've been included because of your vast strategic knowledge, cunning tactical sense, a beautiful personality, *and* we hear you make your own clothes."

He'd just described a homely high school girl that one of her friends was trying to set up a blind date for. I waited with what I hoped was a stern face, but it was really hard.

He had the grace to look embarrassed, although not very. "*You* sign the supply chits now, remember?" he said. "I was just making sure you didn't forget something important, that's all."

"Okay," I said. "So, tell me this: where's the grapefruit juice coming from?"

He gave me a perfectly innocent look. "From grapefruits?" he said.

I couldn't help it. I spluttered into laughter. Then stopped when I saw Captain Benson coming up the hill as the casualty convoy made preparations to get under way with its dismal cargo of broken nineteen-year-olds.

Let the record show I did take care of business, *and* that the good captain didn't bat an eye. Chief Higgins stood ten feet away, nodding his approval. I felt a sudden surge of pride. When a chief approves, you know you're doing all right.

SIX

Boss Cushing came to see me the next morning in the medical bunker. Apparently Chief Higgins had done a little bragging about *his* foresightedness and Boss was worried that I'd had my feelings hurt. I reassured him that there was no offense taken and that I was grateful to be kept in the loop about the bigger picture. Even some of his own skippers didn't enjoy that privilege. A sailor interrupted us with the news that a Mike boat had dropped its ramp at the PT boat pontoons with a load of medical stuff from Cactus, along with two new docs and two new hospitalmen fresh out of school. Those two worthies had news: newly promoted Commander Garr had been sent back to Nouméa to take over one of the departments of the rapidly expanding field hospital operating there. I was saddened to no end, but then they told me that there was scuttlebutt about bringing our whole MTB bunker team from Tulagi back over to Cactus. Boss perked up at that scary rumor and then said he'd go see Captain VanPiet.

Chief Higgins and I went down to the pontoon to supervise a working party who'd been tasked to move the supplies up to the bunker. Sure enough, there were four wooden boxes of something labeled SURGICAL STERILIZATION FLUID $CH_3\text{-}CH_2\text{-}OH$. I immediately recognized that formula as ethanol, which indeed would make an effective sterilization fluid but also a perfectly acceptable screamer. I asked Higgins: "Really, where the hell do you get grapefruit juice?" He took me aside and then, somewhat reluctantly, explained how MTB squadrons obtained supplies, both authorized and unauthorized.

Food, as we all knew to our digestive torment, was provided from the United States Army. Even the Marines had to eat Army chow, which they truly resented. Warships were supplied by the Navy at sea, and their food was far superior to the canned-everything that the Army was famous for, mostly because ships had freezers. Beyond basic field rations, the MTB squadron didn't receive much support from the Navy, mostly because they were based ashore on a series of islands. The Navy resupplied its fleet ships from under way replenishment ships built for that purpose. When a carrier task group refueled it also reprovisioned. Spare parts, frozen food, ammunition for guns big and small, avgas for their scout planes, bombs, replacements—all came aboard through ship-to-ship transfers at sea, usually at night because two large ships tied together by fueling hoses, wire transfer rigs, and personnel highlines, *and* steering a straight course at constant speed for sometimes a few hours was a submariner's dream target.

The result was that the Navy's MTBs were the orphans of the Navy's own supply system. They basically had to beg and scrounge for anything they needed outside of the world of torpedoes, ammunition, and replacement engines. As Chief Higgins explained it, the MTB supply system had become something of a criminal enterprise. If the Navy couldn't, or wouldn't provide, the torpedo boat squadron's midnight requisition team would go into action.

"Do I really want to know about all this?" I asked him.

"We-e-ll, you know those generators that provide for the underground bunker?"

"Yes, of course. The Seabees—"

He shook his head. "The Seabees did what they could, and they made us a by-God first-rate bunker, but providing generators isn't in their mission statement. For that we had to call in Alibaba and his forty thieves."

"Oh, God," I said. "Now I *know* I don't want to hear this." Visions of courts-martial were glimmering in my head.

"C'mon, Doc," he said. "You *do* need to know this, 'cause this is how things really work out here. You've met the supply officer, right?"

I had. Ensign Frank Lang Worcester, SC, USNR, was the scion of a wealthy New England family who'd been slipped into the Navy Supply Corps based upon his finance degree from Yale, probably with the naïve hope that he would thereby avoid combat. Ensign Worcester was a tall, thin, effortlessly effete young man with the appropriate Ivy League accent and academic credentials. He went through life confident that, when all this "Asian unpleasantness," as he called it, was over, he'd soon be a partner in his father's Wall Street firm. Ending up here in the Solomons must have shocked the shit out of him, but I'll give him this: he was nothing if not game. On the other hand, his ignorance of "how things *really* worked" was as great as mine. The old hands, and especially the chief storekeeper for the squadron, one Chief Petty Officer Eli Caswell, quickly saw a use for this highly presentable Supply Corps officer, who was technically his boss. In the Navy, a ship's supply officer was called "the Chop" because the Supply Corps collar insignia looked like a gold pork chop. A very junior supply officer was called "the Lamb Chop."

Chief Caswell, whose nickname was "Alibaba," ran an informal crew of enlisted men who made up the forty thieves. His best operator was a commissaryman second class named Roosevelt Young, a sleepy-looking and somewhat older black man who hailed from Harlem, New York City, where his family had run a bootlegging operation during Prohibition. Black men in the Navy were restricted to only a few ratings, such as cook (commissaryman), wardroom steward, or ship's serviceman (laundry) because segregation was still the law of the land back in the States. Alibaba and his forty thieves went into action any time a cargo ship, troop transport, fleet supply ship, or destroyer tender came into Tulagi. Their mission was to midnight requisition anything they could on the "gotta have" list. Batteries, cans of engine lube oil, radar parts, tools, food, hydraulic oil, canvas, rope, toilet paper—all necessities for a squadron of fighting boats but unattainable through regular supply channels.

The procedure was as follows: They'd send the Lamb Chop aboard the target ship in the harbor, where he would dutifully submit a whole bundle of requisitions to the ship's supply department. The target's storekeepers would then look over the requisitions to determine if they had what was being requested in their storerooms. They'd then approach their Chop to get his approval. That worthy would then have to come to the supply office and inform our Lamb Chop that none of the things he was asking for were authorized for the motor torpedo boats. Lamb Chop would always ask if that was because the ship didn't have any of those things. Oh, yes, we do, but the MTB squadron isn't on our list of supported commands. We have all these things, or most of them, but we simply are not allowed to issue them to *your* squadron. I'm sorry, but regs are regs, you know? You need to go back to your parent command for these supplies.

Bastards of the fleet that we were, there was no parent command, at least not west of the Panama Canal Zone, where our training center was located. Lamb Chop would come back to the squadron and report the dismal results. Alibaba, on the other hand, now knew that this particular ship—cargo ship, replenishment ship, repair ship—had at least some of the stuff we needed. The only problem now was to find a way to relieve said ship of those materials.

I told him to stop right there. What I didn't know I could absolutely deny. He was not persuaded.

That was the point where Roosevelt Young came in, he continued. One thing a big ship would not deny a small ship or outfit was a food handout, requisition or no requisition. Our XO, Deacon Haller, would make the first approach. He'd go aboard the visiting ship and speak to her XO. We need food, he'd say. Not much, but something besides C-rations. Can you spare some? Of course, we can, the ship's XO would say.

Wonderful, Deacon would say. I'll send over one of my cooks. His name is Roosevelt Young.

Roosevelt would make his way after dark to the supply ship on one of our boats and go aboard, saying he was there to see some of his friends down in the galley and to pick up some chow supplies. Forewarned by the ship's XO, they'd let him aboard. There was no reason for concern because everyone knew that the black guys liked to get together to visit with each other. Besides, he was just a cook. His boat and crew would stand off out of sight of the quarterdeck, usually back at the stern. When no one was looking, they'd creep in and tie up to the anchored ship's quarter, opposite of where the officer of the deck maintained his station. Roosevelt would then wander innocently through the ship, nodding politely to officers and chiefs that he encountered. He'd wear his cook's white jacket, which made him even more inconspicuous.

The supply ships that came into Tulagi off-loaded their cargo on a nonstop basis, with working parties inside the ship moving a constant flow of material to large hatch openings in the ship's side. Roosevelt would go all the way back to the stern and then pass down a rope, which allowed some of the forty thieves to send up a rope ladder. They would then climb aboard. Roosevelt would lead them to the staging areas for the side hatches, and the PT boat crewmen would casually join the working party going down into the ship's storerooms and bringing all sorts of "stuff" up to the side hatches. Only not all of it would make it to the side hatches, as individual thieves would get "lost" on the way and then make their way back to the stern, where they'd lower their treasure to the waiting PT boat. Then they'd rejoin the working party.

This would go on for perhaps an hour or so, and then the thieves would decamp back down to their boat. Once the thieves were safely aboard the boat, Roosevelt would appear on the quarterdeck and make obsequious thank-yous to the OOD and his quarterdeck watch as the PT boat approached the sea ladder. They'd ask about the food supplies, and he'd tell them there'd be a Mike boat coming over in the morning. He, himself, was obviously not removing anything from the ship, so they'd send this itinerant cook on his way, just another "invisible" black guy.

A variation on this was carried out when an actual repair ship came into Tulagi. This time the thieves would be enginemen and gunners who were on the hunt for scarce engine parts or things like machine-gun assemblies. They'd be led by Alibaba himself, only he'd show up on the quarterdeck with some canvas bags and ask for the head of the Chief Petty Officers' mess. He'd be taken down to the Goat Locker, as the CPO mess was known, where he'd sit down with his fellow chiefs for a friendly cup of coffee. Then he'd open his bags and reveal some interesting Jap souvenirs, acquired during his occasional trips over to Cactus, ostensibly to scrounge for parts but also to collect stuff Marines had looted from the battlefield. He would "pay" for these things in 20 mm ammo, which was in desperately short supply over at Henderson Field. We, on the other hand, had loads of the stuff because the 20 mm cannon, unlike the 50s, used only about 275 rounds per minute; the 50-calibers fired 750 rounds per minute. That math was part of the conspiracy.

Alibaba would tell the chiefs what he needed, in return for forgetting to take his bags, containing his collection of Jap pistols, bandoliers, uniform hats, and occasionally one of their small ceremonial swords. One of the ship's chiefs would quietly excuse himself, returning in an hour after having organized a quick working party to load the PT boat with whatever they'd come for. Alibaba would then make his manners and head for the quarterdeck, where that PT boat, now riding somewhat lower in the water, would approach the sea ladder to retrieve him.

Alibaba wasn't above organizing raids on the actual supply dumps on Tulagi Island itself. Sometimes the supply ships would be able to off-load a lot more stuff than the small fleet of amphibious boats could carry over to Cactus, inspired by the knowledge that each sunrise could bring Bettys. All of this material was assembled near the pontoon docks for easy onloading to Mike boats the next day. Chief Higgins played a role in these forays. The supply dumps were guarded by Marines, doing seriously boring duty as sentries. Higgins would supply the raiding party, which would go out after midnight, with canteens of joy juice—usually reconstituted powdered orange juice enhanced with medicinal alcohol.

Three boats would approach the back side of Tulagi and plant their noses into the sand at the beach. The thieves would then walk over to the supply dumps on the other side, each carrying burlap bags. They'd gather near the supply dump, start a small fire, and then pretend to be having an unauthorized late-night party. The Marine sentries inevitably would come to see what was going on, only to be offered some joy juice—in return for looking the other way. Tulagi had been declared secured, so Marines who otherwise would have refused in the face of possible enemy attacks, happily joined in. Some of the thieves would have been designated to "maintain'" the party, while the rest would swiftly go through the pallets of war matériel destined for Cactus and confiscate what they needed.

I just stared at Higgins when he was done with these revelations. He grinned, and then told me that there were still other gambits being employed, but since these were under the personal direction of the XO, Deacon Haller, I probably didn't need to know about them. I heartily agreed, already wishing I didn't know as much as I did.

That afternoon the entire squadron was told to stand down in the cove. Something was up and the admiral commanding the waters around Guadalcanal didn't want PT boats complicating his tactical picture, whatever that meant. After a spiffy meal of Spamburgers, reinforced with some of the locals' fermented fish sauce and hot peppers, evening prayers convened, but with beers for a change, if only to put out the gastric conflagrations. I asked Boss about the supply problem.

"What supply problem?" he asked. "We have beer, don't we?"

"The chief told me that we were orphans when it came to getting repair parts, new gear, or anything much out of the Navy's supply system."

Cushing brushed off the question. "Don't worry your head about supply problems, Doc," he said. "Need another beer?"

In other words, none of your beeswax, sonny, or, more probably, what you don't know you can't tell. I took the hint and had another beer.

Sometime that night there was a hell of sea-fight over toward the northwestern horizon. I could hear and even feel the rumble of really big guns, even down in the bunker. I climbed out of my cot and went topside. There, way out beyond the infamous Savo Island, big ships were duking it out in a vigorous display of yellow and red lightning and, more ominously, bulging clouds of yellow, oil-fueled fires, all of it accompanied by a steady rumble of thunder. Some of the boat skippers had come out of their tents to cheer the Navy on. I hoped and prayed that victory was what we were seeing. I made a mental note to grab Chief Higgins first thing in the morning to tell him to get ready for mass casualties.

By the time I got down to the bunker with coffee in hand the next morning I found Higgins was way ahead of me, as befits a competent chief petty officer. He had a working party out exhuming extra bandages and other materials from the various underground dispersal stashes in the palm groves. The Cactus air force was already out in strength, probably bent on taking care of any Jap cripples from the action last night. An hour later I got word from Cushing's Quonset hut that there would be destroyers coming in shortly with the wounded.

"Any idea of how many?" I asked.

"*Very* many, from what I'm hearing," was all he could tell me.

Chief Higgins and I had talked about what we would do if this situation arose here on the Tulagi side. Captain Benson had wanted all large casualty situations to come directly to Cactus, but what if they couldn't, for whatever reason? I'd then asked Benson for two large medical tents, each with hospital cots for fifty men. We'd put them up with the help of the redoubtable Marines just inside the nearest palm tree grove. They were clearly marked with big red crosses, although the Japs, bloodthirsty bastards that they were, seemed to enjoy bombing those when they found them. The Marines brought up black sand from the beach to "pave" the interior, and they set up a way to catch and store rainwater. Then we buttoned them up to keep out bugs and other critters.

Thank God we did. At around noon three battered-looking destroyers, whose gray-painted five-inch gun muzzles were burned black, eased into Tulagi harbor. Their decks were still littered with brass powder cans, amongst which lay more than three hundred wounded sailors. The same destroyer commodore who'd come in to yell at us was among them. We tried to elicit some help from Cactus only to find out they had even more of their own to deal with. Six-hundred-plus casualties: what in the name of God had happened out there?

We didn't have time to find out as the depressing process of triage began yet again. Our two new doctors were overwhelmed by what they saw, and not just by the scale of it. A gun battle at sea is a special horror unto itself. Every man in the ship with the exception of the bridge crew and the signalmen is locked into a honeycomb of steel compartments, with steam lines, electrical cabling, ammunition, high-pressure air lines, and flammable fluids of all descriptions keeping them company. When big shells start arriving there's no diving down into your slit trench. At sea there was also no withdrawing to a safer position on the battlefield once the fleets engaged in a gun battle. An eight-inch-high explosive shell going off in a boiler room meant that everybody down there would be roasted alive by escaping 600-psi steam in about five seconds. The real hell of it was that you, personally, couldn't do much about keeping alive. You had to trust the captain, the officers, and the gunners to keep that eight-inch shell from making that direct hit in the first place.

No one could explain exactly what had happened out there last night. As best we could tell from all the rumors flying around was that an American cruiser-destroyer formation of some fifteen ships had steamed right into a similar Jap formation, resulting in a melee that Admiral Lord Nelson would have recognized (and probably welcomed). Ships on both sides had maneuvered wildly in the dark at one in the morning to avoid physical collisions, while others drove past each other at ranges of a few hundred yards, trading salvoes whose projectiles probably hadn't gone far enough to even harm. Some of the destroyer sailors were telling tales of firing 40 mm anti-aircraft cannon directly into the windows of those massive, black pagoda superstructures of the Jap heavy cruisers. Even more ominously, there were mutterings about American cruisers firing into each other in all the confusion. An eight-inch shell of uncertain origin had smashed its way into the flag bridge of one of our cruisers, killing an admiral and most of his battle staff. *Whose* shell was now a matter of some interest, but there were rumblings that USS *San Francisco,* a heavy cruiser, was the culprit.

The PT boats were pressed into service to ferry the most seriously wounded across the sound to Cactus. Even though Captain Benson had his hands full, they had a better chance over there than down in my pallet-lined bunker. We thought we were relatively safe from a Betty bombing attack since the morning sky had been filled with Navy and Marine planes hunting Jap cripples. Somebody failed to tell the Jap bomber command. A baker's dozen of Bettys made a surprise bombing run on Henderson Field, coming this time up from the south. Their mission was to suppress the launch of fighters, and then they came over to Tulagi to attack the three destroyers that were still anchored there. I was up to my armpits in gore when the air raid warning went off so I didn't get to see what happened next, but Doctor Hobbs, one of the new arrivals, had gone topside for some fresh air and a coffee, and got a ringside seat.

A mighty roar of gunfire erupted seemingly right over our heads out in Tulagi harbor. The three destroyers mustered fifteen five-inch guns among them, plus 40 mm quad and 20 mm twin mounts. From the sounds of it, whatever PT boats were still inport had also joined in. The noise was so overwhelming that I had to stop what I was doing and then quickly drape our patient because the vibration was shaking our log ceiling so bad it was raining dirt. After what seemed like a long time but was probably only five minutes, a white-faced Hobbs came back down and told the story. He sat on an overturned trash can, shaking like a leaf.

"I think those destroyers cut loose their anchors somehow," he began. "Because all of a sudden they were moving *and* shooting. Honest to *God,* they just disappeared in flame and smoke when all those guns got going. I never saw the bombers except when they came flaming out of the sky. One of the bombers came down with both wings on fire and tried to hit one of the destroyers. They just shot it to pieces before it could get there, but, God*damn*! Pieces of that plane still landed on the ship and bounced right off."

He stopped for a moment to take a breath, obviously still beside himself. Then he went on. "One of those bastards launched torpedoes, *big* goddamned torpedoes, but it was crazy. I saw a torpedo land on the hill above the pontoon piers, slide all the way down to the water, chewing up sand and dirt all the way down, and *then* take off like a striped-assed ape, popping up and down and then finally going back down until it blew up on the far side of the harbor. I saw—I saw a bomber get chewed up by the shell fire, nose to tail like a buzz saw had 'em, until it just flew apart. I saw Japs—honest to *God*—individual Japs, flying through the air and splatting into the harbor like rag dolls."

He paused again to take a breath. "The worst, the absolute worst, was when the last bomber crashed into the palm grove, you know, just beyond where those overflow tents are? He was burning from one end to the other, and when he hit the ground the fuselage started spinning like a pinwheel, spewing bombs, crew, and torpedoes into the grove before it finally stopped a hundred yards from the first tent, where it turned into a gasoline bonfire."

He stopped again, eyes closed, fists clenched, breathing through his nose with a scary sound and starting to shake. "There was this one Jap," he whispered. He took another labored breath. "Came staggering out of that mess, on fire from head to toe and screaming his lungs out, literally. Every time he screamed, I saw fire come out of his mouth. Something in the wreckage went off and knocked him flat and then he just curled up like a bug in a bonfire. Jesus, Jesus, *Jesus H. Christ!*"

Chief Higgins took over and shepherded the hysterical doc over to a corner of the operating room where he sat him down on a cot. He looked back at me and I nodded. A syringe flashed and Hobbs finally started to calm down. The other new doc, named Carter, was looking at me as if he wanted to bolt.

"Remove the drapes," I ordered, pointing to the dirt-covered mound on the table. He just stared at me. "Hey!" I shouted.

He blinked and then came back to the problem at hand. We could all hear Hobbs sobbing over in the corner. Carter removed the drapes and then looked up at me.

"Scalpel, Goddammit," I hissed. "I can afford one hysteric but not two."

"Yes, Doctor," he said. "Sorry."

I tried not to laugh. He was looking at me as if I was the Chief of Surgery at a major hospital. Then from up above there came the thunderous roar of a really big explosion. I recognized that sound from the day the LST had blown up in the harbor. Higgins had come back to the table by then and we just looked at each other, sick with the knowledge that even more casualties would be coming.

SEVEN

Hours later we all just suddenly folded up and sat down. My hands and arms were so tired I was no longer safe with a scalpel. My "assistant," Dr. Carter, had sprawled onto the floor, apologizing profusely because his legs weren't working anymore. I didn't even know what time it was, but what I did know was that we were finally out of everything: bandages, sterile instruments, morphine, syringes, sulfa powder, and even sponges, for God's sake. Chief Higgins lay sound asleep.

Then Captain VanPiet showed up, with about two dozen medics and an equal number of stretcher-bearers. He informed me that a light cruiser had come into the harbor for the express purpose of gathering up as many wounded as possible for a high-speed run to Nouméa. Another cruiser was anchored off Henderson Field, on the same mission. I wanted to get up and tell them about each patient, what we'd done for them and what I thought they needed. Then the cruiser's medical officer, a full commander, appeared and motioned for me to sit back down.

"We've got this, Doctor," he said. "You guys have done some amazing stuff. We're going to load as many patients as we can possibly carry and then we're going to do a full-power run for Nouméa. We can get them there in twenty-six hours. This is Chief Hospitalman

Carrons, who's going to check the three of you out and then give you something that will help you get back on your feet as soon as possible. Again, well done."

I was so tired I couldn't formulate an answer, but by then the commander had moved on, organizing the collection of as many patients as could stand to be moved. Chief Carrons and two hospitalmen ushered the three of us out into the triage area, where we were each gently invited to lie down on a bloody cot. The chief gave us some fresh water, brought in from the ship, and then conducted a quick vitals exam. We weren't injured, just exhausted. I vaguely remember a brief sting and that I tried to object, but then a wave of cool darkness swept over me. Who was I to object, I wondered, as my eyes crossed and down I went.

By the time we resurfaced it was two hours after dark. I'd been awakened by the sound of familiar voices. I discovered that Boss Cushing and the usual suspects were seated on ammo boxes around the operating table, digesting the news that the squadron was being moved up the Slot to an island called Santa Isabel. I sat up on my cot and then had to wait for my fuzzy brain to focus and reestablish comms with my arms and legs. When Cushing saw that we were stirring, he dispatched one of the skippers to the galley, where Cookie Young rustled up a batch of powdered eggs and canned bacon, accompanied by his own special hot sauce creation, which he called Sweet Jesus. Higgins, Doc Carter, and I were famished. None of us could remember when we'd last eaten. Boss very nicely had three beers waiting for when Cookie's hot sauce began to pickle our tonsils. I never did find out where Doc Hobbs went after he was transferred.

Half the squadron was now out on patrol just north of Cape Esperance, where the Japanese garrison was hunkered down waiting for supplies. An LCU, a bigger version of a Mike boat, was scheduled to come over in the morning to restock our medical supplies. Captain VanPiet sent over a working party to take all the cots out of the bunker and the two overflow tents and run them down to the seashore. They set up what the Navy called a Handy Billy, which essentially was a gasoline-powered water pump. They blasted everything with seawater, then sprayed an antiseptic solution over all the cots and the mountain of bloodied bedding. Back home we'd have disposed of every bit of it; out here in the weeds of the Solomon Islands, we didn't have that luxury. They hung everything out to dry, cots and all. It promptly rained.

I found out that the big explosion last night had been one of the destroyers. The Betty attack had started a fire and then a magazine had gone up. That said, things were improving, if only relatively. The flights of Bettys thankfully dwindled and then stopped entirely as the summer morphed into early October. Infantry engagements over on Guadalcanal were becoming more infrequent. The Jap army units had withdrawn into a heavily defended enclave up around Cape Esperance. The Marines reportedly had decided to lay siege to the enclave but not try to invade it. The word in the weeds was that the Japs were starving and the Marines had had quite enough of the daily meat-grinder firefights against consistently suicidal defenders.

Perversely, our MTB squadron began to see more action than ever before. The Japs were trying frantically to resupply their encircled and starving troops. They used everything: destroyers, barges, and even submarines. Destroyers provided high-speed deliveries, but they usually lost one or two on the way back north. The subs could get through undetected, but they carried a pitiable amount of food and medicines when compared to the need. Most of the supplies and reinforcements that did get through were on those amphibious barges. Roughly half the squadron went out nightly now, hunting intermittent radar contacts that popped up and then faded because they weren't heavy cruisers. The guys had seen these craft before and knew they'd get perhaps one chance to run in and shoot up a group of barges before an escorting destroyer turned on its searchlights and returned the favor. The barges weren't shy, either. They were armed with 20 mm cannon and heavy machine guns, too. They traveled in groups of four or five, which meant a lone PT boat attacking a group would face a substantial response. And, of course, all of this happened at night.

It was a familiar pattern: the Japs owned the night; the Allies the day. They'd secrete their flotillas of small transports in coves and bays all along the Slot, taking sometimes up to three days to get close enough to Guadalcanal to make the final dash across Iron-bottom Sound. Our planes would search for them by day, having finally gained control of the sky. The *daylight* sky. At night, everything changed. The supply craft would venture forth from their hides and stream across the Sound to land as much as they could in terms of food and ammo to the remaining garrison. They wouldn't actually land on the beach. Instead they would get close in to the shore, dump everything into the surf, and then hustle back across the Sound and into hiding before American air patrols lifted off from Henderson Field at dawn. By that time, the barges had gone to ground in the jungle-covered coves and creeks of the hundreds of small islands littering the Solomons. Once it got dark, they'd resume their way north, back toward Rabaul and New Georgia.

Only the PT boats, as it turned out, could follow them into shallow waters and hunt them down. Our cruisers and destroyers had to stay out in known deep water or risk running aground. Their navigation charts dated back to Captain Cook's day and described large areas around the Solomons simply as "dangerous ground." If there were Japanese destroyers lurking in the darkness, our bigger warships knew all too well what the Long Lance torpedo could do. This led to our boats becoming *gun*boats instead of torpedo boats. The supply barges weren't worth the expenditure of a torpedo, so the boats reduced their loadout of four tubes down to two in favor of adding some more guns.

Boss laid out the changing situation at our first meeting after the cruisers had evacuated our mass casualty situation to Nouméa. The reason for moving us north became clear when he showed us the proposed new base on the lower half of Santa Isabel Island, some fifty miles northwest of Tulagi. We needed to intercept as many of those supply barges as possible, and if we were based farther up the Slot, above Guadalcanal, we'd get two licks at them. Deny the Japs food and ammo and they'd be weakened to the point of ineffectiveness. Hit the barges filled with their sick and wounded from Guadalcanal on their way back north and there'd be fewer Jap soldiers facing us when the Allied armies went north in force to drive them out of the Solomons entirely.

"This long island north of here is called Santa Isabel," he said, tapping a pointer on the map of the Solomons. "We're looking at a tiny coastal village called Tanabuli, which sits on a natural harbor almost at the southern tip of the island."

"Facilities?" one of the skippers asked.

"Nothing," Cushing replied. "Except: real estate. It is a natural harbor and there's a village, which means there's fresh water. Shelter will be important when the typhoons come and fresh water, as we know from experience right here, is doubly precious."

"Natives friendly?" another skipper asked.

"Don't know," Cushing said. "General Vandegrift will send an advance Marine recon platoon to find out."

I raised a hand. "Let's check with that coast-watcher group over on Cactus," I suggested. "They know everybody up and down the Slot."

"Great idea," Boss said. "Will you find out from VanPiet how to do that?"

"Got it," I said, glad to have something to do. "And will we be moving our medical station along with the squadron?"

That question prompted some discussion. We had a pretty nice setup here near Tulagi; the problem was that it was fifty miles away from where our guys would be getting into trouble.

I couldn't reasonably expect the Seabees to do it all again at yet another island. Cushing said he'd ask them. I said this might also be a matter for the medical command over on Cactus to decide. Boss wasn't sure about that. He was of the school that said he'd rather be chastised for something he did than ask permission and be told no.

"If I just order you and your medics to move with us to Tanabuli, I might get a blast from Cactus. But I don't think they'd recall you, which would mean I'll have medical help on the new island."

Later that night Cushing made an interesting point. "Guadalcanal," he said, "is right now the end-all, be-all of our existence. But the real objective is Japan itself. We're not just gonna leave Tulagi for a long stay at Tu-whazzit. Once the Marines stomp on the Japs on Santa Isabel, we'll head north again on whatever route it takes for us to chase these bastards back to their home islands."

"Then the Navy is going to have to figure out how to take major medical care to sea," I said. "The Pacific is huge. We can't go building field hospitals on every damn island as we push them back."

"Don't count on that, Doc," Cushing said. "We might end up doing exactly that."

I made my way back to my bunker by the light of an uncertain moon. My bunker, I thought. Of course, Cushing was right. We weren't going to stop in the Solomons. Higgins met me at the entrance to the bunker. "Boats are coming in," he said. "They ran into Jap destroyers."

I swore and we went below to get ready.

PART II

PART II

EIGHT

The natives *were* friendly, thanks be to God. Friendly and actively interested in driving Japs out of their home islands. My assignment to find a coast-watcher who knew the area had paid off. The Australian coast-watcher coordinator on General Vandegrift's staff had come up with one Woolson "Wooly" McAllen, seventy-three, who had managed a rubber plantation on Santa Isabel Island for thirty-plus years. He'd had to run for it when the Japs invaded the Solomons, rubber being high on the list of their badly needed strategic materials. He knew the entire island and had promised to rustle up a guide for us. He lived in Darwin now, a widower, and technically he was too old to come back to the islands to join the war effort.

Somebody forgot to tell Mr. McAllen that. A week after my query, a Mike boat coming over to Tulagi from Cactus deposited this little scarecrow of a man with a flowing head of white hair, a full beard, and the sun-creased face of an aging imp of Satan. Captain VanPiet happened to be down on the pier and learned that this apparition was demanding to see one Doctor Andersen, who needed a scout for an upcoming move to Tanabuli. It could reasonably be said that the move of the MTB squadron from Tulagi to Tanabuli was a military secret, so VanPiet was somewhat surprised to hear this Aussie civilian talking about it like it was barbershop news. He decided to accompany McAllen to the PT boat base across the harbor, where the two of them sought me out. I took them both down into the bunker after explaining who McAllen was to VanPiet, who could only shake his head in wonder.

McAllen had brought along a small rucksack of what I assumed were personal items. He was wearing knee-length khaki shorts, a short-sleeved khaki shirt, a well-worn slouch hat, and a whopping hip-holstered British Webley .45-caliber revolver that looked like it should tip him right over, except it didn't. I thought I caught a faint whiff of a fruity aftershave or cologne when I stood near him. He reached into his rucksack and produced a regulation-size baby bottle filled with a clear liquid. The nipple had been replaced by a metal cap. Chief Higgins' face lit up and he quickly fetched glasses. McAllen poured each of us a one-half-inch measure.

"This is croaker," he announced. "Our abos make it back of beyond in the bush. Ticket to Dreamtime, they call it. Slowly does it, mates, and to your good health."

I'm guessing the proof was on the order of 150 to 180. Maybe even more, I thought, when my fillings began to react. I'd taken barely a sip and wondered if I was drinking aviation gasoline, except it had a faintly sweetish flavor. A second sip went down easier, probably because of the anesthetic effect of that first sip. McAllen was watching us approvingly as we sampled his housewarming gift.

"Speak to me," he said.

VanPiet tried but could only manage a croak.

Croaker, I thought. Got it.

My voice was entirely out of commission. Higgins was letting his half-inch trickle down his throat, one drop at a time, with a beatific expression on his face. He didn't even bother to croak. By then McAllen had recapped the baby bottle. His three victims took their time to absorb whatever the hell this firewater was. He had downed his in a single gulp and seemed none the worse for wear. Finally, there was a collective sigh and we were able to breathe and also focus back on the matter at hand, namely, what McAllen could tell us about Santa Isabel, Tanabuli, and its people.

"They're rich," he began. "By Solomons standards, anyway. There's a volcanic ridge just west of the village and it stands between them and the sea. There's a cave in this ridge, maybe a hundred feet above sea level. Looked to me like a volcanic lava pipe of some kind from long, long ago. In the cave there's a spring, a really big spring, which comes out of the cave in this lovely waterfall, so strong that it has carved a pool into the cliffside. So: they are rich in cool, clean, fresh water. A mile from the village there is a cleft in the coastline, as if some bloody giant stood astride the coast and swung an axe between his legs. A hundred feet across and twice that deep. Inside the cleft is a solid wedge of ancient sea salts. So, they are twice blessed: unlimited fresh water and the bloody world's supply of rock salt. You can understand how valuable those two things are in an island world that lives on dried fish and in a climate that beggars bloody Hades for heat and humidity."

"I'm surprised the Japs didn't tumble to all that," Boss said. His croaking was wearing off, down now to a throaty squeak.

"Oh, but they did," the old man said. He hoisted the little bottle to see if anyone wanted another shot. Three simultaneous headshakes, which ignited a gathering headache. The bottle went back into the rucksack. Gently. McAllen resumed.

"Came in like the bloody samurai warlords they all think they are and told the Tanabuli natives to scarper. Get lost. The water was theirs for the duration. Everyone in the village was forced into the jungle. About a week later a platoon of naval infantry showed up on my rubber plantation and a couple others, some twenty miles north of the harbor. By then I'd gone bush and was making my way off the island by boat. Found out later my workers were rounded up and told to start harvesting latex. Field boss told 'em that it was the wrong time of the year to slash the trees. Got his face slapped good and proper. My boys got the message and slashed the trees. Of course, there was no goo and then the trees began to die. Head Jappo blamed that on my boys. Rounded up all but one, who escaped, and shot the lot of them. *That* news got back to the Blind Man."

"The blind man?" Boss asked. Chief Higgins was taking a nap by now. I was just starting to feel my teeth again. VanPiet looked like he was chewing gum, but I hadn't actually seen any gum.

"Aye," McAllen replied. "And he's the only potential problem you could face setting up a torpedo-boat base in Tanabuli. You could think of him as a yowie if he lived back in Australia. Half-man, half-spirit. Shape-shifter. Witch doctor. Shaman. Pick your bogeyman. Supposedly lives way back in that cave which produces the spring. Been there over a thousand years. If you dare to lay eyes on him you become blind, like him. Has magical powers for both good and evil. No one has ever seen him, of course, and yet they all believe he exists up there, somewhere in that cave. You get the picture, right?"

"Well, sort of," I said. "But you said the Japs killing the plantation workers got this bogeyman's attention?"

"Apparently, it did. The one boy who got away from the plantation massacre made his way to where the Tanabuli villagers were hiding out and told the headman what had happened. By then the Japs were bringing in barges for water, so everyone was keeping his bloody head down. The headman took the boy up to the cave the next night and the two of them snuck past the sentries. They went to something called the talking stone. The boy whispered the story to the stone and asked for the Blind Man to do something about it."

"And now you're going to tell us something happened to the Japs who killed the farmworkers," Higgins said. I hadn't realized he'd returned to the land of the living.

"Well, laddie, as the story goes, the Jap major in charge at Tana-buli got word that the platoon had bollocksed the rubber effort and sent a message for them to report to him in the harbor. Now: there's one road that runs the length of Santa Isabel, north to south, halfway between the seashore and the central ridge of the island. Not really a road, actually; more of a glorified path through the jungle. The platoon never showed up. The major then sent a squad up the road to find them, and find them they did. Or at least their heads, all neatly impaled on bamboo poles out in the middle of a small river. Just the heads; no bodies. As far as the locals were concerned, the Blind Man had done his bloody job."

"Or somebody had," Cushing said. "Like maybe the farm work-ers' families followed the platoon down the road and took care of business."

"Aye," McAllen said. "Most likely that's *precisely* what happened. The Jappo major was madder than hell about this so he sent two squads back to where the heads had been seen, some ten miles up the trail, and told them to find the bodies; bring 'em back for a proper Shinto burial. When that lot didn't return, either, the major got spooked and the whole lot decamped across the Slot to one of their bases on the Russell Islands. Listen, the point of my story is this: when you-lot move into Tanabuli, be aware that the locals believe in this Blind Man fella absolutely. Don't anyone make sport of the legend. Pretend to accept it, and do so with respect. No reason to shoot yourselves in the bloody foot right from the start, now, is there."

"Got it, Mister McAllen," Boss said, nodding. "Any chance you'd like to come with us? Our intel people tell us there are no Japs on Santa Isabel except for a seaplane base up at the north end of the island."

"Wouldn't bloody miss it," the old man crowed. "And by the way, please call me Wooly." Then he turned to me. "By the way, Doctor," he said. "Did anyone tell you that when I first came out from England that I'd been a physician?"

I shook my head.

"Please note the past tense," he said with a grin. "Haven't prac-ticed for years, have I."

It turned out he'd gone to the university medical school in Glasgow, joined a practice, practiced for five years, and then got struck off for "improper behavior" with one, or possibly more, of his female patients. He was then encouraged to emigrate to Australia. The Aussies wouldn't license him unless he agreed to provide medical services in the northwest territories to the aborigines, because the government couldn't get any licensed physicians to go out there. He went to Queensland instead for five years, where the Aborigines in turn taught him their version of natural medicine. He then wrote a book about that, causing an uproar in the Australian medical community. The government suggested he emigrate again, but this time to the Solomon Islands, which were under the colonial administration of Australia and where the sole white doctor in that island chain had died a suicide.

Captain VanPiet called Boss aside as the meeting broke up. He asked Boss when the squadron would make the big move.

"Thinking day after tomorrow," Boss replied. "Need to get some stuff together for the trip up. I'll probably send a two-boat patrol ahead to scope out the lay of the land."

"Well," VanPiet said, looking around to make sure no one was eavesdropping, "there's a civilian cargo ship coming into the harbor late tonight. Gonna be here for three days, working on a boiler problem. Civilian crew."

"Is that so?" Boss said innocently.

"Yeah, and I'll probably let 'em go ashore tomorrow night for a little beer muster, over on the Cactus side of the island."

"Where they'll be out of sight of the ship for a little while?"

"That's possible," VanPiet said with a perfectly straight face. "There'll be some of my boiler techs left onboard, but they'll be down in the engineering spaces."

Boss stared down at the sand for a minute. "And in return for this priceless intelligence," he said, finally, "we will leave *your* stockpiles alone. The ones up on that little hill over there. Where the Marines sometimes gather for a midnight wiener-roast."

"Those very stockpiles, yes," VanPiet said solemnly.

"Deal," Boss said. "And thank you very much. For everything."

"I'm gonna miss evening prayers," VanPiet declared.

"Not if I leave a small cache in my Quonset hut," Boss said. "Under one of those overturned ammo crates. Just to tide you over until you can make your own arrangements, that is."

"Wonderful," VanPiet said, beaming as only a Dutchman could, knowing that certain necessities of life were not going to suddenly dry up.

NINE

Three days later, the squadron rumbled into Tanabuli harbor at dawn, where we were met by a platoon of Marines and our two advance boats. We'd traveled all night, staying close in to the shore where possible and keeping the speed down to minimize wakes. The boats were piled high with all the squadron's stuff, so we were in no position to get into a fight. The harbor was beautiful: a long, narrowing estuary of crystal-clear water, *white* sand beaches for a change, and a small collection of huts and longhouses scattered along the curving beach. There were no facilities, just fishing boats drawn up on the sand, dense palm tree groves, and curious locals staring in awe at the dark gray torpedo boats rumbling up to the beach and then dropping anchor twenty feet offshore. To the east was the low rise of the tree-covered central spine of Santa Isabel Island, twenty-five miles long. Behind us and not more than a couple hundred yards across the harbor was that wedge-like cliff of black rock, 150 feet high and perhaps a mile long. A bright, wide waterfall fell ten feet into the sea from a pool at the base of a long slit of a cave in its face. Unlike Guadalcanal, there were no looming mountains on Santa Isabel, only that long ridge of green trees and jungle that disappeared north into the humid mists. It was hot and muggy, as usual, but somehow the air seemed cleaner now that we were away from blood-soaked Guadalcanal.

Our MTB pushed its nose right into the sand along the beach and Boss, Wooly McAllen, and I hopped off to meet the Marine first lieutenant and the village headman. Having Wooly along proved to be a Godsend. The locals recognized and, better yet, welcomed him. He spoke to them in a mixture of pidgin, English, and some native dialect. The Marine lieutenant told us the area appeared to be secure, with no Japs around as far as they could tell, and that the locals were glad the Japs were gone. They said the Japs had left suddenly and gone across the Slot, not to the Russells, but to the big Jap airfield at Munda, northwest on New Georgia Island. They had stripped the village of all food supplies before leaving and had seemed to be in a big hurry, as if they'd been expecting an attack. The Marine first lieutenant was taking no chances, however. He kept patrols out day and night in the surrounding woods.

He and Cushing then began talking about where we could build a camp and also where we could disperse the boats in anticipation of a Jap air attack. I took Wooly aside and asked him how I could get up into that cave.

"Want to go see the Blind Man, then, do you, mate?"

"No, I'm looking for a safe place for a medical aid station. Especially one that has running water."

Wooly asked permission from the headman, who assigned a boy to show us how to get up there. We took a fishing skiff across the harbor to the bottom of the cliff next to the waterfall. From across the harbor the cliff had appeared to be flat faced, but up close we found that the waterfall had carved a notch into the face some fifteen feet back. There was a beach of sorts on either side and a ledge leading up to the lip of the waterfall. Two young women were in a boat right under the falls, collecting water in jars. They paddled away when they saw Wooly and me, but with much giggling. Our boatman scolded them, but they didn't seem to take him very seriously. We walked up to the ledge above to find a semicircular pool that was fifteen feet wide and almost twice that long. At the other end of that pool was a wet, slanting face of rock down which the real waterfall, which surged out of a crack in the rock above, sheeted down into the pool. The cave appeared to be more like a grotto, but it did offer shelter because the face of the cliff above the waterfall substantially overhung the pool. The air was fresh and cooler up there than on the beach where we'd landed. I could easily envision up to a dozen beds.

"We won't have any religious problems turning this area into a small hospital, will we?" I asked Wooly.

"Don't think so," he said. "Especially if you offer some medical help to the village, yes?"

"Brilliant," I said.

The next morning two destroyers arrived, bringing yet more "stuff." They couldn't come into the harbor because it was too shallow, so the Marines organized the villagers to use their boats to ferry in materials. Suddenly the tiny village of Tanabuli was awash in stacks of fuel and lubricant drums, ammo crates, C-ration boxes, and all the rest of the things needed to support a clutch of motor torpedo boats. It became apparent that there was no way in hell that this tiny, primitive village could absorb the onslaught of logistics that was upon them. I kept waiting for a Jap reconnaissance plane to come over and do a double take at such rich pickings. That night, however, brought salvation in the form of a Navy cargo ship, escorted by two more destroyers. That ship began dropping amphibious boats into the water from offshore filled with the solution to all our problems: Seabees and their noisy toys. Even better, they were led by Tiny Tim, who immediately proposed to move everything across the long, narrow, and of coursed damned bay and away from the cramped confines of the Tanabuli village.

Cushing agreed. The estuary on which the village sat was barely a mile across, but on the other side there was nothing but miles of white sandy beach and trees of all descriptions. We could widely disperse the boats, supplies, tents, and fuel dumps while still enjoying the advantages of a protected harbor. Even better, I could construct an aid station above the waterfall. The Seabees had been ordered to construct a seaplane ramp across from the village. The Navy's Catalina flying boats could then stage out of our base and provide the MTBs with scouting assets over a wide swath of the Slot, as well as ferry casualties back to Cactus if needed. My only concern was what the Japs would do once they discovered what was going on at Tanabuli. We all had a pretty good idea.

By now it was early November and the rainy season was setting in, which didn't help the Seabees. It did, however, make flying conditions miserable, with an almost continuous low overcast. That meant Jap recon flights were less likely to see what was happening at Tanabuli, or at least that's what we fervently hoped. The high command had ordered that the boats stand down so as not to alert the Japanese until the base was up and running, so there was a period of intense maintenance, personnel changeover, and training. Word got around that the Jap army had gone totally on the defensive on Guadalcanal, although that was definitely not the case in the seas around that bloodied island. I heard that the medical command over on Guadalcanal had taken over my beloved bunker on Tulagi harbor and, apparently, just in time for some of the fiercest naval battles of the campaign.

Tim assigned a team of eight Seabees to my aid station project and they had us up and running in five days. They suspended a roof structure from cables like a big awning over the upper pool, with the cables anchored in the cliff face. Under that we were able to drape rolls of insect netting over an area large enough to contain fifteen cots and a bare-bones surgical tent. During the construction effort I'd taken the opportunity to go up into the actual cave. The entrance above that wide, wet slab was quite narrow, but then it opened up into a cool vault fifty feet high. The spring water rushed down a crack in the cave's floor with some force before pushing down to meet the slab. I found what I assumed was the talking stone, a plinth of black obsidian two feet square, three feet high, and leaning just a bit. There was clear evidence of a footpath leading up to the stone, but no other signs of either mystic or religious paraphernalia.

The floor of the cave rose gently behind the stone into an ever-narrowing defile leading into darkness. The light from the front of the cave seemed to dim perceptibly at this point so I decided not to push it. I don't know if it was fear of running into the Blind Man or just reluctance to walk into darkness without a flashlight, but something told me to turn around, and so I did. Nothing like the power of suggestion, I told myself, but still . . . I stopped on the way back down. There was the faintest breeze blowing from behind me, which for some strange reason raised the hairs on the back of my neck. I considered that breeze for a moment. It had to mean that the passageway behind me led either to an opening in the top of the cliff or at least somewhere in the seaward side of that strange volcanic formation. A call from one of the Seabees broke the spell and I hurried back down past the stone, to the activity below.

TEN

Operations resumed the day after Christmas. Four boats went out to see what they could see in what were new waters, although the monsoon winds promised a mostly dismal, choppy night out in the Slot. Cushing stayed in to decode a lengthy message from Nouméa about what was going on in the campaign to take back the Solomon Islands. The boats of the squadron had been dispersed along the length of the estuary in groups of two on the shore opposite from the village. The Seabees had anchored buoys for the boats to tie up to, which meant that they didn't have to wait to hoist an anchor in the event of an air attack, a measure we all thought was long overdue. The boat crews stood four-hour anti-aircraft watches during daylight. One boat would be ready to open fire against low-flying aircraft immediately, while its partner on watch would be ready to man guns and start shooting in sixty seconds. The squadron's supplies of fuel, ammo, food, and parts had also been dispersed all along that five-mile-long shore.

Our Marine security force maintained constant patrols out in the forests on the chance that Jap raiding parties might land up the coast and come pay us a visit. They also set up an observation post on the seaward side of the rock formation where I had established the medical station. It was nothing elaborate, just a bamboo shelter where three Marines with a radio and their rifles could keep watch on the seaward approaches to Tanabuli harbor. Cushing and *his* radio people were operating out of a kludge of four tents set out in a palm grove. The Seabees had promised him a proper bunker headquarters but they had been suddenly withdrawn for some more urgent project. Still, we had a better situation than we'd had at Tulagi, if for no other reason than that we enjoyed unlimited fresh water.

Cushing had asked Tiny Tim if there was any way they could pipe fresh water from the cave along the shore to the area where the boats were congregated. The operative word was pipe. The Seabees' inventory didn't include pipe. Tim had an idea of how to solve this problem. Bamboo. There were large stands of mature bamboo trees, many up to ten inches in diameter, along that road that led north to upper Santa Isabel Island.

"Cut a bunch of that damn big bamboo down," he said. "Make uniform sections out of the damn trunks, marry them together, and you got yourself a damn pipeline."

"But the bamboo trunks have these woody membranes inside," Boss pointed out. "Water can't flow through that."

"You got damn 20 mm cannons on them spitkits, right?" Tim asked, splashing a chaw of red tobacco into the weeds. "Fire a damn 20 mm round through the damn trunk, and water *will* by God flow, I damn promise it."

After some trial and error, we set up a jig that allowed a single round of 20 mm to blast its way right through a fifteen-foot length of bamboo. Since the upper pool was above sea level, we were able to lay a "pipeline'" all the way around to the area where the boats were tying up. That's when we discovered there were lots more people living near the Tanabuli harbor than we'd known about. I'd always thought that water would have been abundant in the tropical forests of Santa Isabel, but I had to admit, the water coming out of that spring was exceptional. There was plenty of standing water in the jungle, but you wouldn't want to drink it. We showed the headman what we'd done and invited him and his people to make free use of it.

At midnight Boss received a radio message from one of the boats. Two of our boats had been sunk, two others badly damaged. What was left of the four-boat patrol was limping back to Tanabuli with casualties and survivors. Boss roused me from my tent out at the aid station by field telephone, and I woke Higgins, the two new hospitalmen, and Wooly McAllen, who'd camped in with us. The two boats returned about two hours later and came directly to the point where those women had been filling jugs with spring water. They jammed their noses into the sand so we could get the wounded off, which is when we learned what had happened. The patrol had detected a group of radar contacts headed for Guadalcanal, just off a spit of land we called Tanga Point. We'd named it because it stood out so well on radar, which was great for navigation.

As all cats are gray in the dark, all radar contacts are about the same size unless it happens to be a battleship. The group had closed in at relatively slow speed to suppress their wakes and see what was out there. That's when star shells suddenly turned night into day and four, count 'em, *four* Jap destroyers tore into the approaching MTBs with five-inch gunfire. The boats frantically went to full speed to avoid the hail of shells only to run into a convoy of those armed amphibious barges, all of which also opened fire on the badly surprised torpedo boats.

The Japanese fire was so intense that the boats simply scattered, every skipper for himself, but not before two of them were ripped apart by five-inch shellfire that ignited their high-octane avgas tanks, providing even more light for the Jap gunners. Realizing they'd caught the MTBs flat-footed, the Japs turned on searchlights. One of the wounded gunners said he fired back but it was like shooting into the oncoming headlights of a train. He'd hidden behind his gun shield and fired blindly in the direction of the incoming fire. He had no idea if he'd hit anything, friendly or enemy. We ended up with twelve seriously wounded casualties and a total of twelve men who never came back. Of the two boats that had made it back, one was going to become a hangar queen, useful only for parts.

Wooly turned out to be a great help. Even before this crisis, he'd been able to direct me in evaluating cases of sickness, which were slowly approaching the battle casualties in numbers. Mysterious jungle fevers with hair-raising names: malaria, parasitical infections, super-aggressive fungal infections, not to mention spider and occasional snake bites—he'd seen it all and knew what to do about it. I learned a lot, and when he introduced me to some of the natural remedies he'd acquired with the aborigines, my eyes were truly opened.

Our first patrol had turned into a total fiasco. Boss Cushing was beside himself, both with anger about what had happened and his losses. The next day a US Navy destroyer hove to in the deeper waters near Tanabuli. They had an appendicitis case and I was the nearest doctor; theirs had been taken down with malaria. They sent the patient in on their motor whaleboat and the ship's skipper, a full commander, had come along. He was of average height but seriously thin, with dark circles under his eyes and a nervous twitch in his right hand. I couldn't tell how old he was. He chain-smoked cigarettes and never stopped looking around for trouble. He was apologetic when he saw that we had our hands full, but I told him it was okay, we'd done what we could for our wounded, so lemme have a look. I operated forty minutes later and then turned him over to my guys for the post-op watch. Boss showed up about then and he and the skipper got to talking. I joined them out on the edge of the pool. When the commander heard what had happened, he had some interesting advice.

"Sounds like you guys are making this up as you go along," he said. "You operate on a shoestring, go looking for trouble, pit wooden boats against Jap destroyers, and then get your asses kicked. Did you train for *this* specific mission?"

"No, sir," Boss admitted. "We just went out on patrol like we always do."

"Well, that's a problem," the commander said. "Especially after you've just made a move to a new base *and* you've been inport for a while. Here's the thing: as we've learned to our bloody sorrow, the Japs are *masters* of the night surface action because they have trained for *years* to do that. That first Savo fight, right after the invasion, was absolute proof of that. The last big fight, where *two* admirals managed to literally collide with a Jap cruiser formation—you guys hear about that?"

"Yes, sir," I said. "We took in some of the wounded; it was pretty bad."

"Exactly," he said. "Let me make some recommendations: don't just go out there to see what happens. Pre-brief your mission: where are your guys going and for what purpose? Who's gonna be in charge? What could go wrong and what do they do then? You want to disrupt Jap convoys? Pick a specific area, concentrate on that area, assign sectors for patrol, and allow no freelancing. Then, and this is the important bit, go out there during daylight and practice it. That's when you find out whose radios and radars actually work, who can stick to the plan and who can't. Then and only then, run the mission. Finally: debrief it—lessons learned, were there new Jap tactics, what guns worked best for the mission and which ones didn't, the whole deal."

Cushing was taken aback. "That's how the destroyer force does it?" he asked.

"That's how the destroyer force does it *now*. We've got a couple of new commodores—Burke, Moosbrugger—who have introduced an analytical approach. We brief until everybody understands what we're going out to do. We train continuously in the basics because of all the personnel turnover. We practice the maneuvers. After that, it's up to the gods, but at least we know what we're trying to achieve, where and when, who's in charge, who's in charge after him, and at what point to bail. *And* who's got our backs when it all turns to shit—who's been held back in reserve to come help if needed."

"Shee-it," Boss said. "Held in reserve? We're just not that organized."

"And that's your fault, Skipper," the commander said gently. "That's your *job*, isn't it?"

I thought that was a bit hard-hearted, especially for a skipper who'd just lost a bunch of people, with several more whimpering in pain up in the cave. Boss, however, rose to the occasion. "Thank you, sir," he said, nodding. "We've been winging it for so long it never occurred to me to, well . . ."

"Remember how *we* learned that, Skipper?" the commander asked with a wry smile. "And here's the good news: when the Japs started this war, they came to the battlefield with everything they had. Yes, they kicked our collective asses, with the one exception being Midway. But now America the Beautiful has turned into America the Really Angry Industrial Beast. The arsenal of democracy, they're calling it. The Japs lose a heavy cruiser and they may or may not be able to replace it. Like at Midway: they lost four big carriers and a hell of a lot of their best pilots. They sent their first team and lost damn near all of it. Our fleet sent our first team to Guadalcanal last year, and they all died. The difference now is that we have three more first teams on the way. The Japs? I think we're going to overwhelm them. Which is why we can now start to think about how we fight, and how to fight smarter. Even you hooligans: you don't need any more nights like last night, right?"

"Right as fucking rain," Boss said. "Sir."

"There you go, Skipper," the commander said. "You guys need anything? We've got ice cream."

I'd been listening from the sidelines. The destroyer captain's words sounded familiar; we'd heard that lesson before from that downed pilot we'd retrieved. It wasn't my place to criticize Boss's operations, but the mess last night, as the old farmer's joke went, was Two.

ELEVEN

Losing two boats and most of their crews, plus the other casualties, resulted in an inquiry. I didn't know this, but every time the Navy lost a ship sunk in battle, there was an inquiry. The loss of an aircraft in battle required a squadron-level report on what they thought had happened. This wasn't to apportion blame but rather to see if anything tactically useful could be learned from the loss. The loss of a cruiser, or, in the case of Savo Island, *four* heavy cruisers, precipitated an inquiry at the flag officer level. As Boss explained it to his skippers in his somewhat diminished wardroom, the so-called chain of command worked both ways. Officers were appointed to positions of command with the expectation that they would do their utmost to achieve victory in battle. If they didn't, the service wanted to know why. He gave an example:

"Well, sir, we had two cruisers and ran into two battleships. We had two options: run like hell, or attack them."

"Which did you do?"

"We attacked them."

"What happened?"

"They flattened us. We had eight-inch guns. They had fourteen-inch guns. We lost both cruisers."

"Maybe you should have chosen option one."

And there it was, in the cold, clear hindsight always exercised by officers who had not been there. The chain of command was also the chain of accountability. The word "chain" had not been chosen lightly. There was *always* an inquiry. There was always a reckoning. That's what came with the titles of admiral or commodore or even captain. Do your very best, but there will always be an inquiry. If you think that's unfair, then don't take the command.

"I'm probably gonna get relieved," Boss said. "And I accept that. I should have been doing what that CO recommended. That's my fault."

"That's *bull*shit!" one of the boat skippers sputtered. "We were sent out here to attack the Japs. We've been doing that since the invasion. Nobody told us *how* to do it, or *where* to do it, or *when*. Last night was no damn different."

"Yeah, it was," Boss said with a sad smile. "Somewhere, some-time, the Japs sat down and said: how do we deal with these damned PT boats? They brainstormed the problem, and then someone said: let's ambush the bastards. Four destroyers escorting a bunch of the barges? You think that just happened by chance? Remember what that pilot told us after the last mess we got into?"

Nobody had an answer for that.

As it turned out, he was right, although the Navy, in the end, pro-vided him with a fig leaf. A captain and a commander came up from Nouméa via seaplane to conduct the inquiry, during which time the boats stayed in. They made quick work of it. The commander called an all-officers meeting on the second day in the so-called command tent, which the Seabees had made up by combining four tents into one. Boss was notably absent.

I thought he looked too young to be a three-striper but there was no mistaking those silver oak leaves on his collar. To me he looked more like a Marine than a typical naval officer: lean, heavily mus-cled arms and shoulders, and just under six feet tall. He had short black hair, pale blue eyes, and an expression on his face that said he was serious as a heart attack. The audience was noticeably sparse. We'd lost four officers out there last night, and I had three more up in my sick bay, one of whom was iffy.

"I am Commander Preston Cogswell," he began. "Lieutenant Commander Cushing is being transferred to Panama, where he will take command of a new MTB squadron fresh out of stateside training. He will take them through advanced training at the boat base in Colon and then bring the new squadron out to the Western Pacific."

"Who's gonna replace him?" one of the skippers asked bluntly. He'd normally have asked that question in a more respectful tone of voice, but he was exhausted and really upset by our losses.

"I am," Cogswell said, just as bluntly. He scanned the faces at the table, watching as that news settled in. Oh, boy, I thought to myself; they've replaced a lieutenant commander with a three-striper? Things are gonna get really interesting here in dear old Tanabuli.

"I'm coming here from being XO on *San Juan*, which is an anti-aircraft light cruiser," he continued. "And before that I was commanding officer in *Emerson*, DD-722. Most recently *San Juan*'s spent most of her time escorting carriers, but I've also done a couple of stints here in the Slot. I've fought Jap cruisers and destroyers up close, and by close, I mean being under eight-inch and six-inch gunfire at fifteen hundred yards. I'm a true believer in the notion that the Japanese navy is not to be trifled with. I also believe that a PT boat has no business mixing it up with their first team unless it's a truly desperate emergency."

Nobody was going to argue with that.

"So," he continued. "The mission is going to change. We're going to remove the rest of the torpedo tubes from the boats and replace them with their weight in guns. We're going to leave the Japs' capital ships to the carrier aviators, and we're going to specialize in sinking as many of those so-called amphibious barges as we can."

"That's what we *have* been doing, Captain," one of the skippers said. "I was out there for this latest fiasco. We weren't there to sink destroyers with torpedoes; we were there to tear up resupply barges. The destroyers were just part of the problem. Four destroyers? That was a surprise."

There were nods around the room. I watched to see how this commander would react. His expression indicated that he was not exactly pleased by the tone of the skipper's voice. He stared at Lieutenant James for a few seconds. I thought we were in for a tongue-lashing, but then he surprised us.

"Yes, of course," he said, finally. "My mistake."

The tense atmosphere changed. I, for one, was truly surprised: commanders didn't apologize to a bunch of lieutenants and jay-gees. The commander continued.

"Let me begin again," he said. "Things are changing. Up to now, these barges have been the main resupply method for supporting the Jap army on Guadalcanal. However, I've just been to Admiral Halsey's headquarters on Nouméa. His intel people think the Japs have decided to withdraw from Cactus."

That revelation produced a murmur of surprise.

"They think they'll establish new defensive lines on New Georgia and Bougainville Island, much closer to their main base at Rabaul. That's the real reason this squadron was moved up here."

He sat down at the head of the bamboo table and took a minute to light up a cigarette while we all waited to see what was going to happen next. Higgins and I exchanged glances. It was clear he was just as apprehensive as I was about the new skipper, especially one who looked and talked like this guy did. Commander Cogswell indicated that if anyone else needed a smoke to have at it. Several did. Cogswell continued.

"This squadron is going to grow. In addition to replacing the boats you just lost, six more are being added to bring us up to a complement of eighteen. Now, then: the MTB force in general has a reputation for winging it, and by that I mean just going out there

in the dark and seeing what you can stir up. Given that there's no
official US Navy doctrine for the employment of MTBs, no one
can fault you for that. Trouble is, this loosey-goosey approach just
cost you two boats, twenty-four dead or MIA, nine wounded, and
two more boats damaged, one of which is a wreck. That's unaccept-
able, so be advised that I intend to introduce a little more rigor to
our operations."

He paused to take another huge drag on his cigarette, then
stubbed it out on an ashtray made out of a cut-down 40 mm powder
casing. "XO," he said. "Introduce the boat skippers to me, please."

Deacon, who'd been listening with rapt attention, seemed star-
tled at being called on and did one of his pelican launch maneuvers
getting up out of his chair, all elbows and knees as he gathered up
his lanky frame.

"Yes, sir," he said. "Well, I'm Deacon Haller, the squadron XO.
Class of thirty-six. One battleship tour in *West Virginia*, second tour
in a four-piper, *Summerfield*, one year at the PG school back in An-
napolis. Going on two years in MTBs. I'm also skipper of the 307
boat, which is an Elco brand."

"Okay," Cogswell said. He wasn't making notes but I had the impression that he was mentally recording everything being said. He
just had that look about him. He then turned that rangefinder gaze
on Hump Newton, who was sitting next to Deacon. Hump swallowed nervously and then gave his brief history in the USNR. At
that moment, one of the boat crewmen stuck his head into the tent
and signaled for me to come out. Higgins came with me. He told us a
Catalina had landed to move our wounded south, so we went down
to the landing and commandeered a boat. Using the boat meant we
could take them directly to the Catalina, which had anchored in the
harbor. We left the officers to the tender mercies of our new boss.

The next week featured what Cogswell called a "safety stand-
down," where all the boats stayed in and the skippers reviewed
damage control, first aid, firefighting, gun maintenance, lifesaving

equipment and a myriad of other things that tended to be ignored due to the pace of operations, with their individual crews. Cogswell personally inspected each boat in company with the boat's skipper. These weren't spit-and-polish inspections. He wanted to operate every feature on each boat and to build a deficiency list of things that needed fixing. For their entire time in the Solomons, when something broke, the boat crews would try to fix it, but if there weren't any parts and there was a workaround, it would stay broken. The commander seemed to have the novel attitude that all the equipment should actually work. He assembled a team of four enginemen who were deemed by the rest of the enginemen to be the best in the squadron. From now on, when any boat had an engine problem, that team would attack the problem, not just the boat's lone engineman. Teams were also formed for electronics and guns.

On his third day, he picked out one boat, the 747, and declared that it would be his command boat. He ordered all four torpedo tubes removed to compensate for the weight of the stuff he was going to add, such as a second backup radar, taken from the boat that had been deemed beyond repair. He also installed extra radios, a couple of destroyer-size signal searchlights, two additional twin fifty-mounts, one on each side, and then he ripped out the crew's berthing and installed a plotting room. We began to think he was just homesick for his destroyer. On the other hand, the skippers caught on fast: if Commander Cogswell was out there with them, on a boat that could see and communicate reliably, and which wasn't directly involved in any given firefight, there shouldn't be any more Tanga Point debacles.

We had the luxury of this stand-down because the weather out in the Slot was horrible, with confused seas, heavy rain squalls, and high winds. Any boat going out would have been in a hang-on-and-survive mode, at best. The only good news was that the Japs faced the same situation, so it wasn't as if they were getting past us. The commander, who'd never been at sea on a PT boat, went out with Deacon into one of the long bays, where the water was relatively calm. He had Deacon put her through her paces, and then he took the helm. He firewalled the throttles and then made some high-speed turns that scared the hell out of Deacon's crew. At one point they reversed course so suddenly that their own wake caught up with them, sending everyone except Cogswell sprawling. The commander remarked that if it weren't for the Japs, this would be fun.

At the end of that first week, Commander Cogswell had taken a fair measure of us, and we of him. He wasn't a jerk or a screamer. He was polite and professional at all times, even when he uncovered something that embarrassed everybody. He took out his ire on the problem and not the people, even when it was obvious that one or more of the people standing there were the root cause of the problem. The enlisted men began to relax and open up when he asked questions because it was clear he was after solutions and not them. The big breakthrough came when he asked Deacon one evening who was in charge of evening prayers. The squadron officers had ended the practice and hidden the joy juice until they saw how the new CO felt about the practice. There'd even been a betting pool established as to whether or not he'd approve or censure the whole idea. I happened to be there when he asked the question. Deacon, God bless him, equivocated.

Cogswell just looked at him for a moment, and then said, "Let me rephrase my question, XO. I would like all the skippers who are available to meet me in the command center for a planning meeting. If someone could manage to supply some grapefruit juice, it would be much appreciated. Grapefruit juice, as you probably know, has lots of vitamin C, and I'm concerned about scurvy. If it could be fortified with a smidgen of medicinal alcohol that would be even more appreciated. Assuming such a thing is possible."

Then he turned to me. "*Is* such a thing is possible, Doctor?"

I followed his lead in speaking in that quaint passive voice so beloved by senior officers in the regular Navy. "Such a thing is eminently possible, Captain," I said. "I will take the matter under advisement and immediate action, if you wish."

Deacon looked like he'd swallowed a frog. Then for the first time, we saw Cogswell's face break into a wide grin. It was a wolfish grin to be sure, but it totally transformed his face. "Well, well, well," he said, "maybe there *is* hope for you sonsabitches. And from now on, you may call me 'commodore.'"

The next day, Wooly approached me in the aid station and said he wanted to explore this Blind Man legend, up in the cave. I told him I'd gone up a little way into the cave, seen nothing of interest other than that talking stone, and then turned around. "It gets pretty dark," I said. "And the footing is mostly a crack in the floor."

He produced two of those olive-drab, ninety-degree-headed military flashlights, liberated, no doubt, from Cactus, so up we went. I'd forgotten to mention that the "path," such as it was, ran right along the edge of that long crack through which the water came down. Our boots were making squishing sounds by the time we reached the talking stone. Wooly looked for symbols on the plinth, but found nothing. He ran his hand over the stone, which was smooth as glass. "This must be from another place," he said. "This is pure volcanic rock."

We continued up the long and ever-darker crevice. The cave ceiling was still way up there, but the walls had closed in and now we were forced to walk in the rushing water. My feet were cold for the first time since leaving the States, and the grade was getting steeper. Then we began to hear falling water. Wooly stopped to listen, and then switched his light off. I did the same and we stood there like a couple of statues, letting our eyes adjust to the darkness. Except it wasn't total darkness. Ahead of us, maybe fifty feet, there was a dim glow, and that's where the sound was coming from. We advanced some more, with Wooly in the lead. The crevice was very narrow now, and my shoulders brushed the rock walls as we took one careful step at a time. We finally got to a spot where the crevice widened out into a spherical cave, some thirty feet or so in diameter. The floor of the cave was covered in a thin sheet of water, which ended up sluicing through a notch in the rock into our crevice.

There was enough light to see pretty well now, and I realized it had to be sunlight. Right ahead of us, across that sheet of water on the floor, was a wide but very thin waterfall, coming over a long ledge of rock ten feet above the floor. The dim light made the waterfall look like a diaphanous curtain. "Bloody hell," Wooly whispered, pointing. "Look at *that*."

I'd been looking at the waterfall, which was truly beautiful in that spectral light, but he was pointing behind the waterfall, where I now could make out the outline of a large, familiar-looking statue, barely visible through the falling mist.

"What is that thing?" Wooly muttered. "And how did someone get *that* all the way up here?"

Then I remembered. "It looks like one of those statues out on Easter Island," I said. "There was an article about them in *Life* magazine a couple of years ago. They called them *moais*, or something like that."

"Ri-i-ght," Wooly said. We stood there just staring at it, both of us wondering the same thing: there was no way anything that big had come up the way we had come. I think we both looked up at the same time, where the light seemed to be coming from. It looked like our mountain ridge had been split, because the source of the sunlight was hundreds of feet up, creating a chasm that could not have been more than ten feet wide.

"So, the spring has to be up above the statue," Wooly said. "Or, all that water is coming down from somewhere above, either in the mountain or from up on top."

At that moment we heard the sound of thunder, which echoed

around that cave in confusing waves of sound. Distant thunder, but unmistakable. Then the light, already dim, began to dim even more.

"C'mon, Doc," Wooly said, grabbing my arm. "Time to get the hell out of here."

I turned to follow him back into the crevice. He was wasting no time, and I had to scamper behind him as we slid our way down through the rushing water, with another thump and boom of thunder behind us, sounding like it was saying: faster, faster. I called ahead to Wooly, who was slip-sliding down that channel dangerously fast, just asking for a broken ankle. "What's the big hurry?"

Then I found out, as the water in the crevice began to swell behind me. Thunder meant rain, sometimes lots and lots of it, falling in great sheets over the jungle so hard that it obscured the trees. That chasm back there was channeling one of those tropical deluges down into that cave, whose only exit was where the two of us were trying to outrun a building flood.

We made it to the point where we could step out of the crack in the floor and get up on somewhat higher, and dryer, ground, but Wooly didn't stop there. I continued to follow him down into the lower reaches of the cave. We finally stopped when we got abreast of the talking stone, turned, and climbed up to its rocky platform, from which we could watch an eight-foot high flash flood muscling its way down to the pool below.

Wooly whistled softly as the flood swept past. "A lot of the abos live in caves," he said above the muted roar of the water. "Some of their caves go on for miles, but they were always stopping to listen. Damn near died one time when one of those"—he pointed at the swift water below—"caught up with us from out of bloody nowhere. That's how I knew to run for it."

"Thank God you did," I said. "I heard the thunder but never made the connection. That crack has to go all the way to the side or even the top of the mountain."

He nodded. "And now that we've laid eyes on the Blind Man,"

he said quietly, "we have to keep that fact secret, mate, for as long as we're here at Tanabuli. Those elders find out we went up there they'll be duty-bound to make something happen to us, just to keep up the legend."

"Got it," I said. "But how in the hell did someone get that big thing up there?"

"Gonna find out," Wooly said, as the flood began to diminish. "But not today, eh?"

TWELVE

The weather cleared four days later, which meant that the Japs would be on the move again. We received specific orders from Nouméa: interdict barge traffic, both ways if possible. Avoid contact with larger forces, also if possible. This was just what Commodore Cogswell had predicted. On the first relatively clear day, he took three boats out in formation with his command boat. Deacon and the skippers had worked up the best formation tactic for attacking a barge convoy, but when they tried it out, the skippers had to pay so much attention to radar formation-keeping that they couldn't concentrate on a firefight should one pop up. They came back in and worked the problem some more.

One of the skippers had an idea: our radars simply weren't precise enough for station-keeping in a high-speed formation. Why not install a Marine 81 mm mortar on the command boat, and use that to fire illumination rounds during the engagement? The command boat would be standing off anyway, directing traffic. That way the boat drivers could do visual, loose station-keeping, while focusing on getting in on the barges and shooting them up. They put Alibaba on a boat and sent him all the way back to Cactus. Ask nicely, Deacon said, but steal one if you have to. He gave the chief a shiny bronze propeller from the hangar queen, whose key slot had been ruined, as barter bait. Marines liked to barter almost as much as they liked to brawl.

The next night Alibaba returned with the goods. Barter hadn't been necessary. The Marines had been forthcoming with the mortar, its baseplate, and two crates of illumination rounds. Alibaba had thought to ask for a box of of high-explosive rounds as well, which they agreed to, all in the interests of killing Jap reinforcements. He'd handed over the propeller as a gesture of gratitude and as a down payment against future urgent needs. None of the guys had ever fired a mortar before, but the gunnery sergeant said it was pretty simple for what they'd be doing. Pull the pin that was notched through the nose of the projectile, leave all the shiny yellow packets of explosive on the tail fins, and drop it down the tube. Drop only one at a time or *you'll* become the mortar meat. They bolted the baseplate to the fantail area of the 747 boat and then tried it out in the bay that evening. Problem solved.

They did one more practice run against an imaginary convoy of barges, including using the illumination rounds. A spare boat had gone out to play the role of barge convoy. The formation chosen by Cogswell, basically a column, turned out not to work, because each boat had to fire in turn as it came abreast of the target. They switched to echelon formation, and now they could all shoot. We hoped there weren't any Japs watching, but the convoys were slow and they hadn't had time to reach our area all the way from Rabaul yet. Tomorrow night would be the most likely time. A belated evening prayers session gave me the impression that the squadron was coming together and finally absorbing this idea of planning, practicing, fixing, practicing again. The next morning, at about nine, six Jap Betty bombers came streaming across the bay to welcome us to Santa Isabel Island. We'd been hoping to get some advance warning from the distant Cactus radars, but no such luck.

On the other hand, the ready AA boat stations dispersed up and down that long bay ate the first three Bettys for lunch, sending them crashing down into the sea just beyond the volcanic cliffs which harbored my aid station. One of them managed to drop a stick of bombs along the flanks of the ridge that shook the hell out of my miniature hospital before going inverted into the sea. The last two Bettys split north and south, but not before scattering bombs all over the harbor. One of them landed in the village with calamitous results. Two families who'd been cowering in their huts were obliterated. I half expected that the villagers would want us the hell out of there after that, but the headman, fortunately, was mad at the Japs, not us, calling them cowards for running away like that. The bad news was that the Japs now knew for certain that there was a new MTB base on Santa Isabel. Surprising the convoys was no longer a likely option.

Cogswell rose to the occasion. We'd send *two* divisions of three boats out instead of just one. Find and attack a convoy of barges with the first division, then leave. The second division, which now would know where the convoy was, would wait at idle until the command boat fired off a second string of illumination rounds, then they would make one high-speed pass. By now the first division, if still able, would get set up to do it all again. From previous experience, the skippers knew that you'd get one shot at shooting up a convoy, because the "barges" carried just about as many guns as the MTBs. Slash and run were the safest tactics. The Japs were used to being attacked once. They likely wouldn't expect a second attack. Just like we didn't.

This time the Bettys stayed high, eight to ten thousand feet, and made a traditional bombing run well out of range of our 50-caliber and 20 mm guns. All our guys could do was run for the bomb shelters. There were five bombers and they laid sticks of bombs in fairly precise lines, hitting nothing except the harbor, the beaches, and the coastal palm groves. It was loud, though, even from my sheltered position in the cave. I'm not sure they'd spotted the medical station, hidden as it was under the overhang of the ridge, but we'd moved as many patients as we could once the bombing began. I didn't want to take any chances that they might come back and strafe our bamboo huts and tents.

Our little harbor was covered in smoke, sand, and dust after they left, which probably convinced them they'd wiped the new base out. Mostly they'd deepened the channel, not that our boats cared. That night Cogswell took his two divisions out into the Slot. The two bombing attacks must have meant something was coming down from Rabaul. We all prayed it wasn't a formation of heavy cruisers, but the night patrol was a complete bust. They detected nothing, not even local fishing boats. The next morning, we got a report from the coast-watcher net, saying that at least fifty barges had been spotted headed south and passing the southern tip of New Georgia, the island right above Santa Isabel, escorted by two destroyers. Cogswell called a quick council of war. The two destroyers made our planned tactics more dangerous, especially with the use of illumination rounds. One of the guys spoke up. Let's send an additional boat out, one that still had all four torpedo tubes. If the mortars lit up a Jap destroyer it would be his job to torpedo it if possible.

Captain Cogswell had to think about that. First of all, it was a new wrinkle to the tactics they'd already practiced. Second, two destroyers could bring a total of ten five-inch guns to the table, not to mention their secondary batteries of 40 mm and 20 mm cannons. They kicked around the idea of *not* firing the illumination rounds and just blasting in and starting a melee.

"Starting a melee and finishing one are two different things," Cogswell observed. Then Deacon spoke up.

"At some point we're just going to have to go out there and attack the bastards," he declared. "We've made a plan. Everybody knows no plan survives first contact with the enemy, but, hell: when star shells start popping over *their* convoy, those tin cans're gonna think we've brought some big boys to the party. Forget the second

pass idea. Blast in there, tear 'em up, and disappear into the night. If
the lonesome-end boat, who's gonna be just sitting out there, gets a
shot, great—torpedo one of those suckers."

This was the most I'd heard Deacon say in one go since I'd
known him. Cogswell looked at him for a moment and then nodded. "I agree," he said. "Any questions?"

The boats went out an hour after sundown. The plan was that
they'd set up the ambush ten miles off the coast of Santa Isabel, on
a line between the island and Guadalcanal, and then just wait. Back
at the base the left-behind skippers congregated at the command
bunker, where we had a radio set up on the formation's frequency. I
joined the small crowd, sipping a mild screamer surreptitiously
in a coffee mug, anxious to see how this would come out. The
commodore had galvanized the squadron since he'd arrived. It
wasn't as if Boss Cushing had done a lousy job, but Cogswell
had tried to elevate the squadron's game substantially. Tonight,
we'd see.

One of the radio rules he'd initiated was that he would talk and
they would listen. The only time he wanted to hear from a boat was
if that boat got a radar contact that the command boat had not yet
announced. Otherwise, he wanted to issue orders, and they were to
acknowledge with nothing more than a blast of static. The boats'
radios were really good at producing static. At just after midnight,
as some of the officers were drifting off to sleep, the command boat
announced that they had multiple radar contacts, bearing 330,
range twelve miles, on a heading of 230, speed eight knots. Cogswell then repositioned the lonesome end to put him in position to
fire torpedoes along the enemy's line of advance.

After that, the command boat began issuing enemy position reports. Bearing 329, range ten miles. Eight miles. Bearing 330. Five
miles. The boats presumably were just sitting there at idle, already
in loose echelon formation, but making no wakes and no radio
noise, either. The command boat had the radar picture and was

broadcasting the developing situation in short, clipped transmissions. The attack would begin when the command boat began firing star shells. The field phone squeaked. It was the Marine post up on top of the ridge. Deacon answered, listened, and then hung up.

"Marines see flares, low on the horizon. Pretty dim, so they're way the hell out there. That radio's awfully quiet."

One of the skippers questioned the long silence. Another reminded him that that's the way Cogswell had wanted it: I start shooting flares, you boys go in on them. Still, from our perspective back at the base, the silence was a bit unnerving. The Marines called again. They had just seen a large explosion on the horizon. They said it looked like an ammo dump blowing up; big red-yellow blast followed by streamers. Still nothing on the radio. Deacon asked the radio operator to check the frequency. Radio's okay, he said. I asked Deacon if he was going to call the commodore, but he said he'd been told in no uncertain terms not to do that. My eyes were heavy, so I bedded down in one corner of the bunker and immediately fell asleep.

I was awakened by activity in the bunker about four hours later. The patrol was coming back in and people sounded excited. I immediately wondered if I was facing a big casualty list, but Deacon assured me the opposite was true as he left the bunker, so I went to find some coffee and something to eat. I was sitting under a palm tree on an ammo crate when the boats rounded the point and headed in. I counted five boats plus the command boat and the lonesome end. Good start, I thought. Seven went out; seven came back. I saw the commodore jump down off the waist of his boat and greet Deacon with a big grin. Then I saw that the lonesome end boat had four empty torpedo tubes. Even better, I thought. Since there was general but seemingly happy confusion down at the landing, I took a hike out to the cave to check on my patients.

I had three in residence, and they were not battle casualties. All three had high fevers and were truly sick. I feared malaria, which was endemic in the Solomons, but I had no facilities to test for it. A Catalina arrived mid-afternoon with mail and some spare parts. I quickly got them to hold until I could get these three guys down to the harbor. This provoked a bit of a spat because they had a full manifest waiting for them over on Cactus. Finders keepers, I retorted. By the time I got this all sorted out and the plane on its way, it was just after dark. I went to the command bunker to report the disposition of my patients. There I found Deacon and the commodore deep in conversation as they reviewed the events of the night before. They had charts out on the table and several of those green-fabric-covered notebooks favored by the Navy on the table. They took a break when I showed up.

"Doc," Cogswell said. "I think we need some professional medical care. In fact, I *know* we do. Can you help?"

I understood immediately. I went topside, found a passing sailor, and told him to go tell Chief Higgins that the CO needed professional medical care. The alarmed crewman took off in a hurry, and soon Higgins arrived with a canvas bag marked prominently with red crosses. Cogswell positively beamed when Higgins then produced two large cans of grapefruit juice and the requisite medicinal additives. Both he and I joined in, of course, and then Cogswell told us what they'd accomplished last night.

"They walked right into it," he began. "We were all just sitting there, waiting for them along their track. No wakes, engines idling, no radio transmissions except mine. Dark as a well-digger's ass out there. I started firing star shells when they were into 1,500 yards, and when the first one burst, all the boats charged in and tore their asses up. Our guys went by them at twenty-five knots to allow time for more heat, and I don't think a single barge returned fire."

"There were two destroyers?" I asked.

"Yup, there were. Our guys swept through the convoy, tearing up every damn boat they could see, and then took off like striped-assed apes in diverging directions. I did the same, but at slow speed.

I headed west, while our shooters all ran east. And then the best part: the lonesome end boat. There were several barges on fire and both destroyers moved into the convoy to find our boats. Fires meant lots of light. Lonesome end, Goody Walsh in the 418 boat, was just sitting there, some 2,500 yards away, bow on to the convoy. One of the Jap destroyers became visible crossing slowly from left to right across his bow. Goody kicked it in the ass and then let go with all four torpedoes. Four went swimming, three hit, two exploded and caused the ship's magazines to go up. The other tin can turned away to avoid torpedoes while the first one just sat there in two pieces and burned to death. Goody took off, as per instructions. It worked, Doc. It goddamned *worked*."

"Congratulations, Commodore," I said. I almost felt sorry for Boss Cushing at that moment for having missed it. For us to bag a Jap destroyer was especially satisfying. They and those scary seaplanes had been our nemesis from day one. Chewing up the resupply barges was satisfying, but sinking a Jap tin can was wonderful.

"Just one thing," Cogswell said. "All of our shooters got a close-up look-see at the barges. They all reported the same thing: there were no troops in those barges. Barrels of whatever they put in them, but apparently, in the past, there's also been eighty to ninety troops. I need to report that fact; tonight, as a matter of fact."

Chief Higgins asked why the rush. "Because," Cogswell replied. "It might be that the Japs are starting to take troops *off* Guadalcanal."

THIRTEEN

The next morning, the commodore was summoned down to Cactus by Major General Patch, US Army, now in charge of the Guadalcanal fight. The First Marines had finally been relieved in November, and an entire Army division was now carrying the water. A Catalina arrived just after daylight, bringing medical supplies for me and a ride for the commodore. The weather closed in that afternoon, so Cogswell didn't get back until the next day. Deacon had a surprise for him: an attaboy message from Halsey himself, who, in his best laconic tradition, said simply: "Good job. Do it again. Often." Cogswell himself also had news, following an operations conference at Henderson Field. His report of no troops in the barges confirmed the higher-ups' suspicions—the Japs were evacuating, and doing so by sea at night from their ever-constricting enclave up along Cape Esperance. Interdicting the barge convoys became *the* mission now.

"Night before last we hit 'em and then skedaddled," he said. "Now they want us to hit 'em, run, but then hang around out there in case there's a *north*bound train coming our way later, and then hit 'em again. We have to figure out how to do that while staying alive."

"Where did you hit them the other night?" I asked, looking over at the wall chart displaying Guadalcanal and the nearby islands.

"Southwest of here," Cogswell said. "They were probably within twenty miles of Cape Esperance."

"That was around one in the morning, right? I'm asking because the math doesn't work."

"How so, Doc?"

"Those barges supposedly can only go eight knots, so from the place where you hit them, they still had two and a half hours to go just to get there. Assuming it didn't take thirty minutes to recover from your attack, they'd get there at oh-three-thirty. Then they had to off-load supplies and onload troops. Say thirty minutes. It's now oh-four-hundred. From Cape Esperance to the nearest islands, the Russells, it's about thirty miles. To New Georgia, which they control and where they could hide for the day, it's another thirty."

"I get it," Cogswell said, walking over to the chart. "They'd still be out on the sea at dawn, sitting ducks."

"Which tells me," I said, "they're arriving at Cape Esperance, off-loading supplies, and then dispersing the barges and hiding them for the day. That night they load up, only now they have eight, nine hours to get to New Georgia before dawn."

"So, there'd be no point in our staying out there," Deacon said. "They're not going to make the return trip that same night. Because they can't."

"And yet," Cogswell said, "there they were, creeping toward Ironbottom Sound at one in the morning. We're missing something here."

Deacon spoke up. "What if we sent out the whole squadron?" he asked. "Half to the route they usually use, coming down from New Georgia while hugging Santa Isabel to avoid our destroyers out in the Slot. The other half on the west side of the Slot, along the most direct route to the Russells and/or New Georgia from Cape Esperance. Get our tin cans to patrol the open waters of the Slot around Savo Island. That way we cover the coastal waters, the tin cans cover the deep water."

Cogswell considered this, and then he and Deacon went to the chart to see how that would lay out. I took my leave. I was flattered when they included me in these evening brainstorming sessions, but I knew when it was time to leave it to the pros. Cogswell stopped me.

"Stick around if you can, Doc," he said. "Deacon and I are both pretty tired and we're gonna make mistakes. A devil's advocate would be very helpful. A sober one even more so."

I looked ruefully at my empty screamer cup, and said, "Yes, sir, of course."

By next morning we were making preparations for the entire squadron, minus one boat with two of her three engines out of commission, to sortie that evening. Deacon was holding briefings for the boat officers, while the crews topped off fuel tanks, tweaked radars, onloaded extra ammo, and razzed the other crews as to who would sink the most Japs tonight. Cogswell had sent out his plan to his bosses, asking for destroyer support. Now we waited to see what the Navy could come up with. If the Japs were actually evacuating their army from Guadalcanal, this might be the last chance to reduce the size of that army, especially since we all kind of figured that once Cactus was secure, our ground forces there would be going north in pursuit. Cogswell was hoping this might get headquarters to move on his request.

The answer came by radio message one hour before sundown. The destroyers, along with two light cruisers, would be operating 100 miles north tonight and had already departed. They wished us happy hunting.

Cogswell was disappointed, but not too surprised. "I can just hear their commodore," he said. "Do we have an operations plan? A communications plan? Have we rehearsed it? Do we *know* where the Peter Tares will be setting up station?"

Just like that skipper had explained to us. I was about to point out to Cogswell that he was proposing an operation that looked an awful lot like what Boss Cushing had been doing. The four boats who'd gone out with him knew the drill, but the add-ons joining the party tonight? On the other hand, the MTBs were the best hope of intercepting a Jap evacuation convoy because they would be seeking the cover of shallow waters, bays, coves, inlets, and river mouths. That was our playground, not suitable for destroyers. Then he surprised me: "Wanna come along?" he asked.

Absolutely, I told him immediately. I'd only been out once before and I'd caught hell for doing it because I was their only doctor. The risk really wasn't worth it. And yet: I was sick and tired of hearing all about their exploits secondhand at evening prayers. I told myself that going out, with the entire squadron this time, would be justified if we got ourselves into a fur-ball. It was BS, of course, but I'd been really impressed watching the commodore tighten up the squadron and then produce our first real clean-sweep victory. A young sailor brought me a steel helmet and a kapok life jacket, and then escorted me to the command boat.

By two in the morning I was barely able to stay awake. The squadron had made a high-speed run across the Slot just before sundown, dropping off pairs of boats at strategic points to get maximum radar coverage. I learned that not all boats had radar, and not all radars worked all the time, either. The plan had changed again. Without destroyer support, all we could do now was try to cover as much of the Slot as we could and hope to intercept somebody. Once we took up a station, about two-thirds of the way across the Slot, we shut down two of three engines and basically just drifted. We didn't want to make wakes in case there were *Kawanishi* around, but we had to keep one engine on the line in case *we* got jumped.

There was time to get a more detailed tour of an MTB and I learned some interesting things about her. Such as: everyone said that PT boats were made of plywood. They weren't—they were made of premium-grade mahogany and, to a great extent, hand-made at that. They were double-hulled and designed by racing yacht naval architects. Sleek, sturdy, overengined, only about the last third of the planing hull actually touched the water when at full power. Even stranger, the third, middle engine faced aft instead of forward like the other two. This necessitated a complicated gearing arrangement to get its power back to the stern.

Once again it was hot, muggy, and really dark out there, with no lights showing anywhere, at sea or ashore. We could see the occasional yellow pinprick of a flare light up in the sky way to our south as the Army skirmished with Jap patrols on Cactus, but otherwise it was so dark we had to cover the instrument panel because it looked so bright. Cogswell stayed down below with his radar plotter. The rest of the crew wedged themselves into various corners or gun mounts and slept. The sea was flat calm for a change, although we could feel a deep swell rolling in from the Solomon Sea to the west of us. The black bulk of Savo Island was invisible to the south, but the memory of the literally *thousands* of men, ours and theirs, asleep in the cold deep beneath us was never very far from any sailor's thoughts out on those waters. They called it Ironbottom Sound for a reason.

The radio speaker up on the bridge made some sputtering noises, and then: "Calico, this is three-oh-two. Radar contact, three-five-zero, range twenty-three thousand yards, composition six, closing."

I heard Cogswell down in his plotting room acknowledge and then rebroadcast the contact report to all the boats, using the collective call sign for the entire squadron, which tonight was Goblins. They all should have heard the initial report, but he was making sure that everyone got it by repeating it. Our command boat crew heard it and suddenly no one was sleeping. In a minute I heard the other two engines light off, and suddenly *I* was no longer sleepy. A cloud of engine exhaust coiled its way up over the superstructure. The helmsman put one engine in gear and turned the boat slowly to move us out of the engine exhaust. Then I heard Cogswell's voice from down below.

"Goblins, this is Calico: Contacts are on course one-seven-zero, speed thirty knots. Intercept time in twelve minutes. All units, converge at low-wake speed on enemy track line."

One of the boats called in. "Calico, these are not barges," he said. "Radar blips too big. These are warships."

I went below, hot as it was down there, especially with a kapok life jacket on. Cogswell and his plotter were hunched over the plotting table, which was illuminated by a dim red light. It wasn't a real plotting table, but rather what had been the fold-down plywood sheet that served as the crew's dining table. Cogswell was talking to himself.

"Not barges, then what?" he asked himself. "Have they sent a destroyer squadron this time to get their people out? Or is this a clutch of cruisers?"

"Range is eighteen thousand; constant bearing," the plotter reported.

Then the westernmost boat, 415, came up on the net. "Radar contacts, in and out, composition six or more, bearing two-four-zero, range fifteen thousand yards, headed northwest."

Cogswell acknowledged. I was looking over his shoulder in the cramped quarters of the crew's mess, trying not to get in his way. Cogswell was plotting the new contacts himself while the radar operator stayed on the ships coming down from the north. These new contacts were going *out* to sea, while the ones north of us were headed right at us. Cogswell picked up the radio and told the 415 boat to head west and visually identify the contacts he had on radar.

"Range is fifteen thousand, steady bearing," the operator said. His voice was just a wee bit higher as these unknown ships closed in on us.

"Can you see the other boats?" Cogswell asked.

"Affirmative," the operator said. "They're closing, but not very fast."

Cogswell had told them not to make wakes until we knew what was coming at us. We waited for those tiny green blobs on the radar display to get close enough for us to pop some flares. If this was a Jap destroyer squadron approaching, that would be the last thing we ever did.

"Range is thirteen thousand; steady bearing."

I suddenly had an idea, but before I could say anything the 415 boat, the one southwest of us, came up on the net. We could clearly hear explosions and gunfire in the background. "Japs, Japs, Japs!" the skipper shouted into the microphone, and then, after a blast of static, he went silent. Cogswell called him but got no reply.

"Multiple contacts, headed northwest," Cogswell muttered. "*That's* the evacuation force. They didn't come down the Slot. They came down west of the Russell Islands, and now they're headed back the same goddamned way."

"Commodore," I said, finally. "Could this northern group be *our* guys coming back?"

"Range is twelve thousand, two hundred."

That was six miles, well within even a destroyer's gun range. If these were our ships, we were already sitting in someone's gunfire-control computer solution.

"Range is ten thousand, two," the operator said. "Still constant bearing."

Cogswell grabbed the radio. "All units, break off, I say again, break off. Turn around and head *away* from the approaching contacts. Maximum speed."

He put down the radio and yelled up the hatch to the deck gang. "Fire six flares, right now, rapid succession. Bearing north, max range."

"Are we gonna run?" I asked.

"No," he said. "If these are our guys, I want their radars to see all those boats headed for them turn around. If this is a Jap cruiser formation, there's no point in *our* running. We're right in front of them."

The 81mm mortar up on deck began thumping out illumination rounds. Then I remembered they'd taken the four torpedo tubes off the command boat. When those illum rounds started popping, only *we* would be clearly illuminated. For the first time that night, I thought this was it. Higgins had been right. Crazy to come out here.

Cogswell directed the radar operator to change frequencies to the one used by American surface forces around Guadalcanal, and then began calling.

"Range is eight thousand, five," the operator said. Four miles, I thought. Surely whoever was coming could see us now. Cogswell kept calling out on the new frequency.

"Range is six thousand, nine," the operator said. "I think they're slowing down."

At that moment the green light on the face of the radio transmitter went red. Cogswell keyed it twice, swore and then flung the handset onto the plotting table.

"Fire six more illum rounds," he yelled up to the mortar crew. I decided it was time to go topside. If a Jap cruiser was about to eat us alive, I wanted to see it. The mortar hurt my ears as it blasted six more illumination rounds into the black sky. When the first one popped, I saw the bow of a large, dark gray ship looming up out of the gloom. Then I saw small white numerals just below the anchors.

American. Now the question was: did they know *we* were American?

Apparently, they did, because the ship, a totally darkened destroyer, slipped past us at only about 500 yards, followed by two more destroyers and then the cruisers. Cogswell never did make radio contact and the column formation steamed past us as if we didn't exist. The final flares burned out and we were alone in the dark, rolling uncomfortably from the passing wakes. I started breathing again. Cogswell came topside and looked around.

"Okay," he said, brightly, as if nothing had happened. "Let's head back and figure out what the hell happened out here tonight. Is there any coffee?"

We got back to the base an hour and a half later. Everyone involved convened in the command bunker for a debrief. Everyone, that was, except the skipper of the 415 boat. She hadn't been heard from ever since that last frantic transmission: Japs, Japs, Japs! I joined the after-action debrief. I didn't know what time it was, but it almost didn't matter. I was feeling a little bit ashamed of myself for having been scared to death. These guys had been going out, night after night, since August of last year, experiencing the same kind of dangerous confusion we'd been through tonight. And often with the same results. I sat back in a corner, not wanting to intrude.

The first order of business for the commodore was to send out a couple of boats to find the 415 and to notify Cactus that we had a boat missing north and west of Cape Esperance. While the skippers were noisily rehashing the night's operation, Chief Higgins popped his head in and signaled that we needed to talk. I went outside into what looked like morning twilight.

Higgins had interesting news. A transport had come into Tulagi just after sundown. The harbormaster had dispatched a Mike boat to our base on Santa Isabel with four pallets of medical supplies and replacement equipment. The Mike boat's skipper, a boatswain mate first class, had told Higgins that the Japs had vamoosed from Guadalcanal. The Army was still chasing down some lone Jap patrols up near the Cape and in the mountains, but the main Jap army was nowhere to be seen. Word was that the whole American force would be shifting north to someplace called Munda on New Georgia Island. As far as Guadalcanal was concerned, we'd won and now the Japs were falling back on their bases to the north.

I told him to come with me into the command center, where he told Cogswell and the assembled skippers the news. Cogswell was bemused. "How the *hell* did they manage that?" he wondered.

No one had an answer to that question, but one of the skippers asked if this meant we'd be moving again. "Absolutely," Cogswell said. "Munda is over a hundred miles from here. The Japs have an airfield there. They're gonna want us closer than that."

"Who's 'they'?" Deacon wondered aloud. "That cruiser-destroyer force went by us tonight like we were just local fishermen. They wouldn't even talk to us. I'm starting to wonder why the hell we're even out here."

I saw Cogswell cringe a little when Deacon said that. The expressions on the skippers' faces confirmed that Deacon wasn't alone in thinking that our squadron was just plain superfluous in the eyes of the Navy command structure.

Cogswell sighed and then told everyone to go get some rest. He instructed the radio operators to keep him informed as to the search for the 415 boat. Chief Higgins slipped away with the departing skippers, leaving me alone with Cogswell. I was more than ready to go climb up into my tree but decided that the commodore might appreciate some company. A screamer would have been welcome but the fixings were all locked up. Even the coffeepot on the side table was cold. With the meeting over, the radio operators turned out the lights and retired to their annex.

"Can't say as I blame 'em," he said as we sat there in the dark. "I sometimes wonder the same thing. And yet they loved us when we tore up that barge convoy."

"That night you produced results," I said. "Tonight was a bust."

"Ow," he muttered.

"Meaning no disrespect, Commodore," I said. "I'm just the squadron doctor. But you got results when you did the planning and rehearsing. Last night we cobbled up a plan and went on out there. I think we're lucky our big guys didn't open fire as soon as we came up on their radars. I was scared shitless out there, to be honest."

Cogswell grunted. "Me, too," he admitted. "But sometimes we don't have the luxury of a couple days of planning. Like the 415 boat—he probably ran into the Jap destroyer squadron that was taking out the last of the Jap army. We all assumed it would be a barge effort until the end, but, no, the Japs sent every destroyer they could get their hands on and they by-God pulled it off."

"Well, then, that's not our fault, Commodore," I said. "We were sent out to attack barges. Nobody bothered to inform the Japs that they were supposed to be using barges."

He laughed, but it was a bitter sound.

"We're gonna have to carve out our own mission out here," I said. "And the basis for that is to make ourselves useful, if not essential."

"Useful how?" he asked.

"That's for us to figure out, Captain, 'cause the big-ship Navy ain't gonna do that for us. We're the Hooligan Navy, remember?"

"We're the Hooligan Navy because no one owns us, so we've had to become goddamn pirates just to survive."

"Survival was the watchword for 1942," I said. "This is 1943. America is going on offense. If *we* want to be part of that, *we* have to be useful. We have to offer something that the big ships can't or don't want to do. Like search-and-rescue for downed pilots. Landing frogmen behind enemy lines. Scouting for minefields—our boats are made of wood; mines eat steel. Hit-and-run raids against enemy bases and outposts. Eyes and ears in the coves, the inlets, and river mouths, where the Japs hide from our aviators. Laying mines in places they'd never expect."

"Those aren't missions for boats with torpedoes," he said.

"You said we were going to get rid of the torpedoes," I replied. "You were right the first time: we have no business engaging in street fights with cruisers and destroyers. But: we can make life absolute hell for the Japs by just being there when they think they're safe because none of our cruisers and destroyers are around. They'll have to have bases just like this one, out of the way, improvised havens, where they can refuel, repair, regroup. Where they know our big guys can't physically get at them. And then a couple of our guys appear and shoot the place up while they're having *sake* and some rice. Think Nathan Bedford Forrest and his professional joy at putting a 'skeer' into the Yanks."

"You make a lot of military sense for a doc," he muttered.

"That's because I was gonna be an historian, a Civil War historian. I belonged to a Civil War history club in premed. We went to battlefields all over the South. Endlessly fascinating, along with the problems of command, military competency, weak generals, strong generals. The problems of the MTB force aren't new."

"Jeez, Doc. I thought I knew what I was doing when I came here. I was gonna straighten this outfit up and do some damage."

"And you did, the first time. The second time the enemy exercised that well-known vote. From my perspective, the Japs are the worst kind of enemy: merciless, fanatic, competent in the field, and willing to die if that's what it takes. Plus, they've been at this since 1937. We're the new guys on the field."

"I know in my heart that we are going to defeat them," he said. "I just know it. I may not live to see it, but things are changing."

"Yes, sir, I think you're right. Last year we were all on our asses, just starting to fight back, Midway not withstanding. But then more and more of our ships were sunk. Carriers, cruisers, destroyers. When I told that Aussie doctor what I'd been doing as a surgeon since August, he was dumfounded. You remember the old Speedy Gonzales joke, where he tells the guy whose throat he just cut, this won't hurt, did it? That's where I think we are right now: the Japs haven't yet realized that they've invoked the Apocalypse. I think you need to go to Nouméa."

"Nouméa?" he exclaimed. "And what, go have a drink with Halsey?"

"No, sir, go see his *staff*. You're the CO of the forward-most MTB squadron. You want to know how we can best help with what's coming, and when they say: uh, how's about *you* tell *us*? Then tell 'em."

He nodded. "Yup," he said. "Makes sense."

"Second thing: we need an advocate at headquarters. We need an admiral who'll assign us missions and also get us the support we need. U.S. Grant was something of an orphan until Shiloh. That was the battle that shocked the nation because of the casualties. People were accusing this nobody Grant of being drunk on that first day. You know what Lincoln did? As horrendously bloody as that battle was, Lincoln asked somebody to find out what it was Grant was supposed to have been drinking, and then ordered that a case of that whiskey be sent to every one of his generals."

"Doc," he said. "You're making perfect sense. I'm just not sure that *I* can make that good of a case. If I do this, you want to come with me?"

"Halsey's staff would never listen to a mere doctor," I said. "But with the Japs evacuating north, shouldn't we have a little breather before they move us? My patient load is light right now. I could, I don't know, write something up for you."

He thought about that, but then his eyes closed and his head began to sag. I realized he was very tired. So was I, for that matter, but I sensed this was important. The unhelpful specter of the 415 boat hung accusingly in the air. I waited for a few minutes and then quietly left him to sleep. The sun was about to come up outside, so I walked down to the mess tent and cadged a coffee and a biscuit. I left the tent and walked down to where one of the boats was tied up to a palm tree on the beach. I sat down on a nearby stump, drank my coffee, and watched the boats grudgingly come to life. The scene was so peaceful I almost expected to see a six-pack of Bettys swooping in. I did notice that the nearest boat had uncovered the 20 mm cannon back aft and that there was a gunner enjoying *his* morning coffee—but in the gunner's seat.

I thought about what to gin up for the skipper. It had to make
military sense if he was going to get anywhere with a headquarters
staff. I asked myself what outfits in the Civil War were analogous
to the MTBs, and the answer came immediately. Light cavalry.
Southern light cavalry, to be specific. Excellent horsemen even before the war, they were all volunteers, young, fit, used to riding fast
and light, many of them foxhunters jumping hedgerows and ditches,
and whose main mission was to scout out the enemy's heavy formations and rob the supply train if they could for food and ammo.
Union cavalry were more like today's tank regiments, with organic
supply trains and even some light artillery. The newsreels of 1939
had been full of German tank divisions, whose size, armament, and
menacing appearance made the boxy, clunky British and French
tanks look like toys. The Reb light horse was more like a bunch of
Comanches, small units skilled in the art of the raid. Just like the
MTBs should be.

So: start with that. PT boats were already being used for some of
those missions when nothing else was available, especially downed
pilot rescue. That wouldn't have worked at Midway, way out in the
vast, open ocean, but now that the American Navy was grappling
with the Japs among the Pacific island chains and joining forces with
Army and Marine units, there'd certainly be a need. Even in my
business: on an island, even a big island, you needed a fast boat to
take your wounded off the front line and get them to an aid station.
At Guadalcanal, shattered ships would crawl back to Cactus, who
would send out amphibious boats left over from the initial invasion,
slow but with a lot of capacity, to get the wounded off before the
ship went down, like the USS *Atlanta* did, right offshore. But now,
as we headed north, there probably wouldn't be amphibious task
forces lingering around beachheads, not with Fortress Rabaul and
the Japanese 2nd Air Army within much closer striking range. A
plan began to take shape, and I decided to get it down on paper before I forgot it all.

FOURTEEN

Three days later, the commodore caught a hop down to Nouméa from Henderson Field. The deputy chief of staff for operations had agreed to see him and listen to his proposal for a new mission for the MTBs. He left at 0530 from Cactus for the six-hour flight. That afternoon, Deacon was summoned to the bunker to decrypt a message from Nouméa. Several of the skippers and I waited anxiously for Deacon to crank through the laborious process of uncorking the message. He was clearly angry when he finally emerged from the code room.

"I just don't get it," he said. "The commodore is on his way down there right now to lay out a new and different mission for the squadron. This—" He waved the message at us. "This is a new mission for the squadron, along with orders for another base move. I ask you: what the *hell*, over?"

"What's the new mission?" one of the skippers asked.

"We're to go to a new pontoon pier the Seabees are building on Lunga Point over on Cactus. Then we'll support the Army security forces remaining on Cactus as they find and eliminate the remnants of the Jap army still there."

"How the hell do we support that mission?"

"I don't know," Deacon said. "Maybe take army patrols around the coasts of Guadalcanal and insert them where they think Japs might be hiding out. I'm sure some general will tell us."

"While everybody else goes north with the real war," another skipper said, somewhat bitterly. "That's garrison duty. In the rear, with the gear."

"Sounds like it," Deacon said. "We must have really pissed off whoever was in charge of that cruiser group."

Personally, I thought that was likely. There'd probably been an admiral riding one of those cruisers and he'd told Nouméa to get those damned PT boats out of the real navy's way.

"Any word on the 415 boat?" someone asked.

Deacon shook his head. "She just disappeared. Hell, if Mickey blundered into an entire group of Jap destroyers..."

He didn't have to finish. I recalled someone saying that PT boats couldn't really be sunk because they were made of wood. Unless they burned.

It got worse. The next day we received a message from head-quarters that Commander Cogswell was being detached and or-dered back to the States to take command of a brand-new heavy cruiser in his new rank as a four-striper. Our new commanding of-ficer would be one Lieutenant Commander Stede Rackham, USN. He was en route to the headquarters on Nouméa for in-briefing and then would be here in about a week.

Weedy Tucker, one of the skippers, sat up when he heard the name. "Stede Rackham?" he exclaimed. "Good Lord, that's Bluto."

Everybody looked at him. Bluto? Popeye the Sailor Man's out-size, bearded nemesis in the cartoon strip?

Tucker was shaking his head in wonder. "Bluto. I can't believe it. Well, I guess I can. Now it really does sound like we're being banished. And I'll bet Bluto is, too. Wow. Wow. *Wow*."

"You obviously know this guy," someone said, impatiently. "So: give."

"I first met him when I was a plebe and he was a company officer back at the boat school," Weedy said. "Even then he was a pretty unconventional character. I forget which class he is, but he was a varsity football player as a Mid. Then we were shipmates on the *Lexington* when I was a boot ensign on my first sea tour. I was in the engineering department. He was the ordnance officer in charge of all the ammunition and the ship's magazines."

"Character-schmaracter," Deacon said. "What's he like?"

"He's big," Weedy said. "Correction: he's *huge.* Defensive line-man huge. Sometimes things would start to bog down when the ship was trying to get a launch off because his red-shirts got behind, you know, hanging the ordnance. Rackham would come up out onto the flight deck and personally start lifting and hanging bombs that usually took three guys to lift, all the while calling his red-shirts ninety-pound weaklings. Once the launch got off, he'd hand out cans of spinach, which was pretty funny. I think that's probably where the Bluto stuff started. The enlisted guys loved him; most of the wardroom officers just shook their heads."

"So how does somebody get command with a background like that?" I asked.

"You know, Weedy may be right," Deacon said. "Looks to me like somebody senior rescued Commander Cogswell from career oblivion, and now they're sending this guy because he, like the PT boats, is a problem."

"Maybe," Tucker said. "But as I remember it, Rackham got a Navy Cross for something he did at Pearl when the Japs hit. There was a story about him leading a team of divers and welders *into* the hull of one of the overturned battleships and getting some guys out of the engineering spaces. I gotta say—if *he's* our new boss, we won't be dropping off Army patrols over on Cactus for very long."

Our new CO arrived four days later after a flight from Nouméa to Cactus. He was every bit as big as Tucker had described, with a bit of a paunch, upper arms like hams, a big black beard, of all things, an oversize face with a great beak of a nose, and a voice like a trumpet. He came to us from Cactus in a Catalina, whose crew were whispering he'd occupied *two* seats. Deacon had asked me to go along to welcome the new skipper. I asked him if he was scared; he simply said, yeah, a little bit.

We met the seaplane in the 404 boat to avoid having to bring him all the way around the harbor to the command bunker. His handshake enveloped my hand like a bear paw, but in a relatively gentle manner. He had bright blue Nordic eyes. I think he must have weighed almost 250 pounds. The 404 boat's skipper, Goody Gushue, nosed the boat up next to the Cat's hull and Rackham hopped down onto the bow. A plane crewman then handed down his seabag, followed by a Western-style gun belt, complete with rounds in the belt loops and containing *two* Colt .45 revolvers. He took a moment to strap on the gun belt, and then walked over to the helmsman's station without so much as a how-do-you-do.

"Back us outa here," he said. We only had one engine on the line, as was the usual case for moving around the harbor. The helmsman did so, and then Rackham ordered the other two engines lit off. Deacon and I had expected to exchange welcome-aboard nice-ties, but Rackham didn't seem interested in talking. The other two main engines lit off in a cloud of exhaust smoke as we backed away from the Catalina. The helmsman, a young boatswain mate, looked uncertain as to what to do next. Rackham pointed seaward. The helmsman engaged all three engines and headed in the direction of the open sea at just above idle speed. We made a practice of keeping wakes down in the harbor because there were often women and children doing their washing right down on the edge of the beach.

Deacon and I were left standing there up in the cockpit like two pieces of furniture. It took three minutes at slow speed to gain the entrance into Tunabuli harbor, at which point Rackham indicated he wanted to take control of the boat. Goody stepped up and offered to drive. Rackham looked down at him for a brief moment and then shook his head. "Lash yourselves down, shipmates," he ordered with a smile, and then, as we cleared the inner harbor, pushed the throttles to maximum power.

For the next fifteen minutes we basically just tried to hang on as Rackham, much as his predecessor had done, ran that boat flat out through a series of straightaways, wide turns, violent turns, S-turns, and then straight ahead again. Goody had brought only a few crewmen for what he had assumed was just a taxi run: the engineman, one gunner, the boatswain-mate helmsman, and himself. This was the boat Cogswell had taken over as the command boat, so the torpedo tubes were absent. That had taken 4,000 pounds of topside weight off the boat, which meant the 404 could flat-*ass* move out, even with the extra electronic gear and guns. The engineman had disappeared belowdecks once he saw what we were going to do. Goody hung on with both hands, as did we. The gunner strapped himself into the 20 mm mount back aft—it was the driest point on the boat—as we hit almost fifty miles an hour on a light chop. Rackham did one 180-degree turn where the boat basically left the water, bouncing through each ten degrees of the turn every time its keel could snatch a second of traction on the wave tops.

Then the engines positively screamed as he pulled the throttle straight through neutral to reverse. The bow plunged into the sea and we were all instantly soaked. As we gathered sternway, he reversed again and spun the helm. The boat heeled sharply, too sharply I thought, sure that we were going to capsize, and then began shooting a big rooster-tail as she came back up to maximum power. This went on for another five minutes before he slowed the engines down to low power and indicated for the helmsman to take the controls. That wide-eyed worthy almost didn't know what to do, so Goody stepped up and took the helm, while Rackham leaned back on the bulkhead and lit a cigarette. He told Goody to take us back to the base.

Deacon and I leaned against the sloping forward bulkhead of the bridge structure, trying to dry off. Rackham stepped down off the bridge and joined us on the forward bulkhead. It was like standing next to a bear. "I talked to Commander Cogswell while I was down at Halsey's headquarters," he said. "I got a full briefing on the squadron. What you've been doing and where, the problems of not being owned by anyone at Nouméa, how you get supplies and parts when the Navy fails to provide. Screamers."

We both laughed at that. Screamers. There was hope.

"They also told me about our new so-called 'mission' of babysitting the big green machine on Cactus." He spat over the side to show us what he thought of that. "Doc, he said you were an excellent surgeon and that he often used you as a sounding board, because you had no Navy career skin in the game."

"We talked often," I said. "Not that I know much about operational stuff."

"He thought otherwise. Said you were a Civil War history buff. That you thought we ought to be acting like Nathan Bedford Forrest. I think I agree with that. XO?"

"Yes, sir?" Deacon replied. We were about two miles from the turn into the harbor estuary.

"Which would you prefer to be: a part of the regular Navy, with a well-defined chain of command, including a squadron commodore with his staff and a schedule of inspections, a regulation channel into the naval supply system, a book of standard operating procedures, fleet regulations, maintenance directives, and a bevy of captains looking over his shoulder all the time—"

"Or?" Deacon said.

"Being part of a uniformed pirate organization, which governs itself. A mob of high-speed gunfighters who are masters of midnight requisitioning, nighttime raiding parties, ambush, machine-gun massacres, and the general terrorizing of the emperor's navy and all its works."

Deacon nodded as he took all that aboard. "Can I still be the XO?" he asked finally.

Rackham roared with laughter. "Attaboy, Mister Haller. And yes, you can still be XO. Now start thinking about who we're gonna send to the big staff in the sky. He needs to be something of a diplomat, preferably with some connections back home."

"I've got just the guy," Deacon said. I looked over at him, a silent question in my eyes. He mouthed back the words: Lamb Chop.

FIFTEEN

Thus began a brand-new chapter in the existence of the Hooligans. We learned that our new boss, after his séance with Commander Cogswell, had gone to see one of his classmates, someone medium high up in the headquarters, with a proposal for doing something very different from ferrying army patrols around the still-bleeding remains of the Guadalcanal battlefields. The key concession as the price for our independence was that we would put an officer on the staff of whoever was running the show as the fleet went north. His job would be to coordinate our activities with the deep-water Navy so that we wouldn't mutually interfere with each other.

Our mission would be to terrorize Jap logistics, drive up in the night to shoot up their shore installations, rescue any of our pilots who'd gone down in waters too dangerous even for the Catalinas, drop off frogmen to do whatever frogmen did to Jap facilities, conduct hydrographic sounding sweeps in areas where the bosses might want to land troops, lay the odd minefield, and carry wounded from the front lines to the nearest medical facilities. In short, we would strive to become extremely useful, with that all-important proviso that we wouldn't do anything until our warm body on Halsey's staff made sure we wouldn't be screwing things up. His classmate had told Rackham he'd see what he could do.

The first order of business was to find a home on or near New Georgia Island. The planners on Halsey's staff suggested *we* go look for someplace suitable actually on New Georgia Island, unless of course we thought the island was too hot, in which case they'd pick somewhere a bit safer. I suspected that somebody down there knew exactly how a guy nicknamed Bluto would react to that. He told them via message that he would select a spot near enough to be no more than one hour from whatever was going on. We found out that the next Allied objective was a large airfield at a place called Munda, on the west coast of New Georgia. That island was heavily garrisoned, its forces augmented now by the evacuees from Guadalcanal. The plan apparently was for the Army to occupy the much smaller Rendova Island, which was a short four miles across a strait from Munda. Once taken, Rendova would provide a perfect place for a battalion of Army heavy artillery to subdue the Japs across the strait holding the Munda airfield, which was the ultimate objective. Once we took Munda, our bombers would be within practical range of Simpson Harbor at Rabaul, where *all* the Jap ships in the Solomons were based.

Once again, I tapped the coast-watcher headquarters, and they recommended a tiny island named Bau, which was located inside the main harbor on Rendova. Bluto agreed.

I was dealing with a sudden surge in malaria while all this was going on. It was the scourge of South Pacific battlefields, requiring the troops to take toxic pills which they often quit taking. I remembered my Civil War history books all talking about disease incapacitating more soldiers than the enemy. If a soldier came down with it, he was airlifted out. Chief Higgins thought that some of the grunts stopped their pills for this reason, without realizing that it could lead to a lifetime of disabling sickness.

The landings on Rendova pitted 6,000 US Army troops against about 300 Japanese defenders, which meant it was a walkover. As soon as Bluto got word that the island was secure and that there were LSTs parked there, he took his command boat, plus one other to act as wingman, and went to Rendova. It was a longish trip from Tanabuli, so they had to keep their speed down when out in open waters, but they still managed to arrive on the next morning, much to the surprise of the Army commander. The skipper grounded his boat's bow on Bau Island, a tiny, wooded islet, and did a quick walk around. There was one cove that would be perfect, so he visited the Army general in charge and said he'd be back with a full squadron of PT boats within three days. They refueled from an LST and then headed back across the Slot to Tanabuli.

The boats were then divided into two divisions: the first division was made up of all the boats that were ready for sea and able to make the transit right now. The second division consisted of the boats that were not ready, for whatever reason. The first division boats were the ones charged with bringing the most urgently needed gear and as much of our ammo and spare-parts stash as they could possibly carry. I went down to the command center to brief the skipper on our malaria cases, the last five of which were being airlifted out that morning. There were three skippers in there complaining about being put into the second division. Rackham was unsympathetic. If your boats were ready to go out and fight, he told them, you'd be in the first division. Remember that next time and now, if you please, gentlemen, comply with my orders.

I thought that was a pretty good lesson and told him so after the three abashed skippers left. Then I asked him about the medical facilities situation on Rendova.

"Right now, there's a bunch of LSTs there, so any casualties will go to them. But I'm not sure for how long the Navy will stick around, because the Japs are surely gonna counterattack. The Army plans to invade New Georgia proper as soon as it can; they really want that airfield at Munda. Rendova was a cakewalk; New

Georgia might be a tougher nut. I think we ought to set up our own medical facility, just in case the deep-water Navy has to run for it. As I understand it, they've done that before."

He was referring to the first few days after the Guadalcanal landings, which the Marines still resented.

"Sounds good to me," I said. "I'll rape and pillage the amphib ships for as long as they stay there. But now I need to talk to you about malaria."

He groaned, looked at his watch, and sat back down.

I made the transit with the first division that night so that we could arrive at daylight. The crossing went without incident, although everybody was pretty apprehensive. As best we knew, Guadalcanal was the first time the Japs had been driven off an occupied conquest since the beginning of the Pacific-wide war. I left behind the redoubtable Wooly McAllen, Chief Higgins, our two lend-lease surgical chiefs, and two hospitalmen, who were going to bring up all our stuff. I thought I was coming up in the world: I actually had a medical staff!

Rendova was a tropical island with a large, supposedly dormant volcano at the center, some 3,000 feet high. The actual harbor was up on a strait called the Blanche Channel, which ran between Rendova Island and the much bigger New Georgia Island. Rendova was going to be a more spartan base than beautiful Tanabuli, at least for the MTBs. No caves, no freshwater springs, no Blind Man, and very little level ground. The only good news was that it was so inconspicuous that the Jap bombers, when they came, and everyone knew they surely *would* be coming, might just ignore it. There was one small cove, which was more of a notch in the shoreline, and that's where the skipper decided to set up his command center. There were two troop transports and five LSTs anchored around the harbor when we arrived. The transports were unloading 155 mm artillery guns, which the Army lovingly called Long Toms. An advance party of Seabees was busy carving out protective artillery emplacements overlooking the Blanche Channel, which would give the big guns a clear shot over the channel to Munda and its defenses. The Japs had to be watching all this from Munda. It reminded me of the denizens of a medieval castle watching siege works going up. They apparently did not have Long Toms on New Georgia.

The next three days turned into a blur of activity as we got set up on Bau and the Army prepared for the cross-channel invasion of New Georgia itself. We found out that a Marine raider battalion was also going to be involved. Our boats found immediate employment, taking Navy underwater demolition teams (UDTs) across the channel at night to scope out the potential landing sites on New Georgia. Word was that there were as many as 10,000 Jap troops over there who'd had some time to dig in and prepare extensive defensive positions, something they were really good at, according to the Army guys. As a surgeon I was called over to the LSTs at least once a day to deal with one medical emergency or another.

The good news was that Higgins was scheduled to arrive shortly. He could then take over supervision of the medical aid station that was going up on our lonely rock. The bad news was that we'd lost Wooly. He'd gone missing during the beehive activity of packing out the base. A search party eventually found him, at the bottom of that big, clear pool next to the aid station. His body was badly battered, as if he'd rolled all the way down from the cliffs above and hit several sharp rocks on the way down. Broken like a stick figure in so many places that his body bag had been round, not straight, was the way the report described it.

I knew exactly what he'd been doing; he'd gone back to that veil of a waterfall to go through it and explore that dark, brooding statue up above. I sent word back to Higgins to see if the locals would bury him on his old plantation, now that the Japs were gone. The next day I got word back that they would *not* do that. Somehow, they had concluded that Wooly had gone into the water cave beyond the talking stone, and thus incurred the wrath of the Blind Man, and that was that. The pack-up party had buried him in the jungle in one of our supply-dispersal bunkers. They'd put a cross above his grave. I wondered how long that would last once we left.

The best news was that the rest of the Seabees had arrived. They joined the group that were setting up the big guns along the channel side of Rendova, but we still got some help building some makeshift wooden A-frame shelters for the boats along the edges of the cove and the makings of a crude ops hut.

We'd barely got our field medical aid station up and running when a cruiser pulled into the harbor. She'd been in a sea fight north of the island and had a lot of casualties, plus the survivors of a destroyer that had been sunk. The LST medical people were quickly overwhelmed, so we got the chance to try out our new tent-city aid station. The only thing that saved us were all those ugly amphibious boats carried by the transports and the LSTs, which could bring supplies and medical personnel shared by every ship there to wherever they were needed.

Fresh water was a big problem. The Navy ships could make enough for their crews and boilers but not enough to also support us. Once again, the Seabees came to our rescue. They dynamited the sides of a rock formation, creating a slanting slab of bare volcanic rock that led from the top of the island, some 200 feet above the cove, down to the water's edge. They then blasted out a slanting fracture line which led to a small open space, filled with clean barrels. Every time it rained, which was often, rainwater would be collected and sluiced into those barrels, giving us basically unlimited fresh water.

On the sixth day the Army commander got a warning from coast-watchers at around sunrise that Jap bombers were coming down the Slot in our direction. The LSTs quickly slipped their anchors and scrambled to get out of the constricted Rendova Harbor. The two troop transports remained anchored. The Army general ordered the torpedo boats to set up an AA screen around the transports. I'm sure they would have preferred destroyers, but, as usual, tin cans were in short supply. Bluto seemed delighted that the Japs were finally coming. He had wanted to make us useful to the New Georgia operation, and here was our chance. He took his command boat out, purportedly so as not to miss out on the fun. I wanted to tell him that Bettys were anything but fun, but figured he'd discover that soon enough. My medical team and I headed for shelter in a log-covered trench near the base of the water-catchment cliff. We sat down on some logs right outside the ramp going down to the shelter, because of course we wanted to see what happened.

We now had a total of ten boats on Rendova. We had no way of knowing which way the Japs would come, so the skipper ordered eight boats to take up close-in stations around the anchored transports, with the remaining two, including his command boat, ready to move wherever they could do the most good. The transports had guns of their own, four 40 mm twin mounts in gun tubs topside, plus some smaller 20 mm Oerlikon mounts. The swirl of MTBs could offer forty 50-caliber barrels plus ten 20 mm guns. If the Japs came in low, as they usually did, that would make for quite a reception.

They didn't, crafty bastards that they were. There were eight of them and they flew in overhead at about 8,000 feet and dropped 500-pounders all over the Rendova harbor. We scampered down the ramp when we saw what was about to happen and huddled in the dank shelter, wishing it was a mile or so deeper. We were then treated to a series of bomb blasts, mostly out in the harbor except for one that landed on our water-catchment slab, thumping us off our log benches and filling the shelter entrance with a rain of dirt and bits of stone. We could hear lots of gunfire from outside, but I knew that none of those guns could reach the Japs at that altitude.

The noise finally subsided and we crept out of our hidey-hole. One of the transports was burning furiously amidships from what had to have been a direct hit; the other seemed unharmed until we saw all the shrapnel holes along her port side from a near miss. Then that cluster of holes went out of sight as she began to list to port. That near miss had surely opened some seams below the waterline.

I counted PT boats, and came up with eight. A thick pall of water mist, smoke, and blasted air hung over the harbor, obscuring the shores on the opposite sides. There were two oil fires burning furiously over near the main Army encampment. Suddenly we heard the sound of approaching airplane engines out over the Blanche Channel to the northeast. Then two Bettys came zooming in at low level and launched torpedoes at the listing transport. She was hit twice and pretty much disappeared in a blast of red fire, towering waterspouts, and flying debris. When the smoke cleared, she was upside down and sinking by the stern. The other transport continued to burn, and I could now see many small black figures in the water around her. Three MTBs had moved in and were pulling men out of the water. The Bettys had come in so fast that not one MTB had opened fire.

Then we heard more airplane engines, but this time from the direction of that dark volcano five miles to the west. The boats were ready, and when the next two Bettys popped up above the western tree line they were greeted by a veritable storm of fire which quickly turned them into flaming wrecks that spun out of the sky and exploded in the harbor. Then we heard the sounds of distant gunfire, which probably meant that the LSTs offshore were being attacked by yet another group of bombers. The Japs may have been driven off Guadalcanal, but Rendova and New Georgia were absolutely not going to be taken without a fight. The closer we got to the hornets' nest on Rabaul, the more hornets we could expect to see. I saw the MTBs heading in toward the two transports. Hoping that the attack was over, I told everybody to get to the partially completed aid station. It was going to be a long day. I prayed that at least some of the LSTs were coming back, because they had real sick bays onboard, while I had essentially a grass hut with an A-frame roof made of palm tree trunks.

Three of them did but not for two more hours. There had been five of them in the harbor when the warning came. Two had been torpedoed and lost. A third had been torpedoed but the warhead hadn't gone off. It still left a huge hole in her port side engine room, so another LST had taken her in tow to get her back to the harbor. They'd been attacked by six Bettys and had shot down three, after which the Japs apparently lost their taste for LST bombing. But as everyone knew, tomorrow was another day and the Japs reportedly had the world's supply of Bettys up there in Rabaul.

The two LSTs which had gone down had already been unloaded, so their precious cargo of troops and equipment was already ashore on Rendova. The loss of two amphibious ships was costly, though, especially in view of the upcoming cross-channel invasion of New Georgia proper. The general commanding asked Cactus for fighters to be on station during the most likely attack windows.

I received word to meet the first LST that came in. All casualties initially would be collected there until we could assess the state of the other sick bays. Each ship had a doctor assigned, but there were no surgeons. Two hours later, I had a boat take me out to the first LST that dropped anchor back in Rendova harbor, the USS *Liscomb County* (LST 1164). We could see a line of holes where she'd been strafed along the tank deck as we came alongside. Her 40 mm gun tubs, the barrels burned black, were still full of empty shell casings. Sailors were picking their way through the casings, salvaging the deformed ones right along with the good ones. Brass was in short supply back home. All spent casings, 20 mm, 40 mm, five-inch, and even six-inch would go back to the States for reuse. One 40 mm gun tub was fully manned and ready while the other one's crew collected brass.

They lowered the ship's front ramp so Chief Higgins, two HMs, and I could jump aboard with our equipment bags. An ensign took us back to the sick bay. I asked about their casualties. He told me they'd had two killed in the strafing run, but otherwise, that was it for *Liscomb County*. He also said that he'd seen what looked like a couple hundred men in the water after the two ships had gone down, but he didn't know where they were right now. Higgins and I looked at each other, knowing what we were probably going to see in the next several hours. I asked about survivors from the transports. He didn't know. One was gone, the other still burning amidships, although it looked as if the fires were being subdued.

Since the LSTs could be tasked with hauling troops as well as vehicles and ammo, they had a bigger sick bay than did, say, a cruiser or destroyer. There was even an operating table, although they had minimal surgical equipment. The ship's doctor was a lieutenant in his late thirties, possibly even forty, with rather long hair for a naval officer. He introduced himself formally as Doctor Ellsworth Howard. He was already in sick bay, and he looked surprised when I showed up.

"They said the MTBs' MO was a surgeon," he said, with a bit of a Bostonian twang. "I'm sorry, but you don't look old enough."

At that moment, the ship's announcing system came up to report two boatloads of casualties were inbound to the *Liscomb County*.

"Let's get ready for triage, shall we?" I said, evading his implicit question.

He nodded, but I could see he wasn't done with his questions yet. "Tank deck, then," he said. "Follow me, please."

The ramp was down as we came out on the tank deck, that large open cargo area that ran down the middle of the ship. An LST looked like a floating shoebox, whose bow could split open and then drop a ramp large enough for tanks to cross. The genius of the LST design was that the ship would approach the landing beach through shoaling water, drop an anchor behind her, and then deliberately run the front end aground, after which tanks, mobile artillery, trucks, jeeps, and finally troops could cross that big ramp and charge up the beach. Lighter now by several tons, they'd lift the ramp, close the bow doors, and then winch themselves off the beach to go get more stuff from ships anchored offshore and out of danger.

Triage was painful, as it always was. The only way we got through it was to remind ourselves that the broken bodies laid out on the steel decks, most of them leaking precious bodily fluids, were in far more pain than we were. We used a tag system: one color for "hopeless—sedate/make comfortable until he dies," another for "immediate surgery/attention," and a third for "he can wait." The two of us would agree upon a determination and tell the hospitalman what color tag to put on the man's stretcher, using the words one, two, or three so as not to further frighten the already badly frightened man. I'd had a lot of experience doing this; Doc Howard had not, but we agreed on almost every case. It was one of the "disagree" cases that brought back the questions.

Toward the end I examined one man whose belly had been opened up by a piece of flying metal. I called for tag two; Dr. Howard said, surely no, he's a one—just look at that....

I told him I disagreed. It looks horrible, I said, but there's a bowel resection procedure that can save his life as long as you have some plasma. He looked at me over the prostrate form between us. Then I told him who I was and, more importantly, *what* I was. He looked even more upset.

"I can't do a bowel resection, Doctor," he said. "Surely, you're not qualified to do that, are you?"

I asked him a question: "You just said you can't do a bowel resection. I can and *have* done more than thirty of them back on Guadalcanal and Tulagi. But we have to move *now* to avoid sepsis. *You* can't help him. *I* can. It's major surgery under less than ideal conditions, so he still may die, but that's the risk they all take by just being there. Well?"

Higgins was watching this little discussion carefully, as was the wide-eyed HM who'd been applying the tags. Doctor Howard stood there with his mouth open, but he clearly didn't know what to say. Then I piled on.

"You know what, Doctor?" I said. "Why don't you assist? You're going to have to learn how to do this kind of thing 'cause I think it's gonna be a long war and there will never be enough surgeons, will there?"

"First, do no harm," he whispered, reminding me of the Hippocratic oath.

"Granted," I said. "But it's wartime. You want to face his parents and tell them you decided to do nothing? That you didn't even try?"

He sighed. Admittedly, it was an unfair question, but I was going to need an assistant. "Okay," I said. "Let's get to it before the real rush begins."

SIXTEEN

As it turned out, Howard was an excellent assistant. He'd gone to Yale for medical school and Mass General for his internship, and it showed. We did three more abdominal repair procedures during the next twenty hours. We saved the first and the third. The second patient died as we were stabilizing the anesthesia. We also did a bunch of thoracic work—punctured lungs, ruptured diaphragms, blunt force trauma to rib cages, and on and on. Howard had never been on his feet that long and finally cried uncle. That gave me an excuse to sit down, too. By then we had two more docs from other LSTs attending the general triage and repair operations. Even the Army sent over a doc, a very young-looking first lieutenant, but he quailed at the sheer scope of the casualties. I threw him out and told him to go back to the Army HQ and continue with his short-arm inspections. It turned out that the Army had waited to set up a hospital until they were sure Rendova was secure. In the meantime, they'd depend upon the Navy, who had been told there'd be an Army hospital on Rendova. Situation normal, etc.

Procedures was perhaps the wrong word. The term "surgical procedure" calls to mind a fully equipped hospital surgery, a surgical staff of doctors and nurses who've been briefed on what was coming, a patient who's been prepped and is preferably not in shock, and a supporting staff of on-call specialists like radiologists and pathologists, a blood bank, a responsive lab, and an unlimited supply of sterile equipment. We weren't doing procedures, not in the traditional sense. We were doing emergency battle surgery, reinforced by the technical knowledge of how it would be done under perfect conditions. We were doing the best we could, just like the field medics, whose only available response would be to hang an IV, dust the entire wound with sulfa powder, and then bandage the hell out of it. Morphine to stop the screaming. Water on his forehead to keep him cool. A cigarette if the morphine was working. A stretcher when enemy fire allowed one.

Outside of the sick bay, there was a major logistics operation going on. Cactus had begun sending Catalinas, so now there had to be a second round of triage, as we docs had to decide who most needed an airborne stretcher berth out of Rendova. The Cats flew them down to Cactus, where a fresh set of medical eyes evaluated them. Some were then sent on to Nouméa; others to the recovery tents on Guadalcanal, still others back into surgery for another try. We thought we were home free after so many hours, but then the burning transport suddenly broke in half. The back half sank. The front half exploded, raining artillery shells and other ordnance all over the Rendova harbor. One large artillery shell actually hit our LST, but, since it hadn't been armed by being fired down a grooved barrel, there was no explosion. The thing slammed down onto the tank deck, bounced, hit again, and then sat there spinning in place, as if practicing for a game of spin-the-bottle for the wide-eyed sailors, holding their ears as they watched it.

The LST in front of us wasn't so lucky. Some other type of red-hot shell hit her farther aft and penetrated a 40 mm magazine, which blew up and took the port quarter of the ship clean off. Several crewmen were flung into the harbor, and we went back to work about an hour later. Most of the cases were burns, so there wasn't much call for extensive surgery. I reverted to assisting the docs who were doing the burn treatment, about which I had a lot to learn, mostly from Doc Howard, as it turned out.

By sundown we had things pretty much under control. We found our way to the ship's wardroom, where there was food, fresh coffee, and most importantly, a place to sit down. The LST's captain, a Navy full lieutenant, joined us. He said that the Army was about a week away from launching an invasion on New Georgia Island, and that there was talk of designating one of the LSTs as a temporary hospital ship. She'd go into the assault landing zone, disgorge her cargo, then back off and set up shop somewhere close enough that casualties could be brought aboard from behind friendly front lines.

"Who'll protect her?" Doc Howard asked.

"There'll be destroyers for the invasion," the captain said. "Plus, the PT boats will be assigned to be close-in AA defense."

One of the other docs asked if there would be additional medical personnel coming along with the main invasion force. The captain didn't know.

I thought an LST would make a damn sight better field medical station than the tree-covered ravine we had now over on Bau Island. Electricity, fresh water, food, clean bunks, refrigeration, insect and rodent control, and the ability to sterilize equipment properly: relative luxuries, all. The only problem I could see was that the Japs might have an easier time sinking a large, slow target (LST), especially an anchored one, than getting a bomb into our ravine.

A messenger from the bridge knocked on the wardroom door and reported to the captain that three destroyers had arrived just outside the harbor.

"About time," the captain said. "We're overdue for another air raid."

The GQ alarm sounded as if to acknowledge his remark. He shook his head wearily and hustled out of the wardroom. Moments later the ventilation was shut off. We could hear watertight doors being dogged shut throughout the ship, so it looked like we were going to sit this one out in the wardroom. I was tired enough that I wandered over to the couch, sat down in one corner, and went to sleep. I thought I could hear the sound of guns but by then the sleep monster had me. The wardroom was quickly becoming uncomfortably warm, but I was beyond caring.

The next thing I knew I was airborne and tumbling across the wardroom and stumbling painfully into the table. I tried to focus my eyes but the room was full of dust. The other docs were, like me, flailing around on the deck. I couldn't hear anything over the roar of a large explosion, followed by the sounds of structural failure—the screeching of ruptured steel, the clatter of falling debris, and the screams of injured men. I tried to get up off the deck but something was wrong—the deck was moving. Things began to topple off the wardroom table, and all of a sudden we found ourselves trying desperately to get off the deck, which now was tilting ominously. The lights flickered and then went out. Battle lanterns came on, illuminating the chaotic scene in their spectral yellow light.

I clawed my way back over to the table and hoisted myself into a semi-vertical stance, pulling the tablecloth off in the process. The other docs were all trying to do the same. By now the list on the ship was at least twenty degrees and things, *big* things, were sliding around outside on the tank deck. Suddenly the wardroom door, which was not a watertight door, snapped open as its doorframe deformed. A water line out in the passageway had broken and was vigorously spraying water everywhere. I staggered toward the door with the rest of the docs and then realized I didn't know how to get out of the interior of this ship and onto a weather deck. One of the other docs did and took the lead. We followed him into a passageway that was lit only by battle lanterns, sloshing through water that should never have been there. Then there was a very loud bang, followed by a gigantic lurch which threw all of us onto the deck and actually underwater. I realized that hadn't been an explosion but the sound of the hull breaking up.

Suddenly there was daylight and an enormous wall of seawater coming straight at us. We were swept back into the passageway, tumbling ass over teakettle in a vortex of foaming seawater, and then swept right back out as that water wave hit watertight doors and rebounded. I found myself underwater and scrambling to get back up to the surface for a breath of air. My eyes were stinging from salt water and I tasted fuel oil. When I finally cleared my eyes, I saw our LST, broken in half and fully capsized. As I watched, the front half disappeared in a howling cloud of dirty air and frothing seawater. I could dimly hear airplane engines through my water-plugged ears and a lot of heavy gunfire, much bigger than the 40 mm AA guns the LSTs carried. One of the other docs surfaced next to me, purple faced and hacking his lungs out as he tried to recover his breathing. I spied a life raft twenty feet away and swam to it, and grabbed on to the netting like a snapping turtle. The netting was covered in fuel oil so I had to try a couple of times. Then I looked around for the other doc, but he had disappeared.

Patients. What had happened to our burn victims and the other patients? I knew the answer but didn't want to acknowledge it. I closed my eyes and concentrated on breathing, blanking out the horrible knowledge that they were all gone. Then I felt that I was slipping out of the life raft netting, so I hooked my arm through the lines and hoisted myself halfway onto the raft itself. It almost tumbled me back into the water but I kicked vigorously until everything stopped moving. By then I was completely entangled in the raft's netting. I no longer had to work at it, so I just relaxed and hung there.

At that moment I heard more airplane engines approaching and then there were smacking sounds in the water around me as those bastards began strafing survivors. Leave it to the Japs to strafe life rafts. By then I was too exhausted to move so I resigned myself to just being killed. As tired as I was, I realized that I was actually ready to die. But then the bomber passed overhead and exploded into a ball of flame as a nearby PT boat raked its belly with 20 mm fire. I hadn't even been aware that there was a PT boat nearby. The bomber flew into the water about a mile away and disintegrated in a blast of fire and white water.

Yay, team, I thought, and then I think I just passed out.

SEVENTEEN

"Oh, shit—it's the doc!" someone shouted. I woke up to feel the mahogany bow of an MTB nudging past the raft, casting me into complete shadow. For a moment I didn't know where I was, or even who I was. Then strong hands were lifting me up onto the boat. The first thing I heard was the dreaded sound of more airplane engines, followed by an ear-splitting racket as the boat's stern guns lit off. The guys who'd been helping me jumped back to the other gun stations. I bravely crawled under one of the torpedo tube mounts and closed my eyes. The boat accelerated and then began the Betty Jitterbug—a series of high-speed maneuvers aimed at throwing off the bombs and cannons of an approaching Betty bomber. Then came a stem-winder of a turn that catapulted me out from under the torpedo-tube mounts and into the hatchway leading down below. I flailed around trying to find something to grab on to when three booming thumps nearby bounced me off the deck and down the steel ladder, pursued by a wall of seawater from the near-miss bomb explosions. I felt like the proverbial rag doll as I was swept up against a bulkhead, where I finally stopped, sitting in two feet of water. The boat's coffeepot was dangling by its cord right over my head, dripping hot coffee on my left arm. I righted the pot, seized one of the mugs that was bobbing up and down in the sloshing

seawater, and poured myself a cup. The guns stopped their noise
about then and the boat began to slow. That's how the boat's skipper eventually found me, sipping coffee, sitting at the bottom of the
ladder, in two feet of water. His face broke into a huge grin.

He asked me if I was okay, and I nodded. It was true—I hadn't
been wounded or really even injured, other than being scared shitless. Evidence of that was, happily, obscured by the fact that I was
soaking wet from head to toe. The coffee wasn't bad, either, if a
bit salty. The skipper offered me a hand up but I chose to remain
seated. The water was warm and there were no Bettys down here.
He shook his head and jumped back up the ladder. Soon we were
nudging into the beach next to our medical aid station. I got to my
feet, took a moment to stabilize my gyros, and then went topside.
Chief Higgins was already there, and he helped me over the side
and down onto the sandy beach. As we walked back up to our private ravine, he told me what had happened out there in the harbor.

Apparently, the Japs had sent a submarine to reconnoiter Rendova Harbor and attack anything it could. The sub couldn't safely
come into the harbor and the presence of American destroyers
just outside made life even more difficult. So, the sub had slipped
around to one of the unguarded entrances to the harbor and un-
leashed a salvo of their Type 93 torpedoes into the anchorage. The
LST I'd been on had eaten two of them, which blew her in half.
Another LST, the one damaged by the first bombing, had been hit
at the same time and had capsized. The Bettys then joined the fun
and scattered bombs and torpedoes throughout the harbor. One of
the torpedoes had run up on the beach not far from the aid station,
where it flipped and flopped around in the sand as its screaming
propellers chewed up the beach. Then it exploded, creating a new
baby cove.

"Can you operate?" Higgins asked.

"Yeah, I think so. I need some dry clothes and a screamer would
do nicely. We got customers?"

"God, yes," he said, with a sick look on his face. "All but one of the LST docs was on *Liscomb County* and he got killed in the water. You're it, Boss Man. The Army docs are dealing with their own wounded. It's bad, Doc. It's real bad."

I focused on his face and saw that he was close to tears. "We've been here before, Wally," I said. "It was battleships last time, remember? Let's get to it. Where's Bluto?"

"He's still out there. Most of the boats are searching for survivors. One of the tin cans got hit by a bomb but she's still afloat. Those Goddamned Japs are watching us from across the channel: the Bettys didn't come in until the morning Cactus fighters had left for the day, but before the afternoon fighter shift showed up."

"Guadalcanal was the first time they've had to withdraw their army from *any*where," I said. "And, we're a hundred some miles closer to Rabaul. If anything, New Georgia's gonna be even harder than Cactus. Get a signal out to the remaining LSTs and the tin cans. Some of them must have a doc. Tell 'em we need help. Hospitalmen, if there's no doc. Get some more hands over to the aid station as the boats come back in. *Jesus*, what a mess."

It took all night to get the situation somewhat under control, and no one on our little island was really looking forward to daylight. Men were asking: where's the Navy? They'd sent a small destroyer force to take Rendova, which really wasn't even occupied. Supposedly a much bigger force was coming to do the New Georgia invasion, but in the meantime, we were getting our asses kicked. Our biggest problem was that we had nowhere to put all the wounded, much less a real operating theater. I finally gave up and got a boat to take me over to headquarters at 2:30 in the morning. Give him credit: the general was up and in the command tent. He was as hollow-eyed as I probably was. I explained what was going on and that we were going to lose a whole lot of men. He nodded.

"We have two LSTs still here," he said. "They're supposed to leave tomorrow to pick up cargo and troops for the New Georgia operation. I'll order them both to 'land' on your island and provide facilities for forty-eight hours. After that they'll have to leave, but that'll give us some breathing room. My facilities are also overwhelmed, in case you were wondering."

I thanked him profusely and hustled back down to the beach and jumped aboard my mahogany coach. As we rumbled back to our little island, the skipper of the boat sidled over. He spoke with a Georgia drawl.

"There's a story going around the boats, that at the height of the bombing raid, after they'd picked you up, they found you down in the crew's mess, sitting in two feet of water and drinking a cup of coffee. Any of that shit true, Doc?"

"I could either drink it or wear it, Skipper," I said. "And I definitely needed it."

"Well, Doc," he said with an admiring grin, "ain't you a hot mess, then."

The general's plan worked, which is probably why he was a general. The two LSTs drove straight into the beach next to our aid station, dropped their ramps, and suddenly we had beds for the most urgent cases, a clean place where I could do surgery, and two destroyers prowling the harbor nearby. Bluto stationed four PT boats around the LSTs for close-in anti-air protection. Just after noon the next day, the general himself showed up to see how we were doing. All in, we had 342 casualties with injuries ranging from concussion shock to God-awful thoracic and abdominal wounds. I really missed my Yalie ace assistant, but he was now sustaining the wildlife on the bottom of Rendova harbor. Damn! What a waste.

We got a two-day respite from the air raids, during which a small fleet of Catalinas showed up and began a shuttle service down to Cactus and beyond. On the third day a dozen or so Bettys were spotted by a coast-watcher coming down the east side of New Georgia to hide from the air defense radars the Army had put up on Rendova. They came sweeping around the southern tip of the island and ran smack into a full squadron of Marine fighters, who'd been playing their own game of hide-and-seek behind the big volcano on Rendova. Not one of the Bettys made it across the channel, with eight bombers being flamed and the rest running for their lives back up the Slot with a couple of fighters in hot pursuit.

This time the fighters were relieved on station to maintain continuous coverage. Sure enough, as soon as the morning's fighters could be seen making contrails back to Cactus, more Bettys showed up, although this time only four. The Marines' afternoon "shift" hit them from behind. Three went down in flames; the fourth, burning under both wings, made an attempted suicide run on one of the destroyers, succeeding in clipping the ship's mast and carrying away her radar antenna. The bomber then disintegrated with both wings coming off, the engines' propellers still windmilling, while the fuselage went end over end into the water, spewing Japs out onto the surface.

That night our squadron was able to collect all in one place for a change. There were still three boats on watch around the LSTs, with guns manned and the crew sleeping on station. Everyone needed sleep after the pandemonium of the past few days. The boat skippers gathered with Bluto in the now-empty aid station. Higgins had managed to root out the makings for screamers, but it was pretty obvious that anyone who tried for more than one was going to pitch over unconscious. There was one lonely candle burning on the main table as the entire island was under blackout orders.

Bluto filled us in on what he'd been able to find out about the upcoming invasion across the channel, and the extent of our losses to the bombing raids. We'd lost two crews to strafing runs, and a third when the *Liscomb County* was torpedoed. Although the crews had been wiped out, the boats themselves stayed afloat. I kept forgetting they were made of mahogany, and, excepting a fire on board, they'd still be there the next morning. One was repairable, the other would become yet another hangar queen.

Six more boats were coming up the Slot in a few days, with eight new crews. That meant that we'd finally be able to set up a duty rotation so that the guys weren't on duty, day and night, continuously. I'd told Bluto that we had several exhaustion cases out there on the boats. He nodded and then said he knew how they felt. We were really starting to admire our new skipper. He'd been *every-where* during the harbor battles, rescuing sailors, blasting away at the bombers, and running into the main island to get help from the Army. He seemed to be inexhaustible, but I knew better. I suggested he walk down the beach to one of the LSTs and commandeer a bunk for the night. Ask for the captain, I told him. Tell him who you are. Get six hours in a real bed; it'll do wonders. To my surprise, he nodded, finished his screamer, stubbed out his cigarette, and headed down toward the beach.

After about an hour, Higgins and I were the only ones left in the tent. We heard waves crashing down on the beach and looked out. The two remaining destroyers were rushing past, headed for the harbor entrance, with definite bones in their teeth. Then we heard booming noises out beyond the harbor. Not guns, but something else. They got a sub out there, Higgins said. Those are depth charges. The ruckus went on for another hour and then subsided. By then Higgins and I had each found empty cots and submerged for the night.

The following morning brought rain, lots of it. That was a good thing—showers for everybody, fresh water sloping down our catchment wall, and shitty flying weather. We took turns going on board the remaining LSTs to get chow. They were turning out to be superb hosts. I was now hoping they'd go through with that idea of using one for a hospital ship. Out at sea the rain squalls kept coming, backed by a warm wind and the occasional rumble of thunder. I noticed that a lot of the guys were jumping when a thunderclap went off, and no wonder.

I spent the morning aboard the two LSTs, checking on the slowly diminishing number of casualties. At noon one of the destroyers was called in to put its bow alongside the LST's stern. Then came the solemn transfer of the men who'd died the previous night. There were far too many of them, but the weather was preventing any more Catalina flights and there simply wasn't much we could do. The destroyer backed off and headed for the channel to conduct burials at sea. The rain began to diminish by early afternoon and I was able to make rounds of the remaining ships in the harbor, using one of the PT boats as my taxi. I was boarding my chariot at sundown to go back to Bau Island when there was a lot of shouting topside on the tank deck.

"Wow!" my boat's skipper exclaimed. "Lookit that."

"That" was a heavy cruiser entering the harbor, followed by three more. They were big, 10,000 tons, and they each carried nine eight-inch guns. They loomed out of the rainy mist, menacing, dark gray, showing no lights, and approaching us in utter silence. They were followed by some smaller ones, which I recognized as some of the so-called anti-aircraft cruisers. They were almost 6,000 tons and sported eight twin-barreled five-inch mounts. Behind them came a line of transports and their escorting destroyers. The big warships slowed and then seemed to disperse to previously assigned anchorage spots. The harbor was soon filled with the sounds of rattling anchor chains. The ships seemed to be all talking simultaneously using their flashing signal lamps. I guessed that the invasion was on.

Bluto confirmed that in his newly erected command tent. He told us at an all-officers meeting that the boats would be going out tomorrow night with frogmen, who were going to blow up obstacles on the beaches selected for landings. The heavy cruisers were going to make a raid on the Munda airfield, which was the objective of the invasion in the first place. Fresh intelligence suggested that the Jap forces on New Georgia had been reinforced, and, unlike Rendova, this was going to be a tough fight. The AA cruisers would be positioned out in the Blanche Channel to deal with the expected air raids once our troops went ashore. A second destroyer division, which was escorting a formation of more LSTs, was en route. They would then bolster the AA defenses *in* the harbor; the light cruisers would stay out in open waters in case the Japs sent their own cruisers south from Rabaul. The Cactus air force would continue to provide continuous daylight coverage of Rendova, the Blanche Channel, and the landing beaches.

The good news for our medical team was that each of the cruisers had a doctor and at least four hospitalmen. Even some of the destroyers had doctors. The bad news was that none of the combatants had much in the way of facilities. The destroyers used their officers' wardrooms as casualty stations during gunfights. The cruisers had sick bays and room to stage casualties, but not much else. I asked about the LST-as-hospital-ship idea. Bluto said he didn't know if the Navy had decided to do that or not. My job would be to tend to MTB casualties, for a change, while the fleet would look after their own. We would remain based on Bau Island within the harbor. The LSTs, of course, would be over on New Georgia with the landing force. It suddenly occurred to me that, as a medical asset, my team and I would be on the sidelines for this one. I told Higgins that I, for one, was ready for a little sidelining.

EIGHTEEN

Wishful thinking. The landings went well enough for about forty-eight hours. Then the army ran into two immovable objects: the terrain, and the dug-in Japanese army. Their commanding general, Minoru Sasaki, had correctly foreseen that New Georgia would be the next American target because of that big airfield at Munda. During the entire Guadalcanal campaign, they'd had the opportunity to entrench every possible defensive position on New Georgia and reinforce their numbers. The American plan envisioned several separate landings around the island, which meant that no one of them had overwhelming numerical strength against the Jap defenders, who began launching small, individual nighttime terror attacks against the American lines. Our casualties began to mount, while progress inland was pretty much at a standstill.

The Japs continued to send bombing raids against Cactus, even though their troops had been withdrawn from Guadalcanal. This cut into the quality and quantity of air support for the New Georgia invasion. Their navy also contested the invasion during several sea battles, some minor, some bigger, in the area of the Slot near New Georgia. Our MTBs were used for all sorts of missions until the night that one of our guys mistakenly torpedoed the flagship of the American amphibious task group, a large transport configured as a command ship. The ship sank and the admiral and his staff had to hit the lifeboats. After that, the admiral involved, known for his hot temper, didn't want to *ever* see a PT boat in his area of operations again. That proscription didn't last because the boats were too useful and there were no acceptable substitutes. Bluto solved it by making sure the boats only went out at night. That way the admiral couldn't *see* them, just as he had directed. His flagship bore some responsibility for the sinking, having opened fire on a passing division of PT boats without so much as a preliminary flashing-light challenge.

New Georgia quickly descended into a meat grinder. The Army, which had relieved the First Marines on Guadalcanal after most of the hardest fighting was over, had never experienced the full fanatical fury of Japanese troops. The butcher's bill rose quickly. An LST as hospital ship had never been followed up, so the mounting casualties were being transported by any means possible to a large troop transport, the SS *Montrose,* which remained at sea except for when she would close on Rendova to load the wounded. The ship was old, having been built in the early 1920s as a passenger liner, and so slow that the Navy had decided to take her out of service on the nearly 4,000-mile Pearl-to-Nouméa run and construct a makeshift hospital on board. A Navy crew would run the ship; the Army Medical Corps would staff the hospital facilities.

As a twenty-two-thousand-ton troopship, *Montrose* could berth 2,500 men, much more than an LST. While at sea she was escorted by a couple of destroyer escorts, smaller versions of the fleet destroyers, but well equipped for anti-submarine work. When she came into Rendova, our boats provided anti-air escort because the Bettys were a more likely threat. The *Montrose* came into Rendova at odd times so as not to establish a pattern. It was considered too dangerous for her to go over to New Georgia, especially since the Army was getting nowhere.

I went aboard the first time she came into Rendova harbor,

escorting a dozen of the more seriously wounded. The patients had to be loaded by one of the ship's boom cranes, with the individual litters being strapped down onto tank-size pallets and then hoisted out of the amphibious craft, up over the side, and then deposited down in a cargo hold. The medical staff could then wheel them into the medical complex without ever having to come topside. I learned that there were twelve doctors on board, including some specialists in burns, radiography, and three general surgeons. There were also twenty-five female nurses on board, shanghaied from the big hospital on Nouméa. The surgical suite was contained in what had been the ship's main dining room when she'd been in civilian service. It was clear that they were still working on some of the physical setup the first time she came into Rendova.

I was met in the triage area, which was Cargo Hold No. 3, just behind the ship's superstructure, by a pleasant if visibly fatigued nurse wearing major's oak leaves on her collars. She introduced herself as Patsy Bergin, head nurse. I introduced myself and told her that I was the squadron doc for the torpedo boats in Rendova. I accompanied her and a young doc while one of their doctors did triage. I couldn't really brief them on these patients because these were Army troops, not my boat personnel. We'd housed them in our makeshift compound for four hours until *Montrose* came in. I'd looked them over, but I was reluctant to offer any opinions now that they were in the hands of a "real" hospital. That was until the doc, an Army captain who was younger than I was, laid down a three-tag on one patient with two sucking chest wounds and a broken leg. I asked why. He said the three surgeons on board had told the other docs what procedures they could and could not do, and that deep thoracic was off-limits. Stabilize, yes, but to open and do chest-repair work on tattered lungs and the plumbing supplying them, and then restore oxygenated blood to the heart, was not in their bag of tricks.

"Um," I said. "They should be."

Patsy made a face and then pulled me aside. She informed me that the surgeons on board were the ones the nurses privately called "the second team" back in Nouméa. All three were straight out of their residencies. Just like me, I thought, with some irony. The first team, surgeons with twenty years or more of OR experience, were still back in Nouméa. They were considered too valuable to risk in an actual combat zone.

"It makes sense," she said when she saw the look on my face. "There has to be a hospital of last resort, with a medical staff capable of doing anything in the modern medical lexicon."

"Well, for what it's worth," I said, "I'm a surgeon, and I've repaired more lungs than I can remember. If you have some good nurse anesthetists, ether systems, and a clean OR, I believe I can fix this patient. If we move quickly."

She stared at me in some consternation. Then her eyes widened. "*You're* the guy!" she said. "The PT-boat doctor who's actually a fourth-year resident who's been doing all those major procedures at Guadalcanal. You're somewhat famous, Doctor, but I'm afraid there's a problem."

"What's his name?" I asked, as that familiar feeling swept over me.

"His name is Colonel Henry Maddox, MC, US Army. He's the CO of the embarked hospital, and he is ..."

"Twenty feet away and closing fast," I muttered, looking over her shoulder.

Oh, shit, she mouthed silently.

Henry Maddox was a fat guy. Double chins, medium ponderous gut, arms too short for his body, and the flushed face that comes with a blood pressure problem. He was short and walked with a motion that called to mind a duck. He was looking straight at me.

"Are you Doctor Andersen of the torpedo boat squadron?" he asked peremptorily. I said, "Yes, sir."

"Come with me, please. Major Bergin, we sail in two hours."

I followed the portly colonel up a passageway that led through the center of the ship. I was halfway tempted to emulate his strange gait but then noticed that other people in the passageway were quick to get out of his way. We finally arrived at what looked like a large lobby, beyond which double mahogany doors led into what had been the forward main dining room. There was a thin strip of very bright white light visible between the doors. They were rolling gurneys into the lobby, and nurses were tending to wounded who I assumed were waiting for surgery. To the right was a cocktail lounge which clearly hadn't seen a cocktail for some time. He led me to a booth in one corner of the dimly lit room and indicated that I should sit down. He then squeezed into the other side of the booth, displacing the tabletop in my direction.

"Okay," he said. "When I was in Nouméa, we began hearing stories about a surgeon at the Guadalcanal field hospital who had not actually completed all of his surgical training. A third-year resident at Duke who was just beginning his fourth year of a surgical residency, fourth of seven, who left school and joined the Navy when the war broke out. That you?"

"Yes, sir, it is."

He nodded. "Well, Doctor: what the hell were you thinking?" he asked.

"When I went in with the First Marines, I was thinking that I'd be doing surgery as an assistant, under the supervision of the older and more experienced surgeons."

"And?"

"Guadalcanal was chaos from about the third day," I said. "There was a big sea fight around Savo Island, where we lost four allied cruisers. Then the landing support ships were withdrawn because of a carrier battle, where we'd lost a carrier. They took with them half of our supplies: ammo, food, fuel, medical. When the Japs saw that, they hit us hard. We had a big surge in casualties."

"Go on," he said. I wondered if he knew anything about the medical aid conditions during the battle for Guadalcanal, situated as he had been among the stately palms of Nouméa, a thousand miles from Guadalcanal.

"We were immediately overwhelmed at the PHS," I continued. "We had Marine casualties and also Navy wounded. All the amphibs and cargo ships had done a bunk. The senior Navy doctor told me to take a table and do what I could, so I did. Over the next few weeks I found myself doing stuff that I had only assisted with at school. Not just once, either. After the tenth time that I did a bowel resection, removed a ruined lung, spliced up a couple hundred blood vessels, they turned me loose. I kept a log, by the way."

He nodded, and then stared into the middle distance for a moment.

"I have orders to find you if I can and to see to it that you're returned to Nouméa, where they plan to open a board of inquiry on how you 'got loose,' as you so quaintly put it. Where is that log?"

"In my seabag over on Bau island. But a board of inquiry? Everything I did I had permission to do. Orders to do it. Reluctantly, at first, but then enthusiastically."

"Between you and me, Doctor, I think that somehow what you have been doing out here got back to BuMed in Falls Church. Imagine the bureaucratic outrage."

"How's about imagining all the men I saved instead?"

"Fair point," he admitted. Then a messenger knocked on the lounge's entrance and delivered a message to the colonel. "Okay," he said to me. "Our departure has been delayed until sunrise due to some new calamity over on New Georgia. Would you please go retrieve your log *and* your seabag, and then return aboard? I'd like you to go out with us to our hideout station, and then I'll have time to review this matter and not be rushed about it."

"What about my MTB crews?"

"I'll send one of our doctors to your squadron while you're with us. He'll be qualified to do what any squadron doc can do; if surgery is required, the patient will be sent to us, won't he."

I took a deep breath. This threat of an inquiry was bullshit, but now I thought that the portly colonel thought so, too. He might even turn into an ally once he saw my log, or so I hoped. If some Washington medical bureaucrat was going to come after me, I'd need all the allies I could get.

I came back aboard at around ten that night. There'd been only three boats in, so I didn't get a chance to clear my departure with Bluto, who was out on a mission with a makee-learn boat skipper. I told Higgins, but didn't mention the board of inquiry—one less thing for him to worry about. He'd been with me practically the whole time and I knew he'd brood about it. I was assigned to a cabin on the top deck. The doctors got the top deck cabins, usually two to a cabin, along with the ship's captain and Colonel Maddox, who had their own private quarters. The cabins below the main deck were all reserved for patients. The nurses were quartered in the afterpart of the superstructure, separate from all the male doctors and ship's officers. I was taken to my assigned berth by a hospitalman third class. I asked him if he had been given any instructions for me. "Not that I know of, Doctor." The cabin was air-conditioned, as was pretty much the entire ship. I decided to just get a good night's sleep and let events unfold.

I awoke the next morning when my roommate came in off the night shift at 6:15. He looked exhausted. The ship had been kept in port because of a surge in casualties over on New Georgia and the night had been very busy. He introduced himself as Tim Forrest, and said he was a dermatologist.

"So now you're a burns expert," I said.

He gave me a tired grin. "Exactly," he said. "And you?'

"Linc Andersen," I said. "Surgeon. Went in with the First Marines at Guadalcanal, and I am painfully aware of what 'very busy' means."

"Pleased to meet you," he said. "We desperately need more surgeons." Then he shed his bloody gowns and headed for the shower.

When he came out, wrapped in a towel, he sat down in one of the cabin chairs. "You that guy from Duke? Starting fourth-year surgical resident who's been doing major surgery out here on his own for the past year?"

"I am," I said, unsure of where this was going.

"Brother, you're famous down in Nouméa," he said. "There was a rumor going around the hospital here that you were aboard. Honored to meet you, Doctor."

"Don't get too close," I said. "Colonel Maddox says there are rumblings in Washington that I'm some sort of bad guy."

"Screw that," he said. "There's a war on. Nouméa is infested with old-time docs and administrators. Chickenshit rules. That's why I volunteered for *Montrose*."

"Can I trust Maddox?" I asked him. "I'm going to show him my log sometime today."

"Porky Pig?" he said with a grin. "Yes, I think you can. He's a surgeon, thoracic, and he's good at it. He puts on this 'I'm a tyrant, so be afraid' persona, but he's been more than good to the medical staff. The ones that are afraid of him should be, but only because they aren't up to his standards."

"Wow," I said. "America at war, and already the bureaucrats are clawing their way back into the action."

"Linc," he said. "If I may call you Linc. Can I see that log? I mean, the young docs back in Nouméa can't believe what they're hearing about you."

"Sure," I said. "But only if you can show me where the drinkable-coffeepot lives in this showboat."

We got dressed, he in fresh medical whites and I in working khakis. He took me forward to a small dining room where there was not only coffee but actual food. A steady parade of docs and ship's company officers came through. Nobody stayed very long. There were portholes and I could see that it was full daylight outside. Normally *Montrose* would have left Rendova around midnight in order to get well to seaward of the increasingly nasty fight on New Georgia. The ship's company naval officers looked worried. We were only twenty miles from Rendova. This was still Jap bomber country.

My roommate perused my log during breakfast. He whistled softly when he was finished.

"What was your mortality rate?" he asked.

"Too high, at first, but it got better as time went on. It was nothing compared to the mortality rate of the guys we didn't or couldn't get to."

He nodded at that. I described our operating conditions. He could only shake his head at what I was telling him.

"Man!" he said. "I had no idea. All we ever saw were the ones that made it to Nouméa. You show this to Colonel Maddox. He'll take care of you."

He headed back to the cabin for much needed sleep. I gave myself an unofficial tour of the ship, with a mug of coffee in hand. I finally got below to the main operating area after several false starts and went through the swinging doors. They'd done an ingenious job of it. The expansive space that had been the main dining room was now subdivided by curtained enclosures, twenty feet on a side, which contained the operating tables and rolling cabinets filled with surgical instruments. There was a wide central aisle right down the middle which had several nurse's stations and even more equipment, especially sterilization machines. The entire space was air-conditioned and well lighted. Surgery, I thought. On a production-line basis.

There wasn't much going on, so I backed out into the welcoming arms of an orderly, dressed in whites. He told me Colonel Maddox wanted to see me. Ten minutes later I was in Maddox's cabin, which was one of the first-class suites from the old days. I handed over my log. He pointed to a coffee stand, which had a small plate of real donuts. I hadn't seen a donut since leaving Duke. The silver tray was vibrating slightly as the old girl did her best to make tracks out into the open sea and away from prowling Jap bombers. I ate one donut and then took its brother and a mug of coffee to a large, upholstered chair near one of the portholes. Bright sunlight was streaming in, and in the distance I could see one of our escorting destroyers bouncing happily through the choppy seas. In silhouette her five-inch gun mounts, all pointed skyward, looked like spines on the back of some ancient but dangerous beast.

It took the captain twenty minutes to go through my log. When he was finished, he, too, gave a low whistle. "This is pretty amazing, Doctor Andersen," he said. "I'm a chest cutter, so I know most of these procedures. How in the *hell* did you manage all this?"

"It was a matter of necessity," I said. "The conditions weren't very good, nothing like what you have here. Hot, not very clean tents, constant rain, continuous gunfire all around us, generators that were running on questionable fuel...Our one and only autoclave broke down on the first day, so the Marines kept two fifty-five-gallon drums outside the tent filled with boiling water. The hospitalmen would dump our used instruments into one of them for ten minutes, and then into the second one for another ten minutes. Then they'd fish 'em out, set the trays, and bring 'em back in. We'd change gowns twice a day, if there were clean ones available."

"But how did you know what to do?" he asked. "Like an aorta repair? That takes a lot of training."

"I probably didn't do it correctly," I said. "But I could improvise. Sew in a tube upstream of the damage and then terminate it below the damage. Clamp off the damaged area, resection, sew it back up, and then release the clamps. Left the tube in place. The real surgeons down in Nouméa could deal with that later. His aorta was no longer leaking. That was the important thing."

He just stared at me.

"I don't want you to think that *I* think I'm a fully qualified, board-examined general surgeon," I said. "You used the word procedure.

To me, a procedure is something you do in a well-run hospital with a full support staff. I've been doing battlefield trauma surgery. If I knew the general outlines of the procedure, I did it. If I didn't, I had my chief hospitalman read it to me from the manual. Like with a descending aorta repair."

He nodded. I went on. He was the first senior surgeon I'd been able to talk to practically since I'd come out with the Marines.

"You make an aorta repair sound like a once-in-a-lifetime procedure. Problem was that I had fifteen more patients, lying on litters on the floor of the tent, with even worse damage. I did what made sense to me at the time. All the other surgeons were elbow deep in gore of their own. I wasn't the only one there doing stuff way outside my training envelope."

"Damn," he whispered. "Just *damn*."

"You think you've been swamped aboard this ship?" I said. "We were swamped five hundred yards from the front lines. We surely didn't save them all. But we tried our hearts out, and I'm proud of what I did do. If your board of inquiry wants to question what I did, bring it on."

He closed the log and sighed. "Having seen this I'm pretty sure I can take care of that," he said. "The board, I mean. You know, or maybe you don't, that any time a military mission gets its own bureau, the pissants are gonna surface, sooner or later. You ever hear the story of the Pearl Harbor anesthesia incident?"

I shook my head.

"The Brits, who've been at war since September of '39, told us there's a story circulating in medical circles there. The sum and substance of it is that our own surgeons killed more men than the Japs did at Pearl. All because of a new wonder anesthetic called thiopentone. The story's anecdotal, but the deal was that this stuff caused cardiac arrest and respiratory paralysis if misused, especially in patients who were in shock, which was pretty much everybody that day. Did you know that in England, anesthesia is performed exclusively by medical doctors, trained in that as a full-fledged specialty?"

Again, I shook my head. All of our anesthetists were enlisted personnel. "We used ether drip," I said. "But it was our enlisted hospitalmen doing it."

"As it was here," Maddox said. "Until we got the nurses on board. The only thing we use thiopentone for here is, well, when we have to let a patient go peacefully to his Maker."

Battlefield euthanasia, I thought. The unmentionable fact of life in combat medicine. "What would you have me do?" I asked.

"Join a surgical team," he replied. "Hell, after looking at this, *lead* one of my surgical teams. The New Georgia campaign isn't going very well at all and we're getting horrible casualties. I'm the only thoracic guy on board; the rest are mostly post-residency docs. You'd be a Godsend, and you're being wasted with that MTB squadron."

"Now, wait a minute," I protested. "Twenty-four hours ago, I was going to be sent back to Nouméa to face a board of inquiry," I said. "You let me operate here, you might be facing the same thing. Sir."

"I'll take my chances," he said. "They're starting to pay attention to mortality rates back in Nouméa. If that log is any indication, having a surgeon like you on the team will make a big difference to ours."

"Okay, Colonel," I said. "I'm just a lieutenant, so I need to go back to my boat squadron, talk to my skipper. If he's okay with this, then I'll be glad to join your team."

"Yes, that's the proper way to do it. In the meantime, I will—"

The ship's interior telephone system rang. Maddox picked it up and then listened. He said thank you and hung up. "That was the bridge watch. The ship's captain's reporting a formation of B-17s is coming through the area at high altitude. He and I have an agreement that he'll notify me of any other ships or aircraft in our vicinity, ours or theirs, so I can alert the medical staff."

"Is this ship armed?" I asked. "I didn't see any hospital ship markings."

"We have a ten-man Marine detachment on board," he said. "They have small arms, basically; otherwise we have no bigger guns to speak of. We're not marked because the Japs apparently have been instructed to seek out and sink any hospital ship on sight. I presume you heard about the Aussie ship one of their subs got. Marked, you know, with all the required red crosses and the big green stripe on her sides. Fully lighted, unmistakable hospital ship. Jap bastards torpedoed her anyway."

"Yes, sir, that was the *Centaur*," I replied. "We did hear about that."

Just then there was a booming explosion some distance from the ship. Then a second. It wasn't gunfire—I knew what that sounded like. Maddox sprang over to the porthole just as a string of six more thumping blasts reverberated through the ship, each one just a second apart and definitely getting closer. I looked out a second porthole, expecting to see our destroyers blasting away at enemy aircraft, but they were still steaming along, although one began belching smoke and accelerating when those dirty white fountains from underwater explosions erupted a hundred feet into the air. There was a brief pause and then more bombs, because that's what they had to be, rained down in our vicinity, one exploding close enough to rattle the bulkheads in Maddox's stateroom. Then we actually got hit.

There was a loud crash aft of where we were standing as a bomb hit amidships. We could actually hear the damned thing smashing through the ship's unarmored decks. I think both of us closed our eyes and held our breath, waiting for the inevitable big blast. It didn't happen. Then there were more explosions in the sea, this time on the other side of the ship, and thankfully going in the away direction.

"It's those B-17s," Maddox hissed in an angry voice. "They're bombing one of their own ships! *Dumb bastards!*"

The bombs stopped coming and then the phone started ringing. Maddox answered the phone with a loud "What!" still furious at the Army Air Force bombers. He listened intently and then his red face went pale. "Oh, God," he said. "I'll be right down. Get everybody out of there—patients, staff, *every*body. And notify the captain."

He hung up the phone and sat down, shaking his head. "There's a bomb parked in the OR. Big bastard, too. Definitely one of ours—green, with English words and numbers on the side. The nose went through the OR deck but stopped there. The tail is sticking straight out of the deck, and there's a little propeller rotating slowly on the tail."

Oh, shit, I thought. The EOD people back on Tulagi had explained what those little propellers were for. "Call 'em back," I said immediately. "Tell them to put some surgical tape on that propeller so it can't move."

"I don't see—"

"Now!" I yelled. "That propeller is a counter. When it reaches its count, it fires the bomb!"

His eyes went wide. He made the call and gave them instructions. Then the captain called and said he was returning to Rendova because the Army had some bomb disposal people there. I thought that was a great idea, because then I could get off and find Bluto. I really wanted to ask him what the hell I should do.

NINETEEN

We pulled in just before sunset. There'd been a bombing raid on Rendova two hours before, but a division of destroyers had arrived that morning to refuel from a tanker anchored in the harbor. Their combined gunfire, even while at anchor, had driven off the raid, with three Bettys splashed outside the harbor. One of our MTBs brought two injured sailors over to *Montrose,* and I quickly thumbed a ride back to our little base on Bau Island. The boats looked a lot worse for wear after their cross-channel operations around New Georgia. The guys taking me back told me that the drive toward the airfield at Munda had bogged down into a bloody slugfest, emphasis on the bloody part. Most of the Army troops over there hadn't been on Guadalcanal for the big show and were learning the hard way what it was like to fight real Japs, dug-in. I asked the skipper what the boats had been doing.

"Everything," he said, wearily. "Mostly night ops in support of the Army. Not much in the way of fighting but lots of people-moving and logistics runs with emergency ammo and food supplies. We've got a second, sort of emergency base on New Georgia, but it's pretty basic. We wanted to be indispensable; we've succeeded, but with the Army, not the Navy. How do you like them apples?"

Bluto was still out when I got to Bau but Higgins was there to greet me. They'd upgraded the medical station a little, but it was clear that *Montrose* was carrying the load. We repaired to the command tent as full darkness fell. Higgins hadn't lost his ability with screamers, so we were pretty relaxed when Bluto came roaring in, turning the air blue about some Army colonel who'd questioned his authority. From what little I could understand, the FUBARmy was the single most screwed-up organization on the planet, in the solar system, in the Goddamned galaxy, which couldn't, etc., etc. Then he spied me.

"And where the *hell* have you been, Doc?" he roared, as if I'd been AWOL. I looked over at Higgins, who looked over at Bluto, who deflated. "Right. You went out on that hospital ship. How'd that go?"

"Well, today we got bombed by our own planes," I offered. "*Montrose* has a five-hundred-pounder stuck in her OR and a new skylight. Fortunately, it didn't go off."

"And lemme guess," he said. "Those were Army bombers, am I right?"

I nodded. He closed his eyes for a moment, shook his head, then hit the screamer pitcher and ordered me to tell him all about it. I did, and then focused on the colonel's request for me to join the surgical team on *Montrose* in return for a doc from the hospital ship for the squadron. He drained his screamer and growled for another, which was quickly provided.

"That makes some sense," he said. "You're a surgeon. You can't do surgery here, but you can on that ship. But still..."

"I'll miss the boats and evening prayers," I said. "But I think they could use some help."

"And it's not like we're doing much in the way of combat operations," he said ruefully. "We're high-speed taxis most of the time."

"Well," I said. "If things are that tough over there on New Georgia, you're probably the only way they can piss on the fire of the hour. Speed doesn't seem to be the Army's strength."

He laughed at that. "Understatement of the year," he said. And then he relented. "Actually, they're trying their hearts out. Sometimes literally. The Japs have gone crazy. Word is they can't believe we threw them off Cactus and now, here we are, on the next stepping stone to Rabaul. Their officers have 'em hopped up on some kind of drugs and they come out of the dark, screaming like banshees, jump into our trenches with swords and knives, all foaming at the mouth."

"What's the Navy doing?"

"They've got their hands full, too. Big night fights out at sea. Some we win, some we don't. It's not as bad as those first few months around the 'canal, but it seems like they're getting into those scary torpedo fights every other night."

"Sounds like MTBs could help with that, if only to throw some shit into their formations."

"They don't love us anymore," he grumped. "If they ever did."

"What happened?" I asked. Then I remembered—the flagship.

"We-e-l-l, one of our new guys torpedoed the amphib commander's flagship as they were going in on New Georgia. It's a long story, which ends with a wet admiral. No, if we're gonna be useful, it's the Army or nothing. I'm starting to miss the night runs around Savo."

"You're all alone there, Boss," one of the boat skippers muttered, to much laughter. Even Bluto grinned.

"So, you think I *should* go to the *Montrose*?"

"I do; so yes, take the offer. Go be a surgeon. From everything I've heard, you got the gift for it."

That was the first time I'd heard anything like that from Bluto. I was suddenly struck by the fact that individuals were being talked about in this sprawling conflagration. That was a little bit scary. The doc on the *Montrose* said I was famous; notorious might have been closer to the mark. What had Major Bergin said? You're *that* guy.

I was back aboard by midnight, seabag in hand. *Montrose* got under way at 0100 after having received the latest clutch of casualties from New Georgia. An hour later I was scrubbed in and going to town, assisted by one of the original surgeons and three extremely competent army nurses. The bomb was still there in the middle of the OR suite, but some Army bomb disposal guys had removed all the fusing components, which rendered it inert. The holes through the upper decks had had temporary plates welded on, but it would take a crane to get the actual bomb casing out. Some wag had put a white Dixie-cup-style sailor's hat on the rear fuse assembly stub.

After doing three fairly complex thoracic surgeries, I changed roles and assisted my heretofore assistant as he did the fourth one, coaching as we went along. He was nervous but he did well. He should have—he'd completed the full scope of surgical training. He knew *what* to do; it was the fact that he'd mostly only *seen* it done before that had made him hesitate. After that procedure, I floated among the individual tables. By sunrise I thought I had a pretty good sense of who could do what and who would need help. The colonel came down around five in the morning and did his own walk-around, then pulled me aside and asked for a briefing. When I'd finished, he nodded approvingly.

"Perfect," he said. "Keep doing what you're doing. I sense a lot more confidence around here."

I went up to the top deck to see about some coffee and maybe even breakfast. I spied the head nurse, Major Bergin, and asked if I could join her. During the night I had seen her circulating and solving problems. Unlike many of the Hollywood-movie head nurses, Patsy was kind, almost motherly, and it was obvious that the younger nurses loved her. Breakfast on the *Montrose* wasn't a whole lot different from breakfast on Guadalcanal, so I'd opted for coffee and the attempt the ship's baker had made at bread for toast. I wondered where the donuts had come from.

"Well, Doctor," she said with a tired smile, "what'd you think?"

"It's all relative, Major," I said. "I started out on Guadalcanal in a big, wet tent with battle lanterns for light, red mud floors, no ventilation, electricity when and if the generators were running, bloody instruments being boiled in fifty-five-gallon drums, and having to duck when the occasional round whacked through the tent walls. This is medical paradise, in comparison."

"I suppose it is," she said. "Nouméa was mostly tents, as well, but no Japs and a pretty good supply chain."

"We came ashore with the Marines and the Seabees," I said. "Unfortunately, the supporting fleet bailed out on us a few days later with half of our supplies, food, and ammo still on board. Triage became a very sad procedure."

"I hate triage more than anything else," she said. "Especially when you know the guy's not going to make it, but you can't tell him that. I cried in my bunk for several nights before I realized that I had to be tougher than that. Still…"

"Yeah," I said. "Still. And then there are the horrible ones where the only option is a thiopentone spinal."

She shuddered. "The colonel put out the word that there was no reason to put someone who'd basically been blown in half but was still sort of alive through the agony of a boat ride to the *Montrose.* Field medics were authorized to do what they had to do, as long as a medical doctor authorized it."

I sighed. I was suddenly aware that I'd been up all night and needed some sleep. We were well out to sea with our trusty destroyer escorts, which meant that there'd be no new patients for several hours.

"You need to hit the sack, there, Doctor," she said. "By the way, I'm hearing the nurse anesthetists were quite impressed last night."

"I'm not the wunderkind that people think I am, Major," I said. "It's just the fact that I've done so many of these operations that makes people think I'm somebody special. There's still a *hell* of a lot I don't know."

"Hold that thought, Doctor," she said, her eyes twinkling. "And, please, call me Patsy."

TWENTY

Bad weather overtook us that day, going from a relatively calm sea to howling winds, heavy rain, and an ugly chop that made even *Montrose* bounce and roll a bit. The destroyers, when we could see them, were underwater half the time, their bulky radar antennas looking like periscopes. Perversely, the storm kept us from going back into Rendova for almost thirty-six hours, which meant that everybody, patients, staff, ship's company could get some real—meaning more than a couple hours—sleep for a change. Colonel Maddox took that stand-down opportunity to do a comprehensive survey of our medical supplies and equipment. He sent out a message to Nouméa describing what we needed, including a recommendation to send one surgeon and two nurses back for failing to make the grade. He let me see the message before sending it out, and I was relieved to see that there was nothing about my joining the medical staff in it. He grinned when he saw my obvious relief.

"No point in waving red flags, now, is there, Doctor," he said. I was beginning to really like this guy, fat rolls and all. I asked him if he actually thought he'd get those supplies.

"Yes, I do," he said. "They've brought two whole squadrons of those Catalinas into Nouméa, with one rotating up to Cactus and the other staying behind. If the stuff's there, they can get it here in forty-eight hours."

We arrived back at Rendova around eight the next evening and found a mess: a destroyer with her bow blown off all the way back to the bridge, courtesy of a torpedo fight near some island called Kolombangara, a heavy cruiser with her forward-most turret in splinters following a turret explosion, and two dozen casualties from my own MTB squadron after they ran into a bunch of Jap barges and their destroyer escorts on the northeast side of New Georgia, where the Japs were landing reinforcements. Fortunately, there'd been an LST, USS *Harlan County*, in the harbor, so there'd been somewhere safe to put all the wounded.

The transfers began immediately. *Montrose* also needed fuel, so the Army harbormaster sent a fuel barge to come alongside and fill her empty bunkers while she onloaded casualties from the LST on the other side. It wasn't long before we had to tell *Harlan County* to hold whomever they had left. We were out of room in both the triage area and the operating rooms. The Army general in charge of the New Georgia operation heard about that and started raising hell, citing *Montrose*'s advertised troop capacity for 2,500 men. The problem was that there *were* that many berths down below, but not all of them were equipped to provide life support for badly wounded men.

At 0200 it was time to clear the harbor. There were still 160 casualties on board *Harlan County*, so the decision was made to have her go out to sea with us. They had one doctor on board and he could begin immediate first aid. In the meantime, I was back at the operating table, given the sheer quantity of the casualties. There was no time for me to just roam through the operating suite, supervising. The nurses moved some cots into the areas outside the curtained tables so that the surgeons could lie down for a few minutes between operations while they cleaned the table and got the next case under anesthesia. I found out there were some Marines among the wounded, which surprised me because I thought that New Georgia was strictly an Army show. The Marines told me they'd been sent in to reinforce the Army division. As one of the Marines boasted, the Army guys gave it a good try but now it was time for the first team to end the stalemate. That sounded right to me, but I still admired his bravado, lying there with one and a half arms and a morphine drip going.

We got out to sea in good order. We were down to one destroyer escort, the other having been pulled into the ongoing sea battles to the north of New Georgia. The seas were calm enough for boat transfers the next morning. *Harlan County* had two bow-ramped amphibious boats on board which could bring us twelve patients at a time. Two of the *Montrose*'s berthing compartments had been converted into post-op recovery rooms, so we had someplace to put the people we'd treated or operated on. The surgeons got some sleep while the transfers were taking place, and we had a fresh set of nurses by the time we went back to the OR. There was a brief scare at noon when an unidentified plane overflew our little for-mation at high altitude. We then suspended the transfer operation while the two ships moved thirty miles to the south in case that plane had been a Jap reconnaissance aircraft.

For the next twenty-four hours we slogged through the patient backlog, operating on the most urgent and then the less so. Not all our patients required surgery, but every one of them required care. Colonel Maddox had begun hounding Nouméa for the supplies. He told them we had only two more days' worth of medical sup-plies for the operating tables, after which we'd be out of business. He'd exaggerated, of course, but not by much. If we got another load like this last one, he'd have been right. Rendova was already asking when we'd be back in. I asked Maddox why they didn't set up a hospital on Rendova. I'd thought *Montrose* was supposed to have been a temporary solution to an unexpected casualty load from New Georgia. He pointed out that any field hospital set up on Rendova would have been subjected to bombing raids. Until we had complete control of the air around that area, we couldn't do much to change the situation. That would require an airfield, and that, of course, was the whole objective of the New Georgia campaign—that relatively large Jap airfield at Munda, from which we could then stage fighters, bombers, and whatever else we needed to advance toward their big nest at Rabaul.

There was little point in our going back into Rendova until we'd cleared our surgical backlog. Nouméa had promised they'd start a Catalina stream, which would stage through Cactus and then land at Rendova to move our wounded out of the immediate combat zone. The planes would bring up medical supplies and take away the patients who were deemed fit to move. It wasn't a perfect setup, but it was apparent to all of us that everybody was doing all they could to solve this knotty problem of how to save the wounded. They wouldn't start the stream until they knew when we'd get back to Rendova.

The following day the weather became iffy, but *Harlan County* had by then put all her patients aboard *Montrose*. She sailed back northeast toward Rendova, disappearing into a set of dark squall lines when she was only five miles away. By this point, we'd done all the urgent surgeries. We were now doing follow-up work, second surgical repairs where necessary, and treating the lesser injuries, with the term "lesser" being very much a relative word. Colonel Maddox did another inventory and then declared that we *had* to go back in. He sent a message to Nouméa to start the Catalina stream, and then informed the Army at Rendova that we'd be returning at just after dark. We then set about determining who was fit to be off-loaded when we got in because we knew there'd be lots more "customers" waiting in Rendova harbor. We were overflown by another unidentified "high-flier" on our way back in, but the captain was confident that the rain-swept skies had kept us out of sight, assuming the plane was a Jap.

We arrived on the western side of Rendova just at nautical twilight. That big, black volcano, which loomed like some presiding
judge over the whole island, was turning a bright orange color.
Our destroyer escort had gone on ahead to get in before we did to
refuel. We couldn't see what ships were in the harbor because we
were coming in from the west, but most of the medical staff and
even some of the ambulatory patients were topside on the promenade deck just to watch the spectacular sunset and get some fresh
air.

We were perhaps five miles from the big left turn into the harbor
proper when one of the nurses said: "Look—a seaplane." Everyone
assumed it was one of the Catalinas until I saw that it had *four* engines, not two. It was approaching from behind us, and it was low,
not skimming the surface but no more than a few hundred feet
above it. It was coming straight at us, with no nav lights showing,
aiming for our port side. Then I remembered all the stories about
the *Kawanishi;* those huge armed Jap seaplanes that were night-
capable. They'd killed many a PT boat. And, they carried Long
Lance torpedoes.

Before I could yell *Japs!* two dark objects dropped from the seaplane's belly, and then she banked hard to the right and began to
make a big circle to the southwest across our stern, no more than
two miles behind us. I thought I heard some shouting from way up
on the bridge and then felt the ship begin to heel to port as *Montrose* attempted to evade the torpedoes that were coming, to no
avail. An enormous explosion erupted on the port quarter of the
ship, big enough to push the old girl deeper into her turn, followed
by a second that hit the port side a third of the way up from the
stern.

Almost everyone out on the promenade deck was knocked down
by the force of the two blasts and, almost immediately, there was a
roar of steam from the ship's single funnel. As we scrambled to our

feet, we could feel the unmistakable lurch to port as *Montrose*, mortally wounded, reacted to the thousands of tons of seawater rushing into her engineering spaces. Within seconds she slowed and began listing as her stern settled. I literally didn't know what to do for one frightening moment. The nurses' screams were drowned out by that blast of steam thundering out the stack as the ship's boilers succumbed to the onrushing water. The ship continued moving slowly ahead even as she listed further to port, her own momentum carrying her forward in a slow right turn, as if she was intent on executing a death spiral into the deep.

Two crewmen came running down the tilting promenade deck dispersing gray kapok life jackets to everyone there, especially the terrified nurses. There was a life jacket locker right next to where I was standing, so I opened it up, grabbed one, and then began pulling more of them out onto the deck. By then it was becoming difficult to stand upright. The ship was sinking by the stern and listing ever more to port. I'd barely got my jacket strings tied up before there was a great whooshing sound from somewhere aft and then she capsized, going all the way over onto her beam ends and pitching everyone topside into the sea in a waterfall of tumbling bodies. Then she slowly righted herself, paused as if to get a final breath, and then began to slide down by the stern. A big wave forced my head underwater. I had to kick violently to get back to the surface. There were bobbing heads everywhere and a sudden smell of fuel oil. One of the ship's officers nearby was yelling *Go! Go! Go!* to everyone around him, indicating that we should start swimming hard to get away from the suction effect that was coming.

I couldn't tell how many survivors were in the water at this point but I could hear a lot of female voices calling for help. The two nurses nearest me were doggedly trying to swim away from the ship. One of them had a life jacket on, the other was clutching hers under one arm as she kicked vigorously. Then I spotted another nurse who was trying to swim, stay afloat, breathe, and get her life jacket on. Her eyes were closed and she was crying hysterically. I changed direction, came up alongside her, grabbed one of her flailing arms, and started pulling her along with me. She screamed when I first touched her but then relaxed when she saw I wasn't a shark. She then tried to help us both make progress away from what was coming, but mostly ended up kicking me in the legs.

I told her to hold on to her life jacket but I didn't think she could hear me over the roar of steam and compressed air coming out of the dying ship. There was just enough of a seaway that my view of everyone in the water was intermittent. The sinking ship was visible, though, and everybody out there was frantically trying to get away from her as more and more of her red underbelly rose into the air. Her cargo booms began to topple over in a tangle of heavy cables and crashing steel. The roar of air leaving the hull increased and then her bow disappeared in a cloud of dust as the forward cargo hatches gave way. Then she was just gone.

I think everyone out there in the water felt the sudden pull of a massive, sucking current back toward where she'd gone down, but, fortunately, it didn't last. The sudden silence was overwhelming, and then the shouting began as survivors milled around in the darkening ocean. There was no more hysteria; everyone who was still alive began concentrating on getting closer to other survivors. A gray life raft popped high up out of the water and then slapped back onto the surface. Then another. And another. I vaguely remembered that the rafts had been attached to the ship by hydrostatic devices, set to release them if water pressure ever entered the devices. I steered my clingy new best friend toward the nearest raft as even more popped up from the deep. She'd been a troopship, so she'd carried lots of rafts. Soon there were small flashlights coming on across the surface as men got aboard the rafts and began helping others climb in. The rafts were pretty basic: balsa wood covered in painted canvas fabric, eight feet wide by ten long, with a netting bottom and more nets strung along the sides for people to hang on to. Then my heart about stopped when I heard airplane engines approaching. The bastards were coming back to finish the job.

We were suddenly enveloped in a blaze of yellow-white light as the plane came in, but it wasn't a *Kawanishi,* thank God. It was a twin-engined Catalina, followed by two more in close succession. They'd turned on their landing lights and began to circle the area as the pilots took stock of the situation and made their reports back to Rendova. One of them expanded his circle and then dropped some rafts to a clutch of survivors who had drifted away from the main group. I became aware that the young woman whom I'd been helping had buried her wet head against my chest and was sobbing so hard I wondered how she could breathe. I tried to calm her, telling her rescue was coming, that we were going to be OK, but she kept on crying. Finally, she got control of herself and looked up at me with an anguished expression on her face.

"The patients," she sobbed. "What happened to the patients?"

I was embarrassed to realize that I hadn't thought even *once* about all those patients, as well as the medical people tending to them, trapped belowdecks. At that instant we both knew what had happened to them, to *all* of them. *Montrose* hadn't lasted more than a few minutes after the torpedoes struck. She hadn't been a warship, with watertight compartments and damage-control measures installed. Those fearsome Jap torpedoes had eviscerated her, opening up probably half her underwater body to the sea. It was certain that anyone not thrown into the sea when she did that one big roll had gone down with her. I suddenly felt sick at the sheer scale of the slaughter. I put my arm around the nurse and then we both wept as we hung on to the raft's netting.

TWENTY-ONE

PT boats were the first to arrive, followed by some destroyers and then a small fleet of LCMs and other amphibious craft. By midnight everyone who'd been picked up was back in Rendova harbor, exhausted but very glad to be alive. The Army created a hasty tent village ashore and gathered all the survivors into one area in a palm grove. I thought that was kind of them, but later realized it was the most efficient way of determining what the real losses had been.

They were substantial. *Montrose* had lost about half the ship's company. The ship's captain and the bridge watch-officers and enlisted men had survived. The engineering department had been wiped out by that second torpedo hit and the resulting steam release from ruptured boilers. Cooks, ship's service personnel—the laundry, barbershop, ship's store, the cleaning staff—had all been lost, trapped as they were inside the ship when she first capsized. Colonel Maddox had been conducting another one of his supplies surveys when we got hit. He'd had the staff's doctors with him along with some nurses to write down what they would need to restock in Rendova. That second torpedo had hit right beneath the big surgical suite, pushing the deck of the suite flat up into the deck above. Fifteen nurses and three docs had survived the sinking, but only because we'd been topside and rubbernecking as we came into Rendova.

Every one of the patients who'd been recovering belowdecks died in the attack. I couldn't imagine the horror: immobilized in a hospital bed with lines and tubes and even breathing masks attached, woozy from pain meds and basically unable to move and then feeling the explosions and being swamped by the onrushing sea. Broken bodies swirling around the flooding compartments like bloody rag dolls, tables and equipment upended, banging into the drowning patients, and then all the lights going out, for the operating room, the ship, and the men themselves.

God, where were You?

We could account for who'd made it, but not necessarily for who had *not* made it. All the ship's records, the hospital records, and everyone's personnel and pay records were gone forever. *Montrose* had gone down in 7,000 feet of water, so there was no possibility of recovering anything at all. The Army might have records of who'd been sent aboard *Montrose,* but we now had nothing to document what had happened after that.

The surviving docs and I made rounds of the survivors but there were few serious physical injuries to deal with. The one common thread were the shocked expressions we encountered everywhere as the survivors, especially the medical staff, absorbed the scale of the disaster and the certain knowledge that death had not come quietly for those who'd been trapped belowdecks. All that effort, the exhausting round-the-clock surgeries, the hour-by-hour aftercare, the hurt of watching men die after we'd tried so hard. Doctors, nurses, the orderlies. The numbing strain of physical weariness, that scolding subconscious voice telling us: quit complaining. You are whole and they are not, and, in some cases, would never be. Those moments when the nurses would look up and say "we're losing him," and then the frantic efforts to prevent that, sometimes successful, more often not. That moment of silence when we had to recognize that we couldn't do anything more. Those moments of sheer joy when we brought one back and then got him fixed up.

All for nothing.

*God*damned Japs.

The news that the campaign's only hospital ship had been torpedoed and lost sent shock waves throughout Rendova and New Georgia. Strangely, the incident was kept close-hold elsewhere. Word was that Halsey didn't want the Japs to know how bad they'd hurt us, but there was no keeping it from the troops. Most of us didn't think we were keeping it from the enemy, either. They'd sent a lone armed seaplane out to find us. That meant that there had to be some residual pockets of Japs on Rendova, left behind with a radio to report what they saw going on in the harbor. Like an unmarked passenger ship embarking wounded every other night and then heading west.

I was the senior surviving medical officer after the sinking, so the Army expected me to take charge and turn the small field medical station on Rendova into something a lot bigger and more capable. Maddox's final message to Nouméa about starting the Catalina resupply train our way meant that we were able to begin stockpiling medical supplies right away. The Seabees also jumped right to it, building log and tent facilities, laying hoses to a nearby spring, and then digging out more bomb-shelter bunkers. The Army docs had been moved over to New Georgia Island itself as friendly front lines finally began to advance toward Munda, but they'd been tasked to provide immediate first aid and then turn over anyone who needed more than that to *Montrose*.

We then had to wrestle with what to do about the nurses. The Catalinas could ferry some of them down to Cactus and beyond, but if we were going to set up surgeries, I needed those nurse anesthetists to remain behind. And then, of course, they'd need separate living quarters. There were thousands of men here and over on New Georgia, and more coming, who'd not seen an American female for more than a year. As it turned out, I needn't have worried about boy-girl problems. The nurses were too heartsick about what had happened to *Montrose* and all those patients to be interested in flirting with the GIs.

After five days, the Seabees had worked their usual miracles and we had a fairly capable facility just off the harbor on Rendova. My former cohorts on Bau Island moved in with us, including Chief Higgins. Cactus sent up a senior Navy Medical Service Corps officer to take over the administration of the facility and all logistics, which was a huge help. Four of the nurses stayed while the rest took Catalinas all the way back to Nouméa. I'd expected that they'd be rotated to Guadalcanal, but there were big changes in the works that none of us knew about. We learned that the hospital on Guadalcanal was going to be dismantled in preparation for the next push up the Solomons. I thought that was premature, given the battles going on across the channel, but then we got word that the airfield at Munda had finally been taken and that the Japs had evacuated their troops from New Georgia. The Seabees immediately landed at Munda and began repairs and new construction to make the airfield fully operational and even bigger.

As casualties fell off with the capture of New Georgia, we were sitting there on Rendova in a log-and-tent facility staffed by three of the surviving *Montrose* docs, one of whom was a surgeon, the four nurse anesthetists, three medical orderlies, Chief Higgins and two hospitalmen from the MTB squadron station, and myself. It wasn't that we were eager for "business" but the speculation about what was next got inventive. The sinking led to an investigation, which was standard procedure. As someone who'd been topside when the attack occurred, I was interviewed along with the four nurses. The investigating officer, a full captain from Halsey's staff, was surprised that I even knew what a *Kawanishi* was until I explained I'd been with the MTBs, who knew them all too well. He was particularly interested in finding out the extent of the casualty losses. We survivors had to sit down and try to come up with a count, which eventually led to some more waterworks from the nurses. We manly men of course maintained our composure, but to be honest, it was damned hard to do so. The captain, to his credit, was sympathetic and treated the nurses gently during their interviews.

"I know you people are hurting," he told us. "If it makes you feel any better, one of our submarines sank a Jap freighter a month ago. We found out last week that it was carrying one *thousand* Allied POWs and civilians back to Japan to the Mitsubishi slave labor camps. They were locked down in the cargo holds when she sank. Think how *that* sub skipper feels."

No one felt better after hearing that story, but it pointed out the fact that when people talked about the horror of war, there was simply no overstating it.

The Army headquarters camp was in turmoil now that New Georgia had been taken and the airfield at Munda was being rebuilt. Then our old nemesis, malaria, reared its ugly head. I went to headquarters again and asked them to request the Navy to send up some APDs, which were destroyers configured to carry troops. Malaria wasn't something that could be fixed by surgery. I needed a way to get patients out of here and down to either Guadalcanal or Nouméa, where the existing medical infrastructure could take the time required to get them back to health. Rendova simply wasn't the place for that. That night, Bluto showed up at our tent.

"Heard the bad news," he said. "Wanna come back and join us for a prayer session?"

"Hell, yes, Skipper. None of us here are doing too good."

"Are those nurses I see over there?"

"They are, but they're pretty fragile just now. The investigating officer just made us come up with a body count of the casualties on board *Montrose* when the *Kawanishi* hit."

Bluto winced. "May I go talk to them?" he asked.

I gave him a be-my-guest gesture, and he lumbered over to where the nurses were sitting at a makeshift operating table. Five minutes later we were embarked on one of the PT boats and headed for Bau Island, along with Higgins, the nurses, and the three *Montrose* docs. Higgins brought along a little black bag reminiscent of the country doctor in his horse and buggy arriving at a farmhouse on the prairie. Bau hadn't changed much since I'd left. A few more pontoons and some better tents for the crews on the hillside. There was now a larger, square tent that had become the squadron's comms center and Bluto's headquarters. Long HF antennas radiated out from a pole next to the tent in a web of wire anchored in nearby trees. The sporadic bombing raids from Rabaul had been aiming at the Army encampments and those big eight-inch guns that had been pounding Jap positions around Munda, and, of course, any shipping in the harbor. One Betty had circled back one morning to strafe the nest of PT boats. There'd been four boats in that day and their combined firepower put him into the harbor in a satisfying ball of fire.

The six of us congregated up in the square tent. Higgins disappeared while the rest of us sat around a long, split-log table on ammo boxes. The comms shack was separated from the main area of the tent by a canvas wall because of the crypto codes. The inside walls of the tent were covered with charts, maps, patrol assignments, and boat-availability listings. There was a single cot in one corner, next to which was a submachine gun and a steel helmet, which I assumed was for our skipper. Higgins came back with cans of grapefruit juice and his black bag. Soon we had screamers.

It was a pretty subdued prayer session. The presence of four American women on the island had not gone unnoticed, of course, and soon we had a procession of boat skippers and crewmen coming to the tent to deliver an "important" message, or an "update" on boat so-and-so's engineering problems, all with serious faces as they tried not to stare at the women. The nurses rose to the occasion, smiling at the obvious fakery and causing not a few red faces.

They were sad smiles, but they knew what was going on and played their part like the troupers they were.

I'm sure everyone assumed I'd been having the time of my life on a converted passenger liner with all those nurses aboard. The truth was that we'd all been too tired to even learn their names, much less engage in any romantic shenanigans. These women were tough as nails, but I knew they'd had their maternal instincts stomped on every time we lost a guy on the table or had to do the final-spinal, as we called it among ourselves. Still, it was a treat to shut off the hospital drama, sit down with uninjured fleet people instead of shattered soldiers, enjoy some vintage 1942 torpedo fuel, and not have to think about anything. At midnight, we were all taken back to the Rendova encampment. The ladies retired to their special tent, and I found a cot and slept for twelve hours. The next day we learned what we were going to be doing next.

TWENTY-TWO

A major from the general's staff came to find me at noon as I tried to fully wake up after being almost unconscious for so long. He had news.

"We're moving the whole circus over to the Munda airfield," he announced. "Command, logistics support, and medical. That airfield will become the launch point for the next phase of the campaign, because now it's long enough to support transports. Somebody important in Nouméa wants to combine the survivors of the *Montrose* with the field-medical-aid assets we have here, and then the Cactus docs are gonna move up to Munda and set up a real field hospital. Nouméa is just too far away. The Navy Medical Corps is gonna be in charge."

"Okay," I said, trying to digest all this after only one cup of coffee. I wasn't exactly operating at peak performance.

"The next objective is Bougainville Island, and we anticipate another tough campaign. But if we can take it and its airfields, our heavy bombers will be in range of Rabaul, and close enough to have fighter escorts at least for some of the way."

"What's going to happen with the PT boats?" I asked.

He blinked. Apparently, the PT boats were not terribly significant on the grand scale of planning for the Solomon Islands campaign.

He had to consult his notebook. "Right," he said. "The PT boats are going to set up shop on Puruata Island, as soon as Bougainville is reasonably secure."

"Well, look," I said, "sounds like you're gonna have a fully staffed hospital in these parts soon. I got shanghaied from my MTB squadron by the colonel in charge of the *Montrose* hospital facilities. That left the boats with a temporary doc. I want to go back to them. *Montrose* didn't have any really experienced surgeons, so I filled a temporary need. This new outfit certainly will. Can you make a case for my going back to the boats?"

He sighed. "I don't make decisions like that, Doc," he said. "That sort of stuff's *way* up my tape." He paused and looked around to see if anyone was eavesdropping. "You wanna go back to the PT boats?" he said. "Just do it. By the time the Medical Corps gets organized and stands up this new hospital? If you aren't there I'll bet they'll never miss you. Get it?"

"Got it," I said. "Thanks for the advice."

He paused for a moment. "On the other hand, people know about you, Doc. Colonel Maddox told the big boss that you did wonders for the *Montrose* staff. We had a Navy captain come up from Cactus to brief us on the medical plan, and he asked if you were in the area. Suddenly nobody at HQ knew."

"So, if I'm going to do a bunk, today might be a nice day for it."

He grinned. "I never told you that."

"Absolutely, Major," I said. "And thanks, again."

I wanted no part of being swallowed up by the oncoming Guadalcanal medical armada. Someone would inevitably question my credentials again, logs or no logs, and this time there'd be a squad of Medical Service Corps admin types itching to look into such matters. The MTBs rated a squadron doctor. I'd been transferred, loaned out, and cross-decked so many times that I doubted the Navy even knew where I was right now. My last formal orders had been to the squadron. If someone came looking, I could just say:

what's the problem? I'm the squadron doctor unless you can show me written orders to the contrary. And as to Bluto's remark, go be a surgeon—I was pretty sure that the Army's grand plans to set up a big-deal hospital at Munda would encounter a hiccup or ten before they ever missed me. Besides, as always, the Japs would get a vote on how this all shaped up.

I needed to find Higgins and make sure he came with me and then get my ass in gear and out of here. My first mission back on Bau would be to find Bluto. There'd be mass confusion at the Army encampment on Rendova as they packed out the headquarters and much of the logistic train for the move to Munda. Perfect time for Alibaba and his midnight minions to slip over from Bau for some discreet banditry.

The squadron was a little bit larger than when I'd left it, with six more boats and a whole new crop of skippers. The boats themselves were also different—most of them had had all their torpedo tubes removed in favor of more and bigger rapid-firing guns. A better radar and improved radios filled out the new kit, especially now that they had the new portable FM-band Army radios, the so-called "walkie-talkies," for close-in communications. Some genius had finally realized that if the PT boats were going to support Army and Marine infantry operations, it would be good for us to be able to talk to them.

Bluto was the same blustering, loud, profane, and nonstop boss he'd been when I left, although about twenty pounds lighter, which is when I realized I hadn't been gone for that long. It just seemed like it, especially after the *Montrose* sinking. It still didn't take much for images of the men and women I'd worked so hard with on that ship to appear in my mind, especially when I hit the sack. They appeared as spectral faces in a fog until I took a deep breath, squeezed my eyes shut, and firmly banished them. Until the next time. Bluto was delighted to have me back, if only for someone to talk to. As the commanding officer of the squadron, he had to maintain a formal separation from everyone in his command. The squadron doctor wasn't part of the line organization, so he and I could talk about things without breaching that formal chain of command.

I asked him how relations were with the "regular" Navy. He just shook his head. "At this moment we're much more valuable to the Army and Marines than the Navy. Sinking the *McCawley* set us back, *way* back, in the big-ship Navy's opinion."

"And she just *had* to be the amphibious commander's flagship, didn't she," I said. "Who could blame them?"

"Well," he said, sheepishly, "if you're gonna screw up, go big, I guess."

The *McCawley* had been under tow after being hit by a Jap air-dropped torpedo. One of our boats had mistaken it for a Jap ship especially after the towing ship fired on them.

"It was an honest mistake," Bluto continued, "and Navy intel kinda set us up for that one with all the warnings about Jap ships operating in that area."

"But the Army loves you?"

"Much more than the Navy," he replied. "We can move people and stuff—fast. We can be a picket station with a radar and a radio when the Navy can't provide a destroyer. When the Japs started using those barges again to reinforce, we were the first ones who could do something about that."

"So, this new operation will be more of the same, then?"

"Yeah, I think so. There's Bougainville, then the Shortlands, then Choiseul, and finally New Britain, which is where Rabaul lives. Although, I heard a rumor over at the Army HQ that maybe they're gonna bypass Rabaul."

"Bypass?"

"Yeah, conduct some carrier strikes, wreck the place, and sink as many Japs ships as happen to be in Simpson Harbor. But don't try to actually *take* Rabaul, 'cause it would be one tough nut. They've got over a hundred thousand troops there, four big airfields, lots a' caves and underground bunkers for fuel and ammo, big guns, mines, *three* Goddamned active volcanoes, the whole shebang. So: Destroy as many aircraft and warships as we can, and then we'll go around Rabaul and invade the Gilberts. Then use subs to keep any supplies, mainly food, from getting through to the garrison. Gotta admit, that's an interesting concept."

"Then why not go around Bougainville?" I asked.

"We need the airfields on Bougainville to reach all of New Britain, with both bombers *and* fighters."

"And are there any useful facilities on this Puruata Island?"

He grinned. "Of course," he said. "There's a million palm trees, a beach protected by uncharted coral reefs, no fresh water, mosquitos, malaria, and probably cannibals inland."

"Sounds perfect," I said. Then I saw Alibaba approaching. "Here comes trouble. I'll leave you and him to discuss the important stuff."

TWENTY-THREE

The next month became a blur of activity from dawn to dusk as two divisions, one Army, one Marines, prepared to go ashore on Bougainville. I'd heard somewhere that the armies with the best logistics would win every time, and now I was a believer. There was little active fighting going on over there on New Georgia, but a trickle of casualties continued to come in from straggler patrols, both there and even here on Rendova. The Japanese simply did not surrender, which meant that, when they were overwhelmed, the survivors redeployed into the jungle, recovered as best they could, and then continued the fight in small guerilla groups or even as individual snipers. They had not endeared themselves to the local tribes, so when the Army sent out hunting parties, tattered figures would emerge from the jungle trails and point silently. There was no effort to take prisoners. They would have presented a logistics burden, and besides, they'd usually kill themselves before allowing the Americans to take them. That fact left everyone, Japanese and American, satisfied.

Nine weeks after New Georgia was declared "secured," Bougainville was invaded. We medics had no picture as to the deployment of forces, where and when they landed, or with how many troops. We caught glimpses of Navy ships out in the channel, including some of the new cruisers that were coming out of the shipyards in increasing numbers to replace our losses at Guadalcanal. The PT boat squadron was ordered to stand by for a movement to Puruata Island. I told my medical crew that we were going to just lay low as the Guadalcanal hospital staff moved into Rendova prior to staging over to Munda airfield. The Japanese did not seem to want to interfere with any of this. All the mess-tent strategists were convinced that they'd decided to withdraw into their bastions on New Britain Island to await the inevitable invasion of Rabaul.

PART III

PART III

TWENTY-FOUR

Puruata Island was even smaller than *Bau*. It was basically a knob of jungle greenery covering a rocky mound about seventy feet tall and sitting four hundred yards off the main island of Bougainville. The squadron made the transit from Rendova at night in one large gaggle, as always keeping our speed down so as not to attract lurking *Kawanishis*. We got a surprise when we arrived at dawn: a ship was anchored in the narrow channel between Puruata and the main island. She was the USS *Tutuila* (ARG-4). We later learned she was an internal combustion engine repair ship, new to the Pacific theater. She looked like a small, converted cargo ship, small being a relative description. She actually displaced 4,000 tons, small for a cargo ship but twice the displacement of one of our current generation of destroyers. Even better, she was going to be the mobile home base for the squadron, a luxury we'd never had before.

I went aboard with Bluto when we first arrived. The captain was a salty-looking lieutenant who, by his age, was probably exenlisted. He met us at the top of the accommodation ladder and introduced himself as Sam Crawford. He welcomed us aboard and then we went aft to his cabin at the back of the ship. It looked a lot like the captain's cabins I'd seen in movies at the back of the big sailing warships, with fake wood paneling, windows instead of portholes, a large wardroom table, its own head, and even a closed-off area for his sleeping quarters. The only jarring note were two black steel columns coming down from the next level on either side of the main cabin. The captain told us they supported two of his *twelve* 20 mm mounts.

"I've got a single five-inch gun and four 40 mm AA mounts as well," he said proudly.

"And you can support my boats?" Bluto asked.

"That's what we're here for," he replied. "We have machine shops for gasoline *and* diesel engines. We can take any engine down to its bare block and completely rebuild it. We also carry spare parts, fuel, ammo, and a dozen torpedoes. There's a radar and radio shop, a gun shop for up to 40 mm, and electrical, hydraulic, and structural shops. We can even hoist your boats on board and cradle 'em for whatever work they need. I can also berth up to sixty enlisted and fifteen officers."

"Sick bay?" I asked.

"You bet, Doc. A ten-bed ward right next to sick bay, and the basics for doing surgery. All I *don't* got is an actual doctor, but my HM chief is first class."

"You do now," Bluto said, inclining his head at me. "And he's a surgeon."

The captain beamed. "So," he said. "Tell me what you need."

"Where do I start?" Bluto said.

"Well, look," Crawford said. "Chief Maloney is the repair officer. Take a day, get everything written down, *and* prioritized. Second thing: the Army is sending up a battery of the new M2 90 mm AA guns from Rendova. They're gonna set up shop over on the main island. Until then, can I ask that you keep a boat ready for AA work whenever they're alongside?"

"Absolutely," Bluto said. "We've got 20 mm and 50-cal. I can have one boat on ready-alert, and another on five-minute standby."

"Great," the captain said. "The Marines told me that this end of B-ville is relatively secure but that they're still flushing Japs up north. They also said to expect an air attack from Rabaul once the Japs discover that we're here."

Bluto leaned forward. "I'm not sure exactly what the bosses want us to do here, but if you get any indication of Jap bombers coming, be sure to let us know. Any boat that can get under way will, and we'll surround you and throw up a curtain of AA fire. We've done it before."

"Good to hear," Crawford said, standing. "Let's meet again at sundown, see where we are. In the meantime, my guys are rigging boat booms. The Marines say the Seabees are coming, and they'll provide some pontoon piers and the emplacements for those Army AA guns."

"It's standard procedure for my boats to refuel and rearm immediately when they come in from patrol. Can we set that up?"

"You bet," the captain said. "Like I said, that's what we're here for, Skipper."

The rest of our day was spent merging the two organizations. I went forward to meet the chief hospitalman, whose name was Jimmy Whittaker, and his assistant, HM3 Beamer. Together we surveyed the medical spaces. They were about the same size as the LST sick bays, but more modern. *Tutuila* was a brand-new ship, not a conversion as we had assumed, and there was medical equipment in there I hadn't seen before. Nor had Chief Whittaker, as it turned out, so we took off the wraps and set to scanning the instruction manuals. They had an autoclave, which brought a smile to my face. I told the chief about boiling instruments in a fifty-five-gallon drum on Guadalcanal right after the invasion. He just shook his head, and then he stopped and looked at me in recognition.

"You're the third-year resident who's been doing major surgery out here in the Solomons ever since the invasion?"

"Guilty," I said. "Although, technically, I was about to start my fourth year when I signed up."

He laughed and extended his hand. "Honor to meet you, Doctor," he said. "I was stationed in Nouméa before getting this assignment. There were stories going around about you doing some amazing things at the Cactus hospital. The older docs were all highly indignant. The younger docs were grinning and saying that was fantastic, as in, why can't we do some of that. And you were aboard *Montrose* when she went down?"

"I was," I said. "That was—terrible."

"I can't imagine," Whittaker said. "So, what the hell are *you* doing here? You should be at that big deal they're setting up at the Munda airfield."

"Yes and no," I said. "If they'd let me operate, yes. But if the old guard put their feet down and said, forget that stuff, Mister *Resident*, you can assist and only on the cases we deem appropriate for your, ahem, limited medical training..."

He nodded. "And that's exactly what they'd do," he said. "The farther the real war got from Nouméa, the more the same old hospital politics came into play down there. I volunteered for *Tutuila* *because* she was going up on the front lines. With the PT boats, no less. I'm dying for a ride."

"I can set that up for you," I said. "But you may not come back."

"If they'll go out, by God, I'll go out," he said, firmly. "We've gotta beat these bastards, all the way back to Goddamned Tokyo."

"That's the spirit," I said. "Now I need to get you together with my chief, Wally Higgins. He does anesthesia."

The next morning the captain showed up in sick bay while Higgins, Chief Whittaker, and I were doing an inventory. He had a message for me.

"From the Medical Command down at Munda," he announced in a grave tone of voice: "They've asked if a Lieutenant Lincoln Andersen, MC, was here and, if so, they want to see you, ASAP."

I groaned. Apparently, my little escape and evasion plan hadn't worked after all. Whittaker gave me a sympathetic look. Crawford apparently realized that there was a problem. "If I can help in any way..." he offered.

I thanked him and told him that I needed to go see Bluto.

"Like I was saying yesterday," Chief Whittaker said, "you'd be wasted here, you being a surgeon and everything."

I could hope, I thought, but my gut told me this wasn't a summons to join the Munda surgical service. I could see that Higgins was thinking the same thing. I took one of *Tutuila's* small landing craft over to the new pontoon nest on Puruata where Bluto was holding court on one of the boats. I told him what had happened.

"Hell with 'em," he said promptly. "If they had to ask *if* you were here, then they don't *know* you're here. I'll have a word with Sam Crawford. As long as he doesn't answer that message, they'll still be in the dark. Messages go astray all the time."

For a moment I was tempted, but only for a moment. If there was going to be some kind of reckoning over what I'd been doing, I'd just as soon resolve it, one way or another. Two hours later I was headed south for Munda on the 655 boat. We passed through several small islands to minimize our exposure in the Slot to Jap air.

The Munda airfield was already in full operation when we got to the tiny harbor. Navy and Marine fighters were coming and going, while contrails in the sky indicated there were more fighters stationed as top cover. An LCI (Landing Craft, Infantry) was unloading some wounded men onto a steel ramp leading to waiting ambulances, so I hitched a ride with one of them over to where the hospital was being built. The site was abuzz in heavy construction machinery when we got there, with Seabees happily tearing up the ground as only they could. The surprise was that they were installing Quonset huts instead of tents.

Even more impressive, they were excavating deep slots in the sandy soil so that the Quonsets would be almost completely underground. One cluster of four huts was already in operation. Only the top quarter of rounded steel showed, and men were busy dragging camouflage netting over that. From the air they should be invisible. The big red crosses were conspicuously absent. There was a cluster of large generators sitting in concrete revetments and covered with netting. The Seabees had left clumps of palm trees here and there. There was a 90 mm anti-aircraft battery hidden in each clump.

The operational medical cluster was in the shape of a cross: two Quonsets in line with two more branching off on either side. I had to walk down a ramp with the stretcher-bearers to enter the first hut through what looked almost like an airlock. Another surprise: they were air-conditioned! No more need for mosquito netting. What a difference eighteen months makes, I thought. The first Quonset was a combination of triage and admin, so I went to what looked like an admissions desk and introduced myself as Doctor Andersen. The weary-looking Army sergeant sitting behind the biggest desk almost said, *and so?* when a younger man in a surgical gown, who'd been doing some paperwork, looked up when he heard my name. He came over to the counter and stuck out a friendly hand.

"Steve Dugan," he said. "Orthopod. You're being assigned here?"

"Not sure," I said. "Unless you're short on surgeons. I was up north on Bougainville with my PT boat squadron when a message came in saying someone wanted to see me."

"PT boats," Dugan said, admiringly. "That must be something. But look—if a message was sent, you probably need to go over to the headquarters hut. Back up the ramp, look up the hill. You'll see a hut with a flag out front. I'd take you over there but there's a meeting of all the surgeons in five minutes. Mandatory training."

"Who's the CO here?" I asked.

"Captain Holland Fraser Whitman Garr, US Navy Medical Corps," he said with a wry smile. Then he saw the look of dismay that was crossing my face. "Let me guess—you know him?"

"In a manner of speaking," I said. "We didn't exactly get along on Guadalcanal."

"I'm shocked—*shocked*—" he said in his best Claude Rains imitation. "Have fun, Doctor. Better thee than me-e-e."

Wonderful, I thought. Garr, of all people. I'd forgotten his pretentious name, but it was absolutely in character. I took a deep breath and went to find the headquarters.

TWENTY-FIVE

"Well, well, well, look who we have here," Garr said. "The Navy Medical Corps' very own Nobel-striker, in the flesh: Doctor Hooligan himself. Please have a seat, Doctor. These gentlemen want to hear *all* about your amazing surgical achievements of the past year."

Garr was sitting behind a standard Navy gray metal desk, looking somewhat plumper than I remembered, but still sporting that purplish face. There were two other Medical Corps officers in his office. One was a four-stripe captain, the other a lieutenant commander. Their faces were neutral but they both had notebooks open on their laps. I sat down in the chair indicated.

"To refresh your memories, Doctors," Garr continued, "this is the third-year resident from the Duke University surgical program, Lieutenant Lincoln Andersen, Medical Corps and USNR, who landed with us at Guadalcanal and then proceeded to pass himself off as a fully certified surgeon."

"Bullshit," I said, quietly. Garr's eyes flared when I interrupted him. "Total bullshit, and you know it, *Doc*tor."

There was a stunned silence in the room as Garr's face did its familiar color change. I decided to seize the moment.

"I did not pass myself off as anything but what I was and you damned well know that. I'd completed three years of the Duke surgical residency program, so I was assigned to *assist* the fully certified surgeons right after the invasion. By *you*, as I recall. It's only when the Cactus medical team became overwhelmed by the sheer numbers of casualties that I was told to do what I could, by *you*, and that's what I did. Especially after the fleet bailed on us and left the Marines to deal with the Japs as best they could. *And*, took all our supplies with them."

"Now you listen here, Lieutenant—" Garr sputtered.

"No, I won't," I said. "I'm tired of your lies. In the two weeks after the invasion of Guadalcanal, I performed more surgical procedures than anyone at Duke would get to perform, probably in the seven years of our academic training. Yes, I did a lot of them on the fly, assisted by chief petty officers and junior hospitalmen who were doing their best to save lives. I did save lives—lots of them. I also lost some, just like you did. Like everyone did. And, I don't remember *you* taking me off the duty roster because I was only a resident."

"Not because I didn't want to," he blustered. "You simply were not qualified!"

"Granted, but after Guadalcanal, and then Tulagi, I *was* as qualified as any cutter out there for the shock-trauma work I was doing. Nothing like having a nineteen-year-old Marine arrive at the table with his innards in his *hands* to inspire you to do not only what you can, but the *best* that you can. I've done emergency procedures which I'd only heard about at Duke, more times than I can count. I took chances. We *all* took chances, from the anesthetist nurses to the orderlies, often to the sound of incoming fire. I'm sorry I didn't arrive with suitable credentials, but there are a lot of young Marines alive because I was there. And *you* started me on that course."

My angry outburst produced another moment of silence. Garr visibly gathered himself to make a rebuttal, but the captain raised his hand. "Tell us, please, about the surgeries you've been doing. Guadalcanal, Tulagi, Rendova, New Georgia."

I took a deep breath. "Don't forget the *Montrose*," I said.

The captain seemed surprised. "You were on the *Montrose*?"

"I was, temporarily, the *senior* surgeon on the *Montrose*," I said. "At the request of Colonel Maddox, SMO. I was on board when she was sunk by a *Kawanishi*'s torpedoes."

Apparently, that was news to Garr, whose expression revealed his complete surprise. He started to say something, but the captain again cut him off.

"How about you just tell us what you've been doing since landing on Guadalcanal," he said. "Take your time. I want it all."

I proceeded to do just that. It took an hour and a half. When I finally ran out of breath, Garr looked like he'd swallowed a frog. The captain and the lieutenant commander, who'd been taking notes, sat there for a long moment. Then the captain had an interesting question.

"Do you have any records of your surgical work?" he asked.

"I did," I replied. "But Colonel Maddox—he was the SMO on the *Montrose*—advised me to send my first surgical log home. He said I'd need it when the war was over. I began a second one after that, but it was lost with everything else when *Montrose* was sunk. I started a third log after that, but when New Georgia fell, I went back to my squadron duties."

Garr's face lit up. His expression clearly said: Gotcha now, you impudent bastard. The captain, however, seemed to have different ideas.

"Doctor Andersen," he said, finally, "I apologize for this surprise interrogation. It's obvious to me that you must be something of a prodigy, and I would have to say that, based on what you've told us, you're a fully qualified battlefield surgeon. Doctor Garr, do you have anything to add now?"

Poor Garr, God love him, didn't know what to say. The captain left him hanging out to dry for a moment, and then took mercy on him.

"Doctor Andersen," he said, "I want you to return to the PT boat squadron—for the time being, anyway. You belong in a surgical department, but I sense that your talents might be, um, somewhat underutilized here. Let me just say this: the hospital here at Munda will inevitably be overtaken by events in the next several months. Once we set up the next big facility, we'll call you back. If you have no further questions for me, you may go now. Thank you for your debrief."

I stood up, a little bewildered by what had just happened. Garr was visibly gritting his teeth, but it was clear that, whoever this captain was, he was absolutely in charge. I had just stepped out of the admin hut when some sirens began to wail. I was almost bowled over by two sergeants and a Navy hospitalman as they ran past me, slapping their helmets on. One looked over his shoulder and pointed to a nearby air-raid trench while the two of them headed for one of those 90 mm AA gun emplacements out in the trees. I didn't need to be told twice: the sound of Betty bombers, a sound I knew only too well, was rising in the jungles surrounding Munda airfield.

The unfinished trench shelter was a full six feet deep, accessed by a crude dirt ramp at one end. The top of the trench was covered in loose canvas over transverse logs, but the "floor" was two inches of red mud where rainwater had leaked down the ramp. There were two long boards along the top edges to keep the sides from collapsing in. I saw some steel helmets and gas masks hanging on pegs along the wall, so I grabbed a helmet. I had just figured out how to lengthen the strap and put it on when three Army nurses in ward uniforms came hustling down the ramp. They, too, donned helmets and then assumed a crouching position, hands over their heads to hold the helmets in place. By then the AA guns had started up, happily drowning out the sound of the approaching Bettys, at least until bombs began to fall. I'd forgotten how terrifying it was to listen to 500-pound bombs going off, each one closer and louder than the one before it. You'll never hear the one that gets you, a Marine had once told me with a cheerful smile. Cold comfort indeed. He failed to mention that you *would* hear the one that almost got you.

There was a sudden, overwhelming, eardrum-cracking compression of the air around us, followed by a blaze of white light and then the sides of the trench gave way under a deafening blast. I was knocked unconscious for at least a minute. When I was able to gather my senses, I was upright, bent over in what was left of the trench, and up to my waist in pulverized dirt with shreds of burned canvas draped over my head. I couldn't hear anything but a painful buzz in both ears. I put my hands up to my face to wipe the dirt out of my eyes. They came away bloody because my nose was bleeding and I'd somehow bitten my lower lip. I looked around for the nurses but didn't see them. Then I remembered—they'd been crouching. I tried to move but the wet dirt had me locked in place. I tried rocking back and forth, like getting a stubborn fence post out of the ground. That worked. Then I was able to crawl through the dirt to where I thought the nurses had been and start digging like a dog on the hunt for a bone. I uncovered the first head and face and heard her take in one enormous breath and then start crying. I left her to it and scrambled to find the next one. She had been able to move a hand to create an airspace, so she was a little less traumatized. By then I was lying flat on the shattered earth and searching frantically for the third nurse.

"Where is she?" I yelled at the other two. The crying one just kept bawling; the other one said something I couldn't hear and then pointed to her *other* side. Dammit! I'd gone the wrong way, looking for her. I clambered back in the direction she was pointing and resumed digging with my bare hands until I encountered one of those reinforcing boards that had been at the top of the trench. I couldn't budge it and I couldn't get around it. By then I was out of breath and exhausted. I closed my eyes to catch my breath for just a moment.

I woke up on a stretcher, lying on the ground. The two nurses were alongside. The crying one had calmed down, but the second nurse was weeping silently, her eyes closed. We were all filthy and my face felt like it was crusted in mud and blood. I could feel activity all around but I still couldn't hear a thing. I looked for the third nurse. That's when I realized we were lying in a bomb crater, whose circular sides were amazingly smooth. I could catch the occasional glimpse of men coming and going above us and I could feel vehicles passing by. There was a huge cloud of black, oily smoke darkening the sky above our crater. Then some orderlies came, lifted us out of the crater, and took us to the actual hospital Quonsets. On the way I saw the HQ building, which looked untouched until I looked again. It had been strafed and it looked like there were stretchers out front. The dirt berms had absorbed a lot of the rounds, but there was a clear track of what looked like 50-cal holes down the length of the exposed top.

Nobody was bored in the triage/admin area this time. There were stretchers everywhere, nurses hanging drips, and two young-looking docs who were apportioning the dreaded tags. A senior-looking nurse, and by that, I mean a woman in her late thirties, came over to where they put our stretchers down. She gasped when she saw the two nurses from the trench.

"Check them first," I said. "I'm not injured."

She stared at my face, which apparently *was* covered in crusted blood and mud. "Nosebleed," I said. "Also, there was a third nurse in that bomb shelter. I dug these two out when it collapsed, but I couldn't find the third one."

The calmer of the two nurses spoke a name, which I couldn't hear, and then the senior nurse's face paled. She shouted something, which, for the first time, I could hear as my ears crackled back to life. She then grabbed an orderly and ran out the door. The calm one wasn't calm anymore. I decided to just get up, but that took longer than I'd expected as I rolled out of the stretcher and lifted an arm at one of the orderlies. He obliged by pulling me to my feet, where I leaned on him for a full minute before getting my balance back. That's when he saw my medical insignia. "You a doc?" he asked.

I nodded. He took me behind the counter and plopped me down in the surly sergeant's chair, then went to get some surgical wipes to clean me up. I sat there and let him do it as the sounds of triage, some good, some not so good, began to rise. When he was done, he had another question. "Sir, are you a surgeon, by any chance?"

Again, I nodded. At that moment a young and really scared-looking doctor wearing a blood-spattered surgical gown came through the double doors that separated admin from the treatment huts. He was being pursued by two nurses, also in OR gowns, who caught up with him and said he *had* to come back.

"I can't do it," he said plaintively. "I'm not a surgeon. I'm a burns guy. I want to help, but Jesus! I'm doing more harm than good."

I stood up, a little more stable now. "*I'm* a surgeon," I announced.

None of them recognized me, of course, but one of the young nurses came right over. "All the surgeons were doing a training session in hut three," she said, her voice rising. I thought she was very close to completely losing it. "A bomb hit, didn't go off, but none of them can do surgery right now. The hut collapsed and then the bomb started smoking something chemical. We've got broken bones, multiple lacerations, concussions, breathing problems, three surgeons are hurt bad, twenty casualties waiting, and we're all going to *die!*"

That last word came out as a hysterical screech, causing a sudden momentary silence in the area. "Calm down, please," I said. "Take me back to the OR. I need clean everything, and then we'll get to work."

At that moment, the senior nurse came back in, minus her orderly. The expression on her face told the tale: they'd found the third nurse, smothered under all that dirt. The hysterical nurse gave out an anguished cry, but the senior nurse wasn't having it. She chided the young woman to get herself together, and then asked who I was.

"He's a surgeon," the young nurse said. "And at the moment, he's the only surgeon."

"Is that true?" the senior nurse said. "I don't recognize you. What's your name?"

"I'm Doctor Lincoln Andersen," I said. "Lieutenant junior grade, USNR, currently medical officer with the MTB squadron on Bougainville."

"So, what are you doing here, Lieutenant? And since when does a PT boat squadron rate a surgeon?"

"It's a long story," I said. "But right now, why don't you come to the OR with me and I'll prove my bona fides."

"Okay," she said sternly. "I'm Lieutenant Commander Helen Carpenter, director of nursing. You better not be bullshitting me, Doctor, or I'll shoot you myself."

"Got it, sir," I said. "Or, ma'am, I guess. Now, I believe time is of the essence."

TWENTY-SIX

The next twenty-four hours were a nightmare, though I must say, the entire staff took a collective deep breath and rallied magnificently. I began with a triage round, accompanied by Lieutenant Commander Carpenter. The facility had three ready tables, so I assigned the three most urgent patients to those tables. Then I went into a side room, stripped down, and let two orderlies pour buckets of water over me while I scrubbed all the crud off. The pressurized water system was down due to bomb damage out along the airfield. I scrubbed with soap, deluged again, and then got into OR gowns.

I felt better. I could hear pretty well, the nosebleed was just a nosebleed, my lip hurt, but otherwise I was ready to go. My hands were steady. This had been scary, but Guadalcanal had been much scarier. I ordered the young burn specialist to my side as an assistant and, to his credit, he rose to the occasion. Lieutenant Commander Carpenter stayed with me for thirty minutes before moving on to be the OR mover and shaker, getting breathing equipment, instruments, anesthesia, and putting nurses in motion before I even needed to ask. She was marvelous—calm, authoritative without being unpleasant about it—and because of her, we were able to process casualties in a relatively smooth and organized fashion, given the chaos outside. It was clear the nurses adored her, and I was beginning to do the same. I rotated among the three tables for two hours, by which time Carpenter, apparently no longer in a mood to shoot me, made sure I had all the nursing assistance I needed.

Then three of the regular staff surgeons showed up, battered and bandaged, coughing and wheezing, but apparently concerned that there was only one cutter trying to handle the avalanche. One of them was much older than the other two, probably approaching sixty. He looked unusually pale and he was sweating, even in the air-conditioning, which mercifully had come back on. He sat down when he got there and asked for water. The other two, who were my age, gave me a friendly nod before going to scrub in. Once they manned their tables, the OR quieted down substantially. I felt a sense of relief. The nurses were used to working with them, so there were a lot fewer orders and hand-me's once they showed up. Then the older doc, whose head was wrapped in bandages and whose eyeglasses had been taped onto his head, suddenly collapsed at the table from what looked like a heart attack to me. The nurses swarmed him but I just kept going, having done these marathons before. I knew if I stopped, I'd really, really want to sit down. I sucked oxygen periodically but no one batted an eye. Then they brought Garr in.

He was a bloody mess. It was a moment before I recognized him, and then the irony of the situation hit me like a hammer. Had he been conscious, I just might have bent over and asked him if he'd like some thiopentone. But then the nurse anesthetist nodded, and I reverted to being a surgeon. I had to amputate his left arm at the elbow, remove his left eyeball, and do the best I could with a slash wound that went from above and behind his left ear all the way down across his face to his right jawbone. Whatever had hit him had shattered *all* the teeth on the left side of his mouth. I didn't have to remove them; they fell out in a bloody mush of white enamel and gum tissue when I suctioned and rinsed his mouth.

Next in was the Navy captain who'd interviewed me, whose

name I still didn't know, who'd been with Garr when the bombs hit. He had a collapsed lung from a through-and-through projectile wound. He was semiconscious when they brought him to the table. I don't think he recognized me when they laid him down, gowned and masked as I was. He was obviously in great pain, and only relaxed when they started the ether. I backed away, shed my gloves and sweaty mask, got new ones and clean instruments, and went to work.

I don't know how many operations I performed that day—and night—but it was many. The other two surgeons had their hands full as well. It had been Carpenter who finally called time on me and made me go lie down on a cot in a corner of the OR complex. I was asleep in thirty seconds. When I woke up, I found myself covered with a blanket. The OR was dimly lit and quiet except for the familiar noises of post-surgery cleanup. I was stiff and my feet were sore, but I was reasonably happy with what I'd done. I smelled hot coffee, and then Carpenter was there, with a mug in each hand. I sat up with a groan but gratefully accepted the coffee. She pulled a stool over and sat down next to me. I sat with my back against the sloping walls of the Quonset hut. The coffee was wonderful.

"So," she said pleasantly, "you told me it was a long story. The nurses are calling you Superman. Give. And call me Helen, if you'd like."

I did. I gave her a much shorter version of what I'd recited to the captain in Garr's office, but then observed that I was getting tired of having to defend myself every time I collided with the medical bureaucracy.

"I know there's a lot I have to learn," I told her. "But when it comes to battle trauma surgery, I think I'm competent enough to save lives, at least for a while. As I see it, I keep them from dying during the first twenty-four hours after they are wounded. I understand that they'll then need to go back to real hospitals and real specialist surgeons with at least a hundred years of experience."

She grinned. "Got it," she said. "And for what it's worth, you're a long way past being just an intermediate stop between a guy dying from his wounds and the work of a specialist who gets to take his time, study X-rays, pull skin grafts, do lab tests, and call in other experts. I watched you work. For a third-year resident, you're quick, confident, decisive, and technically very impressive. I was a surgical nurse before I got old and they kicked me upstairs to be the Nursing Dragon. I know what I'm talking about. Your problem is political, not medical."

"Do tell," I said. "But, honestly? At this point, I'm ready to give it up and go back to my boat squadron and do pecker-checks and annual physicals for the duration."

"Don't you dare," she said. "This war is spitting out revolutionary technical change. Weapons, airplanes, radar, *and* medicine. The old guard's gonna react like it always does: 'that wasn't how we did it in *my* day, by Godfrey.' You're gonna be somebody in the next generation of surgeons. Did you keep logs of what you did?"

"Yes, I did. But listen, you're making it sound like this war is nothing more than a grand-scale global residency, at least as far as we docs are concerned."

"Bingo," she said triumphantly. "From what I've read, all wars are."

Her eyes were practically blazing. I almost asked her how old she was, because I really couldn't tell. I knew that all the nurses worked hard *not* to be sexy, attractive, or ever seen as "on the make." An operating room or a ward full of bloody, battered, and whimpering soldiers and sailors was no place for war paint or even a hint of perfume, and I was confident that Helen was a dedicated enforcer of that rule. And yet, I found her intensely attractive. Maybe it was because she was on my side. Maybe it was because an attractive American female was sitting right here, talking to me. It made for a nice change after months of nonstop tragedy.

I think at that moment she realized we were dallying with intimacy. Not sexual, so much, but just the kind of intimacy that exists between friends, where you can let your hair down and tell someone how you really feel about things. Except I was a man and she was very much a woman. She straightened up in her chair and momentarily turned her eyes away. Oh, boy, I thought. Doctors and nurses. I knew better.

"How's Garr doing?" I asked. She seemed relieved when I broke the "spell," which probably only existed in my own tired brain. I felt a pang of regret.

"He's hurting and he's scared," she said. "His nurse made the mistake of letting him see himself in a mirror."

"Well, that was inevitable," I said. "He's going to have to go all the way back to Tripler hospital to fix that mess. He needs a plastic surgeon and maxillofacial surgery."

"He needs more than that," she said. "As in, a swift kick in the ass. God, Almighty, but that man was a pimple on the ass of progress."

"I remember him well," I said. "He was my boss on Guadalcanal, a hundred years ago. And that captain? I never got his name."

"*The* captain," she said. "His name is Robert Chisholm, and he's actually a flag selectee. He'll be the senior medical officer for the whole Southwest Pacific. He is—formidable."

"And a good guy?"

She nodded. "Yeah, I think so. Where did you go to med school?"

"Duke," I replied.

"Wow," she said. "Duke Medical? That's up there. I would have thought that a surgeon at Duke could have gotten any deferment he wanted."

"Well," I said. "Is there any more coffee? Then I'll tell you a little bit about me."

She obliged, and then I began. I'd been finishing up my third year as a surgical resident at Duke University Hospital in Durham, North Carolina, when the war started. Both of my parents are medical doctors; my father is a vascular surgeon and my mother a radiologist. Life was just about perfect back then. My parents, both established experts in their respective fields, were paying my way through the grueling process of becoming a surgeon. Unlike many of my contemporaries, I had the luxury of being able to focus entirely on my studies without having to worry about student loans, outside night jobs, and sharing living facilities with other financially strapped residents.

I had "only" four years to go to become a "real" surgeon. I'd already spent four years at a premed college, four years at medical school, and three of the seven years as a rising resident. I was thirty-one years old, beginning to bald a bit, and just starting to wonder if all this endless, day in, day out training and school was going to be worth it. I would have been thirty-five years old when I finally got to take the big Boards. That was a sobering fact, not to mention those nagging questions, such as: when will I ever have time to find a wife, or have a family? I'd already seen the work hours junior surgeons were subjected to. I hadn't dared to express any of these concerns to my parents, who were footing the hefty bills.

And then one day there'd been a great commotion in the residents' lounge over news reports that the Empire of Japan had attacked Pearl Harbor and virtually destroyed the US Pacific Fleet. After studiously avoiding the growing calamity that was Europe, the United States had been plunged into a global war. Hitler and all his machinations had stayed 2,500 miles away for the past two years, kept that way by a nation of parents and grandparents who vividly remembered the last time America was dragged into a European war. But now, as black-and-white newsreels depicted the horrors of the attack in Hawaii and the scope of Japanese treachery, political sentiment in America, ever fickle, had morphed rapidly into a call for national revenge.

I heard about other residents taking leave to get commissions into the Army and I wondered if this might be a good way to deal with my doubts about a medical career. I knew I couldn't present myself as a surgeon, but apparently the Army was taking just about anybody who could show a diploma from an accredited university med school. I went down to the local Army office recruiter in Raleigh, where I joined the surprisingly long lines of men volunteering to make the Japs remember Pearl Harbor. When I finally got up to the desk of a harried sergeant and told him I was a third-year surgical resident at Duke, I was immediately whisked away to another building to meet an Army Medical Corps major.

"Sure you want to do this?" the major had asked me. "I mean, hell, you've got a residency at *Duke,* for Chrissakes. I can get you waivered for at least two years, if not longer. You'd be a lot more valuable to the Army as a Duke-trained surgeon, not to mention preserving your medical career."

"I know I can't be a surgeon in the Army, but surely I can be an MD in wartime. I really want to do my part."

The major just stared at me. "Don't think you won't be doing surgery in the Army, especially when you get to the field. You're gonna get more hands-on training than you'd ever get at school, even at Duke. Let's do this: go take the physical. If you pass that, you'll get a reserve commission as a first lieutenant, then get some training on how to salute, and then you'll get assigned to a field hospital somewhere. Tell me, what did your faculty advisor say when you told him?"

"He said: good for you."

"I'll just bet he did," the major said. "But did he sound sincere?"

In fact, my advisor had tried hard to talk me out of it, but I persisted. I took the Army physical and failed it. Flat feet, a small heart murmur, less than 20/20 vision, and elevated blood pressure. "Go back to school," the major told me. "When things get bad, we'll come find you, trust me. This is gonna be a long war."

On the way out I heard one of the other recruiters telling a volunteer that he, too, failed the physical. "Try the Navy," the sergeant was saying. "They'll take anybody; they just lost three thousand guys at Pearl Harbor." I tried the Navy, told them about my physical. The recruiter listened patiently and then asked if I'd ever been con- victed of a felony. A week later my father pinned on my bright silver lieutenant (junior grade) insignia and I was off to Newport. By mid-1942 I found myself on an Army transport ship to Hawaii, along with a whole bunch of Marines. Scuttlebutt around the ship was that there was an invasion being planned; the target was some island called Guadalcanal.

Helen listened attentively. "Well, I think that Army major was right, but we are all very damned glad you were here yesterday. Oh—speaking of Captain Chisholm: he wants to talk to you."

"Is he in any condition to talk?" I asked. "He had a punctured lung. It was a dirty bullet hole. Infection is likely."

She shrugged. "He's conscious and wants to talk to you. You up to it?"

"Me?" I said. "Why, I'm Superman. I leap tall buildings in a sin- gle bound. I—"

She grinned and looked ten years younger. "Spare me," she said.

"So, where's Lois Lane?" I asked. "Somebody's gotta help me walk." Then she surprised me.

"Right here," she said, and took my hand. Amazed, I put my other hand over hers. "To be continued," I said.

She smiled then. It was a chaste smile. Tentative, demure, hope- ful but not too hopeful. I squeezed her hand. Then someone banged into the OR and announced there'd been a big sea fight and that ships were coming in.

She closed her eyes. "Fuck," she growled through clenched teeth.

"Hold that thought," I said. She giggled and then we both started laughing before we realized people were looking. Then the doors opened, people began swarming into the OR, and the lights went up. Still, for the first time in this war I felt good. Then I remem- bered that Captain, soon-to-be-Admiral, Chisholm wanted to talk to me. Helen disappeared into the crowd that was filling the OR complex. I asked an orderly when the casualties would arrive. "Two hours," he said. "But this time, word is, they kicked some Jap ass for a change."

Wonderful, I thought. I got up, swayed for a moment, hit the head to de-coffee, and then went to find Captain Chisholm.

The captain was in the recovery ward, in one of the crosswise Quonset huts. He had an IV drip going and there was an oxygen apparatus on standby. His color was fairly good but he lay there like a boneless doll. His eyes were shut and his eyelids fluttered every ten seconds or so. I stood by the edge of his bed for a full minute and then massaged his right hand. He woke up and struggled to recognize me. Then he did.

"Doctor Andersen," he said in a weak voice. "Thank you."

"You're going to be fine," I said. "Next time, learn to duck. Sir."

He exhaled a long, chemical-smelling breath. "So, I hear you're Superman," he said.

I laughed out loud. "Nurses," I said. "They like to give docs nicknames. If I was Superman it wasn't for very long. Three of the hospital surgeons climbed out of their sickbeds and came back to work, thanks be to God. Should I be calling you Admiral?"

"Not yet," he said with a tired grin. "Listen; I told you to go back to your squadron, right?"

"Yes, sir, you did."

"Do that," he said. "Munda is temporary. We're going to bypass Rabaul. Let all those thousands of Japs up there just wither on the vine. Next stop is the Gilberts. Tarawa. Makin. Then the Marianas. Saipan. Tinian. Guam. You stick with your PT boats. Keep your damned head down. As soon as Halsey decides where the next big hospital will be, I will be in touch."

"Get well, Captain," I said, not wanting him to spill any more secrets. "You pop a fever, say something. Whatever went through your lung was probably dirty. You get a headache, sweats, aching bones: bitch and moan. Okay, sir?"

"Yes, Doctor," he said with a weary smile. "Keep the faith, young man. You're better than you know."

I walked back down the aisle between all the beds. At one level I was scanning the wounded, looking for crises. At another, I felt humbled. There were too many people believing in me, and I was scared to death that, inevitably, I was going to disappoint. Just before the intersection with the other three Quonset huts I spied an empty bed. I stopped, looked around. No one was watching. I sat down on the bed, then stretched out. It was a whole lot better than the OR cot. I closed my eyes and thought: I'll just catch a quick nap. The last image in my mind was of Helen's face when she pulled back. Gotta work on that, I thought. Then I remembered her hand on mine.

I'd had no time for med-school romances back in Durham. None of the residents did. They were either already married or, like me, just so submerged in the program that the only women they saw were surgical staff. My mother was from a prominent family in Raleigh, and she had given up trying to introduce me to "suitable" young women in the capital's social set. I'd had the occasional weekend fling with a couple of the nurse anesthetists, but there'd been no romance involved, just the healthy needs of young professionals. I knew now that the chances of my ever seeing Helen Carpenter again were truly slim. But one could hope. I really liked her.

TWENTY-SEVEN

"'Bout Goddamned time," Bluto grumped when I showed back up on the *Tutuilla*. "What'cha got for bunions?"

"Torpedo tube grease, twice a day. And bigger boots. Japs bombed Munda, tore up the airfield, killed some docs and nurses, amongst others."

"Just their style," he said, and spat into the trash can. They'd given him his own stateroom, and he was a lot cleaner than the last time I'd seen him. "Godless monkeys that they are. You back for real?"

"I think so," I said. "There's a new medical boss in town. Says we're gonna bypass Rabaul; next stop is some islands called the Gilberts?"

"Gilberts-Schmilberts," he snorted. "All these Goddamned islands look the same to me. Palm trees with snipers in 'em. Red dirt. Fucking volcanoes. Waters full'a reefs. Rain and more rain. Bugs. Malaria. Trench foot. Bunions. " He sighed. "One of the Navy guys said it'll be better when we get to Japan. They get snow there in the wintertime."

"That seems a long way from now," I said. "We're still here in the Solomons. That's closer to Australia than Japan proper. What are the boats doing?"

"Usual stuff," he said. "Running errands, like retrieving AWOL squadron doctors from supposedly secure islands. We did manage to ruin some barges up on the north end of this island. Nobody knows if they were comin' or goin', but they're all fish bait now. A destroyer came in afterwards. CO said he watched it all on radar. Wanted to know if we wanted some ice cream."

"Ice cream," I said. "What's ice cream?"

He laughed. Then his face sobered. "The Navy's finally got a mission for us," he said. "I don't know if I wanna do it."

"That's a first," I said. "The Navy wanting *us* to do anything but get out of their way."

He nodded. "They hit Rabaul with a carrier strike," he said. "Then the Army sent bombers. Word is, there were a lot of ships there. They want an MTB to go into Simpson Harbor and see what they actually accomplished."

"That's crazy," I said. "Into Rabaul's harbor? Where they have, what: lebenty-thousand troops? Hundreds of planes? Mines up the ass?"

"Which is why they don't want to send destroyers, or even submarines, for that matter. Supposedly, this is coming from Halsey himself: he wants a couple of MTBs to creep into Simpson Harbor at night for a look-see. He also wants the boats to leave a message. A life raft, with an American flag on it."

"You're kidding.'

"I am not kidding. And that's not all: he wants the boat crews to take a crap in the raft. Toilet paper and everything. Apparently, that's the biggest personal insult you can offer a Jap. To crap in his presence."

I had to laugh. Halsey. God love him. Commander of the entire Central Pacific war effort, responsible for managing the logistics, the armies and the navies, taking the time to deliver an insult to the Jap hordes based at Rabaul.

"And you have volunteers for this crazy thing?"

"Only every boat skipper in the squadron," he said proudly. "I'm gonna lead it."

"Want a doctor along?"

He hesitated. "Yes, and no," he said. "I've been hearing things about you, as a surgeon. They'd kick my ass if I risked taking you along for this ride."

"I'll kick your ass if you don't," I said. "I wield a mean scalpel. Creep up here in the middle of the night, expose something important, slice, slice."

He grinned. "Okay, okay," he said. "It's a dangerous mission. I guess I should have a doctor along for the ride. Just in case."

We looked at each other and started laughing. That excuse would protect him for a good three seconds, at best. But I really wanted to go along. This is what the MTBs were for, doing the outrageous. I knew the medical establishment out here would be outraged, but that same establishment hadn't been all that good to me. And besides: I knew I was good, but not *that* good. If a never-ending siege of surgeries taught you anything, it was that there was an infinite supply of deadly surprises waiting for you when you first picked up that scalpel, starting with the scalpel, if it hadn't been properly sterilized. The truth was that I was in the truly productive phase of an extended surgical residency. Helen had hit right on it: war was the best incubator of medical technology. I think even Garr would have been proud of me for saying that, even if he would never have admitted it. He was probably going to sue me for "mutilating" him, once the war was over.

The MTB mission to Simpson Harbor departed our comfortable nest alongside Mother *Tutuila* two days later at sunset. Two boats, one with Bluto in charge, the other with one of our more experienced skippers, Lieutenant Bruce Ponts, at the helm. Ponts was one of those guys everyone liked. Funny, profane, a hellcat on liberty, but a skipper who'd never abandon you in a pinch and who liked a good brawl. A third boat came along, carrying a deck-load of fifty-five-gallon drums full of high-octane gasoline. Her job was to refuel the two mission boats about twenty miles out from Rabaul and then run for home.

Bluto had briefed the mission in great detail before we left. Simpson Harbor was Fortress Rabaul's harbor. Ashore, there were nearly one hundred *thousand* Japanese troops, five airfields, a vast warren of caves and tunnels, and the remains of the Japanese 2nd Air Fleet, the source of all those Betty bomber attacks we remembered so fondly. The harbor was a natural deepwater haven, surrounded on three sides by impressively active volcanoes. The Japs had seized it early on in the war, fully understanding that it was the logistical key to all the Solomon Islands to the south. And the Solomons were important because they could provide Japan with an unsinkable aircraft carrier that could interdict American supplies going to Australia.

Our recent airstrikes had wrecked the airfields, but we all knew that airfields could be restored in as little as one night. The strikes had also destroyed dozens of Jap planes, and that was the more important result.

"The intel people are telling me that the Japs expect us to invade at Simpson Harbor," Bluto had said. "They've been shrinking their defensive lines throughout New Britain Island in anticipation of this. Some genius decided we'd let them withdraw into their fortress, and then drive right on by. Remember, the objective is Japan itself. We need bases out in the Central Pacific, for both our ships and some new bombers called the B-29. General MacArthur is advancing up the coasts of New Guinea. Admiral Nimitz is advancing up the Central Pacific island chains. The whole idea is that both commands will join up in the Philippines and then take the whole shootin' match to the Japanese home islands."

One of the skippers had raised his hand. "You're telling us that Guadalcanal, New Britain, and now Bougainville—these were just stepping stones?'

Bluto had sat down with a heavy sigh. "I'm telling you that the Pacific Ocean is huge, vast beyond comprehension. The Japs started this shit back in the nineteen-thirties when they invaded China and Manchuria. Then they went through southeast Asia like a dose of salts. They destroyed MacArthur's whole air force and then captured all his troops. They sank British battleships, overran Singapore, and then captured all the British troops. They sank whatever US Navy that was out here except for some subs that had to vamoose all the way to Australia. Singapore, Indochina, China itself, the Dutch East Indies, Malaya, Burma, New Guinea, the Philippines, the Solomons, the Marianas, the Gilberts, and a bunch'a smaller island chains: what they accomplished is nothing short of amazing.

"But: they are seriously overextended. Look at that map over there: the Japanese home islands are tiny in comparison to what they've bitten off, and some of their 'possessions' are literally thousands of miles from their home base. Our strategy is all about rolling up their empire until we end up on their front door. We've pushed them off Guadalcanal. We pushed them off New Georgia. We pushed them off Bougainville. That's how this war is gonna go, boys. We're going to push the little bastards all the way back to their home islands, one island chain at a time, *and* we're only gonna get stronger while they get weaker. Then we're gonna flatten them."

The expedition boats refueled from our version of a German "milch" cow, and then we headed in toward Simpson Harbor. We knew the Japs had laid minefields all around the likely approach routes to the harbor, but they were aimed mainly at US subs. Besides, we were riding wooden boats. The navigation was pretty easy: two of the volcanoes that loomed over Simpson were raising hell, with sheets of red lava flowing down their cinder cones and a continuous rumbling that filled the air—and masked the sound of our engines. We kept to the southwest side of the harbor, hoping that any shipping would then be silhouetted against the lava flows. Our mission, besides the insult, was to determine how much damage had been done to shipping during the carrier strikes. We were looking for ships that had been intentionally grounded to prevent them from sinking, or masts sticking out of the water.

Bluto was taking no unnecessary chances, knowing that there might be Jap patrol boats or even a bad-tempered destroyer loose in the anchorage. He ordered the raft inflated and suitably "anointed," then put it over the side on a sea painter, which we towed as we made our reconnaissance. The docks, piers, and warehouse facilities were seven miles up the five-mile-wide harbor, so we stayed in the lower reaches, where the carrier bombers had worked over a fairly large collection—thirty-six ships in all—of anchored cargo ships, troop transports, oil tankers, and even a couple of cruisers. It was a spine-tingling excursion—two MTBs prowling around the outskirts of the Japs' biggest base south of Truk. Halfway around, a heavy rain squall swept through the harbor, creating an impressive red cloud of steam that bloomed above the volcanoes. Dante would have loved it. But then a big, carbon-arc naval searchlight flared to our north. Bluto took that as an invitation to declare victory and exit the area. We cut loose the stinky raft, with its brave little American flag and noisome cargo, and then we turned toward the sea and Mother *Tutuila*.

We never knew, of course, if the Japs even found the little raft, but word of the expedition quickly spread around the troops mopping up on Bougainville. We had also sighted several wrecks along the coast, which must have pleased the carrier admirals no end. Both boats got back safely. The next morning, however, we learned we were moving. Again.

PART IV

TWENTY-EIGHT

Battleships. The word hung in the air like a verbal time bomb, with everyone in the briefing hut afraid to say anything lest they set it off.

Bluto, now a full commander, sighed and nodded. He didn't look all that well these days. He'd lost some more weight over the past year and a half, as many men in the squadron had. Gone also was the profane bravado of Rendova, when he'd taken a boat out into the harbor to eagerly go head-to-head with a flight of Betty light bombers. He hadn't slept much over the past week during the landings on Leyte Island and his hands were trembling a little from all the caffeine he'd been ingesting just to stay vertical.

"That's the word," he said. "The intel people are saying that a formation of battleships left someplace called Brunei and are headed east. The formation includes the two biggest battleships in the world, the ones with *eighteen*-inch main guns. Battleships, some heavy cruisers, and of course some destroyers."

He nodded to one of the radiomen standing next to a large chart with a sheet covering it. The radioman pulled the sheet aside to reveal a map of the southern half of the Philippine Islands. Bluto walked over to the chart.

"This here is where we are right now, in Leyte Gulf. To the right, or north, is the main island of Luzon. Across and northeast of where we are is the island of Samar. The great bulk of the Jap armies are up on Luzon, from the city of Manila on north. They've been there ever since they chased Dugout Doug out of the Philippines."

He moved to the left, or western part of the chart. "This is where Brunei is. It's the anchorage where the Jap capital ships have been holed up for the past year. It's eight hundred miles from Leyte. If they're going twenty knots, they can be here in two days. Naturally, Halsey and his carriers are gonna hit them as soon as they're within carrier bomber range. He's got six carriers' worth of bombers, so they oughta be able to put a pretty big crimp in their style."

"So, what will *we* be doing," one of the skippers asked, "going somewhere else?"

"Hold your horses, Pancho," Bluto replied, as the nervous laughter in the hut subsided. "I'm gettin' to that."

He moved back to the right side of the chart. "This stretch of water"—he pointed to a gap between the main island of Luzon and the next one down—"this is called the San Bernardino Strait. Intel thinks the Japs are planning to go through San Bernardino two nights from now and then turn south to come here and tear up all the amphibious shipping as well as blasting away at our troops who are already ashore on Leyte. Some of you might remember when they did that to Cactus."

I remembered. It seemed like a hundred years ago. But I vividly remembered it, as did anyone over on Henderson Field who'd lived through it.

"Intel is calling the big battleship formation the Central Force. But, apparently there's a second battleship formation coming, which they're calling the Southern Force. This one has two battleships, some cruisers, etc., and it's supposed to go south of where we are, penetrate the Surigao Strait, which is right here, and then turn north and join the Central Force coming down from the San Bernardino force. The Army would call this a pincers movement."

"How the hell do we know all this?" one of the newer skippers asked.

"The Intel briefer did not share that with me," Bluto said. "But you gotta remember, we've got subs all over the Western Pacific now. We've probably got one, maybe even two sitting off that Jap anchorage at Brunei, keeping tabs on all those big boys. Anyway, Halsey and his carriers are supposed to take care of the Central Force. We will be part of a blocking force that's being put together to make sure that those two battlewagons in the Southern Force never get through to Leyte Gulf. Halsey is gonna go after the main force with carrier air. Admiral Oldendorf is gonna head up the defense of the Surigao Strait. He's the admiral who's got all those old battleships they raised up from Pearl Harbor. You've seen 'em— those big gray shapes way out there lobbing fourteen-inch shells into the landing zones for the past eighteen months?"

Everyone nodded. That was a good description. Those elderly dreadnoughts sat ten miles out there in the smoke and the mist, barely visible until their main battery muzzle-flashes revealed their presence.

He asked the radioman to put up a second chart.

"This is a chart of the Surigao Strait, which cuts between the bottom half of Leyte Island and an island called Dinagat. The Southern Force is supposed to come into the strait right here, next to Panaon Island, sometime after midnight two days from now, then turn left and come toward Leyte. Oldendorf's blocking force will consist of four layers. The first layer is us—MTBs hiding along the coves of Panaon Island, right—here. We'll launch torpedo attacks against the entire formation—two battleships, three heavy cruisers, two light cruisers, and four or more destroyers. We're gonna take the entire squadron in—all sixteen boats."

"Once we attack, we're supposed to get out of the Jap formation any way we can and regroup behind them, just to the west of Panaon Island. That's because two of our destroyer squadrons will be coming down from the northern end of the Surigao Strait, one squadron on each side of the strait, for a coordinated torpedo attack. Once they get done, they'll get out of the way and then the four heavy cruisers stretched across the strait will get their turn. And once the cruisers open up, the battleships, lined up above them at the top of the strait, will start shooting. I think there's gonna be six of 'em, lined up right *here* across the top of the strait, shooting fourteen- and even sixteen-inch shells under radar control."

There were quiet mutters of "Jee-zus" and "God*damn*" throughout the briefing room.

"Like I said, some of those battleships are the ones the Japs sank at Pearl," Bluto continued. "They were raised, repaired, modernized, and sent out here to provide gunfire support for all these invasions we've been doing. This will be their one and only opportunity to get revenge for Pearl. Think about that."

One of the skippers raised his hand with a question. "If we have that much firepower blocking this strait, what the hell are *we* doing there?"

Bluto took a moment to light up a cigarette. "Well," he said. "Our chances of actually hurting those big boys are pretty slim. But: they're gonna come into the strait not knowing anything about what's waiting for them. At one, two in the morning. Suddenly there's gonna be a bunch of us spitkits roaring at them, launching torpedoes and gunning their bridge windows, which means they'll probably have to break formation, turn left, turn right, speed up, slow down—while they swat us out of their way. And while they're doing that and then reforming, about twenty destroyers will be coming at them from both sides of the strait, each carrying ten torpedoes."

"So, we're what—the distraction?"

"Pretty much," Bluto replied. "And who the hell knows—sixteen boats, four fish each—one of us might get lucky. But our main objective is to rattle the hell out of 'em. If nothing else, they'll realize that the Americans know they're coming, and that's not exactly gonna be confidence-building news."

Then he got that familiar gleam in his eyes. "This'll probably be the last time we're going to get to be torpedo boats and go up against something bigger than a goddamned barge. There's a reason the whole Jap battle fleet—not their carriers, but their big gunships—have been anchored in Brunei Bay, because without air cover, they're just targets. You heard about what the flyboys are calling the Marianas Turkey Shoot—four, five hundred Jap planes shot down in two days? Just east of here? We didn't get their carriers, too, but it hardly matters. What's a carrier without planes and pilots? Just another target."

He looked around the room, searching, I think, for any faces showing apprehension about this mission. "Listen," he said. "Anybody doesn't want to go out on this little adventure, come see me, no questions asked. That said, *I'd* personally hate to go back home one day after this war is over and admit that I bowed out of what's probably going to be the last time in history that battleships duke it out."

He gave them a moment to absorb his offer, and then announced that Deacon was going to walk through the tactical arrangements, initial station assignments, comms, and the search-and-rescue plan.

That was my signal to ease my way out of the ops hut. Bluto went back to his desk and sat down to finish his cigarette while the hut full of junior officers tried to be brave as they absorbed the enormity of the plan. The Seabees had come ashore for two days as soon as the Army infantry had pushed the Japs back five miles. The amphibious navy had figured out how to ship Quonset huts in such a fashion that the Seabees could erect them in a few hours, so now there were five huts positioned under the tree canopy along the captured Tacloban Airfield. The "Toot" was anchored offshore about a half mile away with our boats riding to boat booms on both sides. The airfield itself was ringed with 90 mm AA gun emplacements, manned by a combination of Filipino resistance fighters and Army guys. After taking Guam in the Marianas, the Navy had decided to reinstall torpedo tubes on most of the boats, since the Philippine invasion would put the whole fleet back within range of the remaining Japanese battle fleet. An ammo ship was due in the next morning to bring torpedoes to the *Tutuila*.

The briefing hut was Bluto's headquarters and, as usual, included a radio room and a place for him to sleep. Another hut provided sleeping quarters for the skippers, with the crews staying out with the boats and using *Tutuila* for housekeeping. The third hut was a bare-bones sick bay, where Higgins, two hospitalmen, and I hung out. We'd dealt with overflow casualties from the airfield's medical station who needed urgent attention before being boated out to one of the *two* hospital ships anchored offshore, along with dozens of other support ships. MacArthur had put nearly 200,000 troops ashore over the past few days, and they had driven the Jap defenders back toward the big volcanic ridge behind the airfield. He intended to surround them with further landings to the south and north and force them into the sea on the western side of Leyte Island.

A lot had changed since those frantic days on Cactus, which now was just a sad blood-soaked backwater almost 3,000 miles to the south. Admiral Nimitz and General MacArthur had agreed to pursue parallel advances in both the southwest Pacific areas and the so-called Central Pacific areas. MacArthur had cleaned the Japs out of New Guinea and the western parts of New Britain, home to Rabaul, where thousands of Japs were starving as the war essentially passed them by and American submarines cut off all supplies.

The Central Pacific campaign, and what was now being called The Big Blue Fleet, had endured some of the most God-awful fighting of the war for over a year as they swept the Japs out of a series of islands whose names would reverberate down through Marine Corps history: Tarawa, Tinian, Saipan, Guam, Makin, and now, Leyte. Both claws of this vast strategic pincer were closing in on the Philippines,

where victory would mean the destruction of the last really large
(100,000) Japanese army deployed outside of the home islands, and,
of course, it would fulfill MacArthur's dramatic promise to return.
Sometimes, when watching our own propaganda newsreels, it wasn't
clear which was the more important mission.

I was still the MTB squadron doctor, but no longer doing
much in the way of surgery. Rear Admiral Chisholm's promise of
an eventual summons to a big top one day never materialized. It
wasn't until we took Guam in July that I had finally found out why.
Our squadron had been summoned to Guam after that island was
declared mostly secure. We were currently based in a remote cove
away from the tiny port of Agana, now the main logistical point
of entry. We were employed in our usual post-landing operations,
mostly inserting Marine patrols who were scouring the higher
hills, looking for Jap stragglers. The Navy had set up a fairly large
field hospital a few miles from the port. The Seabees were then
ordered to build an actual hospital right next to it, because Guam
was apparently going to become a central staging point for the two
campaigns: the push on the Philippines, and a strategic bombing
campaign by the B-29s against Japan itself. The Seabees had carved
out a large airbase at the north end of the island for that mission.
The B-29 had a combat range of 4,100 miles, and Tokyo, itself, was
"only" 1,500 miles from Guam. There were even rumors that Admiral Nimitz was going to move his headquarters to Guam.

Three weeks after the major fighting was over, I went up to that
hospital. Basically, I was looking for work, not having much to do
now that Guam was ours. We'd had plenty of action during the
approach to the Marianas, of which Guam was a part. Now, however, we'd been told to refit and train in anticipation of going to the
Philippines "soon." As usual, nobody told the medical people very
much about planned operations. Guam was where we'd learned
that the boats were being refitted with torpedo tubes.

I was surprised to find that the hospital wasn't very busy, either.

The casualties from the invasion fighting had long since been evacuated to hospital ships and then taken back to Pearl. There was a
small staff at the field hospital who were busy supervising the Seabees as they constructed a real, bricks-and-mortar hospital building
in anticipation of the serious fighting yet to come. Everyone understood that, as tough as the island campaign had been, an invasion of
Japan itself would be quite the undertaking.

I'd wandered around the field hospital without introducing myself. I was just another doc in khakis admiring the speed at which
the Seabees were getting that building up. I finally ended up in the
mess tent around lunchtime. The food on offer was an improvement from those days in the Solomons where variations on SPAM,
captured Jap rice rations, and hot sauce were the only choices. I
was finishing a cup of coffee when three Navy Medical Corps full
commanders came into the tent, got their lunches, and sat down
two tables away. Other people were wandering in and out ran-
domly, including some dust-covered Seabees who'd discovered the
mess tent. The threesome started talking about the construction
project and some of the staffing problems they were anticipating.
One mentioned a young surgeon they'd had to send back to the
states for overstepping his qualifications during the height of the
fighting for Guam.

"He was a decent-enough surgeon," one of them said. "Although
he'd only been licensed for two years before coming out here.
Problem was he decided to do a major abdominal repair on his own
when the protocol called for a team. One of the nurses pointed that
out. He yelled at her and then proceeded, but ended up making a
hash of it."

"The patient make it?"

"Nope," the first doc said. "Major bleed, not enough hands. Guy
died on the table. He was pretty badly wounded, but still..."

The third doc, who looked older than the other two, nodded.
"We had a guy like that in late forty-two, back in the Solomons. I

was at Nouméa, and we kept hearing stories about a third-year resident surgeon on leave from Duke Medical doing major procedures
at the field hospital on Guadalcanal, and then later, over on Tulagi.
Doing stuff way beyond his formal training, and the strange thing, he
was apparently doing it with the approval of the local chief surgeons.
Some of the surgeons began calling him Superman."

"So he was that good?"

"Well, hell, I don't know. Must have been to get that nickname,
but still…Anyway, the rumors persisted, and finally, Admiral
Chisholm—he was still a captain then—decided to go have a look
in conjunction with a trip he was making to Cactus, New Georgia,
and Munda. He took an experienced surgeon with him. They interviewed this Superman guy and then they all got caught in an air
raid on the hospital. Chisholm was wounded, and the SMO there,
a grouchy old-timer named Holland Fraser Whitman Garr, if you
can believe it, was really beat-up. This resident guy ended up operating on both of them because the staff docs had been injured by a
building collapse or something. Chisholm recovered, but Garr had
to have an arm *and* an eye removed. He lived but later claimed the
resident should never have done that, and that a more experienced
cutter would have found a way around the two amputations."

"Well, now, that's a tough call to make from a distance isn't it?"
one of the other doctors said. "You don't amputate for the fun of
it. This Garr guy probably had an arm hanging by its skin or the
threat of gangrene. Sounds like the resident didn't have anybody
else to turn to, right?"

"Well, yeah, and I wasn't there, so I know I shouldn't judge," the
older doc said. "But I remember Chisholm coming back to Nouméa
after he'd recuperated from surgery at Munda. He was still convalescing when he insisted on bringing in the hospital department
heads and briefing them on his various findings up at the front. One
of the things on his list was that he'd taken care of the Superman
problem. Said he'd blown some smoke up his ass and then told him

to go back to his boat squadron and wait for his casting call, which, of course, Chisholm had no intention of ever making. He did say that the guy was a damned good surgeon, but no hospital would let the guy operate independently, and so there was no point in pulling him from his squadron."

"So, where's this 'Superman' guy now?"

"Who the hell knows," the older doc said. "Garr was medically retired, which some folks thought was a blessing, and the resident is back in the medical weeds."

The other two docs shook their heads. Then another, older doc came in, nodded to the threesome, and walked over to the chow line. The guy who'd been telling the story nudged the other two and said, "*That's* who everybody's saying will be the CO once this hospital gets built."

I'd stopped listening by then, hoping that my red face wasn't showing. But I'd finally found out why I never got the call. Chisholm, now the head honcho of Navy medicine in the Central Pacific theater, had masterfully defused my indignation at Garr's accusations by promising he'd fix the situation. And he had—he'd put an end to my brief career as a surgeon and banished me to the sidelines, where the Navy felt the PT boats belonged anyway. We were nothing but hooligans, after all.

I should have known, although it was possible that I'd been a bit too full of myself to not anticipate Chisholm's decision. I wasn't the only one pushed out of the limelight, though, as the Navy and Marines clawed their way up the Central Pacific in one bloody clash after another. The MTBs had less and less to do in terms of mixing it up with Japanese fleet units. For one thing, the Japanese fleet hadn't been much in evidence as Nimitz's plan to roll up their island conquests played out across the Central Pacific. Some of the landings created grotesque casualty counts, like Saipan and Tarawa, but there were no more Jap destroyers escorting reinforcement barges or trying to extract defeated garrisons from those islands.

We'd participated in every one of the landings, but our mission was to do everything we could to help the grunts ashore, as opposed to going out to torpedo Jap cruisers and destroyers. It was telling that we didn't even show up on one of these island invasions until the Marines were already ashore and grappling with an enemy that was basically trapped, having been abandoned and told to fight to the death by their commanders in Tokyo, and which is exactly what they did.

I'd become increasingly bored with only the routine injuries and illnesses of life in the tropics to deal with. The island invasion casualties were being whisked directly to hospital ships purpose-built for the job, and I, of course, was not going to get invited aboard one of them as long as Admiral Chisholm was in charge. So, I started to go out on the boats, using the excuse that something just might happen that would require immediate medical attention. Bluto knew better, but he was, as always, amenable; I suspect he was as bored as I was with what seemed like menial missions compared to the heady days of watching battleships fight off Savo Island. I learned how to drive the boats, work out a torpedo-firing solution, interpret a radar picture, and actually operate all the various guns on board. On two occasions it turned out to be fortuitous that I was aboard when we picked up some downed naval aviators who were pretty badly injured. When we pulled alongside one of the hospital ships for transfer, and the ship's hospitalmen came down the accommodation ladder to get them, the boat skipper told them that I was a doctor. The hospitalmen nodded politely and then got the wounded men back up the ladder. I'd often wondered after that if they'd known who I was.

But now we were finally *in* the Philippines. Our trusty mothership *Tutuila* had returned with a cargo of torpedo tubes, which she then reinstalled on all the boats while we were still on Guam. Torpedo tubes had to mean that somebody, however reluctantly, anticipated that the boats were soon going to face the Imperial Japanese

Navy again. We'd finally found out where and when at this morning's briefing. It was only sixty-five miles from our shore base near Tacloban Airfield to the bottom of Leyte Island. The Southern Force was expected two nights from now, so we'd probably transit down to Panaon Island tonight. There was still the threat of Jap bombers during daylight, although the Turkey Shoot had reduced that threat significantly. I assumed *Tutuila* would follow us down, because we'd need fuel both before and after whatever happened in the strait.

Higgins and I decided to transit in separate boats in case we got jumped on the way to Panaon Island. We left the two hospitalmen at our tiny sick bay hut near Tacloban. Bluto informed me that none of the skippers had taken him up on his offer to stay behind. He hadn't given them much time to stew about it; they spent the afternoon getting their boats ready for the transit and loading food, gas, and other supplies. He'd brought them all back to the briefing hut to conduct a refresher course in how to shoot torpedoes. Higgins and I packed battle dressings, pain-control medications, and a bare-bones surgical kit. If any of these things became necessary, they'd have to find an island somewhere to put us ashore; a PT boat had no room for casualty care beyond immediate bandaging. We left just after sunset and headed south along the east coast of Leyte Island. The crew of my boat was subdued, with none of the usual going-out-on-patrol banter and jokes.

Battleships. That was a sobering prospect.

One of the Army sergeants who'd been helping us with truck transportation shook his head when he heard what we were going up against.

"You're brave, I'll give you that," he said. "Not very bright, I reckon, but certainly brave."

TWENTY-NINE

The transit was uneventful thanks to good atmospherics for our radars, which made navigation a lot easier. The night was black as ink and the atmosphere felt like it was loading itself up for some kind of obnoxious weather. It was the beginning of typhoon season, after all. The humidity was intense and the temperature hovered at eighty-five degrees. Our sixteen boats anchored off a little islet. Bluto set up a rotating radar watch among three boats; the rest of us got some sleep. The waters were flat calm, almost as if the sea itself knew that something momentous was about to happen.

Tutuila showed up at dawn and immediately refueled the boats. Crews took turns going aboard our "tender" for a hot meal. Bluto called a meeting of the skippers on board at around noon. There was a message in from Halsey that his carriers had made several strikes against the Central Force and had even sunk one of the super-battleships. The rest of the force, many with bomb and torpedo damage, had been seen turning around and heading back west. We wondered if that meant we were off the hook, but then a second message came in, this time from Admiral Oldendorf, addressed to all units involved in blocking the Surigao Strait. The Southern Force had *not* been sighted by Halsey's aircraft. It was possible, even probable, that they, too, had turned around, since it was supposed to be a coordinated pincer movement. Nevertheless, our big boys were moving into position across the northern end of the strait and all other units were directed to take previously assigned stations, just in case the second Jap formation was still coming on.

Bluto then laid out his final battle plan. Two of our boats would be stationed at the southwest corner of Panaon Island as radar pickets. His command boat would take station just around the corner, on the south side of Panaon, a few miles from the pickets. All the other boats would spread out in a rough line abreast on either side of the command boat at a distance of 500 yards. When the lead ships of the Jap formation crossed a line of bearing 230 degrees true from Panaon, he would give the execute order. All the boats except his would come to full power and head in, firing torpedoes when within 2,000 yards of any suitable target.

"If possible, run through the Jap formation. Bob and weave as soon as they start shooting, but keep going if you can. Run right in front of them or right behind them and strafe 'em wherever you can with your guns. I'll be right behind you and I'll be shooting illume rounds from my 81 mm. They'll turn on their searchlights as soon as we're spotted, but the illume rounds ought to spook 'em. To the Jap navy, flares popping in the sky means cruisers are out there. They'll start maneuvering, so there's no formal attack plan— cowboys and Indians, just like in the old days."

"Won't those illume rounds light us up as well as the Japs?" one skipper asked.

"The Japs' searchlights will do that anyway. I'll be shooting the illume rounds to pop at three thousand feet, which will give our oncoming destroyers a visual to home in on. Now: understand this— just before I transmit the execute signal, I'll inform the destroyer squadrons that we're going in. They will execute their own plan right then. So, once we've had enough fun inside the Jap formation, everybody run west toward the *back* of the Jap formation. In other words, don't linger. We don't want to be there when our tin cans come in, because they'll be shooting at anything that's moving and they can't distinguish us from the Japs."

"With cruisers *and* destroyers shooting at us, I think we'll be lucky to make one pass," another skipper said.

"Don't forget the battleships," one wag pointed out.

"That's all the admiral is expecting," Bluto said. "Jump 'em, Hooligan style, raise a bunch'a hell, and then run for cover. While they're sorting out their formation and changing their skivvies, our tin cans will come in out of the dark and hit 'em from both sides of the straits with a shit-pot full of torpedoes. By then we need to be gone. The eventual join-up point is where we're anchored now."

"What if we get hit?" someone asked.

"Sound off on the radio and then deal with your damage. If your boat goes down and you gotta swim for it, stick together in the water. We'll all be out looking for you, so make sure your vests have those little flashlights. You can turn 'em on after about thirty minutes, because by then all those Goddamned Japs oughta be dead."

God willing, I thought, but there was a better than even chance that we might be, too. Battleships, for Chrissakes.

"We'll go on station at twenty-one hundred," Bluto said. "After that, it'll be hurry up and wait for the pickets to squeak." He paused for a moment. "Just like old times in the Slot."

Deacon and two skippers were nodding. That's when I realized that the rest of them had never even *seen* the Slot. I'd left Higgins in the boat he'd come down on, so we met to make sure we each had about the same amount of stuff. Then we went aboard *Tutuila* for some chow. One of the hospitalmen in her sick bay asked if he could come along for the big show. He'd gone in with the First Marines at Guadalcanal and said he was bored out of his ever-loving mind on *Tutuila*. We told him to go see Deacon for a boat assignment.

After chow I got one of the boats to take me around to each of the other boats to make sure everyone was okay and also to hold a little school-call on emergency actions for wounded personnel. It was dark by the time I made my "rounds," so the boat dropped me off on Bluto's command boat. Like everyone else, I tried to get some sleep, but it was just too hot and sweaty, even above-deck. Sleeping down below was out of the question. The usual night breeze had not materialized. Bluto finally showed up, courtesy of one of *Tutuila*'s boats, at around 2000. He'd stayed aboard *Tutuila* because her radio shack maintained our communications guard. He didn't want to miss any last-minute-change orders from Oldendorf, who by now should have been twelve miles or so up the strait from our station, overseeing a line of six battleships: *West Virginia, Maryland, Mississippi, Tennessee, California,* and *Pennsylvania.* The cruisers should be lining up at the ten-mile point, and two squadrons of destroyers were probably already loitering along both sides of the strait at around six miles from us.

At 2100 all the boats heaved up their anchors, lit off one engine, and rumbled out to the other side of Panaon Island. Once Bluto was satisfied that *he* was where he needed to be, he turned on the command boat's stern light for one minute. That was the signal for the other boats to spread out on either side. We weren't trying for any sort of precise formation, and once the boats had opened out, everyone turned his engine off and we just drifted. With no wind and a flat-calm sea, the boats stayed pretty much wherever they shut down.

And then it was hurry up and wait.

THIRTY

I was dozing when the initial report finally came in.

"Radar contacts, bearing two-eight-zero, range twelve miles and closing. Composition many."

"Track and report," Bluto replied. Then he gave the order for all the boats to light off. All around us big marine engines cranked up, creating clouds of smoke in the night. Our own boat frequency was different from the battle-line ships, meaning Bluto had to switch to our second radio so he could come up on the HF frequency of the main battleship force. He then reported the contacts to Oldendorf's flagship. The cruisers and destroyers gathered up in the strait copied that frequency, so everyone should have been alerted that the Southern Force *was* coming on after all.

Our radar pickets now both had contact on what was headed for Surigao Strait at an estimated speed of twenty knots. Bluto ordered both of them to rejoin the MTB attack force by coming around the back side of Panaon Island. I looked at my watch. It was just after midnight. Bluto told our boat's radar operator to stop his cursor on 230 and report when he got contact and then when the lead Jap ships crossed that bearing.

Engines were rumbling all around us. Clouds of engine exhaust drifted across our loose formation even though we were a quarter mile from the nearest boats. The approaching Japanese formation would stay in the radar shadow of Panaon Island until just about the last moment. One of the picket boats came up on our tactical net and reported that there appeared to be two columns of ships, with one very large radar contact in each column. We waited. If they were doing twenty knots, they should appear around the southern tip of Panaon in about thirty minutes. They didn't, which meant they'd slowed down. Had one of them intercepted our radio transmissions? Or detected us? We'd been told the Japs had radar now, but that it wasn't very good.

Bluto ordered his crew to roust out a dozen illumination rounds for the mortar and stack them right next to the tube. "When I give the order," he said, "fire them all, one after another."

I volunteered to hand the individual rounds to the gunner so that we didn't have to leave a gun unmanned.

"Radar contact," the operator down below announced. "Bearing two-four-seven."

The double-ratchet sound of 50-cal machine guns being chambered echoed through the darkness. The gunner picked up the first 81mm round and pulled the safety pin on the nose. I could just barely make out the little yellow packs of high explosive taped to the tail.

"Bearing two-four-zero."

Another minute passed.

"Bearing, mark! Two-three-three."

"Execute," Bluto said into his handset, then hung it back up. All around us the roar of engines erupted as the boats headed out into the strait. Bluto waited until he could see wakes out in front of him, and then I was sent ass over teakettle to the deck as our boat accelerated. I'd forgotten to hold on.

Now there was a breeze as the boat came up on the step and began planing at about thirty-five knots. I could no longer see any of the other boats, but I could see the torpedomen setting switches on their tubes and then cranking them out ten degrees for launch. I stayed down on the deck just below the conning station, right next to the mortar, tightened my life jacket straps, and clamped a steel helmet on my head.

The Japs were absolutely *not* asleep at the switch. We'd closed in at top speed for no more than a minute before the first searchlight blazed in our direction. Bluto yelled for the mortar gunner to commence firing. He dropped in the first round, which thumped away. I pulled the pin on the next one and handed it to him. He dropped that one in and was reaching for the third when the first shells came howling out of the night, passing so close overhead that I could actually feel them before they exploded behind us in red-tinged fountains. And then a truly amazing searchlight came on and began traversing the waters ahead of us. This was a carbon-arc light, blue-white in intensity, and much bigger than what we were used to from destroyers. It reminded me of the searchlights that Hollywood used at their premieres. Now I could actually see some of the other boats, or at least their wakes, as they charged in among the great black shapes ahead of us.

I dropped the next mortar round as Bluto made a high-speed dodging turn just in time to evade a trio of shell bursts on our port side. The gunner scrambled to pick it up and dropped it in the tube. I'd forgotten to pull the pin so that one was wasted, but by now flares were popping in the sky. Then all of our machine guns opened up, and I caught a glimpse of a pretty big ship flashing by us as our tracers stitched the night, searching for their bridge windows and the topside AA gunners. One of the torpedomen shouted "Stand by!" I looked ahead and saw the outline of a very big ship with a huge pagoda superstructure dead ahead. There were flashes of red light all along her side as she came on.

"Launch, Godammit!" Bluto yelled.

All four of our torpedoes whooshed out of their tubes. The gunner slapped his hand on my helmet.

Rounds. He needed rounds.

I picked up the next mortar round, pulled the pin this time, and passed it to him. He dropped it into the tube and then we were both thrown to the deck as Bluto turned hard right to dash down the port side of the battleship, for that's what it had to be. I hit my head on something and felt a sharp pain in the top of my skull, even with the helmet on. The mortar fired but we were heeling at such an angle that the round went directly into the superstructure of the ship and burst in a shower of fire. I was thunderstruck for a moment as I took in the size of that ship, no more than a hundred yards away from us, sliding through the dark sea like a mountain of black steel and with what seemed like a hundred small guns firing in our direction. Then we were past it and turning again, everyone just hanging on as we felt the bottom of the boat bouncing sideways in the turn until finally, she gained traction and bolted out into the darkness.

I looked behind us and saw a maelstrom of gunfire, explosions in the water, and tracer fire slashing everywhere. Our own guns had gone silent as Bluto executed a wide turn back toward the formation, which is when we saw several familiar-looking gasoline fires low down on the water. We'd gotten clear, but it looked like some of our boats had not. I didn't see any ships burning, just black shapes headed away from us, up the strait, their wakes painted orange by the burning PT boats behind them.

Bluto slowed down. I had this terrible feeling it had all been for nothing, but then one of the smaller Jap ships, probably a destroyer, blew up in a white-hot fireball, revealing the entire Jap formation like a flash-camera as she broke in two. And then the remainder of the first destroyer squadron's torpedoes began to arrive, with at least two and possibly even three hitting the leading battleship, which spouted fire down one side.

Bluto slowed even more because we were spectators now as the approaching destroyers ran at the Jap formation, firing five-inch guns and drawing return fire from five-, six-, and eight-inch guns. Our mission had been to disrupt and distract the Japs; the destroyers did a much better job as we saw Jap cruisers suddenly turning sideways and their own destroyers trying to get out of the bigger ships' way. I saw what looked like one of their cruisers colliding with another, but there was so much noise and so many gun-flashes that I probably imagined it. As we watched we suddenly saw a torpedo coming straight at us from the melee up ahead. Bluto didn't even have time to move the throttles before the damned thing buzzed right underneath us and sped off into the night. Then star shells began to pop above the madly maneuvering ships, which were some five miles from us now, as the first American destroyer squadron cleared away and the second one came in, running down the wakes of their own torpedo salvo, which claimed another Jap destroyer and yet another hit on the bigger of the two battleships.

Bluto turned again, this time back toward Panaon Island and the numerous gasoline fires still flickering out there. One of the gunners yelled: "Hey, look!" He was pointing up into the sky, where small *things*, glowing dark red, were descending on the Jap formation. None of us had ever seen battleship projectiles before, and certainly not near the receiving end, but they were unmistakable when they went off all around the two Jap battleships, raising shell-splashes that rose as high as those pagoda towers. They were followed by more, many more glowing objects that came down out of the sky and blasted entire chunks off their targets, or disappeared into their hull with a small flash, followed by a booming explosion deep within the battlewagon's hull. We were transfixed by the carnage taking place in front of us. Then one of the battleships blew up, broke into two halves, and then disappeared.

Bluto yelled at us to look for survivors, bringing us back to the reality of what happens when PT boats go up against the massed fire of cruisers and destroyers. We stopped next to a patch of flaming gasoline, and then Bluto maneuvered the boat slowly to put the fire between us and any surviving Jap ships so as not to be silhouetted. We then started looking for swimmers, but found none in this patch of gasoline, whose fumes stung our eyes. He then headed for another patch some five hundred yards distant, and this time we recovered four men. All four were wounded and unable to get themselves aboard. Two of our gunners went over the side to bring them to the gunwales and help lift them up to the deck. I was tending to the first one aboard when a rifle shot rang out, followed by another, as the rear gunner drove off a shark.

The rifle shots produced some shouts from the darkness closer to Panaon Island, so we drove over there and found an entire crew hanging on to the bottom of their boat, which had overturned during the battle. At that point our radar operator reported a contact closing on us, which turned out to be one of our boats. Bluto decided we'd form a two-boat search line to go look for more survivors. All the shooting had stopped up in the strait, which I hoped meant that Bluto's prediction had come true. I had an increasingly bad headache as I tended to the wounded out on deck as best I could. One man sat up suddenly, puffed out his cheeks as if he was going to vomit, and then collapsed, unleashing a river of blood from his mouth as he died. Bluto ordered the crew to put the man's corpse over the side and then resume looking for other men in the water.

By dawn we had thirty-five survivors stuffed aboard our two boats. Five boats had rejoined us just before sunrise, reappearing from the coves of Panaon. Seven out of sixteen; it had been a bad night, although what had happened to the Japs seemed even worse. We laid alongside *Tutuila,* which had spent the night tucked into the back side of Panaon, and got our wounded into her sick bay where I could do a much better job. Bluto radioed in his report and requested a destroyer to come take off our most seriously wounded. The flagship did not respond to that request, but then, five minutes later, reported that a Jap battleship force was in Leyte Gulf attacking the invasion shipping.

We stared at each other in astonishment. That's when Bluto saw the two holes in my helmet, one on each side. "Doc?" he said. "You okay?"

I couldn't figure out what had prompted that question until he came over and tried to get my steel helmet off. One of the crewmen moved over and undid the chin strap, but the helmet seemed stuck on my head. When they managed to pry it off there was an ugly sucking sound and then a pretty big blood clot slid down my cheek. The crewman stared at the helmet; there was an entry hole on one side and a clear exit hole on the other, way up at the top of the rounded steel. I felt my head and discovered a sticky mass of bloody hair running from one side of my head to the other in a straight line. Bluto swore and sent for soap and water. I remained seated on the front of the console, wincing when the soapy water hit that line. It didn't help my headache much, either. I gobbled two APC tablets while they bandaged my head.

Bluto ordered the surviving boats to join up with *Tutuila* and refuel and then our much-diminished squadron headed back toward Leyte Gulf at twenty-five knots. No one had any torpedoes left, but if Jap battleships were shooting up the Leyte Gulf landing area the boats would be needed, if only to pick up survivors. I stayed aboard *Tutuila* with the rest of the wounded, so I ended up being the only one in the squadron who got breakfast.

THIRTY-ONE

One more man died of his wounds as *Tutuila* headed back toward Leyte Gulf. We buried him at sea with a small ceremony. There was a hospital ship waiting when *Tutuila* finally pulled into the landing area, so we went directly alongside the much bigger ship, which was anchored a mile offshore. I supervised the transfer of the casualties from *Tutuila* to the hospital ship. I'd gotten used to my head-scarf bandage although there was a thin hot line of fiery pain where the bullet had grazed my skull. Thank God for the helmet.

When I came back topside from accompanying the wounded to the triage area, *Tutuila* was pulling away. Something urgent must have come up, which probably involved Bluto and his remaining hooligans needing fuel. For a moment I didn't know what to do or where to go, which is when I realized I was *probably* exhausted. The hospital ship had a long promenade deck filled with reclining deck chairs. I walked past recuperating sailors until I found an empty chair. I sat down, pushed the back all the way down, and closed my eyes. The warm tropical sun for once felt wonderful, although the headache seemed to be getting worse. Thankfully, I fell asleep, to the accompaniment of visions of alien ships being torn asunder.

When I came to, I was in a brightly lit hospital ward. My "scarf bandage" had been replaced by a complex set of bandages that completely swathed my head. An IV set was stuck into the back of my right wrist and I stared at the tiny beads of liquid dropping into the tube for a minute as I tried to gather my wits. The headache was still there but numbed by some kind of painkiller. Those white lights hurt my eyes, so I closed them and tried to drift back off to sleep.

"You back with us, Doctor?" a female voice asked, and then I felt a soft hand pick up my other wrist to get a pulse.

"No," I said, apropos of nothing.

She giggled and then told me to open my eyes.

"Hurts to do that," I replied, but then I did what she asked. She was young, impossibly young, I thought, but she was wearing the uniform of a registered nurse.

"No surprise there, Doctor Andersen," she said. "You have a linear skull fracture going across the top of your cranium."

"Hairline fracture?" I asked.

"No, Doctor. Not huge, but not hairline, either. The surgeons cleaned it up, put some staples in, and sutured the scalp."

"I thought the brain couldn't feel pain," I said, somewhat stupidly. My brain hadn't been injured. Or had it?

"Correct, but the skull absolutely can. You'll have a groove across the top of your skull once it heals. Now: they've asked me to check motor functions. Can you move your extremities?"

We went through a hands, fingers, and feet check. Everything moved when commanded to do so. Then I tried to move my head. My head informed me that was a bad idea. She saw me wince.

"Yeah," she said. "We're going to put you in a neck brace. There's nothing wrong with your neck but that bullet or whatever it was did a number on your skull-bone. Did a sniper get you?"

"Actually, I think a Jap battleship got me. Down in Surigao Strait."

The blank look on her face told me that the hospital staff didn't know much about what had been going on for the past forty-eight hours. Then a familiar female voice spoke up from behind the nurse. "Told you about that kryptonite, but would you listen? No, you would not."

I looked over the nurse's shoulder to find Helen Carpenter smiling down at me. I didn't remember anything about kryptonite, but I was very glad to see her. She tapped the young nurse on the shoulder and then traded places with her.

I closed my eyes again, even though I wanted to keep them open. Whatever was coming down that IV was really working now. "I need to get back to the squadron," I said, finally. "Chief Higgins can manage my wound and the bandages."

She squeezed my other hand, the one without an IV line. "Your squadron days are over, there, Superman," she said quietly. "We're one day out of Leyte and on our way to Guam. Your hooligans will be all right."

That got my eyes open, although my eyelids felt like they were made of lead. "We're *what?*" I asked.

"You're on the hospital ship *Refuge*. She's taking wounded from the Leyte invasion and some from the carrier *Princeton*. We'll stop at Guam, and then we're bound for Pearl."

"But I can't just leave," I said.

She touched the top of my head with the tip of one finger. Lightning ensued. "Yes, you can. And will. I do believe your war is over, Doctor Lincoln Andersen. It's not like you didn't contribute."

My war was over? My brain tried to grapple with that idea. I vaguely saw her reach up to the IV bottle, and then I got my wish. My eyes closed like a trap and everything got better.

THIRTY-TWO

She came to see me a day later. My head had been feeling better until they had to change the bandage. Part of that change involved peeling the final layer of gauze off the miniature Grand Canyon running across my scalp. Apparently, I'd reacted badly, so I'd been given another round of whatever came in those IV bottles with the green stripe down the side. I knew what that stuff was, but for the life of me, I could *not* dredge up the clinical name.

"How're you feeling?" she asked.

"Weary," I said. "Which, considering I've just been lying here, doesn't make a lot of sense."

She nodded. "I talked to the senior neurosurgeon this morning about your case," she said. "There might be more damage than they first thought. Something about hydrostatic shock, caused by a piece of metal moving across the top of your brain at twice the speed of sound. Can you raise your right arm?"

"Yes," I said, and then lifted my right forearm into the air.

"Now," she said. "Make a fist."

I made a fist, except I didn't. My fingers curled in but then stopped well short of a real fist.

"What the hell," I muttered. For the first time I felt a tinge of fear about my head wound. I think she saw my reaction.

"Look," she said. "I've got an interesting job aboard this ship. I'm called the Patient Coordinator. That title means I go through the wards and evaluate each patient as to the *consequences* of his injury. Not the current medical situation, but what their wounds mean in terms of returning to service. Or not."

She let that sink in for a moment, then continued. "The docs have the last say, of course, but my job is to make recommendations as to what I'm seeing when those scary white-coats are not standing around some badly hurt GI."

"I thought you'd be the head nurse," I said. "Like at Munda."

She smiled. "I'm a full commander now in the Navy Nurse Corps. I'm actually senior to the head nurse in the great scheme of things. But that's not important."

"What is?" I asked.

"They know who you are," she said. "The senior medical officer of this hospital and his heads of department."

"Who *I* am?" I asked. "I'm nobody, ever since that Chisolm fella put me in my place after the attack on Munda. After I operated on him and my beloved Doctor Garr. I haven't touched a scalpel since then. And to tell the truth, after the way Chisolm treated me, I haven't much missed it."

"Bullshit," she said. "You are a natural-born surgeon. I know— I've seen you in action. Now: you need to listen to me, and trust me. We're three days out of Pearl—and Tripler Hospital. You need to lay low, whether you're getting better or not. Some of the old guard—and our present CO is one of those—would like to hang you out to dry. But only if you rise up and demand to become a surgeon again. A *Navy* surgeon."

I didn't know what to say. I actually hadn't thought much about what I'd do after getting back to Pearl and, more importantly, if she was right about my war being over. She saw my confusion.

"Here's what you do," she said. "Go passive. Don't say anything about the future. I'll get you to Tripler with a recommendation that you are physically unfit for further wartime service. They'll go along with my recommendation; I can promise you that. That means discharge from the Navy, by the way."

"But—" I protested.

"No 'buts,'" she said. "The Japs are being pushed back to their home islands by the day. We're going to win this thing, one way or another. *You* have to start thinking about what you're going to do, no, what you're going to *be*—when this war ends."

"Be?" I asked.

"Yes," she said. "Be. You gonna be a surgeon? Do you want to be a surgeon?"

"Well," I said. "That is the question, isn't it? I've been a surgeon and a pretty good one. My reward for that was to be sent back to my sidelined hooligans, with the clear understanding that I was not ever to operate on anybody."

She shook her head. "You're missing the point, my dear Superman. You managed to touch the flypaper of the Navy's medical bureaucracy, and it wasn't a gentle touch. What will that matter once the war ends? If you go to war with the Navy Medical Corps, they'll destroy you. So, *don't* go to war with them. Be quiet. Be agreeable. Be just a little physically impaired. Wounded, physically and perhaps a little bit mentally. When they hear that, they'll forget all about you, and then you can go home and resume your medical career."

"As what?" I said. "As a fourth-year resident at Duke?"

"Show your mentors at Duke those logs," she said. "Trust me, when they see what you did out there in the Solomons and beyond, your 'residency' will be one of the shortest in history."

She saw that I wasn't entirely convinced.

"Dammit, Lincoln Andersen. You're angry at how you've been treated, and I don't blame you. You gave it your best effort and you saved lives. The best revenge against a medical bureaucracy that doesn't like you is to become a full-fledged surgeon with a ticket from Duke Medical. Am I right?"

"I know you are," I said. "I guess that's not what's really bothering me."

She took my hand. "I know. Brain injury. Can't make a fist. Can't hold a scalpel. All you can do is to push that brain of yours to rebuild and regroup. Brains do that, but only when they're pushed."

"Where will *you* go when this is all over?"

She gave a small laugh. "This ship will go back to Guam and then some islands called Palau in another month. I'll go with her. The Japanese consider Okinawa to be a home island. We've been told to expect a lot of 'customers.'"

I nodded, and then remembered that I should limit my nodding. That line of fire across my scalp helped me to remember. "I never got to ask you—where are you from, originally?"

"Omaha, Nebraska," she said. "Farm bred, corn fed, and proud of it."

I smiled then. I could still smile, which was nice when all these gentle people came around to tend to my frailties. "Ever been to Durham, North Carolina?" I asked.

She shook her head.

"When this is all over, come to Durham. It's a nice town. Tobacco town. Got some good hospitals there, too."

She gave me a long, pensive look. "Deal," she said. Then rounds began and my doorway was filled with white coats. Funny, I thought. In all my wartime adventures, I'd never worn a white coat. Maybe that's why they were mad at me. She squeezed my hand and left.

THIRTY-THREE

One year later I was sitting by myself in the Surgery Program director's conference room at Duke Medical. It was a beautiful fall day outside, especially with the trees beginning to turn. The Pacific war against Japan had ended almost two months ago and the entire country seemed to be catching its breath and wondering what was going to happen next. I know I was.

I'd come back to Durham just before Christmas, '44, to the great relief of my parents. My stay at the Army medical center in Pearl called Tripler Hospital had been mercifully brief. Helen's recommendation that I be discharged from the Navy Medical Corps as physically unfit for frontline medical service had had the desired effect. I'd been given a thorough medical exam by the neurosurgical department, which concluded that my injuries would eventually heal and that there did not appear to be any cognitive damage. They established that by bringing in a senior surgeon who asked me a zillion questions about surgical procedures. When we were done, he sat back and said that I was cleared to continue as a surgeon as far as he was concerned. I didn't tell him who, or, more importantly, what I was in terms of surgical certification. He assumed and I just let him. I made sure to take a copy of his medical report with me back to the States.

The trip back was laborious and somewhat tiring. A troopship to San Francisco. A transcontinental train ride to New York, and then another train down to North Carolina. My father met me in New York and rode with me for the trip home. The Navy's casualty-reporting system had informed them that I'd been wounded, so he was greatly relieved when I appeared to be relatively okay. The suture line across the top of my scalp had turned the hair white, so I now had a dramatic tiara, but physically I was better off than most of the troops I'd seen aboard the troopship. The thought had crossed my somewhat bruised mind to offer medical help aboard the ship, but Helen's warning about laying low prevailed. The ship had been escorted by two destroyer escorts against the possibility of Jap subs lurking on the Pearl-to-San Francisco route. To see them pitching and rolling comfortably abeam brought back memories of the *Montrose*. I was pretty sure we were finally out of Betty range.

Memories were a real problem. I waded through a veritable sea of memories while convalescing at home. I still felt guilty for "abandoning" my hooligans. I sent a long letter to Bluto to explain what had happened. I don't know if he ever got it, but I felt strongly that I owed him and the squadron some sort of apology for just disappearing like that. And yet, I'd seen all too many men just disappear from the squadron just like that, or worse. Patches of flaming gasoline on the waters at night. Exactly like that. We'd miss them, but we couldn't dwell on them. Replacements would inevitably show up and then we'd turn to the business of getting them up to speed. That said, the pictures of badly wounded and burned MTB sailors floundering in the bloody waters off Savo Island, never to be found or seen again, were not easy to suppress.

My father didn't ask me about my experiences "out there," somehow knowing that I wouldn't open up about them until I was ready. I'd gone in with the First Marines in August of 1942, and I'd been invalided home in late October 1944. It didn't seem like two years. It seemed more like a flickering series of days: good days, terrible days, sad days. Horrible days. But then, as if to compensate, there were memories of screamers, nighttime raids with Alibaba and his many thieves, watching the Long Toms on Rendova pound the Japs over on New Georgia, seeing Marine pilots happily flaming Bettys over Tulagi and then doing victory rolls, and that brief moment when Helen Carpenter had realized that something might be possible between us... well.

A surgeon must have a very good memory. That's good news and bad news in wartime. My father, God bless him, seemed to know this instinctively. My mother, on the other hand, immediately began plotting ways to introduce me to "suitable" young women in the social set in Durham and Raleigh. There was, apparently, an overabundance of them. That led to more ducking and weaving on my part, much to the vast amusement of my father. It wasn't as if I was being loyal to my memory of Helen Carpenter, who, for all I know, was back in Omaha, looking up old boyfriends.

What Dad did do was to nudge me back to a career as a surgeon. I hemmed and I hawed but eventually had to admit to myself that I couldn't keep living at home like some kind of leech. I knew deep down I had some decisions to make. He suggested a long weekend down on the coast where he had a beach house. It was a ramshackle affair, typical of beach houses that faced hurricanes on an annual basis. It was early November. He said we'd go fishing; the tourists were long gone and the fish were actually more plentiful. I'd tried as a youngster to embrace fishing, but it just seemed to take too long to pull in something that was available right down the block in the fish market. Fishing for fish wasn't his objective, of course, and on the second night there, as we huddled in front of a wood stove pretending it wasn't cold, he produced a bottle of some evil substance called Armagnac. Leave it to the French: I finally told him my story.

Eventually, I was talked out and a wee bit drunk. Screamers had nothing on Armagnac. His only comment when I finished was to say thanks for telling him all that. Good, now that's over, and so I stumbled off to my bedroom, thoroughly boiled. The next morning, over coffee and a hangover, he had some interesting things to say.

"I read your logs," he began. "The ones you sent home?"

I'd forgotten about the logs.

"If you still want to be a surgeon," he said, "and I think that, deep down, you do, those logs may be your ticket back into the medical world's good graces."

"How so?"

"I think you should pay a visit to the med school. First, go through the residency admissions office and apply to resume your studies. They admitted you once before, and I assume you left in good standing. But they'll have a problem trying to decide at what level you'd restart—first year, third year?

"While they're trying to sort that out, put a call in to the chief of surgery's secretary, asking for an appointment with the boss. You want to resume your studies as a resident, but there's some history about your two years out in the Pacific that might bear upon the school's decision. She'll tell you to go through the admissions office, that the chief doesn't make those decisions."

"Right," I said. "That's exactly what she'd say."

"Yeah, but," he said, "you reply that you've done that, and that admissions doesn't know what to do. Ask if you can drop off some documentation for the chief's perusal, so that he'll have a heads-up when admissions comes to him for a what-do-we-do-with-this-guy question. She'd be right in redirecting you to admissions, but you're offering to give her boss advance warning that an issue is coming. Most secretaries are protective of their bosses, and I'd predict she'll tell you, fine, but I can't guarantee he'll look at it. He's the chief, remember? He's a busy guy. Etcetera, etcetera.

"Then, prepare a cover letter laying out your situation and that you were thrown into a sink-or-swim situation during the Solomons campaign, starting with the invasion of Guadalcanal. Include the first log. Also include all the places where you performed surgery beyond the level of a third-year resident. And, finally, declare that you're not asking for carte-blanche credit for your wartime service, but only that you be allowed to demonstrate what you do know to the faculty as a means to decide where, and under what rules, you reenter the program. I think the moment he looks at that log he'll be intrigued enough to call you in. Maybe even open a board to review your situation. After that, it'll all be up to you and the faculty. Whaddaya think?"

Thinking was hard right then, but it seemed like the best, and perhaps the *only* way to get my foot back in the door at Duke Medical. I nodded.

"And," he said, "if you can't pay for it, I can. And will. There's also a new law called the GI Bill that will help you with tuition."

I'd done what most officers had done with their paychecks when deploying to the Western Pacific: take a few bucks in cash every two weeks, but leave the rest "on the books'" until you came home, and designate who would get the money if you did *not* come home. I really had no idea of how much money I had on the books, but it could certainly pay for my first year. I explained that to Dad.

"So, give it a shot," he said. "And if it doesn't fly, you still have M.D. after your name. Even with millions of GIs coming home from the war, there won't be millions of docs. You can get a job anywhere."

Like Omaha, I'd thought, and then laughed silently at myself.

But now, here I was, a year later and waiting to learn my fate. My father's plan had worked. I'd been readmitted to the surgical residency program right where I'd left off, and during the past few months, I'd been doing stuff with the fifth- and sixth-year guys, and mostly waiting for the decision-makers to put me up for the general boards.

The conference room's doors opened and in came the director

and two other doctors from the faculty. Looks like a board to me, I thought as I stood up to greet them. The director was not a surgeon—he was a Ph.D. medical research academic who specialized in a new field dealing with overcoming infections in hospitals in general and surgeries in particular. He had a reputation for being brilliant but also a positive and encouraging influence within the department. He led off after we were all seated.

"Doctor Andersen, I think we have a solution for your unique case," he began. "And it is indeed unique, more than I or the faculty imagined when we first looked into it. I know it's taken a year, but we felt we had some digging to do."

"I understand, sir," I said.

"We first contacted the Navy Bureau of Medicine and Surgery in Washington to establish your bona fides as a Navy doctor. They confirmed your naval service in the Pacific and that you were honorably discharged last year in Pearl Harbor, having been wounded in action at Leyte Gulf. That was relatively easy to do—they have an entire division that certifies service for returning doctors and nurses.

"Determining exactly *what* you had been doing out there was more difficult, since, from your service record, you'd been assigned to a squadron of PT boats, as opposed to an established medical facility."

"Well," I said, "I *was* assigned to the medical group that landed with the Marines on Guadalcanal in August of forty-two. Then I was transferred to the naval command at Tulagi, and after that, to the MTB squadron."

"I see," he said. "But there are no records of that, unfortunately. The Navy said that was not uncommon, especially for service members who were in the Guadalcanal campaign."

I nodded. "Battleships will do that," I said, remembering that nothing had been left of the medical admin tent after that bombardment. I had to explain that to the director.

"Yes, well, be that as it may, the certification division said there should be records of your fitness reports. You were a Navy doctor but also a naval officer, and that there should be some fitness reports on file at the Bureau of Naval Personnel. So that was our next stop."

I vaguely remembered that everybody got an annual fitness report, although I'd never seen mine. Supposedly, whether or not you got promoted in the Navy depended on what those fitness reports said. A promotion board would meet in secret annually, read those reports, and then decide whether or not you got the next stripe.

"When we contacted the personnel bureau, they told us, after a month, that they did have two fitreps, as they called them, but they couldn't release them to anyone, since they were now part of a promotion board's record of deliberations, which stayed secret. They said that you ought to have been given copies of the reports. Were you?"

"No, sir," I replied. "And if I had, they'd be somewhere on the sea bottom near an island called Rendova, in the Solomons."

"Right," he said. "But my assistant who handled your case asked the bureau if they could release the names of the officers who had signed those fitness reports. We would then see if we could track them down and interview them. Two weeks later, we got a letter back, naming two officers who were lieutenant commanders at the time, one Peter Cushing, and the other, Stede Rackham, both line officers. So, then we asked the bureau if we could write a letter to each of those officers. They said no, but that we *could* write a letter to the bureau, asking them to forward our request to the individuals concerned."

"Now I can see why this took a year," I said.

The director smiled. "By this time, my assistant considered this a personal mission. And, she convinced her contact at the Bureau of Medicine that he should, too. Long story short, we got answers from both of them, and also some more names to contact in reference to your actions as a surgeon. An admiral named Chisholm, a captain named Horace Benson, a retired captain with a mouthful of first names, surname Garr, all three Navy doctors, and another captain named"—he looked back down at his notes—"Willem VanPiet, a line officer. Are these names all familiar?"

"Yes, sir, they are. That's amazing."

"I'll tell you what's amazing," the director said. "All of these names were found because Commander Rackham put you in for some medals: a Purple Heart, a Bronze Star, and a Silver Star."

"What?"

"Yes, he did, and as part of that process, he had to list the names of other officers and chief petty officers who knew you, as references for when the award recommendations were considered. They told us that the awards and decorations board is backlogged, but someone will be contacting you to set up an awards ceremony."

I could only shake my head. A Purple Heart I could understand, but the others?

"Now then," he continued. "Everyone we interviewed gave you highly commendatory grades. By the way, that's when we learned that we should have been addressing you as Superman all this time you've been back with us."

My face turned red. But everyone? Including Garr? I asked the director to confirm that. He nodded and went through a file of letters he'd brought in with him.

"Yes," he said. "Doctor Garr reported that when he got back to Tripler Hospital after being badly wounded at, um, some place called Munda, his surgeons told him that he'd been extremely lucky to get the surgical care he did out there. He admitted that he had had a big problem with you, a third-year resident, doing the things you'd been doing in various surgeries, but that he had to finally admit that he was wrong. And, he says at the bottom of his letter, quote: 'Tell him I said that. He probably won't believe it, but tell him anyway.' End quote."

I was too surprised to say anything. The director gave me a moment and then continued.

"So, what are we going to do? First, we'll recommend that you are qualified to take your boards for certification as a general surgeon and for a medical license. As soon as you're ready. Our faculty agrees. You might think that a waste of time, but the law is the law.

"Second, there's a new medical field gathering steam across the country, at least at the premier med schools. It's called emergency shock-trauma, and it has led to some of the teaching hospitals setting up actual shock-trauma centers within the hospital, with doctors trained to handle automobile accidents, plane crashes, building collapses, hunting accidents, criminal shootings, and the like. We're setting one up here at Duke Hospital. We think you'd be the perfect candidate to stand it up for the university."

I was stunned. Ready for boards? Yes. Becoming a department head at the new Duke Hospital? Wow.

"Do you have any questions for us, Doctor?" the director asked, after giving me a moment to digest all this.

"No, sir," I replied. "Just a bit overwhelmed, I guess."

"I can just imagine, but we sincerely hope you'll take on that job. You are singularly qualified. One last administrative note. Commander Rackham wants to talk to you, urgently. Something to do with the medals, I think, but he said there was a personal matter, too."

He handed me a piece of paper with Bluto's current duty station, which was in Norfolk, Virginia, and a base phone number for his ship. Still in a daze, I thanked him. Then I went home to tell my folks the good news. Dad, who I now suspected had called in some favors at Duke Medical, was delighted. I told him I needed to go down to Norfolk. He said he'd drive me—it was only about three hours. He'd go fishing, and I could take as much time as I liked with Bluto.

THIRTY-FOUR

We met up at the Officers Club on the Norfolk naval operating base. Some of the wartime security measures were still in effect, so I couldn't actually go down to the piers. He caused a bit of a stir when he came into the bar, which wasn't surprising since he was by far the biggest customer. He looked great, and he'd put some of his bulk back on. We each got a beer and then retired to a corner table.

"You first," I said. "What happened to the hooligans after I left?"

"After you abandoned us, you mean, right?" he grumped but with a twinkle in his eyes. "Just like some damn girl with her knickers in a knot. Just walked away. Disgraceful, that's what it was."

"Okay, okay, so I abandoned you," I said. "Terribly sorry, but this"—I pointed to my halo—"had a bearing on that."

He pretended to examine my scar. "I know twenty women who'd find that sexy, there, Doc. Think of the stories you could tell, and some of them even true."

"The hooligans?" I asked.

"Yeah, well, we got back to Tacloban in the afternoon. The big show was already over, but we'd lost three tin cans and two escort carriers, plus the light carrier *Princeton*. Bull Halsey may have seen those bastards turn around after his air strikes, but if you can turn around once, you can do it again, and that's just what the monkeys did. Showed up the next morning with a six-pack of battlewagons and all their friends. Started shooting eight-, fourteen-, sixteen-, even *eighteen*-inch shells at all those baby flattops covering the invasion force ashore on Leyte."

"Jee-zus," I said. "How did anyone survive that?"

He polished off his beer and signaled for another round. "Thing was, we had about a dozen of those little jeep carriers out there. They each carried maybe twelve, fourteen planes. Their admiral thought Halsey had battleships covering the San Bernardino Strait. Halsey and all his battleships were a hundred miles up north, beating up on some Jap carriers. So, our admiral told all his jeeps to head east—and to launch everything they had. They got some hundred or so planes into the air who then started to bomb and strafe the big Jap ships. Jap admiral panicked, turned around, hauled ass back through the San Bernardino Strait. Nobody really knows why, but they did, and it was all over. We spent the next three days looking for survivors out there in the waters off Samar. Whole Goddamned thing was just unbelievable."

"Wow," was all I could muster.

"Then we went to Okinawa," he said, his face sobering. "Talk about a bloodbath. Do you know that the Navy lost more people than the Army and Marine divisions ashore *combined*?"

"That was the kamikaze attacks, right?"

"Yes, it was," he said. He shuddered. "Anybody who was at Okinawa doesn't wanna talk about it. Period. Me included. But when the A-bombs finished the bastards off and the Navy finally stood down the MTBs, I got orders to be the CO of a tin can based here in Norfolk. You may now address me as captain."

I grinned. "Yes, sir, Captain." I almost saluted. "And the hooligans?"

"Scattered to the winds," he said. "After Okinawa, they kept some of them to rescue downed pilots, but the mission was pretty much over for us. Most of the squadrons were disbanded. The Jap fleet had been destroyed, and everybody knew it was just a matter of time before the war wrapped up. Our academy officers were offered new duty stations; the reservists were allowed to go home. The gunners all went to carriers because of the kamikaze problem; the enginemen were mostly sent to amphibs with all their boats and the prospect of invading Japan, itself. Thank God for those A-bombs, is all I can say. Everybody was afraid to even *think* about invading the home islands after Okinawa."

"Well, I wanted to thank you for the good words when the Duke Medical School called. It helped a lot. And medals? I never expected that."

"You earned them, Doc," he said. "Sorry they even had to ask, but there's a lotta jungle bunnies and sailors alive today because of you, despite all those bureaucrats."

Then he reached into a pocket and produced an envelope that had been folded in half. "This came for you a coupl'a weeks ago. Addressed to me, but the sealed letter inside was addressed to you. From some commander." He passed it over.

Some commander? I looked at the return address. The letter and the envelope were made of that tissue paper–thin material that we'd all had to use during the war for mail in order to save weight on the transport planes going back to the States. Bluto was giving me an arch look. "Of course, I didn't read it," he said. "But it might be important."

Might be? The return address was in Omaha, Nebraska.

"Yeah, it might," I said, trying not to tear up. With any luck at all I had another trip to make.

"Found out something when I got back," he said. "You call the telephone company operator, give them a name and address? They can get you a phone number. So many people trying to reconnect after this Goddamned war. Bunch'a lost souls out there in America these days, you know?"

"Yes, I do," I said. "I think I'm one."

"Na-a-h," he said. "You? Never. You're Goddamned Superman." Then he leaned forward. "Now, then, Superman. Go find her. As Tiny Tim would say, that's a damn order."

THIRTY-FIVE

Three days later I was sitting in the lobby of the Magnolia Hotel in Omaha. I'd checked in earlier in the day after a long, overnight train ride from Washington, D.C., taken a nap, and was now waiting for Helen Carpenter. I was fortifying myself with a whiskey in hand.

I hadn't opened her letter until I got back to Durham after seeing Bluto. My parents were away at a conference, so I had the house to myself. A glass of Scotch in hand, I'd sat down by the fireplace and opened it. I felt like a coward for not opening it sooner, but I was afraid she'd be telling me all about her new husband. I smiled when I saw the salutation. *Dear Superman.*

She went on: *I hope you got back to the States safely, and that all is well with you. I made it as far as Okinawa, which was Hell on wheels, but you've probably heard all about that. That island, and the war itself, are things I'm trying to forget, if that's humanly possible. I've developed a taste for whiskey to dampen the nightmares.*

I'm writing to tell you that I probably won't be coming to see you in Durham. I've just completed a long and painful convalescence, having lost the bottom half of my left arm during the Okinawa campaign. I wish I could tell you that it was a heroic battlefield injury, but, sadly, it wasn't. I cut my left hand in the OR one night, which resulted in a ghastly infection they simply couldn't control.

Gangrene loomed, so they amputated my hand. And then my lower arm. So now you can call me Stumpy.

I wish I had better news. I'd love to correspond; there's no one to talk to unless they'd been out there, and anyone who'd been there, well, you know. Do reply. Fondly, Helen.

I'd sent her a telegram that night, telling her I was coming out. And now, here I was.

She came into the lobby wearing an overcoat; the weather out on the Great Plains was colder than what we were seeing in North Carolina. She stopped, looked around, then spied me sitting over in a corner of the lounge. As she approached, I thought she looked a bit older, and, truth be told, sadder. There were shades of gray along her temples. I stood up as she approached the table. I offered to take off her coat, but she seemed reluctant.

I looked at her. "Okay, Stumpy," I said. "You've got to take it off sometime."

"I don't want to," she said. "I hate what I look like."

"Oh, I get it," I said. "You're damaged goods now, is that it? Lemme see: maimed, disabled, crippled, and therefore totally un-attractive, right? Tell me this: if I kiss you right now, then will you take the damned coat off?"

That brought waterworks. I pulled her in close to me, hugged her as hard as I could, and then I did kiss her. At first, it was a one-way deal, but then she responded and kissed me back like she meant it. A guy walking past muttered—"hey, you guys, get a room, awready." That broke the spell, but broke it with a laugh. We sat down. She still hadn't removed her coat.

"I've got a proposition," I said. "How's about a date? A real date, not just some midnight dalliance in a wartime OR. This place has a good dining room. Let me take you out to dinner. Talk. Catch up. I've got lots to tell you, and it's all good."

"Sounds wonderful," she said quietly. "I'd like that very much."

"Then we'll go upstairs," I said.

"You mean that?" she said.

"I absolutely mean it, Helen. I've really missed you. But you'll have to take the damned coat off, if only because I want to see what one of those mere mortal surgeons did to your arm-bone."

"Well, then," she said. Her face was a study in longing, which is when I realized she was really hurting, emotionally and maybe even physically. She looked smaller, and vulnerable. And beautiful, I thought.

"Let's take this thing slowly," I said. "I don't have a lot of experience with women, and I do *not* want to screw this up."

She nodded. "But not too slowly, Superman," she said. "I'm not as fragile as I look."

"And that's why we gotta find you a hook," I said. "A nice, stainless-steel hook. And you're gonna have to learn how to say *A-a-a-r-r.* I mean, if you're gonna go back to nursing, especially as the Head Dragon, think what all those lamby-pie nurses will think when they see you coming down the hallway?"

She collapsed into silent laughter; her eyes closed but her shoulders shaking. Attagirl, I thought. This is gonna be okay.